CAMARA

A SHORT STORY CYCLE BY

A SHORT STORY CYCLE BY

JAKE CAMARA

ISBN 979-8-218-25948-8
@TheDevilsLeague

To my visionary Graphic Designer, who helped bring the characters I'd created to life - and in several ways, improved on them.

To my Marine Biologist, who gave insightful information about how the fictional creatures I'd described would live, act, and exist in a realistic setting.

And finally, to my Editor, who acted as a second set of eyes when I was stuck using only my own, and would not rest until every Oxford comma was in its proper place.

All three of these people are Alyson Mello. She remains one of the most uniquely talented people I've had the pleasure of knowing.

Now stands my task accomplished, as not the wrath of Jove,
Nor flame nor sword, nor the devouring ages can destroy.
-Ovid, Metamorphoses

CONTENTS

INTRODUCTION

It would be a little unkind to present these tales without just a word of friendly warning.

The Devil's League refers to the monsters and creatures that, despite their prevalence across myth and folklore, are not believed to have existed in human history. This boundary between what we know to be true and what we don't is precisely where this book takes place: The supernatural pocket of historical plausibility.

There is a prologue, twenty-two short stories, and an epilogue after this message, many of which take place across the entirety of human history. Many can be read and enjoyed as independent, self-contained tales, but there is an internal chronology and an overarching narrative that builds upon what's come before. Reading these stories as presented is much more rewarding to the reader, but it is not the only way that they can be read.

There are no aliens present in these stories. These creatures have been right here all along, sharing this vast planet with us, and through various reasons have never been discovered by mankind. Some are sentient and smart enough to deliberately avoid the public eye. Others leave few survivors to spread word of their existence.

There are no uses of obscenity that a teenager wouldn't be familiar with. There are no sequences of violence more graphically depicted than what you'd find in Homer's *Odyssey*. This book deals with topics and themes such as life, death, pain, transformation, isolation, and other aspects of the mind where inner horrors might reside. It is accessible to all, but crafted for a specific few of you who thrive in this gothic realm of the human psyche.

To a first-time reader, the preceding information will be expanded on further over the course of the story, and this book is designed to be read as if you knew none of this preexisting knowledge or context.

To those who have already experienced this book, and liked it enough to return to this page...

Welcome back.

PROLOGUE

When Abraham Ross passed away in the early winter of the previous year, the boy named Waylon inherited the secluded cottage he'd been raised in in East Freetown, Massachusetts, along with the rest of his father's real estate holdings across the North American continent.

East Freetown was the sort of place that was somehow a twenty minute drive from everything except a gas station. Boundless forests as far as the eye could ever see with one, expansive vista of woodlands and the occasional dirt road. These counties were where the Pilgrims first landed centuries prior, when they built roads not in a practical, grid-like way (like the West would exemplify) but in a slew of random pathways down, up, over, and around hillsides and pond shores. The roads of men mattered little to Waylon, who always made his own pathways wherever he lived. Pathways treaded on foot to places unseen. Pathways unique only to him.

The boy had just entered his twenties, which for him, meant that he was boundlessly ambitious, yet hadn't found the difference between confidence and arrogance. The Ross family had a history of hunting and poaching that went all the way back to the Gilded Age, back when the word "von" would precede their family name. Waylon's heritage was a great source of pride for him. His father instilled that into him from a young age.

Waylon missed his dad with every passing day. He'd shown Waylon every hunting skill he'd ever attained, even chaperoning several excursions to faraway lands and prey. His finest memory of his father was when Waylon, who at the time couldn't have been more than six or seven, asked why his father's jacket was made out of a bear. Abraham told Waylon to do the same when he was older "with the strongest one you've hunted."

Waylon brought the caged bird home to his father's cottage, now *his* cottage. He still hadn't adjusted to thinking of it that way. She was the kind of eagle so endangered that one would be arrested for having anything to do with it. In the cottage's extended patio, where most would throw a table and loveseat and be content, Waylon had made a small habitat for his critters and unconventional pets. It started with certain endangered types of plants, through which he'd procured rare seeds and potted them side-by-side. Then, he expanded into cold-blooded creatures in a nearby tank. The eagle was his fifth endotherm here, and third who could fly.

To watch them all work in tandem with one another brought an insatiable satisfaction to the young poacher, unlike any euphoric drug or partner's love could ever give him. He'd taken the rarest of Earth's creatures and plucked them from their deadly environments before they'd gone completely extinct, and forged a community out of them. They stayed well-fed, and so none fed on each other. Those who caused problems for their neighbors lived caged until housebroken. It was a grand domestication, free from the natural world's abuse. A sanctuary of mother nature's most prized possessions.

He knew he couldn't keep his collection going at this rate. The world's list of endangered species was ever-changing, and this cottage was feeling less like a home and more like an artificial habitat with each new beautiful creature. Waylon had been prolonging the day where he'd have to visit all of his father's international assets, because he'd have to make two difficult choices: Which one to permanently reside in, and which ones to sell off.

Their locations didn't matter so much to him. Waylon spent his youth traveling on foot as far as his curiosity would take him. Sometimes, it took him several towns over before his father tracked him down and spitefully drove him home. Abraham used the family's fortunes on globetrotting adventures with Waylon to hotspot islands, eclectic jungle terrains, deserted plateaus in the East, frigid northlands where the Sun rarely visited, and even wilderness and woodlands like back home. In his adulthood, Waylon had been carrying on this legacy. The eagle had been caught somewhere between Alaska and Canada, and smuggled back to Massachusetts like most of his patio's other inhabitants.

His patio was unsustainable both in size and location. Most of these plants and animals preferred consistently warmer weather, and New England's weather ranged from scorching heat waves in the summer to frigid snowstorms in the winter, sandwiched between accompanying Nor'easters in the off-seasons. Each creature represented a part of the world he'd visited, and only *four* were from this state. None were from this town.

Waylon decided to change that.

If his menagerie of endangered houseguests were to move to another of his father's holdings - probably one of the mansions - then he would find one animal representing the untold town of East Freetown. The place so insignificant it could only be described to somebody by saying "an hour south from Boston" for them to understand.

He dwelled on this idea, and smiled the more he did.

One more... and then, we move.

It was later that very same day when Waylon found himself satisfying that initiative. Despite the waning sun, daylight still illuminated his path deep in the thick of one of the town forests. At the end was a clearing where the ground beneath Waylon's feet smelled of badgers and musty old soil. Each footstep trudged through vibrantly green flora, predominantly vines and weeds. A careless misstep would've tripped him straight away. Waylon breezed through it, stopping briefly to stabilize with his deliberately lightweight loadout. The piping plover he'd been tracking had flown to a branch slightly too far from his grasp if he were standing at the base. He slowed himself down, approaching the tree with extreme caution. The reaction time of birds far exceeded that of terrestrial creatures like himself, or even potential prey.

Waylon heard the snapping of a tree's bark from behind him.

Quickly, he dashed behind the tree he'd been approaching. The piping plover flew away, never to be caught by the crazed poacher, but that wasn't important to him right then. There was something closeby with an unnatural sound... *Footsteps*, almost. But not steady or traditional. They kept stomping the ground with quick, rapid movements, and not in any purposeful direction.

There were two of them.

Two men in broad daylight, struggling in some unarmed conflict not far from Waylon's position. Waylon stayed hidden by the tree as the noise of the scuffle continued, clamoring into fallen leaves and nearby shrubbery. It was only when the noise of the struggle ended that Waylon decided to peer out and get a glance of the victor.

That victor, unmistakably, had to be a story tall, and in his hand was the opponent who seemed puny by comparison.

The tall man held the body of the other - whose size was comparable to Waylon's, maybe six feet tall - by the neck with one of his hands. With the other, the tall man produced a wooden stake, and plunged it into his opponent's chest.

Waylon watched as that man's entire body crumbled into ash amidst the tall man's fingers.

Silently, Waylon looked down at his gear and considered his options. He grabbed the rifle from his jacket, and loaded it with a non-lethal round.

I

RETRO-ENABLEMENT

Dr. Rebecca Chamberton.

That didn't look right to her.

Dr. Chamberton.

No, that sounded like a man's name. This is why she wrote in pencil, not pen. She'd become used to correcting her mistakes.

Dr. Rebecca Chamberton. July 11th, 1963.

My employers are one of the largest producers of medical supplies in the country. For legal reasons, I will refrain from disclosing their name in my notes, and will instead refer to them as "Company X." What Company X has allowed me access to, without their direct knowledge, is a collection of artificial stem cells derived from a variety of regenerative life forms on Earth.

Now that's a solid start, she reckoned.

The means by which I've procured these samplings were highly illegal. The purpose of these notes is to further scientific boundaries, and a byproduct of that is my own implication.

These notes were supposed to be objective. Rebecca erased parts of what she'd written, then refocused and continued.

Individual cells from the collection replicate and replenish adjacent neighboring cells they come in contact with, not unlike human stem cells from a fetus. A blood stream composed of these types of cells, if the body were wounded, would quickly regenerate whatever part of it was lost via its own surrounding cells.

To confirm this, I've combined a drop of the cell collection with a drop of my own blood under a microscope. When observed, the cells started to metamorphose into white blood cells. Discernibly human.

Discernibly hers.

The thought troubled her deeply. But she wasn't finished.

Subject 6, my son Adam Chamberton, is 3 years of age. He was born with missing chromosomes, resulting in Down's syndrome. His father, Edward Chamberton, has been away in Vietnam, leaving me to care for our immensely troubled child. Adam will require extensive care when he is older to carry out daily functions. That care simply does not exist for him, and if Edward does not make it back from the war, Adam's fate is that of an institutionalized inmate.

Almost there.

Starting tonight, I plan on injecting the rest of the artificial cell collection into Adam's bloodstream. If the cells operate as I've observed them to with my own, the working theory is that over a large period of time, my son will gain the missing chromosomes in his body and, as he grows, he will slowly transpose into the strongest version of himself. I've dubbed the experiment "Retro-Enablement."

Good.

It's written down.

Rebecca's theory was no longer an idea. It'd become a plan. Plans could be revised if needed. What mattered now was that she had one.

Adam Chamberton laid sideways in his crib, peering through the bars to see the lava lamp on his mother's desk. It was a gift from Edward before he left. Neither him nor Rebecca knew how fascinated their son would be by it during his sleepless nights. Rebecca turned from her notes and saw Adam eyeing it, following the little blue globs bounce slowly from top to bottom as if propelled by magic. This mysterious object was his nightly fascination, and watching her son be mystified by it was Rebecca's.

The desk of Adam's mother was scrambled with notepads and textbooks, all of which bore messy and terrible penmanship. Though she had graduated from university years ago, she still looked as if she were dorming, with casual clothes for a body that rarely left her house. Her field gave her no female colleagues to talk to. Nobody to vent to without enduring unwanted, unpreventable sexual advances. She was the first woman in her family to become a doctor, and with that came a societal isolation not mentioned in any of her textbooks.

Henry was the house's third and final tenant while Edward was away: An adorable cross between a Husky and a Labrador. As Adam slept and Rebecca took her notes, Henry would usually bustle into the room, his claws muffled by the carpeted floor. If Rebecca were making something in the kitchen, she would hear Henry coming from miles away on the hardwood floors. It usually bothered Adam, who hated unexpected noises.

In the middle of her desk, the icebox containing the cell collection condensated in the humid air of her study.

Rebecca readied the syringe and plunged it into the vial, extracting the oil-like goo from inside. Watching it flow through the needle, passing each notch as it filled the glass, was mesmerizing to her.

Adam caught sight of the needle from his crib as his mother's hand crossed his view of the lava lamp. He whined a little.

"Shhh," Rebecca whispered, stroking the thin fuzz of hair on his head. She locked eyes with the boy and took his attention away from what her other hand was doing. As it stabbed his leg and shot the artificial cells into his veins, Rebecca shushed him again and made a silly face. Adam was uncomfortable, but did not cry. Any minor perturbation could set the young boy off. Rebecca had to navigate this state of uncertainty carefully, lest she not sleep for the next hour amidst his wailing.

It was done.

Rebecca discarded the needle and used both hands to cradle her son. Henry poked his head over, curiously. Rebecca rocked the boy gently, softly shushing him. As she moved in closer to calm Adam, her body stopped obstructing the lava lamp from her son's line of sight. Adam calmed, and empathetically, so did Rebecca. His pain was hers to bear. Now and always.

Dr. Rebecca Chamberton. July 27th, 1963.

Subject 6 has had no apparent reactions since the first night. This is good news; It means the boy's body hasn't rejected the substance, which was an unlikely fear I'd been harboring. Eating patterns are normal. Heart rate normal. Sleep cycle slightly erratic, though that's unchanged.

The more time apart from her husband, the more lonely she anticipated to become. Edward Chamberton had been overseas for a few months now, and Rebecca didn't feel impacted in any strong way. It was something she didn't dwell on.

Metamorphosis is usually lethargic, she penned quickly. *A part of me wants to speed it up.*

She took her notes from the couch while watching him play. Adam had the parts of his Mr. Potato Head sprawled all across the living room's carpet. The Chamberton's den was warm and inviting, though so few were ever invited. Photographs of life achievements decorated the flowered wallpaper that ran all the way into the kitchen, stopping only at tile. Rebecca's graduation ceremony. Edward dropping on one knee to propose. The first picture of their beautiful son in his mother's arms.

Since Subject 6 is still very young, the formative nature of the pluripotent cell collection should have a stronger influence on the boy as he begins to grow. It could be beneficial to administer another dose of the artif-

The nose of Mr. Potato Head hit her leg.

She looked to the source of the attack: A tiny little boy with big eyes and a confused expression. Adam smacked himself in the face.

"Adam!" Rebecca said as she leapt out of her seat. Adam got in a few more smacks before she restrained him. It was the stimulation that Adam desired, and self-administered pain brought it tenfold. Adam screamed intermittently as Rebecca held back his arms and tried to wriggle free. Henry ran into the room at the noise, and stopped as he watched his owner practically wrestling with her son. Rebecca had to carefully dodge the bits of Mr. Potato Head that littered the ground as she did so, for she happened to be barefoot.

Seeing him hurt himself reminded her of the reason she'd started down this unconventional path: His benefit. Adam deserved a life the same as anybody else his age. To exist in this world, which would treat his condition as lunacy and admit him to an asylum, would be analogous to letting Adam die. He'd be stuck behind the bars of a looney bin as a guard would occasionally bring meals and administer a straight jacket upon seeing one of Adam's fits. A cold, empty padded cell awaited him, and nothing more.

Adam's screaming subsided. Rebecca shifted from restraint to a more nurturing cradle of her son, and he conformed to it. She held him close and shushed him softly.

Henry cocked his head, unsure how to react. Though this wasn't the first of Adam's outbursts he'd seen, Henry still never knew what to make of it. Once Adam finally quieted down, Rebecca released him and stood up once more, watching as he grabbed Mr. Potato Head's nose. His favorite piece to throw.

Rebecca sighed as she made her way to the couch. She picked up her notebook and reread what she'd written. Something gave her pause. After a moment, she grabbed the eraser to delete the last half-formed sentence...

Rebecca stopped this, too.

She flipped the pencil around instead, and continued writing, expanding on her earlier thoughts.

-icial cells, which is why I'm doing so again now. The next entry in these notes will not be until a significant change has taken place.

Rebecca stood from the couch again and watched Adam as he threw Mr. Potato Head's nose at the television's screen. It wasn't even on. Perhaps the reflection made him do it. Perhaps Adam had no target in mind at all. Musing on this, Rebecca looked to the open door of her office and saw the sterilized syringe on her desk. She started toward it, and a dutiful Henry followed her into the office.

Dr. Rebecca Chamberton. September 2nd, 1963.

In her bedroom, Rebecca frantically scribbled the header. She desperately needed to record this.

For the past few months, Subject 6 has become increasingly disinterested in his usual hobbies and habits. His primary activity now has been watching television. Without it being tuned in to any channel. Pure white noise captivates the boy, unlike anything I've ever seen, and I have not tried to dissuade him from doing so. Considering his old habits included activities such as smacking himself in the head and unexpectedly shrieking wildly, there seems to be no harm in his recent interests.

Before heading to bed, I'd left one of my textbooks on the couch. It was one on Mathematics, something I was browsing when formatting the serum's dosage. It was the only one I'd left open, I believe. That must've been what prompted him to take it.

He's scanning the thing up and down, slowly and diligently. I can't tell if he's actually accreting this information or just studying the text's wording. Reading was never my son's strongest suit, nor did he have the patience to better himself at it. But here, as I can observe through the crack in my bedroom door, Subject 6 is sitting on the living room couch, diligently reading this book in what would seem to be a deep contemplation.

Rebecca popped her head back up from her notes to double-check the screen in front of Adam.

The television, in the background as he reads, is on with its usual white noise. I can't tell if it's-

But before she could finish the sentence, she noticed Adam's head perk up from the book. Slowly, he turned around, as if to catch her curious eyes.

Rebecca quickly and quietly closed her bedroom door.

"What's wrong?" Rebecca asked at the kitchen table, sitting right across from him.

Looking only at the plate of food in front of him, Adam said nothing back to her.

"Did you already eat?" Rebecca asked.

Adam shook his head.

The little boy remembered all of the meals that he'd been fed over the past five years. *All* of them. Every single one in exquisite detail, every bite he took, every grinding of his teeth as the food disintegrated among the saliva, puddling up into a mushy paste that he would swallow... The thought was repulsive to dwell on, and he couldn't stop dwelling on it.

Rebecca was disheartened, not that Adam seemed to care. She looked over at the notebook by her side, kept deliberately out of Adam's sight.

"You may be excused," she relented.

Adam stood straight up and left for his room as though the table were about to explode. He went straight to his bedroom and promptly closed the door behind him, almost robotically.

Rebecca sat alone with both plates of food. She looked at Adam's untouched plate across from her, wisps of steam still rising off of it. With Henry at her side, Rebecca gave his food to the dog and pulled out her notebook while the details of what just happened were still fresh.

Dr. Rebecca Chamberton. September 5th, 1963.

Subject 6 has stopped eating the meals I've been feeding him, with balanced amounts of proteins and carbohydrates equal to the amount of calories the average six-year-old male is recommended to consume.

Rebecca noticed that Henry had already finished the entire plate. She scratched the back of his neck.

Subject 6 has never had an issue with his usual diet in the past. It wouldn't be as concerning except for the fact that, as of the past three days, I have no idea what Subject 6 has been eating. If anything at all.

Rebecca glanced at Adam's bedroom door, making sure he wasn't watching. He'd left the table promptly and cordially closed the door behind him. Behavior she'd never imagined from him.

Subject 6's skin has darkened into a smooth gray, reminiscent of concrete or cement, and with a similar texture. His body has begun to change shape as well, closer and closer every day into one of peak fitness for a teenage boy. This is exciting for several reasons, but concerning mostly for this one: He's still only six years old.

Her pen drove deep into her notebook's pages. She tried to relax, failing immediately at it.

While Subject 6 is asleep, I plan to carefully extract a piece of his DNA for further clarification.

Dr. Rebecca Chamberton. September 6th, 1963.
The present time is shortly after midnight.
The physical changes of Subject 6 are clearer upon closer examination of the blood sample drawn: The body has grown by an estimated five or six inches in height, brought on by the artificial cells course-correcting his impaired shape. The spinal issues associated with his condition have started to disappear; His spine has spent the past several days trying to adjust itself into an upright position. Every day that passes shows progress towards this eventual end-goal.

Further analysis of Subject 6's DNA suggests that the boy's missing chromosome has returned. His skin, while coarse and grainy, allowed a needle to puncture it while he slept, though it produced no dollop of blood upon the needle's removal. The wound was not visible mere seconds after removing it. The data I've gathered starts to suggest a change on the level of-

The sound of something grinding came from outside of Rebecca's room, probably somewhere in the kitchen.

Rebecca put the pen down and stood up from her desk, dressed only in pajamas. She tried not to make any noise when investigating the source of the sound.

She turned her knob so slow as not to produce any rattling or creaking.

Peering through her bedroom door, Rebecca saw the faint light of the outside city peering in through her windows, casting a dim haze over her house. No lights were on, yet it wasn't unseeable.

She followed the noise's source, which remained faint, but became marginally clearer: The grinding sounded wet, almost. The living room wasn't the source of it. As Rebecca walked closer to the kitchen, she found a putrid smell accompanying the noise, growing more powerful the closer she got. The noise had to be coming from behind the kitchen's island, somewhere on the tiled floor beneath the refrigerator.

No cabinets were open, and the refrigerator's door hadn't been touched.

Rebecca stepped so carefully as not to disturb whatever the noise's source was, placing the tip of her socks first onto the cold floor, then leaning in cautiously as she brought each step onto her heel. She paid conscious attention to how she walked, and for the most part, it actually worked. The source of the noise hadn't found her yet.

Rebecca turned the corner of the kitchen's island.

The first notable sight was the backside of Adam, hunched over the floor like an impish troll. Beneath him was the source of the stench: Henry, the loyal dog's body, laid out across the kitchen floor with his stomach torn open and his blood pooled up where Adam was kneeling.

Instinctively, Rebecca gasped, her breath catching in her throat.

Adam spun around.

The crazed face of a hungry boy glared back at his mother, with Henry's blood dripping profusely from Adam's jaw. In the boy's hands were half-eaten chunks of organs and flesh.

Adam gulped what was left in his mouth right down, and breathed calmly.

"What did you do, mommy?" Adam asked with perfect diction.

Adam pounded against his bedroom door. It was locked from the outside, where Rebecca stood and ignored him.

"YOU DID THIS TO ME!" Adam screamed at his mother. "YOU DID THIS TO ME!!!"

Dr. Rebecca Chamberton. September 6th, 1963, Continued.

"WHAT DID YOU DO?!" Adam yelled, continuing his battering. "WHAT DID YOU DO TO ME?! WHY AM I LIKE THIS, MOMMY?!"

Subject 6 has displayed increased aggression since consuming Henry.

"I'M A *FREAK!!!*" Adam screamed desperately.

Rebecca looked up from the notebook.

She'd been presuming that by simply ignoring Adam, his frustrations would die down. It'd always worked in the past. But this thing she'd created, or at least had a strong regenerative influence over, didn't resemble her son very much anymore. To her, this was both good and bad. She wasn't sure which overpowered the other.

"WHY DID YOU DO THIS TO ME?!"

"I didn't!" Rebecca yelled back.

Adam stopped pounding at the shock of hearing her voice. He didn't expect to at all.

"What's happening?!" Adam managed to say amidst the building tears and mucus. "I can't stop thinking about everything I've ever done. I can't fall asleep anymore. I'm too busy staring at the ceiling thinking about the time that I took my first steps. It was in the kitchen, and I used daddy's hand for support... *What did you do to me, mommy?!*"

Rebecca hesitated with how exactly to word it.

"I made you better," she finally said.

"What?!"

Rebecca unlocked the door.

"I'm sorry," she said face-to-face with her son, whose height now almost eclipsed her own. "Your cells are artificial. They replicate and replace the ones that were there, one-by-one, until you're fully..."

Rebecca stopped herself, realizing that he was still just a boy.

"I'm sorry, Adam. What I mean to say-"

"Undifferentiated regenerative pluripotency," said Adam.

Adam's comment hit Rebecca like a train.

"Y- yes..." Rebecca muttered.

Adam studied his own hands and arms, watching the pores stretch as he spread his fingers. It was exactly the same as before, but with articulation and dexterity he was never capable of.

Rebecca regained her composure.

"It's going to let you live a good life," said Rebecca with clear sincerity.

Adam turned to her, confusion all over his tear-streaked face.

"What life?" Adam asked in a choked-up voice.

"Imagine if something happened to me while daddy's away," she explained. "There's no life for you like this. You'll be institutionalized. All that'll be left of you is a young boy hitting himself in the head, yearning for a television with nothing on it. They'd end up drugging you into sedation until you die. No son of mine deserves that fate. I won't allow you to have it."

"You'll allow something like *this* instead?!"

"It's the only way that-"

"You didn't even *ask!*" Adam interrupted, his rage now returning.

"How was I supposed to ask the boy who screams instead of speaking to me?" Rebecca yelled.

"That doesn't give you the right!"

"Adam!" Rebecca said with a newfound rage all her own. "Look at how you've changed! You're walking upright, you're forming complete sentences... You're not *hurting* yourself every day. You can't honestly sit there and tell me that whatever you've become is somehow worse than the *thing* that you used to be!"

Rebecca regretted it the very moment that she said it. She cursed herself for even thinking it.

Adam became overwhelmed with his brewing emotions. No longer could those immutable feelings of sadness and self-hatred be held back.

"I'm so sorry, Adam," said Rebecca. "I didn't mean that. I didn't. I *loved* you, before and after what I did."

Adam's face went blank as he stared back at his mother.

"Adam, I..."

Rebecca couldn't find any new ways to apologize. Habitually, she pulled out her notebook and continued her entry.

Subject 6's memory has-

Adam snatched the notebook from her hand.

"I'm not your goddamn experiment," Adam mumbled. "I've always been some *thing* holding you back from your work. Some unwanted burden."

"Adam, that's not true-"

"You only care about me now because I *am* your work," he continued. "You've transformed me from a burden into a lab rat... but you've treated neither of those as your son."

Rebecca noticed how Adam's hands had clenched themselves into fists, and how the veins on the boy's neck now bulged out amid his rapidly-accelerating heart rate.

And so did he.

Adam stepped forward towards his mother. In response, Rebecca quickly shut the door and locked it again.

Adam pounded away at it.

"LET ME OUT!!" Adam screamed, no longer in desperation. It was just a blinding rage that compelled him.

The wood of the door splintered in front of Rebecca, and from both sides of the door, the two of them simultaneously realized what exactly was about to happen.

With a few more crashing fists, Adam forced his way through the door and out of his room, sending small chunks of wood and dust everywhere into the living room. Rebecca ran to her room, but slipped on Henry's blood when passing through the kitchen, collapsing on the nearby cabinets. In the panic, Rebecca caught a glimpse of Henry's torn-open body still lying there.

The dog's body was twitching, putting itself back together piece-by-piece.

Rebecca got to her feet and tried to run again, but Adam was now in her way. She noticed how his knuckles, split open from pounding at the door, were almost finished healing the same way as Henry's body.

The room was dark when the man entered. Though the sun hadn't risen yet, Adam left every light in the house off. His eyes preferred it this way.

The man changed that immediately.

As he walked through the door, he flipped the switch and illuminated the living room. This gave him pause. It was the first time he'd been here in what seemed like ages, and yet flipping the switch was still muscle memory. A reflex carried out without thinking. He never realized how much he truly missed doing it, and it made him smile as he came in, finally glimpsing the inside of the house he'd been separated from for all those years.

"Honey..." Edward called out.

The war was not over by any means, but First Lieutenant Edward Chamberton had been granted a long-delayed visit home. He wanted only three nights: A night alone with his wife, a night on the town with what friends he still had, and a night playing games with Adam, his now eight-year-old son.

"Honey?" Edward called out again.

The house fell into its usual silence again, indifferent to Edward's voice.

Edward noticed that the door was open in Rebecca's room. Just as he decided to make his way towards it, a noise came from the couch in the living room. He recognized it instantly.

"Henry!" Edward called out to his dog.

Enthusiastically, Henry leapt into Edward's arms. He hadn't felt his owner's embrace in many years, and relished in the pets and scratches and attention.

"He missed you," a deep voice called from Rebecca's room.

Edward turned back and saw a fully-grown man standing in her room's entryway. This man was much taller than him, his head narrowly missing the top of the threshold as he entered the living room. The man's gray and ghastly skin enveloped an incredibly muscular figure, and that figure was wearing a fresh change of Edward's clothes, along with his nicest black blazer.

Edward assumed a defensive stance.

"Who are you?" Edward yelled out.

As Adam stepped forward, Edward squinted his eyes and came quickly to the ambiguous truth: Beneath all of that gray skin and extra few feet of height, Adam's face was very much ingrained into that man's head, albeit with more striking, superlative features.

Edward was petrified.

Adam calmly walked over to the living room's couch and sat down, calling Henry over to him. In one hand, he scratched the side of Henry's neck. In the other, Rebecca's notebook opened to one of the first pages.

"This was her notebook," said Adam.

Edward was unable to speak, his mind's eye still trying to *imagine* what his son used to look like.

"*Subjects 1, 2, 3, and 4 all failed to survive preliminary trials,*" Adam read aloud. "*Subject 5, a dog we've adopted named Henry Chamberton, was a resounding success: His eyesight's returned in both eyes, and the missing thumb on his hind leg has fully regenerated.*"

Looking up from the notebook, Adam nodded to his father, gesturing towards the seat across from the couch.

Edward didn't move.

"You'll want to sit down, dad."

As if straining to move, Edward migrated over to the chair and sat down, never taking his eyes off of his son.

"What happened?" Edward asked.

"I was Subject 6," Adam admitted.

Edward processed this, still scanning the visibly gray skin on his son's face and hands.

"Before you left for the war," Adam began, "you were falling out of love with her, weren't you?"

"That's not true," said Edward. "Who told you that?"

"Nobody."

"Somebody had to," Edward insisted. "You were two years old when I left."

"I was."

Edward was visibly confused.

"The night you left," said Adam, "there was an argument between you two. Something about how your love had run its course... It was hard to hear from my crib."

Henry left Adam's hand and went back to Edward, who hesitated to embrace him again.

"Why did you stay in a loveless marriage so long?" Adam asked.

And finally, Edward's defensive demeanor broke down. He started to tell the truth, for fear of what lying might do in the presence of his seemingly omniscient son.

"I always loved her," said Edward. "I still do. The thought of her and you waiting for me when I came home... It's all I've thought about since they granted me leave. That fight, it... That fight..."

Edward struggled to bring back those memories. They were toxic to him.

"I asked her why she didn't seem like she would miss me," he continued. "It was light-hearted, at first. But it sparked this whole... This whole back-and-forth, I don't know. I think she loves me as much as she's capable of loving another person. I think that's it. She's not right in the head, Adam. I don't think she's ever truly, I mean *truly*, loved anybody. She'll say it, you know, because it's normal. Because you're supposed to when you start a family. But I think it's a lie."

Adam sat on this for some time. He thought back to every time Rebecca said 'I love you,' cycling through each individual moment. They came once, twice a week. More if spirits were high, around Thanksgivings and Christmases. Was that normal? He had no frame of reference to compare it. He only had his own memories.

"Did you kill her?" Edward asked with trepidation.

Adam shot his father a demeaning look.

"I'm not insane," said Adam. "She's alive and well. She's just not going to be around anymore."

"I don't believe you," said Edward.

"I don't care," said Adam. "The funny thing about the truth is that it's accurate *whether or not* you believe in it."

"What did you do to her?" Edward asked, now more stern.

Adam became frustrated.

"It's always *her,* isn't it?" Adam taunted.

Edward stood up from the chair.

"Where is she?" Edward asked almost in a scream.

"If I write down the address," said Adam, "promise me never to come back."

"What?" Edward reflexively replied.

"I don't want anything to do with you. You weren't a father then, and you won't be now. Not that I really *need* one anymore, anyway."

At first, Edward didn't know how to take this, but Adam read his face as he made his decision. The answer was becoming clear.

"Tell me where she is," said Edward.

Adam bowed his head.

From the table, Adam picked up his mother's notebook and tore out a blank page. He scribbled the address down and gave it to his father. Edward spun around in confusion when Adam started walking towards the front door.

"Where are you going?" Edward asked.

"Keep the apartment," said Adam through gritted teeth. "Find somebody other than your wife and your son to think about when you're coming home."

Edward looked down at the address, then back up at Adam and said the first thing on his mind.

"You're not my son."

Adam stopped, the door partially open, and closed his eyes. He swallowed hard as he took that statement in. Finally, he took a large, deep breath, and closed the door behind him, sealing every trace of his life behind it.

II

BLOODLUST

In its prime, the Colosseum enjoyed the title of Rome's tallest and most bombastic structure by a wide margin. This place was designed for theatrics and bloodshed, where Rome's craziest came and went for glory, retribution, and oftentimes a sense of purpose. It was Galerius Domitius who emerged as that day's victor against Augustus of Rhodes by way of a carefully-timed fakeout and a swift beheading. The crowd cheered this grizzled man clad entirely in armor, and he embraced it with all of his silent ego.

When the games had ended, Galerius retreated to the passage past the cells where the weapons were kept and carefully selected, and began to clean Augustus' blood from his blade.

"Gladiator!"

Galerius did not recognize the voice that called for him. He turned towards it, seeing armor of another country being worn under a cape made of fur. A general, no doubt, holding his helmet by his waist and revealing his face: Aged handsomely, but not without flaw. The wrinkles implied having seen many years come and go, many battles waged and won. The hair was almost completely grayed and white, but the hairline did not recede. This general's visage was a mosaic of perseverance and lost time.

Galerius put down his weapons and approached the man who called for him with a minor belligerence.

"With respect, you're not allowed to be here," said Galerius.

"With respect, Gladiator, I wasn't named general for obeying where I shall and shall not be."

The comment disturbed Galerius, but he had no argument against it. The general approached Galerius and extended his free hand.

"General Braktermos of Alexandria," he continued. "I'm here, partially, as a fan. You were unstoppable in there."

"Thank you," Galerius said, accepting both the handshake and the complement.

"It will be a sad day when your life is taken by a better opponent," said Braktermos.

"Then for your sake," said Galerius, "I'll die of old age instead."

Braktermos smiled at Galerius' rhetoric.

"It seems you're as quick with your wit as you are with a blade," Braktermos told the man. It felt as though every comment he made further confused Galerius.

"What's the other part?" Galerius asked abruptly.

"How's that?" Braktermos responded.

"You said you were here *partially* as a fan. Why else have you come to a place where you do not belong? To talk of my demise?"

Braktermos broke his cadence. Galerius could tell that there was some history behind whatever was on the general's mind.

"A request," said Braktermos.

"For?"

"I'm sorry," Braktermos said firmly, "but it cannot be asked until you see what I have to show you. What you can know is that I greatly need your help."

Galerius laughed. He shook his head as he processed it all. How did this general from so far away even get in here? Who was he to ask favors from a man he'd never met?

"Then show me now, general," said Galerius. "My patience for your games is thinning."

"The only games you've played today were inside the walls of the Colosseum. Gladiator, I assure-"

"My name is Galerius," he firmly said to the general.

Braktermos humbled himself. "Galerius, champion of our great city, I assure you what I'm asking is not only worth your while, but just as well worth the Roman lives at stake at this very moment. Something happened last night, and because of it, everybody in that crowd that you've spent your life entertaining hangs in the balance between fate and an untimely death."

Galerius didn't know if his response should be one of sympathy or a strong sense of doubt. The only way to validate his feelings was to give in to that lingering curiosity.

Day-old blood sporadically decorated random items and areas in the terrace that Braktermos and Galerius approached.

The architecture implied a grand design, with curved masonry and a splendid assortment of balusters holding up a guardrail, shaped like human hands. Things that hung daintily on the walls were spread across the floor and shattered to bits. What puzzled Galerius most was that, upon looking up, somehow the ceiling was also affected, as though somebody had been dragged across it and tore up the wood and tiling it was made of.

"The killer moved inhumanly fast," said Braktermos as he pointed to a mark on the ground. What seemed to be a footprint was almost *smeared* across the ground, cracking the floorboards beneath it as the being dashed forward.

Galerius dropped down on one knee to better observe it. He touched the cracks with his fingers and felt the imperfections.

"This is the third murder that looks this way," Braktermos continued.

"What's *this way?*" Galerius asked, his eyes still transfixed on the horrifying details of the scene.

"These are the patterns of a vampire."

Galerius stood quickly, turning to Braktermos. He saw straight through him.

"I've heard of those creatures," Galerius scoffed. "They bring terror to the hearts of little boys who are naive enough to believe in them."

"Have care how you speak to me," Braktermos retorted with a snide look.

"Have care how you regard my intelligence, general. *Vampires don't exist.*"

"Tell me, Gladiator," said Braktermos mockingly. "What did those stories tell you of those non-existent vampires? What traits of theirs can you recollect?"

Galerius furrowed his brow. He complied:

"They have fangs. They drink your blood. They are warded off by Sacred Water, crucifixes, sunlight-"

Braktermos grabbed Galerius by the strap over his chest and yanked the man to the edge of the terrace's railing. Galerius instinctively caught the railing with both hands, and saw below: A thinly-spread pile of ash coated the grass, the size of a man.

"This was the third attack. The man who lived here was drained of his blood shortly before dawn. The two creatures stayed inside the house. Perhaps they thought nobody would come looking for the one they killed. That man was my *friend.* It wasn't until I arrived that it attacked me as well," Braktermos grumbled to an off-put Galerius.

Galerius pushed himself off of the railing, but continued studying the ashes. Up and down, over and over, as Braktermos spoke:

"I sparred and grappled and threw one of the beasts from the doorway, into the light of day. The thing *vanquished.* The other fled amidst a tunnel beneath the house."

Galerius had no response. He could only look at Braktermos, no longer with animosity.

"Do elaborate how naive those who believe in them are," Braktermos finally said.

The tension between the men slowly dissipated. A mutual recognition of what the other person felt.

"What do you need from me?" Galerius asked.

"Assemble your finest men," ordered Braktermos. "There is a cave from which the beings sleep. When the sun first rises tomorrow, we will storm it."

Galerius mulled this over. "Give me a day to decide," he requested.

"A day will yield another body," Braktermos pointed out. "Your decision must be made before dawn tomorrow morning, and you'll need to bring three more men like yourself."

Galerius eyed down the general, whose words were quick and adamant.

"And if I decide not to assist in your hunt for this beast?" Galerius asked, reasserting himself. Braktermos did not yield.

"Then bring four instead, and let men with courage handle the issue."

As Galerius entered the palace of Cicerus, a long-dormant feeling of nostalgia struck him unexpectedly. The walls of the lead-in were just as he remembered from years long passed, with long, white curtains that flowed aside stiff marble walls. This was a place of peace and luxury, and Cicerus had earned every bit of it.

Galerius and Cicerus had been close friends in the fighting pits, but that did little to calm Galerius' nerves. It was Cicerus who left when he was at his highest, indulging himself in the riches and beauties of Rome as Galerius continued in those pits. It'd been years since they last spoke.

And Cicerus saw him.

The years had treated Cicerus kindly, save for a few pounds around the waist and some straggling grays in his hairs. He was garbed in silk robes head to toe, which was a far cry from the Roman armor Galerius was used to seeing on him. He was heading out for an errand when the very sight of Galerius stopped him in his path. This, in turn, stopped Galerius too, and as the two fools were frozen in place, a mutual recognition and recollection of their shared history flooded their minds.

"Galerius Domitius," said Cicerus with some strife.

Galerius bowed his head slightly, as if to apologize for his presence.

"Good fortunes, old friend," Galerius spoke formally.

Cicerus eyed him up and down, as if the reason Galerius had come were somewhere in his wardrobe. He finally relented.

"Good fortunes, old friend," replied Cicerus.

"Old friend," said Galerius, "I know my sight is long-lost-"

"I don't remember the beard on you," Cicerus said, cutting him off.

Galerius stumbled in his words for a moment. Was this a test? Cicerus simply watched Galerius comprehend the words, all the while Cicerus kept the same stoic expression as though Medusa herself had turned him to stone. Finally, Galerius eyed down his opponent, piercing the charade.

"I don't remember that gut on you, either," Galerius responded.

Cicerus was shocked, so much so that the laughter that'd been hiding deep down inside finally burst out of him. The thunderous cackling forced Galerius to do the same. At heart, they were still the two foolish youths who met in those pits long ago.

"The gods have been favorable to you," Galerius said as he approached him with open arms. Cicerus accepted the embrace warmly.

"You moreso," Cicerus responded, "and you very well know it. Word has spread of your recent victories. You haven't changed a bloody bit."

"And you've changed tremendously, *Cicerus the Savage*."

The term struck Cicerus like lightning.

"Now there's a name I haven't heard in..."

"Don't strain yourself trying to figure it out," said Galerius quickly. "In truth, I am here for more than just pleasantries."

Cicerus smiled. It was the exact same Galerius he'd always known. Sharp as ever.

"Come," said Cicerus as he gestured inside. "Tell me why the gods have brought you to my doorstep on this day."

"Weren't you leaving?"

"The wine and whores will always be there, and so will I to meet them," Cicerus said back to Galerius. "Whatever brought you here has all of my attention."

Cicerus sat atop his bench that had been fashioned like something of a throne. It was surrounded by pillows and embroidered designs and details by many well-paid carpenters. Galerius sat across from him in a comfortable chair. A fine Corinthian table laden with fruits and trinkets separated them.

An hour had passed since Galerius' arrival, and only recently had he revealed to Cicerus the reason he was here.

"Rather hilariously," Cicerus spoke with a grand joy, "I have never toyed with the idea of returning to that life of mine."

"You mean the life that brought you this fortune?" Galerius responded, marveling at the home he'd been welcomed into.

Cicerus shot him a snide look. One that didn't deny anything.

"There is simply no purpose for it," Cicerus said back to him. "We won the fights. We won the crowd. We won the approval of the Senate. Hell, we were *slaves* once. You and I won our way out of that one, too."

Cicerus leaned closer to Galerius, changing his tone, and asked the question foremost on his mind: "Why didn't you leave like I did?"

The question hit Galerius in an uncomfortable way. He'd encountered the choice long ago to live life as a free Roman man, yet remained active in the crowd-pleasing battles of the great Colosseum. He was married to it.

"It's not easy to say," Galerius said. "I kept waiting for one day to wake up and feel as you do: Proud of what I've done. *Content* with it..."

"You're damn proud and you know it," Cicerus said to him. They shared a bit of a laugh. It was a laugh that faded quickly.

"Certainly," replied Galerius. "In truth, I'm not sure how to feel. I never wanted to leave... I still don't."

Cicerus leaned back in his chair and left the subject alone.

"So it's men you want, then? For your vampire hunt?" Cicerus said, shifting his tone.

"It's not my hunt," said Galerius.

Cicerus reached for the dagger in his belt. He pulled it out, inspecting it, and said: "If you kill a man in the ring, it's not the Senate's victory. It's yours."

"Fine," Galerius conceded. "I need men for my hunt."

"For your vampire," added Cicerus, pointing with the dagger. "Knives like these won't be of much use with those."

Galerius glared at him.

"Cicerus," Galerius relented, "I need three of your strongest men to accompany me in killing a magical creature."

Cicerus burst into laughter at the absurd point he had pushed Galerius to, and Galerius joined in on it. This time, the laughs did not die down.

In the widespread fields adjacent to the metropolitan cities of ancient Rome, five men conglomerated. Three of their names were Lutatio, Helvius, and Aemilius, and these three stood before Galerius and Cicerus, garbed in the same Gladiatorial armor as Galerius himself, with emotionless expressions. Cicerus knew that Galerius would be selective about his companions in battle, so the fact that Helvius didn't look nearly as strong or as brute as the other two was concerning to him.

Looking to Galerius, Cicerus spoke for the three men:

"You'll notice how Lutatio and Aemilius are significantly larger than Helvius. That is for good reason. Lutatio is a soldier among the finest of Rome's ranks, and you'll recognize Aemilius from-"

"I know," Galerius interrupted. Though him and Aemilius sparred briefly in the pits of the Colosseum, neither held any grudge against the other. Men acted very differently outside of that place.

Cicerus recognized this. He feared that if the moment continued, their alliance and acceptance would be short-lived.

"Helvius will join us," Cicerus said, hastily moving on. "He's trained minimally in combat, but his experiences are what will bring us value."

Galerius came up to Helvius, who looked to be no more than twenty-three of age.

"How well will your experiences fare against a mythical parasite?" Galerius pressed.

Helvius bowed his head slightly. It was as though he were now free to speak.

"I've spent a great deal of my upbringing studying them with my father," said Helvius in a wavering tone. "It is the reason he met his fate."

Galerius turned to Cicerus with concern.

"Marcus Verilius. The vampire's second victim," Cicerus spoke empathetically.

Galerius took this in. He then placed his hand on Helvius' shoulder.

"My boy, I recognize your desire for revenge. But the group of us may share your father's untimely fate." Galerius held Helvius firmly as he spoke, as if instilling the words into him. A powerful warning from an unlikely friend.

Helvius respectfully removed Galerius' hand from his shoulder.

"I am not childlike," Helvius said.

He produced a small book from his garments. The pages were strung together with yarn and string, from years of constant revision, whose title read only one word:

PRODIGIOGONY

"My father intended to finish this book and share it with Rome. Then elsewhere. He wished to etch its findings on every hearthstone of every household."

Helvius shuffled through it, stopping at a page early on in the book. One of the first entries that the Verilius family recorded: *The Vampire.*

"The world is owed an awareness of the gods, monsters and miscreants that prey on the worlds of men," the boy continued. "I don't believe my father died because he had particularly appealing blood in his veins. I believe he was targeted."

Galerius almost shook his head in disbelief. But he refrained from it. When Braktermos threw him against the railing and revealed the ashy vampire's body, Galerius made the choice to no longer outright doubt the absurd, lest he continuously waste the time of everybody around him.

But there was one important point to be made.

"Aemilius," Galerius said to his former opponent, "our blades have crossed more than once. Would you say my intent studying of my opponents saved me from a Gladiator's death in Elysium?"

Aemilius played along, and answered quickly: "Not at all."

Galerius then turned to Lutatio.

"Great Lutatio, who has been described to me as among the *finest of Rome's ranks,* are you standing here today instead of bleeding out on a battlefield because you created a tiny booklet with theories and highlights about the armies you fought?"

"No," spoke Lutatio with a deep, gravely voice.

"Tell the son of Marcus Verilius why you have lived," said Galerius.

"Training. Winning. *Losing.* There are certain parts of me stricken with scars that run so deep that they no longer give sensation to me. But there is a woman who has found and accepted me for all of my damage, and with her I have borne two beautiful children. When I must kill, I think of my family waiting for me to return with new scars, and this gives me strength to fight once more."

Helvius bowed his head, all traces of confidence having left his spirit. Galerius saw this, and finally smiled. He turned to Cicerus with bravado.

"Old friend, I'll take all three of them on this hunt," said Galerius. "The men will use their skills to kill this creature, and the boy will learn to gain them."

Helvius was agasp. Before he could ask why, Galerius made his intentions clear: "Survive tomorrow morning, Helvius Verilius, and transition from an aspiring sage to an avenger of innocent men. Only then will people study your writings."

Braktermos waited impatiently by the cave's entrance. It was as though the daylight that had just begun was somehow about to turn to dusk in a matter of minutes.

From the nearby Roman village that'd been plagued by a vampiric infestation, four men rode towards Braktermos on horseback. Braktermos saw them approach, but did not feel any relief. Not yet.

As the four men arrived and dismounted, Braktermos took in Galerius' new companions, and judged them harshly in his head.

"General Braktermos of Alexandria," said Galerius sternly, "your courageous lot is at your command for the morning."

Braktermos took notice of the unusual weapon on Galerius' side: It was a knife not of steel or iron, but of the wood of a white oak. Galerius saw this and smiled, drawing it and handing it to the general.

"It took hours to sharpen properly," said Galerius.

Braktermos was fixated on the craftsmanship behind it. He smirked, and handed it back to Galerius with a higher respect for him than he previously had. Dedication to this type of cause was in short supply.

Helvius, unlike the others, did not carry a weapon. Instead, only the book he'd been constructing, and a torch which he'd just lit up. Braktermos caught him by the arm.

"Boy, what exactly is your plan in there?" Braktermos asked adamantly.

Helvius abided rather normally: "Well, general, from my understanding we're all here to kill a vampire."

Helvius freed his arm from the general's grasp.

"General," Helvius continued, "you may have called this party to action, but they'd be ill-equipped without this book."

"Then why don't we just take the book?" Lutatio asked rhetorically. Aemilius laughed at the remark. Helvius was unphased, and walked right past Braktermos to Galerius, who'd made it to the front of the cave.

It was immeasurably deep.

The shining rays of dawn's sunlight could never penetrate far enough to reveal the true breadth of the tunnel. Only the modest flames of Helvius' torch could even attempt to do so from the inside. The five men converged together at the entrance, and with a hearty slap on the shoulder blade, Braktermos ordered Galerius to "head in first."

Galerius couldn't believe his ears.

"When recruiting me and calling me cowardly, you spoke with such arrogance and bravery. Where has it all gone during our ride up to this cave?" Galerius scoffed, as if egging the man on.

"I'm not the one who beheaded Augustus of Rhodes in front of a crowd of cheering souls," snapped Braktermos at him. "Every man in Rome would agree that you'd fare better than I in that bloody cave."

Galerius looked to his colleagues, as if asking their opinion. Helvius was the only one who responded:

"I'm one of 'every man in Rome,' and I must align with the general."

Galerius shook off Helvius' comments and ignored his better judgment, heading inside. His peers followed suit, and after them, Braktermos with a spear.

The eerie onlook of the cave became darker and darker as they progressed, and they didn't need to progress far for Helvius to open his mouth again:

"They thrive among darkness. They're averse to the Christian Cross. The blood of men sustains them. Perhaps their most popular trait is being weakened by sunlight."

Galerius laughed.

"Weakened quite a bit, I'd say. The damn thing turned to ash," said Galerius to a pedantic Helvius.

"To ash?" Helvius asked, coming closer to his side as they walked.

"That's what the general said. He threw it from the terrace into the sunlight, and it eviscerated in front of him."

A moment passed as Helvius thought to himself. Finally, against everyone's wishes, he verbalized those thoughts.

"That's odd," said Helvius. "They've never done that before. The sun's light weakens them, and greatly limits their power. I've never heard of it being fatal."

Galerius stopped walking. He turned and addressed Helvius directly.

"It's not lethal?" Galerius asked.

"Galerius, I've been doing this as long as I can remember. I know what I know."

Aemilius and Lutatio stopped as well, following Galerius' suit. Galerius looked to the back of the group at the one man still walking. And so did everyone else. Braktermos removed his helmet, revealing the grin of a man who had won, and laid the spear down on the rocky floor of the cave. He did not need to use it. Setting foot in the shadows of the carefully-chosen cave brought an air of calm to the deceiver, for General Braktermos felt the sunlight's limitations on him no more.

There was no warning for what happened in that cave.

With the speed of a falling star, Braktermos jettisoned toward Helvius before anybody could blink. A blur of darkness accompanied his trail, as though the dark armor he wore painted a ghastly swipe across the canvas of their field of view. Braktermos swatted at the throat of Helvius with fingers now clawed. He turned and pushed Aemilius with a godlike force that launched the warrior toward the walls of the cave, and moved towards Lutatio to implant his fangs in his throat.

In a period of time too small to easily measure, three noises occurred in rapid succession: The slimy puncturing of Lutatio's neck as the demon's fangs plunged themselves inside, followed by the thud of Aemilius' shell-shocked body impacting the rocky wall and splitting apart the bones and organs inside, and finally tailed by the smack of Helvius' withering body hitting the ground, uncontrollably spewing blood from the hole in his neck.

The torch clattered beside them, still lighting up the cave.

Braktermos restrained the fighting arms of Lutatio as he quickly drained the blood from his body, fueling his strength further, and forced him to watch Aemilius' lifeless corpse tumble to the ground. The luxury of a brisk death befell him. Helvius, coughing violently, was experiencing the opposite. Lutatio's eyes rolled backward as the parasite drew the remaining life out of him at a terribly inhuman pace.

Galerius couldn't move. In the Colosseum, he was faster than most and thought quickly on his feet. But all of his opponents had been human. The sight of the general rampaging through his peers with more power than any living creature in Rome *froze* him, and Galerius did not attempt any heroics.

Helvius and Lutatio bled out homogeneously. One donated it rapidly to the cave's inhabitant, and the other shot it wildly across the cave's floor. Helvius died next, partially from the impact he'd taken. The dream-like final thoughts of his children's smiles passed through Lutatio's mind as he lost enough blood to no longer remain conscious, and his body was the last to fall to the ground beside Aemilius and Helvius.

Only several seconds had passed. Galerius, still, did not move. Braktermos wiped Lutatio's blood from his mouth, flicking the excess from his hand. It spattered along the corpse of Aemilius. Galerius looked up at the monster who'd done this and saw the face of a man much younger. The grays in Braktermos' hair had turned black, and the wrinkles had smoothed away, revealing a man in the prime of his life. Galerius raised his wooden dagger defensively. Braktermos smiled, as if to laugh, and Galerius lowered his guard once more. Uncertainty flooded his mind. He was shaking quietly from the experience, but the expression on his face was stoic. Purposely emotionless.

"You'd have it easier striking God with a crossbow."

Braktermos' voice echoed through the boundless interior of the cave. He'd made this place his home, with channels and nooks and open spaces spreading out the deeper one went into the cave. It was some twisted cross of a labyrinth and a dungeon, made only from mother nature's rocks and stones. The internal beauty of it was much too dark for human eyes to see, barely lit up by the withering flames of Helvius' torch on the ground. The space only manifested in the echoes of one's voice.

Galerius laid his dagger on the cave's floor. The sharpened wood met the growing pool of his friends' blood. It dampened slightly, as the pool was almost at Galerius' feet.

"Why me?" Galerius asked, his tone too soft to be audible.

But the wicked ears of the vampire heard him.

"The blood of a civilian is common and dull," Braktermos said as he took a step forward. "The blood of a king is riddled with disease..."

Braktermos stepped carefully over the bodies of the gladiators as he approached Galerius. Galerius watched, and did not flee.

"The blood of a warrior... is *divine*. It courses through the body with a voluminous, youthful energy. And it brings a succulent taste to the tongue."

Braktermos was now inches from Galerius. He ran his sharp fingertips down the side of Galerius' cheek, stopping at the man's chin. Braktermos raised it, exposing the neck.

Galerius did nothing but comply.

"The ash on the ground?" Galerius asked quizzically.

Braktermos smiled, then spoke the truth: "I burned the body after I fed from it. Insert one strand of truth into a web of lies, and men are quick to believe the entirety."

The vampire did not even need to look at Galerius' neck. He simply sensed the way his blood moved through his arteries. The pace remained steady, unaffected by any fear.

From the bloodied ground, Braktermos picked up Galerius' blade, studying it further.

"You didn't attempt to save them," Braktermos pointed out. "Why?"

With no reason to lie, Galerius looked his opponent dead in the eyes.

"The moment we set foot in this cave, our lives were compromised," said Galerius.

"But not even a reaction?" Braktermos retorted.

Galerius bowed his head. He saw now how the pool of blood had started to stain the garments of his shoes.

"I long for bloodshed," Galerius mumbled. "The way a man's blade befalls them, twisting them in ways they weren't meant to move. Prying the muscles apart. Spraying the walls with it. I don't know why I've been made this way, but I know and revel in death... I *crave* bringing it."

Galerius looked back up at his opponent, who cocked his head in curiosity.

"I'd joined the fighting pits of my own accord, and told the masses I was a slave like them," Galerius continued. "It was the only place my desires would be met with applause, not crucifixion."

The vampire was the first to hear Galerius admit this secret. Of all the victims he'd preyed on in all the countries he'd silently invaded, none had stayed so calm in the presence of a vampire's slaughter. Nor accepted defeat so plainly.

"If you are to kill me," said Galerius in a more prominent tone, "then cause me little pain. I feel as though I've experienced enough of it."

Braktermos waved his wrist toward the entrance of the cave. Galerius turned his head to see what he caused: The four horses that the men rode in on conglomerated at the entrance. The smell of these beasts now permeated the cave, mixing with the repulsive odor of fresh bodies and blood. The horses stood strong as they blankly faced the cave's entrance, as formal and diligent as an army of men, and stared back at Galerius with cold, voided eyes.

Pocketing the wooden dagger, Braktermos started toward the cave's exit, his footsteps sloshing the blood beneath them. All three bodies still hadn't stopped producing it. As he passed over the body of Helvius, he reached down and picked up the incomplete book, shuffling through its bloodstained pages on his way to the cave's entrance. Once there, he threw the book on top of Helvius' torch, letting the pages catch the flames.

"My intention was to visit Cicerus and share word of your death," admitted Braktermos. "He would most likely attempt to avenge you, and his blood would spill all the same."

Galerius turned around to face the exit of the cave. It was the first time he'd moved since the attack.

"I will leave him be," said Braktermos with a nod.

After a moment, Galerius nodded back. It was a mutual recognition of two very different types of monsters, neither of which disrespected the others' actions.

"The dagger was made with passion," said Braktermos as he touched his pocket. "I will give it to the first man who knows of my existence, and responds with peace instead of violence."

Defeated as he was, Galerius couldn't help himself.

"It's a good thing you're immortal, demon... because that day will never come."

Braktermos lost his usual cadence. A deep sense of disappointment took its place.

"The blood of these three men will last me quite some time before I move on to yours, Gladiator."

The relief that Galerius felt had vanished as quickly as it came. His words had moved Braktermos, but they did not save him. The spider still needed to feed on the ensnared housefly.

Galerius glared back at the vampire, seeing the shine of daylight illuminate him and his diligent string of guardians from behind. These animals would stay and keep the gladiator here while Braktermos was gone, keeping the man in his trap. Though Braktermos' body was normalized by the light, with human fingers and a fangless mouth, he could still stare back at the gladiator with a red light of triumph in his eyes, and a smile that Judas in Hell would be proud of.

III

THE APE-WOMAN

Dr. John Sigmund wheeled the stretcher out into the middle of the circus tent. For the third time in the past five minutes, John made sure that the straps on the sides on the stretcher were tightened to their absolute peak. Nobody's mind in 1887 was quite ready to see what lay under that large, white tarp, and the man who created it knew that all too well.

"Success?" a voice cried out from behind John, startling him. He turned, seeing the face of his benefactor smiling intently.

"Yes, Mr. Walters," said John reflexively, as though snapping out of a trance. "The past six months have brought wonders, tenfold more than imagined."

"I asked for it in four," said Mr. Walters as he approached the stretcher.

Mr. Walters' three-piece suit was purple and festive, as it was every day that he walked into work. Even when temperatures skyrocketed on scalding summer days, Mr. Walters' jacket never came off. He had a massive show to run and made sure to dress the part. John was less vain, and had no knack for showmanship at all. He knew what he knew, and that was decades of biological research power-packed into that brilliant mind of his. The two had been a good team because of it, contrasting each other wonderfully in skills and expertise.

Seeing Mr. Walters' hand go for the tarp, John instinctively grabbed it, stopping him from seeing what was underneath.

"Forgive me," John said plainly, "but you did ask for *The Most Ghastly Freak Show Ever Concocted By Man* when you asked me to do this. I assure you that I've delivered."

Mr. Walters shook free from John's grasp.

"Doctor, you've cost me a tremendous amount of time, resources, and frankly a bit of my patience," Mr. Walters said, eyeing over the tarp. "Do you expect me to take your word as to its completion?"

John smiled, almost to himself.

"Just make sure you're ready," John said cryptically.

Mr. Walters chuckled. Then, before he could be told not to, removed the tarp from the body. John did not try to stop him this time.

Thick, black fur ran up and down the thing's monstrously large body. The frame was savage and muscular, with gigantic arms and paws of a feral beast at its disposal. Through all of this, to the one who created it, this beast still somehow possessed the *physique* of a woman. A human one. The very image of it would jar an onlooker for days, depending on their mental fortitude. It was a hybrid born not by nature but by an aspirational man of medicine, brought forth by fusing the bodies of a recently-deceased prostitute, and a western lowland gorilla.

"You were warned," John reiterated.

Mr. Walters did not remove his gaze. *Unhuman* would be the most appropriate word to describe the appearance of John's creation. Mr. Walters was plainly awestruck, and almost unable to breathe at first.

"Your warning was horseshit," said Mr. Walters.

Mr. Walters looked to John with a void of terror in his eyes. As if through some strange error, the man's mouth slowly formed a smile, contrasting the fear in his gaze.

"You've done nothing but *wonders* here, Doctor," said Mr. Walters with a crazed expression. One he would not lose anytime soon.

John sat in Mr. Walters' tent three days before their show was slated to reopen. His hand was starting to cramp from the non-stop signing of extensive legal forms, agreeing to certain profit shares and ownership issues relating to the carnival. Mr. Walters sat back at his desk and, rather calmly, kept elaborating on their show:

"One could say we've been *lacking* a draw like this. We have a freak show or two, undoubtedly: The Strongman, some siamese twins, some people with unusual parts of them pierced. All good stuff, surely. But everybody's seen them now, and there's no real reason for our patrons to return."

John half-listened to Mr. Walters' ramblings. These contracts were frustratingly boring to read. Even trying to *skim* them was annoying.

"Your man-made beast is the kind of feral, untamed creature that'll smash itself against the walls of its cage," raved Mr. Walters. "The kids and parents who spend countless afternoons here are sure to be drawn towards it, solely to satisfy that burning curiosity if not for their admiration."

This caught John's much-divided attention.

"Admiration?" John asked his employer, looking up from the contracts.

Mr. Walters blinked hard.

"The mad doctor *speaks,* does he? I was beginning to lose myself in the sound of my own voice. Not an awful place to be," said Mr. Walters, leaning forward and setting his elbows on that recently-purchased mahogany table.

"Whosoever looks at my creation and feels a sense of admiration, may God heal their damaged vision," boasted John.

"Come now," said Mr. Walters as John buried himself back into the contracts. "You don't admire what you've created?"

"Of course I do," said John with enthusiasm. "It's a triumph of science over nature. It's *unprecedented-*"

"I don't need the spiel again," said Mr. Walters, putting up his hand. "You're overselling what's already sold."

"It's still true," John continued. "She's the most intriguing creature I've ever seen walk the face of the Earth."

"Intrigue and love are not mutually exclusive. You of all men ought to know that."

John froze. Mr. Walters immediately recognized the line he crossed: "I'm sorry-"

"It's fine," said John quickly. Shutting him down.

"I didn't mean any-"

"It's fine," John repeated just as fast, as if it'd been recorded and replayed.

John went back to Mr. Walters' contracts. He was almost finished with them now. Six months ago, when Mr. Walters came to Dr. John Sigmund for this task, he'd caught the man amidst a rather nasty separation: Bethany Sigmund, though she'd never go by that last name anymore, had finally given up on dealing with John's shortcomings in the marriage and left him. John didn't put up a fight when she proposed it, and that only drove her away faster.

Mr. Walters had meant the joke in jest, but now the atmosphere had surely gone. John signed the final bit of the many, many papers, and passed it off onto Mr. Walters' brand-new desk.

"Split the profitability 60-40, your favor" said John. "I'm to receive these in perpetuity, and as payment for keeping her well-kept here on these premises."

"That all sounds well and good, Doctor," said Mr. Walters. The usual smile returned to his face.

"Excellent," said John as he rose from the seat. "I'll be here in the morning. The asset will be needing her morphine injections."

"That's an ugly name," said Mr. Walters.

"I think John is rather bold, and daring," said John back to him, attempting to return the light-hearted mood. This almost got a laugh out of Mr. Walters.

"You know what I meant, Doctor. What person in this world would pay to see our *asset*? That's not a name you can plaster on the marquee of a freak show."

Dr. John Sigmund had a think. Marketing was not his strongest suit.

"The naming conventions of freak shows are often absurd," said John. "You'll call my ape-woman something ridiculous, like Captive Wild Woman, and pass her off as something she's not."

"Certainly not," said Mr. Walters. "A good name conveys what the audience is going to experience. Try and imagine a bunch of small children begging their mothers to take them to see it, saying the name over and over again 'til their parents can't take it anymore, pacifying them with their wallets... Truth be told, Doctor, I'd much sooner call her exactly what you said she is."

THE APE-WOMAN

The freshly-painted letters could not be large nor bold enough for the sideshow's overhang. It replaced the Strongman's exhibit, taking up the largest sideshow venue in the freak show. The Strongman himself was not consulted about the sudden change. He found out the morning of, and was not given a chance to voice his grievances.

As foreseen, the unorthodox name drove a decent amount of intrigue, with bachelors and families alike crossing through the threshold this title was plastered over. But the show itself would have to live up to its unorthodox name in order for these people to return, and respend their earnings on it.

Thus was Mr. Walters' grand plan. This man had two particular talents in this world, and fused them brilliantly.

He was a ruthless businessman with an eye for power and fame. At a young age, he convinced kids on his school's playground to give him what was theirs for loads of false reasons. As his peers grew older, their gullibility subsided, and Mr. Walters matured to match that.

His second talent, which was also innate in him, was that of a charming, charismatic host who could entertain and stall a crowd for so long that they'd start to forget about their real-world obligations. Those only existed outside of his traveling carnival. This very powerful skill of immersion, it was hoped, would be used to great effect for today's unveiling of Dr. John Sigmund's twisted creation.

From behind the stage, John sat and readied the syringe with a precise dosage of morphine. The process by which he'd fused these two bodies into one, hybridized creature still brought her pain, and the drug substantially dampened it. The beast wasn't strapped or harnessed down, but rather, as the two sat alone in this dimly-lit stage room, she was laid out onto a dressing couch as John kneeled over her. The vein he chose for the morphine was the largest and most obvious near her elbow. Once it became unusable, he would move on to the other arm.

"Easy girl," John said as he stroked the fur on her head, trying to calm her down.

She had been nervous ever since regaining consciousness. The world around her was a mystery, and her past knowledge of either lives was blurred and fragmented. Her mind was a blending of the intelligence levels of human and ape, but carried no memories from either. Today was the second day of her life, the first day of her own showcase, and the second injection of this strange medical substance that she didn't understand.

Once that syringe pierced her skin and brought that drug into her animalistic veins, her trembling practically vanished. A glorious reprieve from her usual state of mind.

"Is she ready?" Mr. Walters asked, entering the backstage area. John had forgotten to shut the room's door, and hadn't yet become used to Mr. Walters sneaking up on him like that.

"*Knock* next time, Walters. I could've been administering her dosage."

But Mr. Walters had already begun ignoring the doctor's words. He stared at his marvelous Ape-Woman once more, drawn to that wicked, ghastly form of hers.

"Extraordinary, isn't she?" Mr. Walters asked.

John shook his head, mildly frustrated.

"She's ready for your show, if that's what you're asking."

Outside, anticipation was built. Chatter amongst the crowd spread rapidly. A byproduct of Mr. Walters' illustrious energy. The people watched as their beloved Mr. Walters stepped out onto the stage with a *leash* in his hands, with the other end leading somewhere off-stage. The crowd hollered curiously at whatever this man was about to present. Mr. Walters smiled at the crowd and pulled slowly on the leash...

It was tied around a gorgeous woman's neck, who posed playfully. The crowd knew her as Mr. Walters' assistant, and they erupted in laughter.

"Not what you were expecting?" Mr. Walters asked facetiously, laughing a bit himself.

Mr. Walters undid the leash from her neck, but didn't shoo her away. She stayed by his side as he spoke, projecting his voice.

"At quite long last, I give to you the most abhorrent abomination to ever walk God's green Earth. Mothers in the audience, please keep your children closeby, and prepare if you must to block their eyes and keep their minds incorruptible. You and your families are about to see the most ghastly freak show ever concocted by man."

Mr. Walters nodded to his assistant, who went over to the stage's curtains.

"I think it will thrill you. It may shock you. It might even *horrify* you. So, if any of you feel that you do not care to subject your nerves to such a strain, now's your chance to uh, well..."

Mr. Walters looked again to his assistant, nodding approval, then back to the audience.

"...We *warned* you."

The crowd was in a full state of uncertainty. Was this all just dramatic fluff? Should they really be so concerned over whatever miscreant was behind that curtain? They would find out momentarily, as Mr. Walters' assistant had already begun pulling down the stage's curtains.

Mr. Walters quickly stepped aside, revealing the long-awaited sight.

The curtains parted and the beast's cage was in sight: Cast-iron, with bars thin enough to not obstruct the view, and large enough to comfortably house a mountain lion. Paula was unbound in her prison, and when finally seeing the crowd, she grabbed the bars of the cage firmly. She'd never seen so many people together before.

The crowd gasped at her sight: Her thick fur covered a hybridized corpse-like entity, with a woman's face holistically morphed onto the gorilla's head. Twisted, unnatural, and most certainly demonic. The chimera bore noticeable scars and stitches and indents throughout her entire body. Neither the gorilla nor the woman's body were used as a base; instead, they were both *equally* represented.

The beast was gorgeously, spectacularly horrifying.

Mr. Walters' abomination looked back over the crowd with a sense of wonder and curiosity, but all they saw was a fearsome gaze of the wild, petrifying Ape-Woman.

Dr. John Sigmund watched from stage right. He knew this would be a good opportunity for her to become acclimated to her new environment of a freak show's attraction. The longer she stared at the crowd and moved in accordance with their shocked little faces - her gaze following the ones who flinched the most - the more she felt what could only be described as an unorthodox sense of joy. The attention was all on her, and she was infatuated with the feeling of it.

John smiled. His creation was being marveled at by a crowd of curious people. By proxy, he felt admired just as much as what he'd created.

Mr. Walters' show migrated from town to town, making the Ape-Woman a moderate success across the vast unsettled plains of the New Frontier.

John had this thought in his mind every time she was brought out on stage and grew a weird fondness for what he'd done. He had no children (making the separation much easier on him) and thought of himself as some type of fatherly figure to her: A young, artless girl whom he'd created and treated kindly, and now raised to showcase her uncanny nature. He'd wanted a child with his wife, and he knew she did too, but only learned after the separation why she never gave him one: She simply didn't want *his*.

To alleviate Paula's growing pains, John administered one regular dosage of morphine every morning, and one more right before she slept. These were her *most favorite* hours in the dressing room she lived in. She quickly developed an association between the face and body of Dr. John Sigmund and the joy of the morphine's effusion. In return, John stared back at her with a great sense of pride, and this power was something he often drew on when he felt alone. That very thought, knowing somebody was happy to see his face... It was a Hail Mary in the Hell that he'd found himself in.

John saw Paula's veins bulge out of her arm as he tightened the belt again, noticing the spots where he'd previously given her the dosage. When this arm ran out, he would switch to a vein in one of her feet, and that would last at least several more cities on Mr. Walters' traveling show. This was torture to him as he reassessed her health, and over time as all of her veins became unusable, it would be infinitely more torturous for her to survive this way. But it needed to be done. Just for a little while longer.

After the day's injection, Paula scampered around the dressing room with her usual glee, that powerful substance coursing its way through her entire body. John admired her passion and energy, but didn't share it, so when she eventually made her way around the room in a big circle and tackled him to the ground, he couldn't help but laugh and push her off.

That's enough, Paula, John said in sign language.

Paula released him and batted the ground near John aggressively. She was in a delightful mood and didn't want him to turn her down today. The doctor had been teaching her a little bit of the language a day, but warned her not to use it when she performed on stage. The thought that the caged beast would be anything more than a mindless beast would disturb the show's audience in a way they didn't pay for.

Why don't we learn something? John signed.

John shuffled around the room for something he'd packed away. It was an old chess board that hadn't seen much use since he was a teenager.

Paula stared back at him, innocently confused.

Hours later, when John finally stopped Paula from attempting to swallow all of the pieces on the board, Paula was finally able to make a legal move on every single one of her turns. That was her *human* half showing through, he reckoned. The half that learned quicker than any monkey ever could. They played a thousand times in a row, or at least it felt that way to him, and yet neither of them ever got tired or bored from doing it.

After a series of games that brought them both past the hour of midnight, Paula finally beat her opponent. She shrieked in joy, prompting John to quiet her down and not wake anybody.

Good girl, he signed.

Paula became excited at the phrase. Like clockwork, she set up all of the pieces on the board in the exact same way. John watched with wide eyes, bewildered at how fast she was able to work. It brought a beaming smile to the doctor's face. He'd created something substantial, with a living body and a beating heart, and it showed signs of excitement as it started to match him intellectually.

Getting late, John signed to her.

Before Paula could react negatively, John picked up her Queen and held it up like a prize. Her wide eyes followed it as he slowly handed it to her.

This is you, said John. *Everyone else... They're pawns and knights and bishops. Paula is a Queen: More powerful than all of them. Don't you ever forget that.*

Paula studied the piece as he spoke, then looked up at him: *King is most important piece...*

John smiled wide. He reached over to her half of the board, then topped her King on its side.

Mr. Walters sat in his tent smoking one of his cigars like he always did after a showcase. The experience calmed him, alleviating the tension and stress that came with trying to run an operation like the one he managed. Conversations, handshakes, the occasional signature. And an abundance of warming up crowds before the acts.

His tent's door opened quickly. John didn't even knock on it.

"What is this, Walters?!" The doctor fumed at his boss. He tossed a small bag of coins and dollars on Mr. Walters' desk in the center of the working space. Mr. Walters barely flinched at it. He'd been expecting this conversation for some time now. *Today's the day,* he thought to himself as he took one final drag of the cigar before ashing it out for later.

"What's the problem?" Mr. Walters asked innocently.

John scoffed. "Don't play me a fool, you bastard. We'd agreed to forty cents on the dollar for my services for any and all of the Ape-Woman's appearances. Every ticket sold to her sideshow. Forty percent is mine."

"Is it not all there?" Mr. Walters asked with wide eyes.

"*Walters!!*" John snapped. "I will not be toyed with by a man who wears the same ridiculous suit every day, prancing around about his show like he's P. T. Barnum, and not just some disgusting scam artist. You've paid me *five cents* on the goddamn dollar, Walters. That bag isn't heavier than my left shoe. You're going to pay me the other thirty-five percent, or I'll take my Ape-Woman to someone who's not a complete scumbag like yourself."

Mr. Walters dropped the act.

"How does it feel to have created something truly unique?" Mr. Walters asked with a rhetorical, sardonic drawl. "She really is the first of her kind, isn't she? There aren't any others in the world like her. What would the law say if I were to inform them of what you've done? Surely, you have prescriptions for everything you're injecting into her every day, lest you be accused of malpractice and animal abuse. Or would it just be *abuse,* seeing as you occasionally treat her like a human being?"

John was flabbergasted. "How dare you-"

"Shut up, John," said Mr. Walters in a grim tone. "You've gone completely *mad.* You're a raving lunatic with a doctorate and an aspirational mind. Those contracts you signed were completely void, because I *am* a scam artist. A disgusting scam artist, at that. Just like you said. I'm scamming the people of this country into paying me to see something they're *revolted* by at a close range. I've scammed every sword-swallowing, fire-breathing, knife-throwing freak I've recruited into my system and operation. I've scammed you into thinking that the man who created the Ape-Woman was entitled to nearly *half* of her goddamn first dollar gross."

Mr. Walters re-lit the cigar next to him. This conversation wasn't going to be anywhere near as stressful as he anticipated.

"You've *screwed* me!" John yelled.

"Five cents on the dollar is plenty," said Mr. Walters before taking a long drag. "Look at the traffic what we're doing is bringing in. More than you ever would've made if you'd said no to me."

"But that's not your decision to make!"

"So that makes it *your* decision, then? Do tell me what you believe you're worth to me now. To anybody. You've created a product, and I've sold the world on it. Your efforts were brief. Mine are ongoing. Every single day. Every single week. Your five cents on the dollar wouldn't exist without my show, but my show would *certainly* exist without you. Understand your value, Doctor. It's *nil* compared to mine."

John gritted his teeth. He stumbled trying to respond: "This- this is blackmail. *This is kidnapping!* You cannot hold her hostage in your circus without my approval!"

"*Your approval?!*" Mr. Walters barked back at the man. "By Jove, don't make me laugh. You have no more consent to the Ape-Woman than the Ape-Woman herself! Have you considered that, Doctor? If we are to treat her like a human, then you must let her make her own decision untrifled by your leanings. But if we are to treat her like the chattel she is, then she is here and there, past and present, *irrevocably mine.* She's no different to me than the tent I display her in. Or the yacht I'm taking this weekend. Or the pack of cigars in my coat pocket. You have just as much claim to any of those as you do to her."

John was defeated. Anything he said would've only dug his hole even deeper, and he was nearing the point where he'd never be able to escape. He analyzed his options: Go to the authorities and crash and burn alongside Mr. Walters and his show... or take the deal and keep quiet.

"And by the way, should you ever barge in here and insult me like this again, I won't have you thrown in prison for drugging your little pet every day. I'll have my Strongman rip your beating heart out of that thin, gangly chest, and we'll feed it to the Ape-Woman for lunch."

Something changed in the doctor right then. It was some weird form of protection over her that motivated it. Perhaps contacting the police or keeping silent weren't John's only two options in this situation. Perhaps, unbeknownst to Mr. Walters, there was a third brewing in John's mind. One much more sinister in order to rival his opponent's.

"Take your bag full of *whatever* I decide to give you and get out," said Mr. Walters finally.

John abided. He swiped the bag, and as he did so, snagged the pair of keys they'd landed near. Keys to the yacht Mr. Walters had just bragged about taking out this weekend.

Mr. Walters was a joke. He'd forged his business on the promises of fortunes and experiences worth the grossly overpriced tickets he churned out before showtime. John meditated on all of this as he made his way down to Paula's enclosure, the key to her door readily in his hand. He fidgeted with it as he stewed in all of his subsided rage and resentment for that lowly man.

John opened her door and saw his creation picking the stuffing out of the couch's cushions. The moment he entered, she excitedly went over to him.

"Paula!" John barked at her, seeing the damage she'd done to the furniture.

But Paula didn't care. She still stormed him with a world of affection. She clutched onto him like it were an attack, not knowing her own strength. John wriggled out of her bind and held her head firmly in his hands, making close, direct eye contact.

"We don't destroy couches," he said sternly.

But nothing could erase the distorted smile on Paula's face. She knew what it meant when her favorite person walked into this room. And additionally, he only *said* this out loud. He'd forgotten to sign it to her.

Paula scampered over to the dressing room's table and mirror and opened a drawer. That act of gently gripping the drawer's handle, John recalled, took hours of practice and training for her to learn. Or re-learn, as it were. From the drawer, Paula grabbed the brown leather belt that'd seen many days of use. She scurried back over to John and held it out to him, freezing in place in anticipation.

John sighed solemnly. This was what needed to be done for her. To keep her happy.

To keep *Walters* happy.

The reality was becoming clear to him: Paula had more than overcome her growing pains weeks prior. She was physically well and fit enough to exist on her own. What John was doing now was obligatory, to satisfy her incredible dependency and Mr. Walters' standards for the fractions of pay from what he was promised.

John took the leather belt from her hand and wrapped it around her bicep. He tightened it, watching her black veins perk out. Too damaged to reinject on this arm. He undid the leather strap and reapplied it on her other arm, confusing Paula.

"It's okay," John mumbled softly as he stroked her head.

Before John could ready the needle, the door to her dressing room opened up, and from it came another of Mr. Walters' freak shows: The Strongman.

"What's this?!" John asked, hating to be disturbed during this process.

"*Outside*," said the Strongman.

Paula had no say in the matter. With a growing fear, John abided and left, signing '*Be back soon*' to her as he walked out the door.

Outside of the dressing room, the Strongman cornered John with his body language, forcing him against the room's wall with barely any space of breathing room between them. His body was as massive as it looked on stage when he lifted those giant weights and objects with a smile. But there was no smile on his face in that hallway. Instead, a hideous scowl met John's neutral, emotionless expression. The eyes of the Strongman were crazed, but John had only just left Mr. Walters' tent. Even if he'd realized the keys were missing, John knew there was no way that Mr. Walters could've sent his Strongman after him so early.

"I overheard your conversation," said the Strongman in a rancher's drawl and an expectedly deep voice. "I didn't know his foot could cram that far up someone's ass."

John remained silent.

"I'm not gonna rip your heart out," said the Strongman. "If he asks me to,

I sure will. But that's not what this is... Walters pays me *less* than the five you're makin', and I work damn hard to earn it. Ever since your gorilla girl started her show, nobody's paying to see *mine.* Anywhere we go. Always the same thing."

"I'm sorry," said John honestly.

"I don't need an apology," said the Strongman. "You're gonna gimme *half* of what you're makin' every week or I'll break her little neck like a twig."

Again, John said nothing.

"*Y'hear me,* Doc?" the Strongman threatened.

"I can't," said John calmly.

"What's that, now?" the Strongman almost sounded confused. He'd never have anticipated this sort of pushback from a man so much smaller than him.

"As it stands, I won't make enough to sustain a living," said John in a diplomatic sort of way. "I'm pulling my Ape-Woman from his show. You'll never see either of us again."

The Strongman smirked a bit. This was better than his own idea.

"You're a smart man, John," said the Strongman.

John smiled and gave a nod in a friendly manner. He hid the terror inside of him with an admirable execution. This false confidence he hid behind broke the moment the Strongman left him with this parting request: "Give me the bag before I leave."

"What?" John asked.

"I've already suffered traveling alongside her," the Strongman insisted. "Give it here and I'll lcave you on your way."

John couldn't part with that bag. It was just what was needed to leave with Paula for some time before he found new work. If he were penniless, the two of them would get absolutely nowhere. It took a great deal of strength for John to speak his mind to the massive man, but it *needed* to be said. There was no other way.

"I can't do that," John insisted, "and you'll need to move out of my way."

Gracefully, as though it were a dance, the Strongman raised one of his muscular arms and firmly placed his hand on John's shoulder, getting a nice grip on the doctor's collarbone.

John thrust the morphine needle into the Strongman's neck. The Strongman cried out in pain, then violently tossed John aside. Petrified, John sprawled to his feet and ran away as fast as he possibly could. He'd lost the ability to coordinate his plan in advance. It would need to begin tonight. It would need to begin without Paula.

The next morning yielded dozens of new customers for Mr. Walters' traveling show, and although the Strongman was suspiciously sick in his tent the night before, everything else was running smoothly for the day's activities to be underway.

The show was about to begin.

Mr. Walters' assistant had the leash prepared around her neck as she hid just offstage. The same old gag they'd always done before showcasing the show's titular beast. Mr. Walters stood in the crowd's view and pulled on the leash, revealing his assistant and gaining the laughs of the audience. He made his same joke, removed the leash from his assistant's neck, and began his introductory speech. The only real change in the entire act over the past several weeks of touring was the audience that they did it for.

The showman's voice could be heard from backstage by the creature that did not understand any English: *"So, if any of you feel that you do not care to subject your nerves to such a strain..."*

The curtains surrounding the Ape-Woman's cage slowly began to part. The day's light reached down and touched Paula's disheveled, patchy fur which she'd begun tearing out in certain places.

Mr. Walters continued: "Now's your chance to..."

He gave the audience a cocky gesture, and smiled sensibly.

"...Well, we *warned* you," Mr. Walters finished as he stepped aside.

The curtains fully parted, and the audience was in shock.

Paula's hybridized body was covered in sweat. Random clumps of her fur coated the cage's bottom. One-half of the cage housed her vomit, while the other had droppings of diarrhea. Her eyes were watery, crying profusely in an uncontrollable way, and the pain in her chest and stomach caused her to be fixed in a hunched-over position. The sunlight had only been hitting her for several seconds, but in her mind, it was the unbridled effect of the Sahara desert, scorching what life was left inside of her.

She cocked her head towards the crowd with dilated pupils and glared at them in a fit of rage and anxiety.

The Ape-Woman screeched from the bottom of her soul and grabbed the thin bars of the iron cage with both hands. Paula shook it violently as she screamed, not losing sight of the audience as she did so. A complete primal wrath was being contained by that cage in full view of Mr. Walters' latest patrons. Mr. Walters watched nervously, knowing that the magnitude of her absurdity would give incredible stories for the families to tell afterwards. Cautiously, he let the show go on.

The iron cage's bars began to bend.

Mr. Walters' assistant noticed before he did. The two were hidden on opposite ends of the stage, unwilling to walk across and distract the audience's grotesque show. They could only exchange looks for the time being: The assistant gave him a confused gesture, to which he put out his hand and signaled for the assistant to calm down. He would see this play out to fruition before risking a refund.

Paula's screams had drawn the attention of other sideshows' attendees now. People began leaving other parts of Mr. Walters' show to find the source of these most dissonant, gruesome sorts of cries. They sounded worse than what people imagined a woman would scream during her own murder. The cage's bars kept bending and contorting as Paula kept shaking with unbelievable tenacity, and some families in the crowd began to leave the scene.

Upon noticing some of them leave, Mr. Walters stepped back out onto the stage.

He came close to her cage and showed himself in a friendly manner, but before he could say any words, the Ape-Woman again passionately screamed and rippled the cage slightly more: It twisted as though it were made of wood amidst a horrible storm. Mr. Walters flinched, now in plain view of the silenced crowd. The boisterous energy about them had completely died down. He turned to see their frightful eyes and saw more of them leaving, as others showed up out of curiosity and fear. The entertainment empire that Mr. Walters had been trying to build was crumbling in his uncertain view.

The paw of the Ape-Woman tore open a chunk of the cage. Mr. Walters turned at the sight as Paula snatched him by the suit and *yanked* him right towards her iron trap. Mr. Walters' assistant screamed, unsure how to help him or anybody else, and inadvertently motivated the crowd before them to share that fear and scream as well.

Families flooded away from the stage of the Ape-Woman as fast as they could. Droves of people stumbled over each other as the massive, confused crowd tried to migrate swiftly to an exit from this horrid place. Mr. Walters peeled himself away from Paula's mighty grasp only by allowing her to tear the front of his purple suit off and gift him with several scrapes and bruises along his chest and arms. He stumbled backward over his own feet as he was flung away by the force of the break, landing on his side and immediately trying to scuffle away from the beast he'd commissioned to exist.

The Ape-Woman broke free of her cage and firstly saw the assistant trying to run.

The assistant almost toppled over her tall high heels trying to rapidly descend the staircase. Coursing through Paula's body was the strength, speed, and stamina of a western lowland gorilla that had never been unleashed since her inception. This arcane feeling, fueled by her unbearable morphine withdrawals, possessed her and motivated her forward on all fours, the tips of her fingers scraping through the stage's hardwood flooring. The Ape-Woman mantled after Mr. Walters' assistant and tackled her at the bottom of the stage's steps. She used her jagged fangs and bit into the assistant's neck, ripping the throat from her body and creating a wave of blood that stuck to everything it came in contact with.

On his feet again, Mr. Walters ran straight for his tent. He bolted through the opposite side of the stage from the monster and fled in a direction that the crowd wasn't trying to go in.

The Ape-Woman dashed forward and grabbed the arm of the closest one in the crowd: A younger man with a thick-brimmed hat and a long, scraggly beard. The man resisted and tried to pull free from her grasp. A hopeless effort. The Ape-Woman pulled him down onto the ground and stepped on his chest, dominating him in a primal way. She used her large toes to grip his rib cage and, with his arm still in her hand, used tremendous force to pull it straight out of his shoulder's socket. The Ape-Woman screamed at him and used the severed limb to beat him savagely on the ground.

Mr. Walters entered the tent and locked the door behind him. In the drawer of his desk, he produced an expensive six-shooter revolver and spent too much time loading the bullets. He'd never been trained in how to use one. His jitters made him drop one of them onto the ground. Panicking, Mr. Walters crouched down on all fours to retrieve it, and as he did so, heard the carnage taking place outside: A massacre only dreamt in the most haunting of nightmares.

His Ape-Woman was loose, and he would be responsible for it.

Mr. Walters rose with the lost bullet and continued loading the revolver. Clicking the chamber in place, he now waited patiently behind his desk for her to enter. His tent had only one window, and it was facing the opposite direction from the Ape-Woman's stage. He could only listen to the Ape-Woman's malevolence and annihilation: Paula's screams overpowered the crowd's as she unleashed her hell upon them. People's bodies were hitting walls and breaking on impact, or being torn apart by her own neanderthalic hands and teeth. This all continued for many moments until the entire crowd either dispersed or perished. Mr. Walters couldn't tell which from inside his tent.

Unassumingly, the noise died down.

Mr. Walters was almost petrified. He held that revolver with a minor shake in his hand. An unusual irresolution had overtaken the man as he took refuge in his tent, whose flimsy walls would not have done him any well against her attack. Mr. Walters moved to the door and unlocked it slowly, careful to not let the bolt of the door make too much noise as it slid out of position. The door peered open and gave him his view of what he'd missed, and Mr. Walters saw his career's end completely actualized everywhere he looked.

Bodies coated the dirt ground below, made up of both customers and staff. The beast's morphine withdrawals had driven her into a frenzy-like rage from which she'd never experienced before, and her retaliation brought an ultimate consequence to the world she'd been born into.

Mr. Walters stepped out from the tent into the all-quiet world. In the plethora of death and bloodshed, he saw the body of his assistant not far from the stage's entry. Her throat had been viscerally removed, and Paula, herself, was nowhere in sight. Mr. Walters continuously looked in all directions and moved very carefully toward her body.

She came from atop the stage where she'd climbed to see a new, more expansive world than she ever had. Her pounce was unheard until the feral landing she made on his chest, using Mr. Walters' body as protection from her fall. Mr. Walters was now pinned beneath her tackle. Several of his bones snapped on impact, being crunched between the thick of the Earth's expanse and the animalistic body of the Ape-Woman. The gun was still in his hand, though the arm couldn't move beneath the massive paw holding it down. His body was fully immobile.

As Mr. Walters cringed in the sudden excruciating agony, he was forced to see into the face of his chattel: The piercing dyad of what was once human and primate, never meant to share the same experience, whose natures both glared right back at him in visible confusion and pain. The shape and skull of her head was the gorilla's, with the skin of the woman's face fused over it like a leech clings to its victim in shallow waters. Those eyes of hers were manic, adorned by the misshapen cheekbones and jawline that gave a surreal experience to all who tried to make sense of her sight. She was an unseeable abomination that had never asked to be willed into existence, for greed nor any other purpose.

As Mr. Walters was forcibly entrapped and mesmerized by the Ape-Woman's considerably close face, Paula twitched weirdly and vomited all over Mr. Walters' head, then groggily stood up off of him and tried to walk away. Before making it very far, Paula staggered disturbingly and passed out.

Paula awoke to a wondrous night sky, populated with an astronomer's bounty of glistening stars. She rose from her dormancy, but coughed when she tried to move, spreading tiny particles of vomit. Remnants of her most eventful showcase.

"Easy, girl," spoke a familiar voice.

John's hand met her shoulder and guided her back down to rest. He used a towel to dab up the particles. She was otherwise clean, something John had focused on after he'd brought her here. He washed her body and dressed her in comfortable rags, and trimmed the thick, unagreeable fur that grew from everywhere. She was an object of fascination for him, and so he strove to achieve her mental and physical well-being.

The boat swayed gently in the untroubled waters of the Atlantic Ocean.

John procured access to Mr. Walters' yacht the previous night, and only saw the aftermath of his disastrous show the following morning. He tossed her unconscious body into a cart and walked the both of them towards the nearest train set for the Eastern Seaboard. There, he acquired a crew of six young, healthy men, and hired them with almost every dollar in that bag. After raiding the locked safe in Mr. Walters' tent when taking his creation back, John doubled his crew and tripled all of their rates. This vessel was The Wind Dancer, and because nobody wondered what happened to the ship's previous owner, it belonged only to Dr. John Sigmund and his seamen.

Paula's head rose up from her bed of hay and empty crates - something John threw together by happenstance for her - and saw his huge, beaming eyes of admiration. Her hand trembled when trying to sign, but John could make it out: *What did I do?*

John took her hand and rested it on her lap using his other to sign back: *You did what Queens do. You took the King... You won.*

As John leaned closer to her, he grabbed his medical needle and brought it into her view. Paula's attention shifted towards it permanently.

"You'll never be in pain again." John said in a whisper. "Not with me."

Along with the yacht, John had stolen a medication that counteracted some of the effects of opioid withdrawal. He tinted it to look a very similar hue as morphine from within that syringe.

Her response was Pavlovian: Seeing and feeling the needle was her melodic lullaby in a chaos-ridden world. John administered it with careful precision into her arm's largest untapped vein. Her smile grew rapidly, and John felt nothing but loved by the sight. To him, nothing quite compared to seeing that simple, powerful smile on her face when he took care of her. He'd forgotten what the feeling was like, and so he smiled, too.

Before she could feel the extent of the drug's effects, John reached behind her head and pulled it towards his, kissing her slowly. Compelled by broken passion, John lingered in this entranced state, and then pulled back simply to watch her eyes move and twitch again. The feeling of the bountiful white liquid surging through her brought a powerful warmth and tranquility to her mind, body, and being. Her expression was blank. Emotions she'd never tapped into before started to emerge; remnants of her human brain telling her to learn more.

IV

HOXTON

The knock on Theia's door shook her in her sleep.

It was dawn, surely, but Theia lived her life in isolation. A life ungoverned by normal working jobs or sleep schedules. She slept when nature called for it, but always woke at the slightest noise. And the knocking at her door wasn't slight.

The witch lived alone in her house of interwoven logs and bricks. It was a hybrid-type cabin, atop a long field of grass in an area that got regular sunlight by day and those perfectly cool, crisp temperatures by night. There was a forest bordering all four sides of the remote, rural landscape, but the area itself was an open field of property, with a hand-placed stone path stretching from a clearing in the forest right up to the modest entryway. The fantastically beautiful yet simply constructed home was purposely secluded away from the cities of men.

The land of Massachusetts in 1693 was unfavorable to her kind. Humanity started to catch on to their ways, but like most issues uncovered by men, the hunt for beings like her reached absurd heights in such an incredibly short amount of time. Theia, the sole inhabitant of this place and a still-practicing witch, used to have friends in her coven before recent events. It was only last year when one of her sisters exposed her voodoo to the townsfolk of Salem and sparked a small genocide.

Once the men of Salem ran out of witches to burn and hang, everything spiraled into a legendary mass hysteria.

They moved on to innocent girls. Dutiful saints and housewives who were untouched by the Devil's black magic. Countless were hanged and burned at the stake, as were the few who tried to help them. Hiding from the public eye took everything from Theia: Her husband, friends, and every detail about her old life had either been destroyed or turned against her. Theia's home was unfound by them, and she'd been to great lengths to keep it that way. The witch hunts of these men were far from over.

Theia quickly rose from her bed and threw on a gown, peering out of her second-story bedroom window at the cloaked figure standing at her door. There was only one. Theia scanned the fields around the house for signs of reinforcements, but saw nothing move except for the morning's blue jays that flew untamed amidst the far-off trees.

The knocking continued as she descended the stairs. At the door, Theia stopped and did not open it.

"Be gone!" Theia called through the doorway at the passerby. She did not have a particularly intimidating voice, but it was undoubtedly stern and robust.

"Please, I need your help," the stranger said through the closed door. "There is nowhere else to go-"

"There is *anywhere* else to go," shouted Theia. She did not expect the stranger's voice to be female. Still, it garnered no sympathy from the forlorn, sought-after witch.

"If you don't open this door, they'll kill him!!"

Theia was about to shout back another foreboding command to leave, but didn't. She remembered moments ago when checking the fields for others accompanying the stranger. It was only this cloaked little girl who stood outside her door, a tad too tall for her age. There was no "him."

Theia grabbed the butcher's knife from the ledge beside her door. The black magic she practiced took much time and energy to conjure. The butcher's knife she'd stolen from her husband was quick, and readily available in the face of dangers that arrived at her doorstep. The door cracked open, stifled by a chain lock from the inside. Theia saw the face of a girl in true desperation, not far from despair. She carried a great domestic beauty under that cloak, and in her hands was something shrouded in garments she'd carried miles and miles from her Puritan village.

"What is your name?" Theia promptly asked. The cloaked girl was shaken by the fact that Theia's door actually opened for her.

"Marie," said the woman, "and his name is Hoxton."

Marie pulled the cloak from the object she was holding and revealed a sight formerly of nightmares.

It was a baby, whose skin had hardened into a cavalcade of dark blue scales and whose facial features protruded too far from the little boy's face. The baby's hands were almost the size of an adult's, and just like the rest of his body, crunched and crumpled amidst the ultra-hard outer layer of skin, segmented into plates where the joints had to bend. Were little baby Hoxton to be born several hundred years later, medical scientists would have labeled Marie's baby brother with acromegaly, gigantism, and a rare type of ichthyosis. None of these terms existed, and so Hoxton was dubbed "cursed" by his now-deceased mother, and "demon" by his now-absentee father.

Theia took care not to scald the tea as she poured the water. Her guest, Marie, sat at the living room's table. It had only two chairs and no tablecloth.

Marie looked around the house and saw an awkward sparsity of household ornaments. Nothing hung from the walls. There were no decorative items atop any of the shelves, except for two small plants and several books of varying sizes. The kitchen was nothing more than the wall of the living room, set up plainly to make only essential food when needed. If this place were ever bought or sold, the new homeowners would find no difficulty in redecorating.

Theia brought the tea from the kitchen with careful, steady hands, and placed it on the barren table in front of them. As the steam propagated through the air between them, Theia slowly sat down and looked her guest in the eye.

"Who told you to come here?" said Theia sternly.

"Nobody," replied Marie, cradling a sleeping Hoxton in her arms. "I learned of a surviving witch from Jessica."

The name impacted Theia, and Marie could see the history there.

"How did you know her?" Theia asked sternly.

Marie understood her hesitations. There couldn't be any connections to the village that massacred her coven.

"She was our mother," said Marie.

Theia looked again at Marie's baby brother, noticing his leg kick in his sleep. She started to pour herself some of the tea.

"I'm sorry," Theia said calmly.

Marie looked up from her baby to match the eyes of Theia, which glowed with a beaming intensity. She understood Theia's pain, and silently accepted her apology.

"Our father had connections to the town's court houses," said Marie. "When Hoxton was born, father believed mother was a witch. Some who were hanged by the courthouses actually *were* witches... but most of them weren't. And *none* of them deserved to die."

Marie looked again to her brother. The horrible memories started to flood back into her mind.

"It was our mother who you'd become intimate with, and I've kept that secret for many years," said Marie. "This is a favor I performed for you and our mother alike. In her memory, it's only right that you pay it back and release her son from this curse."

From across the table, Theia reached over to Hoxton's head, and rubbed it gently. The coarse scales grooved against the tips of her fingers.

"Child of Jessica," said Theia, "there is not a single element of magic afoot here. This boy is deformed. I cannot remove a curse which does not exist."

"You told my mother of your plan to come here," said Marie back to her. "You spoke of this place as a safe haven for your coven. Built of brick and stone, and charmed with a hex to deter evil."

Theia was shook at the memory. It was one that she forgot was still there. Theia said back to her. She almost smiled at Marie, grateful to have another piece of her old friend back in her mind.

"She told me the witch's name was Theia," Marie continued, "and that any who knew her could expect a warm embrace on our arrival."

Theia bowed her head and took another sip of her tea.

"That was years ago," Theia said plainly. "Before the hangings."

A low groaning hum emanated from Hoxton.

The noise was inhuman. The sound was of a wild boar slowly dying alone with nobody around to help it. Theia looked up from her drink with great concern. This noise the baby made equalized all sounds in Theia's home, for it reverberated off every wall and surface around them.

Marie rocked Hoxton once more. The waking baby made the powerful noise again, and what felt like many moments later, Hoxton again fell into his deep sleep.

Theia set her tea down on the table and leaned closer to the baby. As his limbs moved, the plates that comprised his skin ground and slid past each other to allow it to happen, breeding immense pain in the young boy.

"He cannot cry," said Marie. "He's tried many, many times but he simply cannot. He can only moan."

"People cry and moan when they're in a great deal of pain," noted Theia. "Is he only calm when he's..."

"Still, yes," Marie affirmed. "The only parts of his life that he can live without pain are in his dreams."

Theia shuddered at the thought, her gaze transfixed on the sleeping Hoxton in Marie's arms. She reasoned that if the little boy's only waking experiences were pain, then it followed that all of his dreams were nothing more than memories of those painful experiences.

Downstairs was a crypt, designed and constructed with atypical talismans bordering the room and ancient Sumerian symbols painted on the wall in goat's blood. The room carried with it an unusually cold breeze that seemed to come from no source at all. There were no windows down there, and the only door was sealed shut. In the center of the room was a podium made of stone, with a perfectly smooth and flat top. It was here that Hoxton slept, still wrapped in his sister's garments for him.

Beside him, Theia rifled through the pages of a book with no cover nor title. It was one of many from the shelf beside them. The only other furniture in the room.

Marie looked around this crypt with concern.

"What are you going to do to him here?" Marie asked cautiously.

"I don't know yet," said Theia offhandedly. She was almost at the page she needed.

"Please don't change him," pleaded Marie. "Change his skin. His body. Everything that torments him in waking life... But make sure he's still my brother, undoubtedly."

Theia stopped at the certain page, and set the book down on the podium next to Hoxton.

"Marie, I can't change the boy," said Theia plainly. "Transmutation and shapeshifting were only known by a few of us, and they're all dead and hanged.

They are not elements of Black Magic I've studied."

"Can't you try?" Marie pleaded.

"There's no guarantee that he wouldn't transform into something even more horrid," said Theia.

Marie looked down at Hoxton, processing what she'd just heard.

"What do you propose?" asked Marie, looking at the open pages of the book she could not read.

"There is a spell that can help the poor soul without repercussions," Theia affirmed.

Marie looked closer at the open pages of Theia's book and saw the only word in English lettering:

K H R O N O M A N C Y

"Your brother will not enjoy his life until his prime," said Theia. "Only after."

"How do you mean?" Marie asked.

Theia raised her hands around her and formed her fingers in atypical fashions, moving her wrists with sudden, jerking motions. As she did so, the talismans laid around the room started to glow, and slowly rose up.

"His conditions will kill him shortly after fifty years of age," said Theia.

The cold draft that came from nowhere started to quicken, cooling the crypt even further.

"I'm going to suspend him," Theia continued.

"*Suspend* him?!" Marie called out, the winds of the room almost drowning her out. She grabbed the podium for support.

It was a clear, sunny day outside, yet the striking sound of thunder awoke the baby.

The Sumerian symbols of blood caught fire on the walls they were painted on. Fire that persevered amidst the thundering force of a hurricane in that room. All that was left was the catalyst, and it came spectacularly as Theia crossed her hands and willed it into existence. The burning symbols that surrounded them breathed a new blazing force of energy; One of lightning, that burrowed down from the ceiling as though it were the sky above, spawning branches of electricity that connected to every person in the room. Theia focused and channeled it all into Hoxton. Louder than the storms, louder than the flaming stone walls, and louder than the crackling of the grand thunderbolts of Zeus, was the intense screams of Hoxton, which Marie had never heard possible from her brother before.

The mutated child surged with celestial energies that any man would have trouble withstanding, and the low warblings of Hoxton's screams almost equalized the room's incessant and chaotic noises. Marie was powerless as she watched the baby endure the pain of a thousand lifetimes, and took solace only in the fact that he could take it, since suffering was all that Hoxton truly knew.

12 years had passed since Theia, the last witch of her coven, was hanged in Salem Village, and her estate left to the Commonwealth of Massachusetts. No living will of hers had relinquished her worldly possessions, but witches who practiced Black Magic deserved no rights and could own no chattel.

Hoxton only partially understood what he was. He knew that his skin was different from everyone else's, and that he would grow in unexpected ways. It wasn't even a year ago when he hit 6 feet tall, shocking his friends who never understood. They were no longer his friends at all.

Marie rang the dinner bell outside of her log cabin in Maine. She took Hoxton and fled Salem after Theia had cast her spell, and prayed the witch hunts would not follow them North. Hoxton was sitting on the large, rocky shore of their cabin when the bell rang, overlooking the lake their house bordered. The boulder he sat on matched his skin's plates in coarseness and density, and so it was his favorite of them all. Hoxton got down from the boulder and made his way onto the porch. He used his hand, which now was larger than a gorilla's, to stop the bell from reverberating after the ring. The noise it made bothered him.

Hoxton came inside and sat at the table Marie had made for him: A pure white tablecloth cloaked the top, blanketing the pristine silver dishes and dinnerware. This place was homely, made wholly and entirely by the hard work Marie spent almost every hour of her life doing. Hoxton was schooled briefly, but proceeded to be taught from home with only his sister. The children at school called him "brute" and "ogre" and many more demoralizing sentiments, but it wasn't until one of them struck Hoxton in the jaw that he was pulled from schooling systems entirely. The kid snapped his knuckles against the plates of Hoxton's face.

A crucifix adorned every threshold, every table, every corner of the home where it wouldn't look out-of-place.

Marie served him his plate and sat down herself, watching him eat with uneasy eyes. Today was the day.

"How do you like it?" Marie asked her brother, who didn't seem as talkative as usual.

"It's good." Hoxton responded apathetically, as all preteens did.

That low, baleful voice was something Marie had gotten used to in these years. Even still, she knew it would further deepen in the short years to come. He was entering puberty, and the pain would increase as the boy's body naturally grew into a man's. This was something he expected to happen. But it was not all that he was destined for.

"Hoxton," Marie said gently to him, "there's something we need to talk about."

Hoxton glanced back up at his older sister, food dangling from his mouth.

"What's the matter?" Hoxton quickly said through the meats she had cooked for him. He desperately wanted no such conversation.

But it needed to happen.

"Do you remember a woman named Theia?"

"No," Hoxton replied as he chewed faster. Soon, he would be out on his favorite rock again, watching waves crash against his shoreline. Marie took a moment before speaking next.

"You know how we lived in Massachusetts when you were a baby?" Hoxton nodded, no longer looking her way. "When you were born, our father was..."

Hoxton stopped eating.

All the years they had lived here and he'd been raised as best Marie possibly could, not once did she speak of their father. Whenever he asked, she said he "left when you were born" and brushed the subject away.

"...Scared."

Hoxton stared at Marie.

"Of me?" he asked her, afraid of the answer. Marie nodded, and reality set in for the both of them.

"His name was Johnathan," said Marie. "He was a good man when I knew him, Hox. He truly was."

Hoxton saw what she was getting at. He knew that people always complemented their loved ones before insulting them.

"He was just so stuck in his ways," Marie pressed on, "and when he saw you, he had no way to understand you. He believed you were wicked and evil."

"What did he do when he saw me for the first time?" Hoxton asked his sister. Neither of them ate another bite of their meals.

Marie bowed her head.

"He gathered his friends in a witch hunt, and he tried to kill mother," Marie said, losing composure. "He thought she had cursed you."

Hoxton didn't respond.

"He thought she was part of a coven," Marie continued.

She noticed that Hoxton didn't recognize what she meant.

"It's a group of witches," Marie explained. "It means they can do really wondrous things with the world around them. Things that you or I can't do."

"Am I cursed?" Hoxton asked plainly.

Marie almost cried at the question.

"Heavens no! You were born different from other people... It's just that when you were born, Johnathan saw your skin and heard the noises you made. That dreadful groaning you did when you couldn't cry. He assumed you..."

Marie couldn't finish the thought. Hoxton forced her to.

"I was what?" Hoxton pressed.

Marie finally relented.

"He called you a demon-child, Hoxton."

Hoxton looked away, unable to cry. His physicality wouldn't allow for it.

"He had power with the townspeople," said Marie. "They captured mother and hanged her. Along with anyone else they suspected. Even partially."

Marie wiped away her tears with the perfectly-folded napkin beside her dinner plate.

"I took you and ran," she finally told him. "Father planned to kill you himself. I stole you and brought you to one of the only witches they hadn't killed yet."

Hoxton turned back to Marie.

"You were so small then. Whenever you woke up, you were in agony. I begged Theia for help, and she gave it to us," said Hoxton's now-emotional sister.

Hoxton slowly stood up, pushing the chair out from the table with his legs. The legs of the chair slowly ground against the hard floor. His height now cast a shadow over the table, and his head almost touched the ceiling.

"*What did she do to me?*"

Maria paused, attempting to compose herself. This was supposed to be done civilly.

"Your body was going to kill you after you turned 50," said Marie, finally.

The statement hit Hoxton harder than anything ever had.

"The pain you feel is because you grow..."

Hoxton waited patiently as Marie finally finished her thought.

"On your 18th birthday," said Marie, "you'll no longer age."

Hoxton leaned forward on the table, looking down at his plate of food. Before this meal, he was content with his life. His immutable agony. No longer, and never again.

"How dare you," Hoxton said sternly to his sister. That unreasonably deep voice, combined with the hateful tone in which he now spoke, brought the heart and soul out of anybody who heard it. Marie, for the first time since Hoxton was a baby, truly feared for her life.

"I say my prayers every night," said Hoxton with conviction. "I pray to our Lord to help me get through the day, each and every morning, as smoothly as possible. You told me my pain was the Devil's work."

"It *is* the Devil's work!" Marie responded.

"Then *why* did you have one of his disciples infect me with Black Magic?" Hoxton almost yelled.

Marie had nothing to say to him.

"Pain accompanies my movements," said Hoxton, losing his composure. "It lingers when I'm still and multiplies when I'm not. The only solaces I have are when He responds to my prayers. And now you sit here, sharing stories of madness and witchcraft, telling me that you've bartered with a Satanic sorceress. Is my life not sinister enough?! Must you place a hex on me to experience this life *for all eternity?!*"

Hoxton slammed his fist down on the table, splintering the wood beneath the tablecloth. Marie jumped when it happened, and recognizing this, Hoxton relaxed. He meant no physical harm. Instead, pure hatred.

"Remember that little boy who tried to strike me?" Hoxton said, his temper subsided. "Do you know what he and his friends called me?"

Marie could not speak.

"They called me *The Brute Man.* I'm neither a man nor a brute, and yet, that term proved popular amongst every student and teacher in that institution. Not a single one of them defended me from the attack that day, yet all of them rallied to have me removed once a boy who looked normal hurt himself against a demon-child's face. *This* is the life I was forced to have. And now you've taken away my death."

Hoxton's words were cold, and Marie struggled to handle them. He turned to leave the house, and her in it.

"Where are you going?" Marie asked him. She got no response, and feared the truth: He didn't care where. Any place but this one would do.

She was to be alone.

"Hoxton!" Marie desperately called for him. "You would die if not for her spell!"

Hoxton stopped at his sister's pleas. He turned his head back to her, the plates of his skin grinding against each other as he did so, but did not look her in the eye. To him, she did not deserve it.

"There are many things worse than death in this world," said Marie's spiteful brother. "This life is one of them, and it can no longer be given back."

In his 17th year, Hoxton was a force known to a close-knit circle of fans. The spectators of the underground fighting ring admired him like a hero. It was only for those in the know, and it existed beneath an average-looking tavern. When Hoxton arrived, the people who ran this place soon realized that the structure of their matches had to change for the fights to get interesting: It was no longer man-vs-man. It was men-vs-brute.

The challenges were offset drastically. Hoxton was paired with three, four, sometimes five or six other burly men, each offered a massive cash prize if they lasted more than three minutes with the notorious Brute Man. Hoxton took the name to spite his childhood, and bringing other men down in this ring proved an excellent way to channel his frustrations and miseries.

Last night, he'd taken on five: Two armed with sledgehammers, two with knives, and one with a firearm. The room smelled of tired, sweaty men; An odor that Hoxton's body did not produce. As the men placed their bets and the prize grew larger, Hoxton made quick use of his gifts and dispatched them promptly, but always took care never to kill anybody. That was a line he'd never cross no matter how large the prize money got. When he kicked, he did so softly towards somebody's knee, fracturing it and bringing them down. When he punched, he always aimed for their arms, occasionally dislocating a shoulder. Tonight, he walked up to the back entrance of the tavern like he always had, but did not hear the cry of fans from inside.

"Hoxie!"

The voice was Irish, and familiar to him. Barnard, the owner and Hoxton's only real friend, came up to him in the nighttime interim. He wore a clean-cut jacket he'd bought with the money he'd invested in Hoxton, which used to pay him lucratively. The fact that it didn't anymore was precisely why he was here today.

"Barney, where are the people?" Hoxton eagerly asked as he wrapped his fists in leather. He did not need to protect his immovable knuckles one bit, but it cushioned his blows and made the ones he fought feel comfortable.

"Hoxie, the fight's been canceled." Barnard stopped Hoxton from wrapping his hands. "And the news is only getting worse."

"Have we finally run out of fools to put in the dirt?" Hoxton laughed at his own cocky query. Barnard, who usually laughed along, didn't at all.

"You're done, kid."

Hoxton gave Barnard a snide look.

"They think I'm to be beaten this time?" Hoxton asked innocently.

"No!" Barnard almost snapped at him. "That's all it is. You've done nothing but best everybody who's ever set foot in there. Nobody thinks the fights are worth betting on. And they're *right,* kid."

Hoxton could not understand.

"Barney, I'm God to these people. They practically worship me."

"They *did,*" said Barnard with a nasty tinge. The arrogance on Hoxton's tongue disgusted Barnard. He spoke much younger than he looked.

Barnard handed Hoxton a black bag, the kind he usually got every week. It was full of silver. The last time he'd be handed payment for what he did.

"Kid," Barnard said, now friendlier, "I mean this in the best possible way: Don't come back here. We're shutting down the fighting for good. Too many men came home to their wives broken beyond repair because of you."

With that, Barnard entered the tavern without saying goodbye.

Hoxton was livid. The only thing he'd ever done since he started fighting was what he was told. *Put them down, but don't ruin them, and you'll be compensated for it.* This was a punishment he was again forced to live with, and again it was because of how he was. The modest crowds in the underground of this place had cheered wildly and championed him. It was the arrogance he lived in that blinded him to the fact that every passing week, those crowds slowly shrank. As soon as people became disinterested in what he was, they moved on to better things with their time. Better people to spend them with. Hoxton could not live a life like they did, with anybody at all, and now he couldn't live the life of *The Brute Man* beneath this place.

Hoxton punched the wall of the tavern.

It cracked instantaneously underneath his fist, giving way to his godly punch. Barnard came storming out of the tavern.

"What's wrong with you, boy?!" Barnard screamed.

Hoxton reached into his bag of silver and tossed him some coin. Barnard flinched as the pieces bounced off of his face.

"That ought to cover it," Hoxton scoffed. He spat at Barnard's feet and stormed off into the night.

It was the eve of the most important day of his life.

Hoxton sat by the shoreline, watching the same waves crash against his favorite rock amidst the glimmering moonlight. The distorted reflection of the vast star-filled sky above wriggled their twinkling essence, almost symmetrically mirroring his widespread vista. Barnard had shut down the fighting ring almost a year ago now, and that was the night where Hoxton had to re-evaluate what he wanted from his temporary life, before it became eternal.

It took years for him to realize how harshly he'd treated Marie, and it killed him to think about what he said to her before he left. He hadn't gone inside yet, because on the walk up to her front door was his favorite view from his favorite rock. And that was worth stopping for.

Hoxton checked the timepiece in his coat pocket. He'd updated his clothing, from the universally soft robes of his youth to a timeless black three-piece suit, head to toe. A newly-bought hat adorned his oddly-shapen dome, hiding some insecurities. The material fared well against his skin, which attempted to shred all articles of clothing he ever wore. The timepiece revealed that he was a few hours away from midnight.

Hoxton turned from the shore of Marie's house to the home itself, and saw how not much had changed. There were many things he wished to say to her, many stories of the lives he'd lived in his absence, and so little time to tell them before the witch's spell took hold over him. He wanted these moments with his sister to be his final minutes of mortality.

Hoxton approached the deck and saw the dinner bell removed. There was no use for it anymore. Still, he placed his hand in the cavity where it was, as if stopping the reverberations.

He breathed in.

Breathing was one of the only things Hoxton ever did that never caused him any pain. The organs were internal, and so no plates of skin intersected or scraped, though his chest widening did cause some minor forms of it. He'd almost gotten used to the feeling, but he knew he never completely would.

Slowly, he breathed out.

Hoxton faced the closed door of the house he hadn't visited nor written to in almost five years. He raised his hand to knock on it, but stopped himself. Would she accept him still? He'd abandoned his sister all those years ago, and the rash, adolescent decision of his hung over him. Many nights were spent praying in penance over that rash, petty decision. He hadn't realized how it manifested in the fighting ring beneath Barnard's tavern, slowly eating away at him as he effortlessly broke what once were good, strong men. But now he did.

No longer could he channel his hatred into their bodies. No longer did he want to.

He knocked with delicacy on the front door exactly five times. It was a specific number, chosen from overthinking his return. Less, and she may not have heard. More, and it would be incessant. Several possible ways this encounter could happen ran through his mind, and he stressed over all of them.

The door opened, and Marie was not there.

It was a woman, dressed in a white sleeping gown, who saw the tall man at her door and screamed at the top of her lungs. Hoxton freaked out, holding his hands up in disarmament, but it further terrified the tiny woman beneath him. She collapsed to the floor, attempting to run back inside of the house, but spent too much time scrambling on all fours trying to get back up to her feet, letting a concerned Hoxton enter the house.

"Wait!" Hoxton bellowed out as he moved towards her. "I'm sorry! I-"

Hoxton barely got words out before her husband ran from the bedroom, and he too saw the Brute Man, backlit by the stark moonlight outside. The massive figure had to duck when entering, so when he was inside, the full breadth of his height was revealed. And it was unfathomably haunting to them.

The husband grabbed a knife from the countertop and ran toward the intruder, jabbing it into his gut. The blade chinked against the unbreakable skin, and Hoxton grabbed the man's arms, trying to calm him. Hoxton's strength was unexpected, and he began bruising the man's biceps.

As the man cried out in incredible agony, his wife finally got to her feet and ran upstairs. Hoxton let go of the man's arms.

"Are you okay?" Hoxton asked the man, who struck him square in the jaw. Just like the kid in Hoxton's class who coined the name "Brute Man," the man's hand split open down the knuckles.

He cried out in pain and held his bleeding hand close to him. Hoxton placed his own hand on the man's shoulder, trying to restrain him from hurting himself.

"Stop!" Hoxton said quickly.

The man grabbed Hoxton's arm with both hands, bleeding profusely on Hoxton's leather coat, and attempted to remove it. In the heat of the vigorous, unexpected altercation, Hoxton clenched too strongly trying to resist the man's struggles.

The man fell to the ground, completely lifeless. It was a grotesque noise as his body impacted the floor, for Hoxton had artlessly snapped the man's neck.

From upstairs, the dead man's wife came down with her husband's musket, stowed away in his closet since he returned from Queen Anne's War earlier this year. Seeing his body in front of Hoxton, she shot the intruder in the chest. It was perhaps the strongest, most painful attack Hoxton had ever experienced thus far in his life, and as it chipped away a piece of his skin, Hoxton was reminded of the anguish he'd been ignoring thus far. It was one of the topics of conversation he'd hoped to strike up with his sister tonight.

The kickback from her husband's gun fractured her hip almost immediately. His wife had never shot nor known how to shoot it, and the force of the gunshot sent her flying backward into the hallway. Her head whacked itself against the ground, and though not dead, she lost consciousness as soon as she experienced the impact.

Hoxton was alone.

He'd been running incessantly now, far and away from that unsuspecting house. Faster than he'd ever run in his entire life. No amount of time spent running, or speed he reached, or intensity in which he ran could allow him to escape what he had done, but Lord did he try. Nothing he set out to do that night was immoral, yet it was him and him alone that caused the man's death. What's more, this couple would only have lived there if the original homeowner didn't anymore, and Marie would never move out of the house she poured all of that time and energy into every day.

She was gone.

His last words to his sister were full of unbridled hatred, and they could never be revoked. After all of these years learning to control himself, he knew he'd lost that control amidst the self-conscious panic of the incident. He'd taken his first life tonight, almost two. Nobody who'd died in that house could be brought back, then or now, and the weight of that bore down on him with an immensity he'd never felt before. Never in all of the years fighting under Barnard's tavern, or in all of the years in class letting his peers lash out at him. None of it compared to that night.

Hoxton stopped suddenly in the breadth of something indescribably spectacular.

He was engulfed in trees from all sides, caught right in the middle of a thinning forest, the moonlight still peering down at him. A new feeling, not of terror or anguish but one of purity, overtook him.

It was strong.

The power possessed him in such vibrant capacity that he fell on all fours, cringing to withstand it. And withstand it he did.

Hoxton fell to his side and rolled onto his back, moaning loudly in the middle of the forest. His voice bellowed out and overpowered the woodland creatures' nightly noises, dominating them. The pain and the hatred and the anguish and all of the pent-up rage inside of his body, mind, and soul all shifted drastically. It was cathartic. An orgasmic sense of divinity and relief befell him greatly, stronger than even imaginable, for as the timepiece in his coat pocket struck the hour of midnight, all of the pain Hoxton lived with every waking moment of his life had righteously vanished.

This feeling could not be the Devil's work at all. It was benevolent, like a gift he'd never known he needed. It was as if all of the prayers he'd spent endless nights making all paid off right there in that moment.

Hoxton could not stand. He felt glued to the ground beneath him, and stuck in a grand awe at the stars above. He wriggled his fingers through the grassy ground, and felt no aching as his joints bent back and forth. He did not know what his eternal life was going to become, but he intended to use it well. Once he rose from his glow of painlessness, he would bring that man's wife to a place of hospitality, and would never return to this place again.

A passion for the natural world grew in him rapidly, and God himself couldn't strike it down if he tried. He could never tell his sister of his sorrows and share gratitude for what she did for him, but he swore on her death that Theia's gift to him would not be squandered. And it *was* a gift, for he could feel its generosity.

Hoxton had no idea what his purpose was. He felt lost when it came to God's plan for him. But he owed it to the Lord to find that plan out, whatever it may be. And he had eternity to do it.

A Wickie's Company

Since New Year's Day of 1796, the wickie had been on this tall tower on this tiny island off the coast of Norway, and *relished* in the isolation that the job brought him. He had a beard composed of many different shades of blacks and grays and a wickie's uniform in remarkably well-kept shape. This man had been a lighthouse keeper for a total of four days, and the only companion he had was a large dog by the name of Neptune, who ran and hid on the stormier nights the lighthouse experienced, and slept by his side as he stayed awake on the calmer ones.

It was his fourth night on the job, and for the absolute life of him, the wickie could not find a way to begin his journal's notes.

Amidst the crisp, frigid air hundreds of feet above the ground, the wickie sat near the bright lens of the lighthouse with his journal in his hands and could not begin anything past the logline of *January 4th.* The wickie stood up from his chair, startling Neptune on this calm Norwegian winter's night by the sea. He exited the lighthouse's lantern room and leaned over the catwalk's railing, watching as the dim light of the moon reached through the thick clouds above and painted the raging waves below. Neptune perked his head up and followed his master with his eyeline, but did not care enough to move. The wickie produced a telescope from his pocket and looked outward into the boundlessness of the night's usual void, seeing several small clouds migrating very slowly from one position to the next.

And something else.

It was a thing resembling a bat or a hawk, flapping its wings as it flew closer and closer to him. Not another seagull at all. The flying critter was completely black, or at least appeared that way in the darkness of night, silhouetted against the foggy backdrop of the night's endless skyline. The wickie became disturbed at this illusive creature's flight path, and how it was strangely aimed nowhere else but the very top of the lighthouse where he was standing.

The wickie turned towards the steps which ran down to the tower's bottom layers. He'd spent most of the previous day exploring the lighthouse's inner machinations. He knew every good and bad step on the staircase, the way the water hit the tower's hollow interior during high tide, and the ax hanging up near the tower's final step on the ground's level. That ax was waiting for him at the bottom of those stairs, but could not be retrieved before this oncoming creature would arrive at the lighthouse's brilliant, shining light.

He turned back and stumbled at the sight. It petrified him; it had gotten remarkably closer than he'd estimated in the time it took him to stare down that long, spiral stairwell. The creature he saw was only a blur in his vision that made him almost fall backward onto the squeaky old wood of the catwalk. Steadying himself, the wickie now saw the true scope of what had almost arrived.

The large beast flapped its wings once with incomparable strength and speed, launching itself higher into the air, then spread them out and proceeded to glide down to the wickie's position.

Neptune leapt up and ran behind the lantern. The wickie hesitantly backed up and made room as the beast revealed itself and landed ceremoniously on the railing of the catwalk right outside the lantern room. It perched with two arms and two legs gripping the railing fiercely, hunching over and stabilizing its body with the weight of its long tail and two massive wings. The beast's body was a deep gray like that of stone - in fact, it *was* stone - comprising the rigid, muscular frame of an adult male's shape and form. The curvature of the body bended and flexed with him, not cracking as stone would, as though through some ethereal cheat against the known laws of physics.

The face, however, was particularly *inhuman.* It had exaggerated brow ridges and temples, and cheek bones that protruded marginally too far. The chin was pointed, brought out to a length one's beard might reach if unkempt for several weeks. The eye sockets, where the wickie expected it to look back at him, had clear, reflective black orbs. No irises, no corneas. They were two smooth, plain black spheroids, and they faced the wickie with conviction.

Rain lightly coated the perched creature's silhouette, sounding softly around them both.

The wickie took in the sight but did not scream. Was this a *real* sight? Of course it had to be. No nightmare he'd ever had resembled a demon such as this. Its wings were large and fleshed out, and contorted the same way a bat's would, and the thing's tail... *My god, watch it move!* The wickie became transfixed by it as the beast slowly wrapped it around the railing's edge, stabilizing itself firmly.

"I bid you no harm," spoke the monster in a welcoming tone.

The voice was unexpectedly normal. Not unlike a friend's would be when casually chatting over drinks at a pub. It sounded of an elegant adult male with cadence, perhaps in the latter years of his prime. The wickie caught brief glimpses of serrated, perfectly-symmetrical teeth as it spoke, filed down to the very tips.

The wickie stood up slowly, never taking his sight off of the creature. It waited patiently for him to do so. There was no rush for it whatsoever.

"What are ye?!" the wickie yelled into the night. His voice was sailorly, and his breath was musty and dry.

"You may call me Gargoyle. For simplicity's sake."

Again, the tone was eerily friendly. The wickie looked behind him to the lighthouse's lantern. His dog's fluffy tail was poking out from its side.

"Whatev'r ye are, ye've frightened Neptune," said the wickie.

"My appearance has that effect," admitted the Gargoyle.

"Are ye a demon?" the wickie asked more calmly.

"No."

The wickie started laughing, his nerves forcing it out of him. The Gargoyle slowly turned his head to one side, examining the wickie more closely. Absorbing the man's intricacies.

"What, then?" the wickie prompted. "Ye look like one."

"You've *seen* demons?" the Gargoyle replied.

The wickie sat with this for a moment.

Behind the Gargoyle, the wickie noticed that perplexingly long tail again, slithering itself through the bars of the railing and adjusting its grip. It moved with both grace and strength, and had tiny little spikes traveling up the spine, leading all the way through the Gargoyle's back and up to his neck.

"Wha..." the wickie tried to ask. He collected himself: "What're ye doin' here?"

The Gargoyle thought to himself. The response was not so easy to conjure.

"D'y'hear me, Gargoyle?"

"Wickie," said the Gargoyle, "I've allowed you to ask a great number of questions in succession. That is fair, seeing as I'm an intruder here. But perhaps, from this point forth, this conversation could not be so one-sided."

The wings of the Gargoyle retracted from their expanded state. He was getting comfortable now. As was the wickie, who looked to the lantern room and saw the chair he'd stood up from.

With a nod, the wickie went into the room and grabbed his chair. He saw Neptune, who continued cowering away behind the lantern's bright light, and whispered: "S'okay, boy." Out came the wickie with the chair in his hands, setting it directly in front of the Gargoyle. The wickie had a seat and met eyes with the monster once again.

"Suppose I agree to this rule o' yers," said the wickie. "A turn-takin' system of questions an' answers. How far would it go until it ends?"

"As long as I wish it to."

"Aye, 'cause yer the only one who can fly away at any time."

The Gargoyle gave the wickie a snide look.

"No more questions will be answered," said the Gargoyle. "Not until you agree to these terms. Or counter with your own."

The wickie did not need much time to think about this proposition.

"Promise me this one, simple thing," said the wickie.

"I won't eat you alive, wickie" the Gargoyle said with disdain.

"That ain't it," said the wickie, "though I'd prefer if ye wouldn't."

"It's a common request."

The wickie perked up an eyebrow. *Common?* How many others have been in his position, speaking to this beast? The wickie pondered whether or not this Gargoyle was having conversations with more like himself, and he was simply next in line.

But those were all questions. So they could not be asked as of yet.

"My stipulation for this game is that ye-"

"Game?" the Gargoyle interrupted.

"What else would ye call it?" the wickie asked. Rhetorically, of course.

"A game denotes competition," said the Gargoyle. "There are no winners or losers here. Just two men, satisfying their curiosities."

"Ye think yerself a man," the wickie pointed out.

Perturbed, the Gargoyle shifted uncomfortably. He'd revealed more than he wanted to. And it didn't even cost the man a question.

"I accept yer game," the wickie continued. "Or conversation, or whatever ye'd like to know it as. But only with this here stipulation: That all answers be wholly truthful and honest. Swear this to me, ye *must!* Or I have no interest in it. Not one bit, says I."

The Gargoyle smirked. It was an uncanny sight, seeing that scowling face raise the corner of its lip slightly. It was a visual faux pas for that sort of Satanic visage, and it unsettled the wickie.

"We have an agreement," said the Gargoyle modestly.

The westerly winds passed them both by in the dreary expanse of their night, chilling the wickie enough to bundle himself more closely into his uniform. For so it had come about, as solemnly hoped by both parties, that a dialogue would be formed between them. One they both hoped to take advantage of.

"So who goes first?" asked the wickie.

"You do," said the Gargoyle, "and you've done a fine job, indeed."

The wickie turned pale. He'd been slighted.

"Aye, that wasn't-"

"Where are you from, wickie?"

"Oslo," said the wickie. "Where..."

No, he reckoned. He would not waste his next question as easily as that, on something so silly as a place.

"...Why do ye look this way, if ye reckon yerself a man like I?"

The Gargoyle meditated on this for a moment, then said: "Supremely bad luck, wickie."

"That ain't fair!"

"How's it not fair?"

"Ye haven't answered nothin," the wickie insisted. "*Wholly truthful and honest,* said I. There'll be no cryptic answers in tonight's talk."

The Gargoyle had no retort for such a rant.

"I was *turned* this way," said the Gargoyle. "Three hundred years ago."

The wickie's eyes widened at his guest.

"What monster would make this of a man?" the wickie asked in disbelief.

The Gargoyle ignored him, and continued: "Why are you alone here?"

Now quite solemn, the wickie shuffled in place.

"Might seem like a job no seafarin' man would ever *dream* of havin', bein' stranded amidst the night's torturous embrace. I was not assigned this job, Gargoyle. I lobbied for it." The wickie turned to his dog, and concluded: "Aside from Neptune, I wish for no companion at all."

The Gargoyle smiled again for a brief moment, exposing those abhorrent teeth.

"My presence must be *revolting* to a man of your sensibilities," said the Gargoyle.

"T'was at first, demon," said the wickie before turning back to the lantern room. He whistled for Neptune, who still refused to come out from behind the blazing light of that lantern.

This thought came into the wickie's mind.

"You have no eyes," remarked the wickie to his guest.

"And you've gone mad in your old age, thinking that's what a question sounds like."

"'Tis an observation," the wickie grumbled.

Distraught, the wickie pondered a little while longer, watching the Gargoyle balance flawlessly on that railing. It was as though he weighed nothing at all.

"What do ye want to know?" the wickie asked.

"A bit open-ended, isn't it?" the Gargoyle replied.

"It ain't yer turn," said the wickie spitefully. "That's a question if I've ever heard one."

The Gargoyle didn't know whether to be proud or angry. In a sense, he was both.

"I've taken many hobbies," said the Gargoyle. "I've built and destroyed buildings brick by brick, plank by plank, nail by nail. All by my lonesome. No experience, no crew. Only brute force until I did so correctly. I've learned dozens of languages. I learned so many languages that I started learning *sign* languages, the likes of which meant only for deaf ears and wide eyes. I've learned writings of all the world's types that I've encountered. I can read all, see all, speak all, in the hopes that one day I will, at once, *be* all. There must be an upper limit to the amount of knowledge one man can accrete, and after three hundred years, I am *nowhere near* reaching it. Nobody else can live as I do, work as I do, for anywhere near as *long* as I do. The only shackle I bare is my disgusting form. I cannot blend into a crowd. I cannot learn of people's customs, nuances, or any of their practices unless from afar..."

"Ye done hearin' ye-self talk?" the wickie replied indifferently. "A million years could pass and ye'd ne'er hear me ramble for anywhere near that long 'bout me-self."

The Gargoyle brushed off the wickie's comments.

"I like to talk," said the Gargoyle.

"Evidently," said the wickie. "*Yer turn,* ain't it?"

The Gargoyle had its next question prepared: "What do you first think of when you look at me?"

The wickie again glanced over the Gargoyle's spectacular form.

"A fire-breathin' demon of Lucifer's imagination," said the wickie.

"You think I can breathe fire?" the Gargoyle scoffed.

"Didn't say that," said the wickie, "nor would I answer it anyway. *My* turn."

The Gargoyle read the wickie's face like an open book.

"You're thinking about it," said the Gargoyle.

"Aye," the wickie admitted.

The Gargoyle's face went blank, confusing the wickie.

Grabbing the railing for support, the Gargoyle slowly inhaled. The monster's huge chest filled up with air as if to reign down a stream of hellfire onto the wickie.

Slowly, the Gargoyle released the air with a chuckle.

For the first time all night, the Gargoyle and the wickie shared a laugh together. It was so brief and unusual that the very sound of it almost frightened the wickie, and it snapped him back into his reserved state of mind.

It was his turn.

"Why have ye come to my Light-House?" the wickie finally asked. "And don't just say no son-of-a-bitch-type o' riddle. I'm asking why exactly ye've come here, *to this place,* and started flabbin' yer wildebeest's mouth about questions and conversations to a man as I."

Something changed in the Gargoyle.

"Ask something else."

The wickie's tongue caught in his mouth. The Gargoyle's words were impossible to digest.

"Now I'm no fool and a fool I ain't," said the wickie proudly. "The terms of this-"

"Ask something else-"

"-of this here conversation-"

"That question isn't-"

"-were such that any and all questions-"

"Wickie-"

"-would be honestly *answered!*"

The wickie stood from his chair, close to throwing his drink into the Gargoyle's face. Calmly, the Gargoyle meditated on what exactly to do. The wickie's hands trembled from all of the commotion, and the Gargoyle noticed it. They'd both become a little too worked up over such a small detail of an otherwise enlightening conversation.

A strong apathy washed over the Gargoyle's mind. His mood shifted back into what it was.

"Forgive me, wickie," said the Gargoyle as he bowed his head.

The wickie stayed standing. Trepidation deep inside of him prevented him from sitting back down. He longed for Neptune's comfort.

"You are owed an answer, as I've promised..."

The Gargoyle moved his gargantuan body down slowly from the railing and crawled to the floorboards between them. He stood tall, showing the full breadth of his devilish body, and his tail followed suit. It curled to the side of them both, drawing the wickie's attention.

"Wickie, I intend to destroy this lighthouse. The problem is thus: By doing so, you'd be without food or shelter for a very long time. I do not wish to kill you in my pursuit of what I need."

The wickie took this all in the best that he could. But it wasn't enough. He paced back inside the lantern room, finding Neptune cowering behind the light.

"S'okay, boy," he said, kneeling down to pet his only friend. It was an embrace both he and Neptune needed.

Destroy the lighthouse? After four goddamn days on this rock? How the Consistory would react if so early on in his job he managed to allow the entire lighthouse to be *destroyed* as such. No right-minded lad would believe some weird Gargoyle flew here, saying he *intended* to do such a thing...

The wickie reckoned himself to be right-minded, too.

"Ye ain't real," said the wickie to his company. "A figment o' mine. Nothin' more."

The Gargoyle stayed out of the lantern room, respectfully. He did not want to be a bother.

"I am no figment-"

"Ye lie!" the wickie screamed. "Ye lie ev'r since ye landed on this rock. Ain't no Gargoyles flyin' 'round the night-time sky, askin' wickies like me-self about destroyin' their towers! Ye lie! Lie! Lie!"

The Gargoyle's wings fleshed out to their true, uncurled length, and enveloped the wickie's entire view of the outside of the lantern room. The moon's dim light cascaded down from the edge of the Gargoyle's wings, silhouetting the bat-like monster in a terrifying pose.

"Ye flyin' away, figment?" the wickie taunted. "Off to chase the flames of St. Elmo?"

The wings batted strongly, propelling the Gargoyle into a low hover.

"Flyin' out me-mind just as soon as ye entered. *Cowardly*, says I. Cowardly and untrue."

The wickie's words wouldn't let the Gargoyle leave. Some misplaced sense of pride lingered in the Gargoyle's mind, and it kept him from leaving that lighthouse. The unhinged thoughts of this wickie mattered to him, whether he realized it or not. The Gargoyle landed just as soon as he'd taken off, planting his claw into the floorboards for support as he did so. The entire lantern room trembled stronger than any storm ever made it.

"I've been nothing but polite and cordial with you, wickie-"

"*Polite?!*"

"Very," said the Gargoyle with unbroken confidence. "Place your rage elsewhere. I need it not."

"Look at ye," said the wickie scornfully. "The might of a thousand men but the character of a small child. Bitchin' for naught."

"This is not how this conversation is supposed to go-"

"TO HELL WITH YE, WRETCH!" the wickie screamed. "Hell with ye tidings, ye words o' the Devil. A pile o' lies taller than Odin himself."

The Gargoyle came so close to the wickie that the moisture from the man's breath collected on the Gargoyle's skin, the condensation gathering amidst the coarse texture of gravely black stone.

And they said nothing.

The wickie was petrified. Wrathful and intolerant, but petrified nonetheless.

"It's yer turn," said the wickie through his teeth.

The Gargoyle backed away. He used his wings to propel himself back onto the railing, wrapping his claws and tail around it once again.

"How long have you been a wickie?" the Gargoyle calmly asked.

The wickie turned pale. "Four days," he replied.

But the color returned to his face. It was his turn once again.

"What is yer problem with this Light-House?" asked the wickie. "Does it not face the mornin' sun at the correct angle? Maybe the floorboards ain't nailed down properly."

"No, I-"

"Or maybe ye hate seafarin' vessels, and wish them all to crash along the rocky shores of this island," said the wickie scornfully. "Watch 'em sink as they join the likes of Davy Jones, lower than any man's ever been and returned to tell tales of."

"Nothing of the sort," said the Gargoyle.

"Then *why?!*" yelled the wickie.

"To retrieve what is buried beneath it," the Gargoyle finally answered. "I am a pacifist at heart. I never kill unprovoked. And that includes innocent wickies and their noble dogs."

The wickie looked back at Neptune, who poked his head out from the light's corner. He was getting used to the Gargoyle's long-standing presence on the railing's edge. All of the best memories with that dog flooded into the wickie's mind, starting from the very first day he'd taken him in, through to all of the times he'd scratch that exact spot behind Neptune's ear, making his back leg kick over and over.

"Ain't no dog e'er been more noble," said the wickie as he turned back to his company. "Perhaps there's another way. Could ye not inspect the Light-House's ground? Dig 'round for yer prize, an' keep the structure intact?"

"Those are *questions*," the Gargoyle pointed out, "but I'll oblige. I cannot get at what I need unless the structure is dismantled. Time has not been kind to what I seek."

The wickie bowed his head, letting the Gargoyle speak.

"How did you meet Nept-"

"Is it money?" The wickie interrupted, his head perking back up.

"No."

"Is it a portal somewhere?"

"No."

"Another beast like yourself?"

"No."

"*Bah!!*" yelled the wickie as he clenched a fist. The more that man spoke, the clearer the desperation bled through in his voice.

"How did you meet-"

"What is it ye desire?!" the wickie screamed into the night. "If it's fortunes, I have a modest saving of gold. It's buried somewhere nearby, not several walkin' miles from here. It was from back in me sailin' days, where I indulged me-self in the outlawed act of piracy. I've never told anybody about it. *Ever in me life.* Fly away from this place now, Demon, and ye can have the *whole lot* of it. Leave this Light-House alone from ye untimely wrath and it's yers. It's all yers!"

The Gargoyle sighed. He didn't need to respond for the wickie to realize that his offer had been rejected.

"What more?" the wickie screamed, his voice giving way. "What exists in this world more valuable than that?"

Though the wickie had gone far, far over the allotted amount of questions on his turn, the Gargoyle was no stranger to pain and desperation.

"A way back," said the Gargoyle. "A way *out* of this nightmarish form."

The wickie's hapless gaze scanned the Gargoyle with newfound curiosity.

"Then why the conversation?" the wickie finally asked.

And the Gargoyle, disregarding the agreed-upon rules for one, final time, complied with the wickie's query.

"I'm immortal, wickie," said the Gargoyle. "I will not kill you, and I will not let you die by anybody's hand. Even your own. I'm waiting for you to expire, and I figured I'd pass the time."

All energy from the wickie's face, passionately angry or otherwise, melted away into a blank void. The insurmountable weight of inevitability took its hold on the wickie's mind and soul.

For a third time, the Gargoyle asked the wickie: "How did you meet Neptune?"

The wickie could not answer right away, still processing everything so suddenly. He wondered if perhaps *that* was why the Gargoyle structured their game like he had. Perhaps knowledge itself was meant to come only in doses.

There was no reason to continue their game.

There was no reason not to.

"I've always had one," said the wickie, the words now pouring out of him. "Parents got a dog just like 'im when I was a lad, and I wanted no other friend but 'im. I longed for no other attention. He was the sweetest little pup, with fur so soft it'd make Poseidon himself weep tears of saltwater, adorning the world with a new sea born only from it. When he died, all I could think of was getting another. Neptune's the *fifth* I've had in these Earthly travels o' mine, and he seems to be the most fear-stricken of all of 'em... No doubt in me mind, the face of a Gargoyle would make the strongest among canines and panthers and bears wince at the mere sight of ye, but even still... This lad's always been the one I confide in, the one I come home to and share musings of the days I've been through. I've never taken a wife. My commitment has been only to the sea for so many years... and now, it's been this here Light-House, the likes of which I truly did intend to die in. The Consistory that put me here needed convincin' to allow but one man to man the Light. I kept no power in high places... Made only enemies in me travels, Gargoyle. Only enemies, says I, save for a man named De Grät. Bestest friend I'd ever knew, if ye could even call it that. I wasn't planning on seeing 'im again, anyway. I always tolerated 'im. Tolerated everybody. Everybody who's ever lived, breathin' the same air as I, I've always *tolerated.* This job was supposed to serve me well. Let me write. Let me think. Let whatever happens *happen* to me, as it were, and happen to all the *rest* of them all the same. Let whatever the gods decide become true in the blithering wake of man's idiocy and contempt, indifferent to the prayers and whims of the lot... I've always accepted this fate. A lone man's death beside a perfect dog named Neptune. To the ocean floor with all the rest... I can't... I don't know how to talk anymore, Gargoyle, but I know *differently* now. I *know* I know differently. To ye, I feel drawn in some unnatural way... Difficult to explain rightly, says I. Ought to be some *sense* about ye, like in yer presence is the first person in all m'life that understands what it's like... I can't rightly say. I *can't.* But yer different, is all. Not just appearance-wise."

Though it was only one answer to only one question, the Gargoyle considered the wickie's debt paid in full.

"Your turn," said the Gargoyle.

Thirty-seven years had passed since the wickie first met that Gargoyle. His body now laid rest in the ground beside the magnificent lighthouse, next to where Neptune had been buried for decades. The Gargoyle had spent several months chiseling a large boulder into a tombstone with nothing but his own claws, and had erected it neatly over the wickie's grave.

Beneath the lighthouse's heaping pile of wreckage, the Gargoyle dug with his thick, dense claws and carefully moved each piece away, layer by layer. He was in no hurry at all. What remained of that lighthouse's base was nothing more than a carefully-laid foundation in the process of being carved away by each careful, methodical movement the Gargoyle made.

With another few hours worth of work, the entire structure was finally gone.

The Gargoyle searched for what he'd been seeking. He knew it to be large, but he also knew whatever it said would be immensely faded with time. This stone was foretold in one of thousands of books he'd read all in one sitting, and of all of them, it was the only one that mentioned a way to undo transmutation. Conceivably, this stone no longer existed. A petty inconvenience to the one who enjoys an infinite amount of time. But those eyes were careful and deliberate, not to miss so much as a trace of the stone anywhere along this shoreline...

And there it was.

The steady hands of the Gargoyle unearthed what lied below the rocky foundation of what used to be a beautiful, towering lighthouse. Rocks and sand and splintered pieces of wood, adorned with sporadic shards of metal, piled in a mucky substance over the runestone's wording. Finally, the Gargoyle had finished clearing it off, and laid eyes upon the message.

The Gargoyle had trouble comprehending what he read. He understood it flawlessly, having spent several centuries accreting these Nordic symbols and languages into his analytical mind, but *comprehended* the message with trouble...

It wasn't the key to transmutation. It wasn't his path back to becoming a mortal man. It was a saga of adventure and defeat, and it ended with a warning.

A very specific time frame had been illustrated on that runestone for the upcoming cataclysmic event. To do anything useful with that information would be to give in to a ticking clock, utterly finite in form and substance.

For three uninterrupted days, the Gargoyle stared at the runestone and pondered what to do next. On the third, the Gargoyle took flight and departed from the forlorn island. He headed towards the Americas with greater speed than he'd ever needed to fly with, because for the first time in three hundred years, the Gargoyle felt that there wasn't much time to waste.

VI
THE HOUSE OF WAYLON ROSS

The moon's light softly grazed the treetops in the dense, remote forest.

Gwen Siodmak had only been in Mexico for a few lonesome hours, and had spent most of her international flight second-guessing her decision to pursue the man's offer. He lived secluded somewhere in Northeast Durango, residing in a mansion beyond the thick forests of redwoods. She traveled light, with only a backpack and a few night's clothes, and navigated what she considered "almost darkness" as she came closer and closer to the building. It was the kind of dark that was seeable only in the minute, finer details of the objects so *scarcely* hit with any light, as though they had a faint, white aura in the vacuum of shade.

When Gwen finally found the manor itself, she still only saw the way the soft edge of the light outlined the top of it, and refracted and defused even further against the night's musky air. *Almost* darkness.

The manor had a gateway like all mansions did, and it was solemnly left unlocked. Gwen approached the many carefully-constructed steps leading up to the massive, church-like doors. This place was either built a very, very long time ago, or made to look like it was, in an eccentrically deliberate way.

Gwen stopped herself from grabbing the door-knocker. There's no way the sound would carry to every room of the house. Instead, she searched for a doorbell. There was none on either side. She thought back to the door-knocker when the sound of a very large locking mechanism *clicked* undone, unprompted by any of her interactions.

The large doors slowly swung open and revealed not a butler or handmaid, but the homeowner himself.

A tall man in black solemnly met her gaze. His features were striking, with chin-length hair and a well-kept beard. The long, leather coat that draped his body had the mane of a large animal at its shoulders: Thick, prominent gray fur stitched into the coat's collar. It served the purpose of a hood or scarf, warming the back of his neck in the springtime air. Gwen caught herself staring at the peculiar man's many features, the last of which being the smile that lingered on his face.

"Am I early?" Gwen asked, confused at his silence.

"Gwendolyn?" Waylon confirmed in a deep Australian accent.

"Yes, we talked about-"

"Come in, please," said Waylon as he ushered her inside. He smiled with a strong admiration of her. It was a masculine desire, but not one of lust. Not entirely.

The interior was beyond what she could've anticipated.

Ceilings rose higher than practically necessary. Staircases coated the interior chateau's beige walls through and up to a balcony with a spectacular view. Tall, slender support beams held the roof over a gorgeously neo-gothic mansion of dark, luxurious fantasy. This place was secluded deep into this thicket of the forest, but it was not at all as imagined from the exterior. The view inside was truly otherworldly.

In the center of the chateau, between those beautiful rising staircases, was a couch, table, and loveseat. It was a life-size version of something a little girl would orchestrate while planning a tea party with her dolls. Very formal, but comfortable. Almost too inviting. Gwen was not a fool to men attempting to manipulate her, and so as Waylon gestured for her to sit down, this sight gave her pause.

"I'm quite alright, actually," Gwen said to the kind man.

"Nonsense," said Waylon. "You must've traveled obscenely far to come here. *Canada,* was it?"

"Hamilton," Gwen said pridefully. "Ontario is quite a ways away from Mexico. Fifty states worth of distance."

Waylon chuckled. It wasn't very funny, but he did not want to embarrass her. He'd been looking forward to meeting her in person for so long that every move he made was careful, and deliberate. Only that man could find a way to be both confident and self-conscious at the exact same time.

"I heard about what happened there," said Waylon. "I'm awfully sorry."

The comment made her uneasy. There was some history there that she didn't want to think about. Waylon quickly changed the subject:

"Please have a seat, Gwendolyn. I've had my assistant brew us some coffee."

Indeed on that table was a freshly brewed pot, still steaming a bit from the spout. Nowhere in sight was any sign of an assistant. Still, Gwen relented and took the couch, leaving the loveseat for Waylon. He would've chosen whichever one she didn't.

Coffee's not a good idea, said the voice in her head.

The man's hands stayed steady as he poured them both a fresh drink. Gwen watched him perform this task with a surgical precision. She was still not settled with this place.

"Actually it's pretty late, I don't know if I can-"

"It's decaf," said Waylon. "How was the flight?"

"Uncomfortable," said Gwen, scanning the rest of the house. Large photographs of exotic terrains hung from the beige walls, far above the trim of white wainscoting: Jungles, beaches, waterfalls, marshlands.

Waylon noticed her.

"Being born wealthy left no dream of mine ignored," spoke Waylon somewhat humbly.

"You've taken all of them yourself?" Gwen asked as she grabbed her drink. It was not very strong, but tasted remarkably sweet.

"Hunting has brought me to every continent not covered in ice," said Waylon before taking a sip.

"What cities have you visited?"

Waylon paused before answering the question.

"I scarcely visit the popular ones," he said diplomatically. "Of course, I've nothing against Tokyo or Paris. I hear they're lovely. But in my journeys, Gwendolyn, I've learned that the most iconic cities in the world lack the respect and appreciation for the very world they inhabit."

"How do you mean?" Gwen asked, putting the drink down. Finally getting comfortable.

"The more remote the area," said Waylon, "the more our natural world is recognized for its beauty. There are certain areas in every bloody country that are like this. They draw me right in. *Those* cultures are where I've tried to take my philosophies from."

Gwen cocked her head curiously. "These cultures you've visited... Is this where you've found others like me?"

Waylon smiled again. That same warm, friendly smile that livened any room it was in.

"There are so many others like you, Gwendolyn, that exist outside of common knowledge," said Waylon with a newfound glimmer in his eye.

Waylon took one more drink of the coffee, then placed it down as well. He stood up from his seat, surprising Gwen.

"Where are you going?" Gwen asked, confused since they both just sat down.

Waylon nodded to someone behind her.

Gwen spun her head around and saw nothing. Nothing but the paintings of Waylon Ross' extensive travels and reputations, their diverse environments looking right back at her. She looked again to Waylon, then back behind her. As if something would appear.

The sound of a footstep pressed against the hardwood floorboards.

Run, said the voice in her head.

Gwen moved to escape, but something stopped her cold. Something that wasn't there at all.

Her coffee fell as her arm was twisted behind her back. She couldn't fight back, since there was no aggressor. The cup shattered at her feet, soaking her pants in the drink and creating the only mess in this pristine building. Gwen hunched over from the force against her upper back, and soon her other arm was forced behind her as well. She was not bound by handcuffs or rope but by human hands, and she aggressively tried to stand up and shake free of this invisible grasp.

"This will only bring pain if you resist," said Waylon, still in that charismatic tone of his.

Her sanity was called into question: She'd seen *nothing*. Even still, as she looked back up at her attacker, there was only the air she'd been breathing. Gwen ignored Waylon's advice and tried to break free, closing her eyes since they could no longer be trusted. Waylon nodded again to the one holding her.

The last thing Gwen did before getting struck in the head was kick over Waylon's table. Waylon sidestepped the debris of the entire coffee pot flying towards him, and watched as it crashed on the ground and added to the horrible mess on the floor. The coffee ran and trailed around his feet. A high risk of staining the ground if not dealt with soon.

Waylon thought on this: Perhaps next time, an opportunity 'not to resist' shouldn't even be offered. His next guest would simply be made unconscious upon entry.

The ceiling above her was the first thing she noticed upon awakening: A fan lightly spun, blowing a calm, light breeze right onto where she slept. She looked at herself and felt the same clothes she already had on. No rips or tears.

Good, said the voice. *Thank god.*

Gwen lifted her head and looked around.

This place had to be part of Waylon Ross' mansion. The walls to her left, right, and backside matched the premium decor of the living room she was in, complete with the beige paint and white wainscotting. No paintings hung, though. The bed she was in was flush in the back of the room, and on it, a small window. In the front of the room, perhaps most curiously, was not a wall or a normal door. It was a caged gateway, similar to a prison cell's.

Beyond that, nothing but pure, boundless darkness.

Find a way out, said the voice.

The ceiling fan provided a dim yellow light for her while she slept. The only other source of light was a window on the wall behind her, opposite the gateway, shining sunlight into the room...

Was it?

The parallax when she moved her head wasn't correct. It wasn't a view of the outside behind that window, but an *image* of it. Gwen looked closer, getting out of bed for a better view. The closer she got, the clearer what she was looking at became: Tiny little pixels amidst a vast, high-definition screen. A television in place of a window.

"That's an OLED," said a voice from behind her.

Gwen spun around to see Waylon Ross, standing in front of her cell's door. He still had his gray fur coat on from earlier. *Not much time has passed,* the voice deduced quickly.

"What's nice about the OLED is that the black pixels actually turn *off*, giving a much deeper contrast in the dark," Waylon continued.

"What is this place?" Gwen asked pertinently.

Waylon smiled at her, then quickly recanted it.

"I apologize for my deception," said Waylon with only a hint of remorse.

"You came here believing you were going to be cured, and instead you've been permanently relocated here."

Gwen dashed straight up to the room's cage door. He did not flinch at her arrival. She grabbed the bars of the cell door and her palms *burned* at the touch. Gwen fell back, now wriggling on the floor dealing with two large blisters that were beginning to form on the palms of her hands.

The gateway was made of silver.

"A precaution," said Waylon. "For your sake and mine."

Gwen could not take her eyes off of her hands.

"Why did you cage me?!" Gwen asked, trembling on the floor.

"Because you are *not* to be cured, Gwendolyn. You are no more in need of a cure for lycanthropy as I am in need of a cure for being human. It is simply an *aspect* of you. Nothing more than that. It's worthy of celebration and respect."

Gwen looked up and met his gaze through the silver gateway. She rose to her feet as he spoke.

"Your latest incident before you came here claimed eight people's lives," Waylon continued. "The *very next morning* you reached out for my help. Isn't a place like this much safer for you, and everybody else in Hamilton, Ontario?"

"Waylon, please-"

"Do you care nothing for the people of your hometown?" Waylon pressed. "Are their lives worth less than yours?"

"*Let me out of here!!*" Gwen screamed at her captor.

A moment passed. Waylon sat with this thought. Then, he turned to his left and nodded.

The silver gateway unlocked itself and slowly opened up. Gwen took a step back. She wanted nothing more to do with whatever entity heeded Waylon's commands. The bars slid across the ashlar floor and hid themselves aside, leaving Gwen and Waylon completely unseparated. From his pocket, Waylon grabbed a remote switch. He pressed some button and lit up the entire room behind him. The vast darkness behind Waylon disappeared, and though Waylon's assistant was still nowhere in view, what Gwen *did* see was breathtaking.

Dozens more cages. Dozens more cells. All in a circle, facing the center of a large, circular crypt of ashlar with a pentagram in the middle. This place was a twisted underground prison, set up like a Medieval dungeon with ancient stone pillars holding the thing together, but eerily modernized for the mansion's style. The remote lights were in the shape of torches on the pillars between each dungeon cell. Much more controllable than authentic flames would have been.

And in these cells were the atrocities, each distinct in their horror.

"If you abuse this privilege, this cage will never open again," said Waylon, extending his hand.

Gwen looked down at the offer, then back up at those cells. The creatures inside of them. The menagerie of demons.

Characteristically, her curiosity trumped her reservations. She didn't wait for any approval from the voice in her head.

Waylon brought her clockwise around the dungeon room's arena-like layout. The artificial torches lit the room evenly, but not brightly. It was a dim aura of man-made luminescence that revealed the crypt's finer details and features: The hand-made nature of the pillars, the ashlar's brick placement stitched together by some concrete or cement many, many years ago. Gwen's cell was adjacent to an empty cell, which itself was adjacent to the only way out or in: A long, winding hallway whose end was lost amid the shadows. She squinted as Waylon led her right past the hallway's entrance, making out the faint shape of a door's threshold some fifty feet down.

Almost darkness, said the voice. It almost managed to make her smile.

"You're allowed to try and escape at any point, mate," said Waylon sardonically. "I don't discourage it."

Gwen looked over to Waylon in a snide way.

If we were to strike him, said the voice, *now would be the time.*

The voice in her head had been there since birth. She'd never shared it with anybody. It was her own personal friend guiding her through life in a way she was surprised was unique. The voice helped her face bullies when she was growing up throughout grade school. It helped her make important, life-changing decisions when they were presented.

Ever since she'd been bitten, the voice had always made sure she'd cover all of her tracks.

Striking Waylon was a suggestion she chose to ignore. She would probably not incapacitate someone as experienced as him in one, simple attack, and even if she could, his invisible guardian would most surely retaliate.

Gwen meditated on this thought as they walked. Not for terribly long, of course, since after the hallway's entrance was the first cell of Waylon Ross' collection, and the very sight of the man inside was breathtaking.

The tall man's suit was custom-tailored, since rarely do humans grow over eight feet. The only parts of his body not hidden by clothes were his large, grotesque hands and face, and they revealed his skin: Thick, brittle, and with a deep blue shade. The fingers were much larger and longer than an average man's, and his nose and lips protruded far down his own face in an uncanny sort of way.

Behind him, his television's screen was completely shattered.

"Please don't be your dreary self, Brute," Waylon said encouragingly. "Introduce yourself properly. You're already dressed the part."

The tall man, whose given name was Hoxton, glared back at him with merciless eyes. He then looked to Gwen with the same disdain.

"I am not associated with this man's zoo," said Hoxton with vigor.

When he spoke, it was as though time itself had stopped cold. Hoxton's voice was deep and gravely, and somehow echoed off of every surface in the entire crypt. Gwen's bones shivered at his speech. She wanted to ask him a question, but feared what a response in this man's voice would sound of.

"This one's our first," Waylon started. "I encountered the Brute Man in an unpopular town not far from Boston. He's as much of a poacher as I am, Gwendolyn."

"Leave me *alone*, Waylon," said Hoxton again, disgusted at hearing that title.

Waylon ignored him: "I was in my twenties then, if you could believe it. And yet, he looked the exact same as this. Wardrobe and all."

Gwen looked at Waylon closely. She surmised that he had to be approaching his mid-forties.

"You've been doing this for twenty years," said Gwen, taken aback.

"There is no skill as rewarding as conviction," he told her calmly. "Hoxton's no stranger to it. He had a vampire by the neck when I found him in that forest. His other hand held the stake. This man, Gwendolyn, had made an everlasting career of finding and destroying the monsters that nobody believed in. Because he was one of them."

Hoxton's fist bashed against the cage's bars.

The reverberation of the solid steel against his knuckles bellowed throughout the entire dungeon, and caused a ringing that lingered in everybody's ears. Even his own. Gwen cringed at the noise, her heightened sense of hearing disturbing her greatly.

"Don't frighten our new friend," said Waylon sternly.

Hoxton looked right to Gwen with conviction, and drilled the words in: "If you are smart, you will strike him. Before he locks you up again."

There was that thought she'd just had, back with vigor and purpose. It was spoken by somebody else other than her mental companion. She knew she wasn't crazy for hearing it.

Hoxton retreated further into his cell. He hadn't seen the outside of this place in a very long time. He made the mistake of repeatedly bashing his gateway to bits and running for the exit, leading to him being bested by an opponent he couldn't see. When the new, reinforced gateway was installed into his cell, it never once opened again.

Gwen looked around and saw that Hoxton's outburst had woken up some of the other of Waylon's guests. Some creatures and beasts she hadn't seen when Waylon switched on his torch lights earlier. Some with spikes, scales, claws, tails, or all and every one of those traits. She looked back to Hoxton, who now went back to his artificial window. His screen was the only one in any of the cells that was purposely turned off.

Waylon turned to her sincerely: "I can't excuse his behavior. At his worst, he attempted to literally break his way out of here. *By hand.*"

"At his best?"

"What you just saw, more or less," admitted Waylon. "I called him *Brute* like many others did, but his given name is Hoxton. I hope that you will come to know him as such."

Gwen was still reeling from the idea of never leaving this place. It felt like a sick dream, from which she would be pulled back into reality after hearing her phone's alarm. But that moment hadn't come, and it never would for her. Or anybody else trapped in the crypt of Waylon Ross.

Escape, said the voice, which she once again ignored.

Waylon led her to the next cell, and when she saw what was inside, Gwen realized just how real this place actually was. No dream of hers would invent such an atrocity.

An unsettling beast made of two distinct worlds.

"This one's origins illude me," said Waylon, "but I have reason to believe that she's man-made."

Gwen looked at the creature in as fine a detail as she could: Some large gorilla so bizarrely twisted with a woman's body, fused as though they were one and the same.

"Where did you find it?" Gwen asked.

"An island," said Waylon.

"Where?"

"Do you intend to *sail* there, Gwendolyn?" Waylon retorted.

The Ape-Woman came closer to the cell door with an innocence in her eyes. It was hard to tell if it was genuine, or a ruse for Gwen to free her. Perhaps to convince her to act on that brief thought of hers.

"Her creator wasn't present when I found her," Waylon explained. "I've taken many samples of her DNA. Whatever process she went through removed the effects of natural aging. She's much older than she looks."

Gwen reached for the bars of the cell, seeing as they weren't made of silver. The Ape-Woman raised her paw and grabbed the same bar. Waylon could only watch in fascination. *This* interaction was precisely his goal.

"You seem confident that she won't tear your arm off," said Waylon.

Gwen retracted her hand from the bar, off-put by his comment. The Ape-Woman lingered a bit longer on it, then slowly let go of it as well.

"How long has she been here?"

"She was the second," said Waylon.

It all clicked for her. Gwen swiveled her head and saw how Waylon ordered these beasts chronologically. The cell next to hers was empty. Whatever he'd catch next would surely inhabit it.

Waylon led her to the next cell. As they moved, she felt a slight wind at her opposite side. A breeze? This deep in a crypt?

Or a passerby to subdue her at a moment's notice.

Her spine shivered again. It was a primal fear that began to stimulate something deep within. Something she kept buried as best she could. Waylon stopped and noticed her body slightly twitching, and saw her consciously course-correcting to look normal or unaffected. She'd been doing it for so long that it now came naturally to her. But not quite enough.

Waylon placed his hand on her shoulder. "You won't turn, Gwendolyn."

There were many unnerving aspects about Waylon Ross and the horrid mansion that he lived in, and she was learning and trying to accept them all rather quickly. But physical contact like that could not be tolerated.

Off, said the voice.

Gwen quickly took Waylon's hand away. She practically threw it back at him.

"You will not touch me again," she sternly told him.

Waylon paused. If he were a younger man, he might have started an argument or locked her away. But she was entitled to what she needed to feel comfortable.

"My apologies. I meant no disrespect-"

"What is your plan with me?!" Gwen exploded. "With all of us? Hoxton and the gorilla girl? Is this chamber of horrors full of living *hunting trophies?*"

Waylon almost grabbed her by the arms to calm her, but halted himself. *She needs to feel comfortable.* Instead his hands went up, as though Gwen had a gun pointed at him.

"Gwendolyn-"

"*Gwen,*" she finally snapped at him.

Waylon nodded.

"There is only one lie I've ever told you," he said softly. "Everything else is the full, transparent truth. Ask Hoxton, or the Gargoyle a few rooms further. They've been here long enough to know."

Gwen calmed a bit. Her defenses were still up.

"This place isn't a trophy room, Gwen. It's going to be a Utopia."

Waylon guided Gwen's attention to the pillars between the dungeons of the crypt.

"There is a hex on this room that encircles us," Waylon explained. "It extends to the back of every cell, and cuts right through the only entryway."

Gwen looked carefully. Each pillar, and there had to be at least a dozen of them, had a symbol on it. They looked to be Latin, or maybe Akkadian, and some were hybridized between ancient letters and strange glyphs or shapes.

"I am no warlock by any means, but I've dabbled in magic. Surrounding this dungeon is an Isolation Spell, through which only human entities may pass through. That means, inherently, there's no reason for these cell walls to exist. Idealistically, this small community should live in harmony with each other... and I believe that with enough time, we will all reach that goal."

There were many new pieces of information to take away from what he said, whether explicit or implied, but only one stood out foremost to her: Whatever invisible assistant Waylon Ross had at his side was entirely human.

"Perhaps this is a pipe dream," Waylon clarified. "But dreaming has brought us this far, hasn't it?"

"You said I won't turn," said Gwendolyn.

Waylon nodded, finally lowering his hands.

"There is no cure, but there is something that *stifles* your transformation for a short while. It's uncommon, tasteless, and doesn't show up in a drug test. And you drank it in your coffee."

Gwen felt sick to her stomach. Before she could fully process this groundbreaking piece of information, Waylon had already nodded and moved on to the next cell in his crypt. She swallowed hard and powered through it. Answers like this would only come if she didn't break his trust.

The third cell contained a large tank with a deeply fogged glass wall, shielding any good look inside with a slimy layer of thick condensation. The encasement took up over half of the cell, and the ashlar flooring of the other half was fitted with a draining system for when the tank's open top spilled any excess. The wall of the tank was in arm's reach through the gateway's bars, but Gwen was hesitant to try and wipe the condensation to see deeper, for just as she'd considered doing so, a large shape of whatever was inside moved through the foggy waters of the tank.

"I plan on extending this one's home in some future revision. It's used to the wide-open waters of the Caribbean... Admittedly, I have no name for the Creature."

Gwen was still thinking about whatever substance he'd slipped into her coffee. She noticed Waylon staring at her, as if expecting a question. She quickly made one up.

"Does it hear us?" Gwen asked.

"It's not deaf," said Waylon.

"Can it *understand* us?"

"No," Waylon assured.

This felt permission enough.

Gwen put her hand through the bars and wiped just enough to see a little bit further into the tank, and saw the blurred backside of a monstrosity. The closest Earthly creature in resemblance seemed to be an alligator, with reptilian scales and spikes running down whichever part of the body this was, most likely a tail or a lower back.

"It isn't intelligent," Gwen confirmed.

Waylon shot her a curious look.

Slowly, Waylon's hand raised as if to greet or salute somebody.

From the area of wiped-away condensation, the figure inside of the tank swayed weightlessly in a whirl, then provided its own hand onto the glass. It mimicked Waylon's position. Waylon beckoned his hand further to his side with a sense of elegance and charm, careful not to move too quickly or aggressively. The Creature mimed his movements against the glass.

"It isn't stupid," he insisted.

Waylon lowered his hand. The Creature did the same, and disappeared again amidst the tank's foggy veneer.

"The Creature has its roots somewhere in the Devonian age," said Waylon. "It's had a lot more of a life than you or I."

"And this one's unrelated to the Ape-Woman? Or anybody else here?"

"Entirely."

The Creature's concealed body slowly slithered through the visible area, which itself was now condensating once again. Gwen could no longer see the scales or the spine on the blurred figure. As it moved, she confirmed it was some sort of tail that waved briefly. A truly magnificent one.

She couldn't stand not knowing anymore.

"Waylon," said Gwen cautiously, "what did you give me when we sat down? The drug that stops my transformation-"

"There's no *stopping* it, Gwen," said Waylon. "It's a rare Tibetan plant that I don't have much left of. I'm not heading that way anytime soon."

But this didn't satisfy her.

"Instead of staying here, why don't one of us simply go to Tibet and find more of-"

"It doesn't work that way," said Waylon.

"Why not?" Gwen insisted. "You've gone to the ends of the Earth to amass these creatures as though they were domesticated pets. How can you neglect properly caring for them?"

"They are cared for here better than they ever are when I find them," Waylon grumbled.

"Oh *please,* Waylon. Do you think this Creature is happy here?"

"*Happier* here, yes."

"In what way?"

Annoyed, Waylon looked to the empty half of the cell and nodded.

Gwen saw a panel open up from a compartment beside the tank - *his assistant was inside of the cell* - and out of it came a piece of meat. In moments, the meat floated upwards into the air, unconnected to anything at all, and found its way up and over the glass walls of the tank. Waylon reached through the bars and re-wiped the same spot, clearing all of the new condensation, but made an even *wider* circle: The Creature rose up like a serpent and a pair of incredible jowls chomped at the floating meat above.

"Careful!" Waylon shouted.

Mucky water splashed violently as the Creature fell back down into the tank. Once the chaos settled, Gwen saw through where Waylon had wiped away: A massive, humanoid swamp monster ravenously tore through the chunk of meat.

As the Creature shredded through its dinner with unbelievable speed, Waylon addressed Gwen one final time on this matter: "To eat a meal nearly that good in the Caribbean, this predator would've had to scavenge the islands for days. Disrupting ecosystems with her invasive nature... Not to mention if she had any young to feed."

Gwen could not look away from the Creature's underwater feast. She watched until the glass's condensation returned, after which she could only see that large, dark green celestial shifting in the deep of its tank.

Waylon observed her and sensed the horror in Gwen's heart. *Comfortable,* he kept thinking to himself. It drove his every action.

"It's called mariphasa," Waylon relented.

Gwen's attention was dutifully his again.

"All else being equal, it inhibits a werewolf's transformation for a couple of hours. The problem is how easily one develops an immunity to it. There isn't enough of it to sustain yourself long-term, nor is there enough of it to try and synthesize... but before I run out completely, I will obtain more. Use it as sparingly as possible, Gwen. It's all that's working in your favor."

Gwen watched as the gateway to the Creature's cell opened briefly, and shut again. Waylon's assistant knew how to move and carry himself almost completely silently. Were it not for the mariphasa coursing through Gwen's system, some of her senses might have made his job of stealth much more difficult than it was.

"Come" said Waylon. "There are more of them to meet."

The next cell's television was on static.

Gwen saw the backside of the one watching it: A large, gray-skinned being with long, black hair. The skin was wretched, yet the body looked incredibly healthy: Too large and muscular and toned to be malnourished or unhealthy. Yet, paradoxically, the thing looked like the exact reverse of human health and condition. It was puzzling to stare at, and Gwen had realized she'd been doing just that.

Waylon stopped briefly, and only said this: "It's a mutant. Genetically engineered, somehow. This one doesn't talk. At least not to me."

"Where and when?"

"Romania. I can't remember the year, but this was the fourth."

"I gathered as much," Gwen bitterly replied.

Waylon caught the snide tone in her remark. He realized that he would have to do much, much better to appease her. Above all else, she needed time to adjust.

"If you'd like to meet the rest later, we can-"

"Show me now," Gwen insisted. "These are my neighbors for the rest of my life. There's no changing that fate."

After having moved not one muscle this entire conversation, the gray-skinned being's head turned slightly at that remark. As if to turn around and see her. Gwen picked up on it, but soon noticed that Waylon had already moved on to the next cell. Completely oblivious.

After a moment, the being's head slowly went back to the static of the television.

The next cell was one of the furthest ones from hers, but with all of Waylon's lights on in this crypt, all of them could be seen. Gwen moved on to Waylon's position and saw nothing but an empty cell.

"An escapee?" Gwen abrasively asked.

"Keep looking."

Gwen squinted and examined carefully. An empty bed. A table and bathroom, like all the rest. And the television only showed a long-running soap opera, transitioning into an ad break.

But something was unusually placed.

The entire floor of the cell was covered in a mucky layer of dirt. Haphazardly placed on top, but evenly dispersed as to coat the floor's complete reach. It smelled somewhat fertilized, as though it could've been soil and bore plants. But none existed. Though she was now irritated, the search for whatever creature lurked inside this dark confinement gave her a sense of calm...

It took a moment to fully manifest.

Like an image being developed, the outline of a translucent man started to fade into existence. The ghastly figure glowed a soft white like a dimmed bulb on its last legs. The shape was perfectly human from the waist-up, complete with arms, chest, and a normal head. No claws or fangs. The anomaly, however, was the lower half, tapering down to a point below that was barely visible, as though the rest had faded away somehow. The jagged distortion in viewing him was perplexing. The wall of the cell behind him could be seen through his body. Gwen noticed his eyes, unlike the others, became transfixed on her features.

"You'll make a beautiful trophy," said the ghastly man in an archaic French accent. "Assuming you keep your current form, of course."

And accordingly, Gwen's rage returned in full fashion.

"When and where did he catch you, Phantom?" Gwen barked at the prisoner.

"Thrilling line of questioning," the Phantom snobbishly replied.

Before Gwen could ask again, the Phantom turned his attention to Waylon.

"Is this protocol, poacher?" the Phantom asked. "Introduce all of your old trophies to your latest victim? Are we supposed to care who she is before you lock her away forever?"

"Infinite time still hasn't given you any manners, has it?" Waylon asked.

"I have infinite time, and yet remain painfully aware when it's being wasted," said the Phantom.

As the Phantom talked, Gwen saw parts of his body from a new angle: His outline housed a black coat or robe tailored many, many years ago. The height of fashion, from whenever he was from.

The Phantom caught Gwen staring at his uncanny form. Ashamedly, Gwen looked elsewhere.

"I echo the Brute Man's sentiments," said the Phantom. "Strike this man dead while you still can. Lest you let your life become nothing but a totem to the mad poacher's ego."

The answer made her uneasy again, but not in a fearsome way as before. The feeling that washed over her now was sadness. Her new reality was starting to set in. The unpleasant truth that she was to live here, and it would truly be forever.

The voice in her head said nothing.

Gwen moved on to the next cell, passing Waylon entirely. Waylon shot the Phantom a glare before following after her. The Phantom shot one back before fading away.

Waylon wanted to comfort her, but didn't know what to say. He couldn't even tell her he was sorry for what he did. He wouldn't have meant it. In his heart, he stood by every decision he'd made regarding that place and those monsters. All he could do was take solace in the idea that whatever depression was starting in her would soon pass with enough time. And time was all she would ever have.

The being was humongous, rivaling Hoxton in size, but even the Brute Man managed to look more human than it.

The Gargoyle had two colossal bat-like wings and an enormous tail of many spikes, starting from the base and traveling all up its spine to the back of its neck. The entire body was made of stone, yet moved in a somehow versatile way when it breathed or walked. The face of the Gargoyle, perhaps, was most frightening of all: It sent many who looked at it into a state of apprehension and anxiety. Twisted fangs came from the mouth, and two smooth black orbs were fixed firmly where the thing's eyes ought to have been.

Unexpectedly, the Gargoyle was the first to speak on their encounter.

"Gwen," said the Gargoyle in greeting.

Gwen stood her ground as though it were an attack.

"What are you?" Gwen asked, diverging from the usual queries.

"He won't share his own name," said Waylon on his behalf. "I've taken to calling him Gargoyle, and he doesn't seem offended by it."

The Gargoyle nodded.

Behind the Gargoyle, the television was tuned in to a news channel, with muted closed captions not to disturb the others. Gwen gathered something else from the Gargoyle's lifestyle and mannerisms.

"You like it here, don't you?" Gwen asked.

The Gargoyle smirked with a horrific smile.

Ask him why, said the voice in her head.

"Why do you like it here... Gargoyle?"

The Gargoyle took a moment. He knew what he was about to say, which Waylon was aware of, would not sound like a normal dialogue of conversation.

"Waylon wants me to spend the rest of his lifetime down here in this crypt," said the Gargoyle. "That's forty, fifty years at most. Twenty *good* years, at that. It's meaningless to me, but it's *everything* to him. It's all he has in this world. He cares more about how he spends his time than any man I've ever met. In that time, he's furthered our understanding of the unnatural world hiding beneath the natural one... It's more interesting to me than how I initially planned on spending these next few decades."

Gwen couldn't help but briefly chuckle. This one was her favorite thus far. Waylon was more solemn; The Gargoyle's words had a way of *really* getting under his skin.

Waylon gestured to Gwen to continue onward. Only one cell remained before the crypt looped back around to her own. The upcoming cell had a tinge of weird, purple-ish light emanating from it.

"I look forward to our future conversations, Gargoyle," said Gwen with respect.

"As do I," he replied.

Gwen nodded to him, and her and Waylon went on to the final cell together.

Ultraviolet lights hung from every corner of the ceiling, blasting the cell with a deep blue tinge. The room's interior radiated this weird, almost purple coloring from afar. The man inside, in purely black clothing, had his back turned to Waylon and Gwen as they approached. He was fidgeting with a small hole in his cell's wall, blocking it from their sight with his body. The hole was no larger than a centimeter across.

"Can you speak?" Gwen asked the figure.

In return, she received his silence.

"He can," said Waylon. "He would tell you his name is Abrem Trosk, and that without these lights, he's the most dangerous guest in this entire mansion."

Abrem Trosk continued paying no attention to them. Whatever was inside the tiny hole in front of him was the only important task on his agenda.

"Ultraviolet?" Gwen asked, looking them over.

Waylon nodded. "They inhibit his power. Subdue him. He's no more threatening than a normal man... You know, when I first told him about this place, he actually started *laughing* at me... I've never heard him laugh since."

Waylon became irritated by Abrem Trosk's silence.

"You are her *last* guest, Abrem. Show some class about it," Waylon implored.

Abrem Trosk stopped fidgeting with the hole in the wall. But still, he did not respond.

"Your silence is useless," Waylon snapped. "You've barely spent one month in this place and are still unable to accept that, for once in your entire lifetime, somebody else holds power over you. Not the other way around. Everybody else will earn their way out of their cells first, and you'll be too busy sulking over the fact that you can't make that caterpillar crawl out of that little hole in your wall."

Something changed. Something inside of Abrem Trosk had been dormant this entire time. And Waylon just woke it up.

Abrem Trosk turned around to face the both of them. Gwen could see now that he wore a black cassock fit for a priest, lacking the white collar around the neck. The details of his face were arresting, with prominent cheekbones and a powerful jawline shaping his pale, lifeless skin. This was the face of a man made memorable by anybody he met, simply by a first glance, and alongside this trait, his eyes had a quality of drawing people's attention to them. Consciously or otherwise.

Abrem Trosk recalled the conversation Gwen and the Gargoyle had just had. He knew that the Gargoyle's existential comments had always disturbed Waylon. It generated an idea.

"What's your mother's name?" Abrem Trosk asked Waylon directly.

Waylon paused, looking to see if this was a trick.

"Florence," Waylon finally said.

"Your grandmother's?" Abrem Trosk insisted.

"Charlotte," Waylon complied again.

"How about your great-grandmother's name? What's hers?"

Waylon thought for a moment, unable to retrieve an answer.

"Your great-great-grandmother's?" Abrem Trosk asked pertinently.

"I can't rightly say," admitted Waylon.

"And yet, without all of them, you'd never exist. That seems awfully selfish of you not to know their names, let alone anything about them. Were they nice people? Did they prefer lunch or dinner?"

Abrem Trosk's dripping sarcasm was now boiling over into full-blown malice. He walked closer and closer to the cell's gateway in such a methodical way as to be unnoticeable by Waylon or Gwen. It was an eerie sight that Waylon didn't pay much attention to, being caught in Abrem Trosk's alluring eyes.

"You are forgotten," Abrem Trosk continued. "Everything you love will fall, and you with it, and as everyone left moves on to someone else, you'll be part of another unimportant generation. You will be exactly where they are now: A nameless, faceless, dead man's memory of a great-great-grandparent."

Gwen tried to draw some sort of strength from Waylon, but he had none to give.

"But not me," said Abrem Trosk cryptically.

Abruptly, Abrem Trosk reached forward and snatched Waylon by his furred collar. He pulled him in right up against the cell's gateway.

"I've been sucking the lifeblood from the necks of your ancestors for thousands of years. I've done it to your family then, and once your knees get weaker and your back gives out, I'll do it to your children's children. I'll work them, eat them, tear them limb from limb if I want to. I'm immutable. And you are a sentient bag of blood with a fading lifespan. So stand there and tell me how much power you hold over me, Waylon. I'm in dire need of a good laugh."

Abrem Trosk tossed Waylon back with an aggressive dismissal. Not just of his character, but of everything that Waylon stood for and believed. The house of Waylon Ross was nothing more than an incompetent joke to him, and it too would fade with enough time.

Finally, Abrem Trosk's gaze turned to Gwen, his newest neighbor and peer in this godforsaken crypt.

Something's wrong, said the voice after a long silence.

"There is a cure," he said carefully and passionately. "Seek it with all of your spirit."

Waylon splashed a small bottle of water through the gateway's bars. Abrem Trosk shrieked at the water's burning touch, which was blessed and Holy. Gwen wanted desperately to help him before Waylon explained: "He'll say whatever he wants you to hear, Gwen. It's what he does."

Waylon gathered himself and adjusted his coat, ushering Gwen back to her cell. He reminded himself just how normal and mortal Abrem Trosk became under those lights. Gwen, alternatively, was not entirely sold on the idea of what Waylon told her... He'd already lied to her once before.

And if there truly was a cure, then Waylon would've been lying to her this entire time.

Waylon gestured for her to head back inside her dungeon, but Gwen stopped in front of it. She turned to her captor with reservation.

"You haven't proven yourself yet," Waylon asserted to her.

"How can I from the inside of a cell?"

"Incrementally," he said. "You did great on your first day out. You never attacked me or tried to escape. But that kind of trust isn't formed over the course of twenty minutes."

From his back pocket, Waylon produced her cell phone. Gwen lit up and grabbed it.

"You'll need to charge it. There's one by your bedside."

Gwen looked to her nightstand, and as she did so, Waylon clarified something crucial: "Within the walls of this place are the makings of a Faraday cage. You'll be maintaining absolutely no contact with anybody outside of these walls."

The defeatism resurfaced in her. It set in so firmly in her mind that all joy from regaining her phone was lost completely. What would be the point of charging it? Already-downloaded games and music? Still, everything Waylon was offering trumped any poorly-conceived attempt at an escape. She wasn't human, and couldn't pass through the Isolation Spell. She'd never be able to defeat Waylon's assistant, wherever he was. She wasn't even able to *touch* the silver bars of her cell's gateway that were about to close behind her.

Gwen entered her permanent residency, letting Waylon's assistant lock the gateway.

"You will be fed three times a day. The door by your bedside leads to a personal bathroom and wash. On the TV are some streaming services, and the stock display are some images of the outside world's beauty. For comfort, mostly. You'll find the remote by your bedside."

Gwen looked around her room again, confirming everything he said in her mind.

Waylon gestured above his head: "The screen at the top of the crypt is a live feed of the sky, real-time. When it shows daylight, my assistant will typically be present. Call for him if you need anything. His name is Jack."

"He's always listening?"

Waylon scoffed. "He'd better be, with what I'm bloody paying him."

Gwen sat on her bed and stared back out through the gateway at Waylon and his unseen assistant. She was growing to accept this place. This new life of hers. As he mentioned, this would be for the betterment of everybody involved. The betterment of the innocent people she preyed on, and her own personal well-being. She'd never have to worry about another outburst again.

Stay, the voice finally relented.

Gwen sat on her bed and stared back out through the gateway at Waylon and his unseen assistant. She was growing to accept this place. This new life of hers. As he mentioned, this would be for the betterment of everybody involved. The betterment of the innocent people she preyed on, and her own personal well-being. She'd never have to worry about another outburst again.

This is good for us, said the voice in her head. *If we stay here, we'll never-*

"Goodnight, Gwen," said Waylon as he began to leave.

"Wait!"

Waylon stopped, turning to her once more. She had something more to say. Some missing piece that didn't add up with the rest.

"You do feel some level of guilt, don't you? You talk about an ideal life for us, but you round us up like cattle and cage us here in a crypt... Are our lives worth less than yours?"

Waylon lost his usual smile. He came right up to the cell's gateway, as close as he could be to her, and never broke eye contact as he spoke.

"To not embrace your game with the respect it deserves would be dreadful," said Waylon, almost insulted.

Gwen looked down at Waylon's jacket. He'd started running his fingers through the fur.

"This coat is made from a werewolf's hyde. When killed, the body no longer transforms back and forth. I always eat what I kill, Gwen. I've hunted Africa's Big Five twice over. Tasted the flesh of countless creatures who've walked, flown, or swam through this Earth. *Countless* of them. *That* is the respect they deserve."

Gwen turned pale. Though safe behind the bars, she felt incredibly insecure. As if at any moment he'd reach through them and wring her neck with those sleek, black gloves.

The man was wearing one of her.

"In all my years of doing what I do, it's started to feel monotonous. Most of the firearms I own could fire one, singular round at any creature who's ever lived, and cripple most. A second shot would usually finish them. What intrigues me are the ones that stand up to weapons like those, and I believed for a very long time that the world had run out of species that fit this criteria."

Gwen could feel his invasive eyes on her. Every part of her.

"So yes, a part of this is selfish," Waylon continued. "You're here in this cell because no game of any hunt could come close to what you are... No matter how much mariphasa you end up using, this is the category that you've permanently found yourself in. You are, irreversibly, one of *them*."

Waylon gestured to the room around him, his smile finally returning.

"*Monsters.* Vampires, werewolves, spirits. The undead mutants and the wicked immortals. They are the Devil's league, and they are the greatest game in the world."

VII

UNSEEN

Vera West, age 5, ran to the living room in search of the perfect hiding place.

It was a game of hide and seek, her father had just told her, but with a twist: 'Find a spot that nobody would think to check, and only come out if daddy finds you.' Vera loved games like these and happily played along. She'd decided on the cupboard under the stairs: A treasure trove of old furniture, cleaning products, and anything else the West family simply didn't have a real place for. She weaved her tiny body through all of it and got comfortable inside.

Though the cupboard door did shut, there was a crevasse where she could look out into her living room and see if her father was near. He was a man named Claude West, who took a great deal of pride in his sixteen degrees from several universities. In his study, he'd aligned them in a four-by-four grid on his wall, showing anybody who'd give him the time of day his beautiful, deliberate symmetry of his prestige.

Unexpectedly, Vera heard her father's voice from the room over from the cupboard. He spoke to his wife, Elisabeth, in his study.

"She's hidden," Claude spoke in a hushed tone. "I don't know when he's coming. For all we know, he could already be here."

"Why can't we take her with us?" Elisabeth responded, clearly more worried than him.

"Because he doesn't know that we have a daughter," Claude said to his wife. "I told her to hide, but I don't know where. So he can't even try to get it out of me."

"He wouldn't want to kill her too, would he?" Elisabeth said to her husband while he finished packing their bags. "Claude, she's just a little girl."

"And George isn't stable. All he wants is-"

A loud bang cut them off, pulling Vera out of her eavesdropping. The noise came from the front door as it was broken open, but nobody was at the threshold.

Vera looked through her crevasse and saw the broken door swing inward, splintered bits of wood landing on the living room's vibrant blue carpet. Nobody caused it, and nobody entered the house.

Claude hushed his wife, and for the first time in her young life, Vera heard the sound of a gun loading from her dad's study.

Vera didn't know what to do. She adhered to her dad's rules: Don't tell him where you hid, don't leave the hiding place, and only come out if daddy says so.

But after the front door broke open and the house went silent, she was starting to become terrified. The only thing she knew for certain was not to let her cries be heard from her hiding spot. She looked through the crevasse again and saw nothing but the broken door, still ruffling slightly from the outside breeze. The break-in had silenced her parents, who now began to move out of the study and into rooms and hallways that Vera could no longer hear them in.

Aside from the visual of the entire living room, all she could hear and feel were the muffled movements of their footsteps. After what seemed like an eternity, she finally began to hear her father's voice again. They were in the kitchen, which neighbored the living room. She did not make out the words of his whispers, but she recognized them as his.

The gunshot shook the house.

Elisabeth screamed. Vera could hear Claude struggling with the man who broke down their front door. Pots and pans began to clash in the kitchen as their bodies were thrown into them. Frantically, Elisabeth attempted to run, and Vera was able to see her mother come through the living room. She grabbed the house phone on the wall and attempted to dial the police when the sound of Claude's gun loading was heard again.

"No!!" Claude screamed, right before it went off for the second time.

Elisabeth fell quickly from the shot, her blood dressing the phone and the wall it hung from. Her daughter could not scream from the hiding place, but a whimper did force its way out of her as she watched the murder take place. In that instant, Vera no longer had a mother.

Claude screamed with immeasurable pain and continued his assault. Whoever it was that broke into their house had killed the wrong person first.

Out from the kitchen, Claude's body tumbled onto the ground. Getting to his feet as fast as possible, he reloaded the gun that had been fired twice already, for a third and hopefully final shot. Pure rage drove the man now. When it was loaded, he aimed it towards the kitchen, and froze for a few moments.

He looked around. The gun followed his gaze.

Claude scanned the room up and down. The man who shot his wife with Claude's gun was still in this house, but Vera didn't understand why he couldn't be found. They were just fighting in the kitchen before her mother was shot. Wherever this villain was, he needed to be stopped if for no other reason that Vera and Claude desired so strongly to cry over Elisabeth until authorities arrived. Authorities that never got Elisabeth's call.

Claude's body rose.

The gun fell from his hand by a force unbodied. Claude grabbed at his neck quickly, and now desperately. Vera watched the indescribable sight of a nightmare from her cupboard: Her father was floating in air, unable to breathe, and hovering towards Elisabeth's body. It wasn't a short death like her mother's, to Vera's misfortune. It was a death that took far too long and had no tangible source. A death no man, woman or child should ever dream of imagining in the darkest corners of their minds. A death that she was forced to witness.

When Claude finally fell from his ethereal position, his body landed next to his wife's, and for a moment everything was immutably still again. The entire house, and everybody in it, were completely silent and motionless.

The last thing Vera witnessed before her tears blocked up her vision was Claude's gun floating through the air from the kitchen, and placing itself intentionally in her father's hand.

Vera West, age 13, had finally escaped from her upper-class foster home. She didn't leave so much as a note when sneaking out from her second-story window. The family was perfectly nice to her when they met and the four months that followed, but that simply wasn't enough. No family ever would be for her.

The house she grew up in was abandoned since the event that the police and every news outlet described as a murder-suicide. It was completely unsellable. Vera was extensively questioned after that day, but said she saw nothing at all. Though it wasn't very far from the truth, it wasn't considered helpful by any of her town's detectives. She hadn't been back at that house since getting wrapped up in this indifferent system that attempted to place her with a family that wanted her time and time again. Systems like those didn't account for the fact that a love between a child and parent needed to be mutual.

Vera went on foot for much of the journey, but deliberately wore shoes that made her look tall enough to ride the bus alone. She was smart for her age, and more mature than her peers in the countless grade schools she was placed in. The bright, morning sunlight did a lot to calm her nerves of traversing the streets alone, since she figured most male predators struck when it was dark. Aside from a few hours trek and the twenty dollar bill she lifted from her foster mom, the trip to her old house didn't cost much at all for her to pull off.

She was here.

The door was repaired so it could be locked again. The paint had more than faded, and several shingles were slipping into the gutter of the house, which itself was clogged and full of wet leaves. She remembered the shade of blue very differently than how the outside of the house actually looked today. Aside from some aesthetic changes courtesy of lost time, it was practically identical to her memory.

Vera trusted her memory more than most. Her memory of that day's events eight years ago was all of the tangible evidence that remained of her parents' murder. Completely inadmissible in a court of law for a number of valid reasons. There was nobody in the world who would help her discover what happened or why it did, and her limited reservoir of knowledge was all that she had to work with.

Sneaking in wasn't troublesome at all. The sliding doors at the back of the house were susceptible to a little *nudge* that jostled them free. Whoever last entered this house years prior hadn't considered locking them properly. In the breezeway, Vera saw the empty spots where all of her family's furniture used to be. They were all sold at a yard sale or destroyed in a landfill. This place, completely, was barren and forsaken.

Vera entered the living room with a flashlight she had brought. Turning it on illuminated the dark corners of the place, and made some tiny creatures scutter quickly away before they were seen by the light. The nostalgia of being here sometimes got the better of her, in the very worst way. That, combined with the house's putrid smell, and the bugs that she had heard moving around her, made Vera throw up on the floor.

She coughed and gagged and composed herself, wiping her mouth with the sleeve of her mother's jacket. Practically nothing on her person actually belonged to her. Not even the house that she just threw up in. Legally, it belonged to no one.

Vera continued towards the cupboard, whose door was wide open and its contents cleared out. Police searched extensively after they found little Vera stowed away in her hiding spot, and everything that had been removed from the space got taken out of the house along with the rest of the furniture. It was empty, and it was so much larger of a space than it led on when it was cluttered. She scanned it with the light, not knowing what she was really looking for in the first place.

She just needed something.

Vera went to her dad's study, finding remnants of an office spread about. The space where his desk used to be now housed a pen and some paper clips sprawled across the floor. The file cabinet in the corner wasn't removed, but the drawers were certainly emptied. The wall that used to hold Claude West's sixteen university degrees, neatly in a four-by-four pattern, was completely blank. Those went back to his parents back up in Maine, Vera believed.

Claude's mother and father were the last living relatives of Vera after the incident. Many times her grandparents tried to claim custody of her. Many times, Vera opted not to see them. To do what she had to do, and find some semblance of vindication, she needed to be alone. It would never be possible if she was stowed away in a somewhat-normal life several states over from the crime scene.

The smell lingered, and Vera used all of her mental fortitude to ignore it.

Vera sifted through the empty drawers of her father's file cabinet. Maybe *something* was left behind before this place was cleared out. Something to point her in the right direction. This was the room that her parents packed their things in that night and prepared to escape whatever killer was after them. It was the place that stored her father's gun.

And where would that gun have been kept?

Surely not in a desk or a cabinet. No, Vera realized that something that was that important to her father probably had its own special spot. Its own hiding place that nobody could see.

Vera turned to the closet of the office and sifted through empty hangers. Nothing on the ledge above but some cobwebs and a long millipede slithering into the ceiling. She checked the floor, which still had a couple of Claude's old pairs of shoes. She didn't touch them for fear of what critters now lived inside of them. Behind the shoes, there was some kind of panel that dangled a short string. It was smaller than a crawlspace, but large enough to be of significance. Vera crouched down and opened it.

There were no bugs or cobwebs in here.

It was a small black box, like a safe without a key. Vera pulled it out and opened it, expecting it to be where he housed the gun. She didn't realize that Claude simply stored the gun itself in the space she'd found, and this little black box was meant for something more.

It was empty.

Vera became frustrated. She was getting nowhere with all of this digging around. Even if she found no clues whatsoever, she was bound to a life searching for truth where nobody else could find it. She felt the insides of the box, hoping to find a button or a latch or something that would give her something real or useful, something *tangible* that she could...

She felt something.

It wasn't anything inside the box, yet that's precisely where she felt it. No secret compartment or hidden key triggered the feeling. It was soft like fabric, and she returned her finger to the spot she felt it again.

It was there. Whatever it was resided in that specific spot, right towards the corner of the box. She stirred her fingers around the ethereal feeling and was compelled to close her eyes, and stop trusting her vision.

It was a piece of clothing.

Vera opened her eyes and grabbed where she felt the thing to be. The thing she couldn't rightly see. She held it up to her flashlight and saw only the closet in front of her, no matter how hard she tried to look at it. She laid her hand flat and let whatever non-visible object it was sprawl itself out on her palm, the edges of the cloth draping over her hand.

She flinched seeing how her hand had disappeared.

It was gone with no warning and no trace. Her arm simply *stopped* at the wrist, and she only saw the floor beneath her when she looked down at where her hand used to be. Quickly, she clenched her disappeared hand into a fist and restrained the cloth into a scrunched-up ball. There, she saw her fingers holding the fabric together, but it still covered her palm. And so her palm was gone, with her five floating fingers holding the space where it used to be.

Vera West, age 19, had been waiting beneath the pine tree's foliage near George's driveway for several hours now.

The soil beneath her dirtied the knees of her jeans, and the bristles above occasionally tickled her and made her sneeze. She'd befriended a colony of ants to pass the time. A lucky few of them had the privilege of crawling up and down her fingers, and she gave them bridges between her hands to make new pathways for them to travel down.

After a great deal of patience, George's garage door opened.

Three years ago, she'd found the name and last known location of this man, who'd quit his lucrative job and moved away shortly after Claude and Elisabeth's death. Vera had spent that time tracking him in several counties across multiple states, with her extensive searching finally culminating last week when she discovered his home. Large, gorgeous statues of Greek gods stood tall over the expansive front yard, which housed a fountain right in the center. The grass was impeccably trimmed and well-kept. The walls of the mansion were pure white, and a large marble entryway greeted all onlookers and privileged guests. It was the place of men's dreams, and the summit of one's domestic imaginations.

As the distance between her and George slowly shortened over the span of the last three years, her knowledge of him had grown tremendously. He lived alone, and always has. No wife or kids. He developed an absurd amount of income that he kept carefully out of the sights and talons of the IRS. Vera had only seen the one bank's footage, but the stature of the home and the intel she'd gained on him suggested numerous more, and just barely a low enough number of them to keep out of rational minds' suspicions. His parents lived in a retirement home in Arizona, a place he used to visit annually. He stopped seeing them, predictably, after the death of Vera's parents, and according to phone records that she certainly wasn't allowed access to, he stopped answering their calls. George was living in a self-imposed isolation ever since that gruesome day.

The vanity-plated car drove off from his driveway. Vera quickly dashed over to the slowly-closing garage door and rolled underneath before it shut. She knew George only had one housekeeper, but she had no idea what room he was in. Vera looked around the garage as she got to her feet. The sun's light peered in through a small window overhead, and as she cased the room, she could definitely say that the housekeeper wasn't in this room. One down, and about a dozen to go.

George's labyrinth of a home was puzzling to Vera, who snuck through the place conspicuously in a dirtied t-shirt and jeans. She made her way up the staircase to one of the master bedrooms, where she stopped short of reaching the top. The housekeeper was inside one of them, though she couldn't tell which room. Casing her surroundings, she moved quickly into the first one she saw.

It was empty.

Vera was relieved, but still alert. She snooped through the drawers as quiet as she possibly could, feeling the fabrics with her hand and watching them closely. *All visible.* She began to open the closet when she heard a noise from behind her, and quickly turned to see it. But she saw nothing. Anybody else in the world would continue to believe that they were alone in that room, except the little girl who watched a man unseen strangle her father in the air.

Vera heard the floorboard in front of her creak ever-so-slightly. That was enough.

She kicked as hard as she possibly could, her foot contacting *something* before her. Whatever it was tumbled backward into the king-size bed and whacked itself on the frame. A loud *thud!* accompanied the body as George's housekeeper fell to the ground and groaned in pain.

Vera ran over to the noise and pinned the body down. She closed her eyes as she did it. They weren't to be trusted.

The housekeeper struggled beneath her, but was simply too stricken to properly react, and Vera finally opened her eyes when she located the man's mask and yanked it off of his head, the fabric feeling identical to the face cloth she'd been holding onto for six years now.

The sight of a head with no body, lying on the ground yet floating in air, was jarring for her. The eyes of the housekeeper locked with hers, finally within her view, as an undetectable punch struck her forehead. He was aiming for her jaw, but George's housekeeper was no experienced fighter and didn't know where exactly his own arm was as he attacked her. Vera, conversely, had seen her fair share of fights, and knocked him square in the nose before forcibly tearing the chest of the suit off him.

"Why are you wearing this?!" Vera asked the half-visible man she had pinned. It took him a moment to recover from the bloody nose she'd given him, and say something back to her.

"It's my job," said the housekeeper. "If anybody broke into this house, I'm supposed to put this on and take care of them."

"Take care of them?" Vera shouted. "How do you plan on taking care of me?"

The housekeeper had no good response, so Vera punched him once more, and he slipped into unconsciousness from it. Her father did not design this fabric to be exploited by sociopaths and murderers. Or their servants.

Vera quickly disrobed the housekeeper and left his body. Claude didn't have another suit, otherwise he would've used it that night before George broke in. So this suit was everything left of his creation. His legacy was in her hands, recently peeled off of his killer's lackey. The blood from the housekeeper's nose stained the outside of the fabric, so she could not wear it and stay to see George's reaction. She left long before George returned, and only dreamed of what George may have done upon coming home and finding his well-paid servant knocked out cold, with the most valuable thing in that mansion now permanently missing.

Vera West, age 24, was nowhere in sight.

George awoke trapped. His arms were behind his back, tied to the chair he was stuck in. His legs were tied as well, and the chair he'd been bound to was haphazardly bolted to the ground. This was no professional kidnapping room, and it didn't look the part: The walls were concrete and moist. The ground below was hardwood, but severely unkempt, having fallen victim to the wild hands of nature and many of its insectoid inhabitants. It was most likely a basement or cellar, George gathered, but unrecognizable and untraceable beyond those details.

There was one source of light. It was from a small lamp up on a ledge to his right, with an air freshener dangling from it. The lamp beamed a fluorescent white light across the damp, ugly room, and revealed a cheap table in front of him.

"*George.*"

The voice was unbound to anyone or anything. It was female, and certainly not one he recognized. George scanned the room around him for whatever speaker produced it, unable to find one.

The voice continued.

"*March 31st, 1999. You murdered Claude and Elisabeth West in their home.*"

George panicked.

"Where are you?!" George screamed into thin air, struggling against his restraints.

Her head simply appeared.

Head to toe, she was hidden from sight. From the perspective of an onlooker, a human head just appeared out of thin air as she took off the skin-tight mask of her father's suit.

Unexpectedly, George calmed down at the sight of a disembodied woman's head. Vera assumed it would haunt him like a specter. But he recognized immediately what was happening, and exactly why he was here.

"You dumb bitch," George lashed out at her. "You think because you stole that thing from me five years ago that you can-"

Quite literally, he didn't see her attack coming. Vera slugged him across the jaw with the speed and power of a flyweight boxer. It didn't shut him up.

"You think you're powerful, beating a man tied up to a chair? Not letting me see what you're doing?"

Vera glared at the man with eyes that would pierce lead. Her hands made invisible fists.

"Why did you kill them?" Vera adamantly asked. George glared right back into the eyes of his kidnapper, completely unyielding.

A moment passed.

The table between them moved on its own, at least in George's mind. It slid across the old hardwood and left a gap between them. The disembodied head of Vera West moved closer to him, before she put the mask back on and completely vanished once more.

George could not brace for the strike to his abdomen, and because he was bound, could not cringe or hunch over when it happened. Vera grabbed him by the back of his head and yanked it back up. Instinctively, he flinched, awaiting a fist he'd never detect.

It did not come.

And then, as his guard slowly fell again, it did.

It was in the temple this time, dazing the man. Concussing his brain. Vera let his head go, and as George composed himself, he coughed strongly, and looked back up at nobody at all. If the Devil had a wife, it would be the invisible woman in front of him.

"Claude wanted to sell that thing you're in," George grumbled back into the aether. "He was going to patent it."

"And that's worth taking his life?"

"The world would change beyond repair," said George, still faltering from the assault. "If everybody had that kind of power, all would fall victim to it. A world of Invisible Men wouldn't sustain."

George composed himself, and glared at where he assumed she was.

"Alternatively," he said to her, "if only one man were privileged with that gift, he would be truly unstoppable."

Beneath that mask, Vera turned pale. It wasn't a thinly-veiled sense of altruism that compelled Claude and Elisabeth West's killer to do what he did. It was a lust for her father's indescribable power. The one he created to lift his family out of the financial hole that they found themselves in, with a straight-shot to success and legacy. George saw this, murdered the creator, and robbed banks with his creation.

The restraints around George were cut.

A knife from behind George floated over to his chair and freed him, top to bottom. George stood quickly. He grabbed his wrists, which had become sore from his bondage, and scanned the room with his eyes and ears.

"They were my parents," the disembodied voice said to George.

His eyes locked on to the only thing they could: The floating knife that freed him. It swayed in the air slightly as Vera adjusted her grip on it, and turned its blade towards her victim.

The knife fell.

George watched as it clanged against the floor, chipping the wood in the process. He made fists from weakened hands, and held them up in defense. Constantly, he kept rotating, paranoid of when or where she would strike. His adrenaline surged as he did so.

The lamp's light went out.

It was unclear if this was by fault, or if she had done it deliberately. Practically, it mattered very little to him. Psychologically, being trapped alone in pure darkness with Vera was nothing short of complete terror.

"You're his daughter, are you?" George yelled to the air that surrounded him. "You want to hit me, just do it! See what happens to you!"

He kept looking around him with useless eyes, unable to see the room around him anymore. Even if he could, it would be of absolutely no help to him. His blood pressure kept rising as the true angst and restlessness began setting in. And those feelings were unbelievably strong, beyond all logic and reason.

"WHERE ARE YOU?!"

George spent a great deal of time in this state of horror and uncertainty. He couldn't possibly have had any way to realize that she had left him, and from another room, killed the power to the light. He would never come to understand that the basement he was trapped in had one door, which he could not locate, and was bolted three times from the outside.

This place was the cellar of her home. It was a place that had been left completely untouched for nearly twenty years, and unlike a brutal, savage death by strangling, Vera had sentenced George to a much darker fate than her father's; A vista of existence where he'd be forced into an endless worry and anticipation of an attack, one story beneath where Claude and Elisabeth West were taken from their daughter. One story beneath where Vera was forced to stay quiet as she watched them die. George was stuck in perpetual, inescapable, frantic anticipation of an assault that would not come. The only harm he'd receive would be death itself once his mind and body finally withered in the depths of that cellar.

James Claude Griffin, age 12, sat across from his therapist like he usually did on Wednesday afternoons: Still, calm, and completely void of emotion. He stared only at the ground beneath his therapist's feet.

"How are you holding up, Jack?" his therapist asked him softly. She scanned his face for telltale signs of how he was feeling, but it felt like solving a Rubik's Cube with eighteen sides.

"I'm fine," replied Jack politely, still dressed in the uniform for his high-end private school. "It didn't hit me that hard."

"Are you sure?"

"Yes," Jack said with a stoic tone. The boy looked up at her with a blank stare. He didn't want to be here, and tried his damnedest to answer quickly and diligently.

The therapist took a moment to breathe. She was going to have to push him.

"You've had three weeks to think about their passing, Jack. You know there was a lot of pain there... Do you miss them at all?"

"I do," Jack answered reflexively. He was prepared for that question.

"What did you do when you found out?"

"I woke up to the sound of a loud bang. That's when I came downstairs, and I saw them on the floor-"

Jack's therapist put her hand on his leg, stopping him. "I know. That's not what I meant."

Jack was confused. He'd recited his carefully-rehearsed alibi to the police when they questioned him, and it'd always worked. He didn't realize that a list of alleged facts wouldn't satisfy someone whose job it was to study feelings.

After a pause, Jack brushed the hand away and didn't offer an explanation why. He closed his eyes and turned his head away.

"You're supposed to make me feel better, right?" Jack asked in a more welcoming tone.

"Yes," she answered, paying close attention to the boy She was careful not to lose this moment. They were too rare.

Jack exhaled softly, then spoke his mind: "I'd feel better if I were left alone."

"Why do you want to be alone?"

"Because people don't like me."

"That's not true," she replied. "Your mother loved you."

"Not anymore."

The therapist took another moment. She was running out of options, angles, and whatever was left of her patience. Meanwhile, Jack looked around the room curiously. Bored of everything.

"That's all you want to share today, Jack?"

Jack looked her straight in the eye, but did not answer instantly.

What the therapist could not know, no matter the interrogation, was how Vera Griffin, age 42, had feared for her child amidst her husband's late-night benders. The therapist could not know the horror that settled into Jack's mother when Oliver's headlights illuminated the front of their house when pulling in too quickly and slamming on the breaks before grinding against the driveway's retaining wall again. The scrapes on the side of Oliver's car were recently buffed out before that night, and this time he'd taken care not to do it again in his intoxicated state.

"That's all," said Jack in a glum tone.

The therapist could not know about how Vera rushed her son into her room and produced a lockbox from beneath her bed. Pulling out something illusive, she handed her son Jack what felt like a cloth and told him to "put this on quickly, then hide." He'd never seen anything like it before in his life, and technically, still hadn't. Even after putting it on.

"Alright," said the therapist before standing back up.

No matter the questions she tried, Jack's therapist certainly could not know of how his father yelled at Vera, his typically obedient wife, about Jack's whereabouts, and her reply of him being "at a friend's tonight." Oliver saw through her lie instantly: *"That little bitch doesn't have any of those. Just like his mother."* The words lived inside Jack's mind from that point forth with that same twisted tone they were spoken with.

"I'll see you next week," said the therapist as Jack shot up from her couch.

Under no circumstance could Jack's therapist know of how Jack stood right beside them as his father smacked Vera into a wall. His father believed him and Vera were alone in their kitchen. Jack watched as Vera's head banged against the corner of a table on her way down, blood spilling mildly. For this reason and many others, it was a floating kitchen knife that stabbed Jack's father in the back, and then the front, and several more places in his torso.

"Bye-bye!" said Jack in a playful voice as he left the therapist's office.

All that the therapist *could* know, in corroboration with the police's story, was that Jack had woken up and harmlessly discovered both of his parents dead on the floor: One from blunt force to the temple, and the other from a knife with no fingerprints.

Gerald Wynne came home from his monotonous day job with a strong desire to use his in-ground pool. The sun would only be out for another couple of hours. His feet ached from standing up all day, and the sweat on the back of his neck could finally contact the air and cool down after he removed his collared shirt.

As he walked through his front door and stripped the shirt down to a tight-fitting tank top, Gerald made his way to the refrigerator before making any further decisions. His wife, Erin, was constantly on his case about drinking straight out of the carton. Gerald grabbed the carton, thinking about how she happened to be out-of-town for the night, and took a long swig from the carton's opening.

He exhaled loudly after lowering the carton.

Gerald returned it to the refrigerator and shuffled through some of the other shelves. In a take-out box was a carefully-wrapped sandwich Erin had ordered from her second-favorite restaurant the night prior. He smiled, then unwrapped his wife's leftovers and took a large bite. He didn't like the place nearly as much as she did, but it was the fastest, easiest thing for him to eat right then. No microwave, no oven.

Gerald looked through the picture window of his living room and saw into the backyard, marveling at his pool as if the chlorinated waters were graced with the properties of the Fountain of Youth. In two more massive bites, Gerald finished Erin's sandwich and took off his pants and shoes. He left them right in the middle of the kitchen.

Before opening the door outside, Gerald noticed his alarm system had been silently blinking since he came home.

He remembered deactivating it before walking through the front door. Interacting with it, the alarm showed that there were no signs of forced entry, but that the motion detectors had been triggered from inside and outside of the house. *Did she stop by and forget to turn it off?* Gerald figured as much, considering how airy she tended to act recently.

Gerald deactivated the security system. He opened his phone and pulled up his contact for maintaining the security system.

"Put the phone down."

Gerald spun around to an empty house. He was in nothing but his underwear, and intended soon to be wearing even less than that, but found himself absolutely petrified before he could proceed. His eyes shifted around the walls, floors, ceilings, even the turns and corners where somebody would have quickly ran away. He knew the voice came from the kitchen - or maybe the dining room - but that it somehow belonged to nobody at all.

Gerald was frozen in place.

He looked again at his phone, seeing the maintenance contact's icon. His thumb hovered over the button as if to call them. As it slowly lowered down, the phone was smacked out of his hand completely.

Gerald reacted, swinging a fist at the air around him. It soared through it and struck nothing.

"Where are you?!" Gerald screamed, turning his head in every direction.

From the kitchen table, a chair slowly pulled itself out. Gerald watched closely as the chair's cushion subtly *compressed* beneath an invisible weight.

"Wh... What are..." Gerald began, never actually forming a question.

From nowhere, an envelope materialized and placed itself on the table. It slid itself over to Gerald.

Gerald opened the envelope and read the details of what was inside: Divorce papers, court proceedings, several long paragraphs of legalese, and a contract that would transfer an exorbitant amount of money to his wife.

"Sh... She wants to *ruin* me," said Gerald.

The chair stayed quiet.

"I'm not signing these," said Gerald, tossing the file back onto the table. "I'll never work again if I sign those pages. I'd be damning myself. My reputation..."

The chair stayed quiet.

"Do you know what's in these pages?! One of them is a signed confession. I can't admit to something like that. Even if it *were* true, I just... I can't do something like that. I'd never have actually... I mean, maybe in the context of the situation, it's possible I reacted and my arm might've... I *never* hit her. I never did."

The chair stayed quiet.

"She's *lying* to you. That bitch is in way over her head. We've had plenty of arguments. All couples do, don't they? What's so wrong about a few arguments..."

The chair stayed quiet. Gerald realized he wasn't going to get anywhere.

"I'm not signing," Gerald repeated with conviction.

Gerald watched closely as nothing happened at all. It was a surreal sight, but he was confident it wasn't a dream or hallucination. This had to be an objective experience.

"Okay," the voice said calmly.

The cushion on the chair slowly decompressed.

Gerald silently panicked. He backed away from the chair slowly, and scanned his surroundings, still believing that his own vision would be of any use at all. There was nothing to help him down here. In his bedroom upstairs, sitting dormant beneath a small box under his bed, was the ammunition to a 12-gauge shotgun resting on his bedroom's mantle above the fireplace.

In nothing but socks, underwear, and a tight-fitting tank top, Gerald suddenly ran for the stairs to the second floor. Making it almost to the very first step, Gerald was knocked back by Jack's undetectably swift movement. Gerald had no idea what part of Jack's body did it, but it felt to be either an elbow or a kneecap that belted him in the stomach and hunched him down onto the floor.

Gerald sprawled back onto his feet and put up his fists, rotating sporadically. He had nowhere to aim it.

One of the floorboards by his side quietly creaked.

Gerald threw a wild punch in that direction, striking what felt like a torso. An audible *thud* came from the ground near him. Using this window of uncertainty, Gerald ran up the steps and entered his bedroom. He locked the door and barricaded it with his own nightstand.

The shotgun was in pristine condition. Gerald had no license to own one whatsoever. He hadn't planned on ever firing it anyway. It merely looked interesting adorning the fireplace, in his opinion.

Gerald could hear the footsteps ascending the stairs outside of his bedroom.

He loaded the ammunition into the shotgun the way that the box's instructions detailed to him.

The footsteps stopped.

Gerald aimed the weapon at his own bedroom door. There was no way inside or out. Not without forcing entry and revealing oneself.

"You're being *lied* to!!" Gerald shouted through the walls.

"I don't care," said the voice.

Gerald was shocked at the response, not only because of what was being said, but at the very fact that there was any response at all.

Is it money?

"Whatever she's paying you, I'll double it," Gerald shouted back.

But Jack remained completely silent, frustrating Gerald further.

The door broke off its hinges with the force of a tornado. Jack had put his entire body's weight into that kick, and placed it purposefully at the door's weakest spot.

Gerald sidestepped the door and fired the gun into his hallway, striking only the hanging picture frames on the hallway's opposite wall.

"You have no allegiance to her," Gerald said to nobody. "Take the bigger paycheck."

Terrified, Gerald turned rapidly at random parts of his room, his eyesight yielding him no results or evidence to follow. Any part of the room, from any area surrounding him, could be the intruder's shelter.

"She already paid the first half," said the voice.

Gerald could not track it. He aimed the gun somewhere near his own closet, but the hanging clothes were still swaying from the wind the door had made when bashing itself down. An invisible man could easily be hiding amongst them.

But if he were, he'd most certainly have moved away by then.

"If you sign," said the voice, "the second half comes out of the transfer."

Gerald reloaded the gun.

"And if I die?!" Gerald screamed defiantly.

"It comes out of your life insurance," said the voice ominously.

A floorboard creaked nearby.

Gerald blasted his bedroom floor, sending splinters up all over the room in something resembling a small whirlwind. He ran for the only window in his bedroom, knowing that it overlooked a second-story drop, and quickly unlocked it. Gerald slid it open and looked back around the room, surprised at the lack of resistance. He stepped one leg out over the edge and planted it loosely on the house's outside trim.

Jack smacked the gun out of Gerald's hand, sending him off-balance.

Before plummeting straight down, Gerald reflexively grabbed the window's frame a fraction of a second too late, slipping off of the outside trim and down onto the windowsill. The wood splintered beneath his hands.

The windowsill held him.

On its own, the windowsill snapped and almost broke off.

Gerald could feel the intruder kicking from inside. Voluntarily, Gerald let himself go and tumbled into the bushes below. Nothing broke or fractured, but his extremely exposed skin became treated to dozens of brand-new lacerations.

Bloodied, Gerald hobbled back onto his feet and tried to run away from the house towards the garage. He looked up at the bedroom window, and upon realizing that nothing was there, turned and ran anyway. Relying on his eyesight was purely habitual. He knew it wouldn't actually help him.

But he *had* to look back again.

The gun floated into view, and fired from his bedroom window.

Buckshot riddled the ground in front of Gerald, slicing and wounding the man's legs. Gerald was forced onto all fours and started crawling away from the house as fast as he could. He looked over his shoulder and saw the window completely empty. The gun was no longer floating in view. Gerald scrambled himself to his feet and ignored the mounting pain that it brought him. He needed to start running again. It was his only shot at surviving this horrid night.

Glancing back over his shoulder, Gerald saw nothing out of the ordinary.

Gerald arrived at the garage and pried the door open by hand. The disarmed security system wouldn't alert anybody at all. A critical mistake Gerald realized much too late. He unlocked the car door and jammed his key in the ignition, frantically starting it up.

Glancing into his rearview mirror to back out of the garage, Gerald saw the shotgun hovering over the car's trunk.

Gerald ducked as the second round of buckshot disintegrated his back window, firing bits of glass and shotgun shells everywhere throughout the interior. Probably injured again, Gerald actively ignored whatever pain he was in and slammed on the gas pedal, reversing with incredible speed.

The car bolted out of the garage and reversed out onto the street, letting Gerald look ahead to see where he'd come from.

From several feet off the ground, the floating shotgun started reloading itself.

Gerald shifted into first gear.

The car roared with fury as it bolted over towards his own garage. Before it collided with anything, the shotgun fell to the ground all on its own.

Gerald didn't feel anything slam into the front of his car when re-entering his garage. He quickly hit the brakes before crashing into the garage's back wall.

Speedily, Gerald exited the car and walked over to the shotgun on the ground. Gerald picked it up, realizing that the assassin hadn't finished reloading it yet. Gerald took the time to do so and spun it around at his own house, scanning the grass of his front lawn for any impressions from footsteps. It was all he had to go on.

"Where are you?!" Gerald yelled, wielding the shotgun maniacally.

His front lawn was once something to be proud of. It was spattered in Gerald's blood from the shotgun's very first blast, adorned with bits and pieces of shells from the gun's discharge. No footsteps could be spotted anywhere.

The security system turned back on.

Cameras covered every angle of Gerald's property, and the house's motion detectors forced the front lawn's spotlight onto the home's owner. Gerald raised the shotgun instinctively, then lowered it again. *The bastard's inside my house,* he thought. Gerald looked to the front door and saw it left open again, but dared not follow where the assassin must've fled. Trapping himself in his own home with an invisible man would be akin to fighting a lion with his eyes closed.

The safest place was out here.

Gerald kept a careful eye on his lawn. There was no wind moving them, no breeze to confuse him. The blades of grass would only move or part for a man's footsteps. None did whatsoever.

Gerald stepped closer to his front door.

The grass in front of him remained perfectly still.

In the distance, a police siren wailed louder and louder. Gerald tried to see the flashing lights far down the road, but couldn't yet. He still had some time left.

Gerald looked to the threshold of his front door, seeing only the lightbulb's illumination. It bounced off of the hallway inside, revealing nothing. Nobody was standing there at all. Gerald forced his eyes to look closer, trying to pick up even a tiny detail or imperfection in the assassin's garb.

Looking down at the grass, Gerald noticed footsteps creating themselves on his front lawn.

The shotgun forced itself up at Gerald's own head. Before Gerald could wriggle it free, the trigger pulled itself down.

Gerald's body fell limp to the ground below him in full view of the front lawn's camera just as the police car's lights became visible down the road.

Jack Griffin, age 22, had completed his very first contract.

VIII
THE CREATURE

1762 was not a year of many pleasant events for Captain Archibald Black. He'd spent his younger years running supplies for traders through the hellish waters of the Caribbean Sea, navigating the most fearsome storms and hurricanes that occasionally plagued his trading routes. Benjamin Black, a buccaneer-turned-pirate and Archibald's uncle, had an encounter with a Spanish warship some thirty years prior, and valiantly fought them off at the expense of two-thirds of his crew. Archibald grew up hearing those stories from his parents, his cousins, and about everybody else in his close-knit circle of friends. Uncle Benjamin lived in his riches now, somewhere far off the coasts of the Caribbean. Presently, Archibald was 37, and amidst his countless months and years spent on these trepidatious trade routes, his pistol had stayed holstered, and his sword always sheathed.

Mundanity made for poor storytelling with his friends. When visiting, they asked him of his sailorly journeys and his replies were middling. "Simple trade route, had to avoid some strong eastbound winds. Tricky when you're heading west, it certainly is. Troubles? Ahh, none today, lads. T'was a straight shot, there 'n' back... 'ow-bout you?" The conversations always shifted away from him with a tinge of disappointment, and Captain Archibald Black was painfully aware of it all. *Archibald Black.* That could've been a revered name, were this the 1710s. Even the 20s. Could've been a name on par with the likes of Blackbeard himself, he reckoned. Indeed, Archibald lived with this perpetual sense of self-worthlessness, and had a multitude of places to put his blame.

This job, initiated by a man named Sam Bertrok somewhere down in Watling's Island, was predominantly like all the others. Smuggle something from here to there, don't ask questions, protect the cargo at all costs. Rules he agreed to many years ago, and to them, stayed faithful as a spouse. It'd made him many types of currencies over the years, spendable in a variety of countries. Nothing comparable to what his uncle had earned according to the stories. It seemed as though every time someone mentioned his uncle's fortunes, it doubled in size. Piracy was not at all extinct, but it certainly wasn't as prominent, and Archibald's fantasies of living up to the legacies of smugglers and scoundrels were simply musings as he continued along his routes, keeping him distracted until something drew away his boredom.

It came rather suddenly.

It was a bright, piercing daylight when he departed from Nassau to Watling's Island, and about a third the way through his trip, the sky darkened slightly, coinciding with his mighty vessel, *Rita,* swaying stronger than usual against the frothing tides below. It wavered and shook more than usual, and Archibald's routine was promptly broken. He grabbed the wheel of the ship from the first mate and steadily spun it around.

"The main sails! Reel them back, boys!" Archibald practically screamed to his men. They obeyed to little avail; that storm had snuck up on them a tad too quickly. The first mate, Iliff Frye, damn-near panicked. He was new to Archibald's crew, picked up not two weeks ago from a port on Cat Island, and was the one who originally gave Archibald the intel about Sam Bertrok and their current mission. Iliff was the only one aboard who knew the contents that they were shipping to Bertrok, and when this storm hit, his heart nearly sank.

Archibald churned the wheel harder than he had previously, and much faster. The "slow bend" he had planned on to avoid disruption did exactly what the name implied, and a much sharper turning of *Rita* was in order. The crew held on and waned at their captain's grasp on the ship, slowly trying to reroute it from the thing that soon lied ahead. Waves crashed against him, half of the sky now a dull gray from the oncoming storm clouds, and off in the distance cracked a silent, heavenly flash of lightning.

As *Rita* descended down the crashing waves, she leaned back in Archibald's favor, and at their lowest point, the bellow of thunder was heard. *Mere seconds after the bolt,* Archibald realized. Their realigned ship was now on course to head through a thin lagoon he'd never been down before on an island he passed frequently.

"Cap'n, we're headed for-"

"*I see it, boy!*" Archibald quickly replied to a dutiful Iliff. "We haven't time to think, only move!"

As Archibald stated, he began to enter the lagoon without thinking. He could see the entrance being wide enough to support *Rita* without damage, but not one soul on board could speak to the legitimacy of a natural way out. It led to a river, and it went on further than the eye can see, deep into a murk of fog and rain clouds. An elaborate mossy rainforest of long, stringy trees coated the surface of the land around the river's opening, bordering the lagoon. This was Archibald's sight dead ahead, directly beneath the bright, sunny sky. To his backside, a looming gray one, and beneath it, a slew of relentless waves. They plowed forward, their broadsides brushing the leaves of some odd trees with no grace whatsoever, as the mighty Neptune's wrath was now much further off than before.

Iliff ran directly to the front of the ship. He needed no telescope. Captain Archibald Black tried not to be taken by the view of the rocky, yet fertile terrain, fusing the beauty of a tropical, forested island with the grave, stoic semblance of an islet's cliffs. He instead maintained focus on his first mate, who turned back toward him from the front of *Rita* and yelled the following:

"Clear waters, sir! We're good to move forward!"

The alleviation washing over Archibald's crew was short-lived. Their captain had solved one problem, sort of, but brought with it many more. The storm likely wouldn't follow them to the lagoon, and if it did, the crew could dock and wait it out. Archibald turned behind him, seeing the inklings of the rousing storm get further and further from his vision, and so he looked up to see a sky still divided; Not fully bright nor dim, but somewhere down the middle.

"Easy, lads! Steady through the..." Archibald wasn't sure what to call the area. A channel? A ravine? It certainly shared traits of both. The boggy waters stayed deep for some time, and as they quickly moved inland towards the cloudy mists, the ways the water forked ahead seemed less like clear paths for a detour and more like a waterlogged labyrinth.

But alas, this was the place.

Iliff quickly returned to Archibald's post, retaking the wheel from him. The adrenaline that surged through him these past moments meant that the fatigue hadn't been truly felt by his body yet.

"Cap'n..." he said, Archibald too distraught to respond. "Cap'n, I think this was a mistake. I don't blame ye, but there's no certainty we can make it through the entire island."

"We either can or we can't," said Archibald. "If we have to, we'll double-back when that bloody storm dies down. But that would make us at least a day late, maybe two. Payment isn't guaranteed then."

With a forlorn realization, Iliff nodded. Though Archibald was driven by factors like his reputation and a large payout for his troubles, Iliff understood the situation more clearly with Archibald's estimates: If Sam Bertrok's cargo weren't delivered on time, the life of Iliff Frye could potentially be threatened.

"It's through the waters, then, Cap'n," said Iliff with a newly sombre tone that caught Archibald by surprise.

With his usual tenacity, Archibald waded through the strong, steady waters of the lagoon for what seemed like an hour. Logic dictated there be an exit to this maze of a swamp, and the island wasn't very large to begin with. He'd told Iliff this, but nothing he said could shake the powerful sense of dread on Archibald's first mate. It wasn't the foggy atmosphere, the eclectic environment, or even the idea that there wasn't an exit that made Iliff so uneasy. It was the very idea that their cargo wouldn't get delivered to Sam Bertrok on the day that was promised, and the consequences thereof.

Iliff kept watch toward the front of the ship and gave visual directions for Captain Archibald and his crew, but other than that he rarely moved. When his arms weren't signaling which route to take, Iliff Frye stood almost defeated in nature.

Archibald recognized this.

"Aye, take the helm for a moment," said Archibald to the crewmate standing beside him. He took the wheel from Archibald and dutifully obeyed his captain's order. Archibald wasn't done giving them.

"Treat our first mate's instructions as you would the gospel," Archibald added before he left his post and headed over to Iliff.

As he walked almost the full length of *Rita*, Captain Archibald Black took in where exactly he was: It was oddly gorgeous to him. It was damp and boggy and smelly and populated by the noise of a thousand tiny critters and their mating calls. But it was pure, and wholesome. On his trade routes were nothing but an endless breadth of ocean and the glorious expanse of an ever-shifting sky. Remarkably simple, but dull and repetitive. *How many others have steered their ship down this eerie lagoon?*

Perhaps I'm the first?

Archibald made it to his ship's front and tapped Iliff on the shoulder, making him jump out of the trance he was in. His body was following the motions of signaling directions, but his mind was thoroughly elsewhere.

"Oh," yelped Iliff. "It's just you, Cap'n."

"What's got you bothersome?" Archibald asked.

He received no response.

"We'll make it through," Archibald continued. "The waters wouldn't flow this steadily if there weren't another opening."

"I'm aware," Iliff finally spoke.

"Then what's-"

"Cap'n," Iliff interrupted, "I admire your empathy. But there's simply nothing to be done unless there's a way through this island."

Seeing an opening distributary ahead, Iliff signaled another direction to the crewman at the wheel.

"Cap'n," Iliff continued. "I know my client well. Too well, many would say. Sam Bertrok is a very powerful individual. The kind that's not... Well... Well I mean it like this, Cap'n: He's not all there. He doesn't make logical decisions like you 'n' me, navigating these unknown straits to avoid a storm. He's crazy. Not right in the head. Not one bit."

"Iliff," said Archibald finally, "I couldn't chance it with that storm. She was brewin' too powerful for Rita to handle."

Iliff wasn't satisfied.

"So your alternative was a harsh turn through a lagoon no man's sailed through before?" Iliff snapped back at his captain.

Archibald had no response, and so Iliff continued.

"Don't bother telling me you've been doing this job in *this* place on *these* waters for as long as you have and not encountered a *wee bit o' rain,*" Iliff grumbled at his captain. There were equal parts fear and disdain in each sentence, and Archibald sensed it.

"Easy there," Archibald said, grabbing his shoulder. Iliff swatted it away.

"No, Cap'n, I'm fine. I tell you, I'm fine. Let's just get there *on the day that we planned.* Not after. Not two days later. Right on time, Cap'n."

Iliff nodded to him, distraught beyond repair. Archibald reluctantly nodded back.

"Best you go now to your helm," Iliff said. "Rita needs your handlin'."

With a pause of regret, Archibald started heading back, leaving his first mate alone, just as Iliff preferred in his time of immense stress and uncertainty. Archibald looked ahead at the helm of his ship, then up at the lush environment he'd lost himself in thinking about earlier. His eyes wandered amongst the branches and leaves of the trees, following each limb sway lightly amongst the cold, misty afternoon breeze.

An unusual noise stopped Archibald in his tracks.

A weirdly low *thud* noise, similar to a mallet striking a wooden log. Whatever it was had struck the side of *Rita* with a force strong enough to make the noise, but with a grace careful enough not to damage the ship. Archibald and two surrounding crewmen turned to the railing from whence it came.

Scuttering.

Teeny, fast-paced little movements sounded from the side of the ship and carried themselves down the outside of the hull, stopping right near the helm.

Archibald and the two who heard the thing shared a brief look, and he saw flashes of fear on his crew's faces.

Without thinking, Archibald moved toward where the sound had stopped near the helm and drew his sword. The unsheathing of the blade drew attention from more of his crew.

"Hold!!" Archibald called out to the crewman he'd handed the wheel. The scuttering returned, accompanied by a visual as it launched itself over the railing and on board *Rita*. A blur of green rage dashed across the floorboards of the quarterdeck and straight into the crewman at the wheel, creating a spatter of blood across *Rita*'s whitest sail as its teeth sunk into his neck and its jowls tore the man's head from his body.

Iliff finally caught sight of it, distracted by thoughts of Sam Bertrok's retaliation. Those thoughts faded quickly upon seeing it.

It towered over the tallest man on board, or ever born, and was somehow thick and muscular whilst lean and swift... Strong, but not at all heavy. The armored skin was a deep green with a black underbelly. Massive webbed claws protruded on each hand. All down the arms, legs, tail and backside were spiked ridges, not unlike a crocodile's, which themselves were webbed together. It switched seamlessly between quadrupedal positions on all fours, or hunched over on hind legs, using its arms and tail for balance. That long and wicked tail as thick as a tree slithered with the speed of a jaguar. The dragon-like head had the face of an anglerfish, with black piths for eyes that never blinked, and a massive underbite that protruded long, unkempt teeth.

There.

Archibald was agasp. It was the thing foretold only in rumor and legend. The Creature that he'd been tipped off lived in this obscure place.

Being one of few souls aboard that ship with an actual firearm, Archibald drew it with gusto and shot cleanly for its head. Like lighting a powder keg, he managed to hit the Creature's shoulder and spur it into a rage.

He'd only ever shot still targets with that pistol. Targets pinned up to tree trunks in the yard of his modest ranch, and after missing what was planned to be a headshot, he reckoned he'd never see that ranch again.

Fear petrified the man. His hands seized up, clutching close to his sword and his gun, which were both drawn for no real purpose. The bravery in his belly that compelled him to open fire on a predatory beast would take some time to return to him. In the interim, Iliff sprinted over to Archibald from where he was standing, almost perfectly timed with the Creature beginning an unruly massacre aboard his ship.

The Creature almost soared with its movements. It was inhumanly fast as it crawled on the deck and onto *Rita's* mast - the same one covered in that crewman's blood - and slashed open another's throat. Just as soon as this happened, the Creature scaled the mast like a spider on its web and leapt onto a Jacob's ladder, scuttering down towards more of Archibald's crew. Only a handful of them had swords. Even less of them had guns.

Amidst the slaughter, the Creature scuttered up the mast once more and moved to the elongated branch of a nearby tree, disappearing amongst the leaves.

An awkward calm settled amongst the crew. Iliff Frye furiously approached his captain.

"*What did you just do?!*" Iliff screamed at his superior.

"I..." Archibald spoke partially, his sight still transfixed on the monster's last known location amidst the foliage of the forest.

"...I made a mistake, Iliff."

Archibald noticed another tree's leaves ruffle quickly. The bravery returned.

"And I intend to fix it," Archibald added, holstering his gun. "You were correct in your earlier assessment. I've seen many *wee bits o' rain,* and I've survived them all."

"You came here... deliberately." Iliff was in shock for many reasons. Betrayal, the primary of them.

"The townspeople of Cat's Island have a price for their secrets," Archibald responded, readying for another attack. "Just like everybody else."

Iliff struggled believing what he now knew to be true. Coming here wasn't a reflexive reaction to a foreboding storm. It was a personal choice, based on intel that Archibald sought out himself. He wished to kill the beast that no man had ever lived to discover, and his name would be celebrated thusly. More than any historical pirate for generations to come.

Captain Archibald Black's Creature burst from the branches, landing again on one of the crew's hapless members.

The rest of them watched as one bite from the disgusting array of teeth rendered him deceased. Archibald shoved Iliff aside and readied a running stance. The Creature swatted another of Archibald's crew with a meaty swing, both slashing the man's body and sending him flying across *Rita*'s deck in one swift motion. His loyal crew were dying in front of him, and he cared nothing for them.

Archibald flurried his sword. The Creature leapt for another crewman, who'd barely drawn his gun. He did not have time to shoot it before losing the arm. As it sunk its hefty jowls into it and yanked it out of the socket by turning its head, Archibald made a daring run towards the impostor on board. He held his sword up high for the first time in his life, and prepared to strike his enemy as he got close. The thrill of pure adrenaline surged through him like lightning through the tallest tree. He saw the Creature distracted by the meal it was making of his men. Now was his window of time. No man could stop him, and no man would, for he was possessed by the arrogant will of the gods he looked up to.

Like a lion tamer's whip, the Creature's long, unrelenting tail cut through the air and struck Captain Archibald Black in his chest, launching him far enough backwards to tumble into the railing on the other side of the ship. The sword he majestically carried fell almost instantaneously from his grasp. It wedged itself into *Rita*'s center, the perfectly sharp tip jabbing through one of the floorboards. It was the first time it had been used.

The Creature didn't even look in Archibald's direction as it completely incapacitated him. It didn't need to.

Iliff watched as the Creature moved on to each passing crewman who tried to fight or run. He'd watched it render Archibald defeated with an instinctive passing thought. On Iliff's person, he had a small shank in his belt and a flintlock pistol in his coat with one round in it, and like Archibald, no time to load another afterwards. Unlike Archibald, he was clever enough not to shoot it.

Iliff Frye ran straight towards the lower chambers of the ship.

The total people on board at the start of this mission was about twenty, and by the time Iliff made it one floor lower than the deck, there were about a dozen left. The sounds of crunching bone and helpless screams of his peers continued above him: Iliff's ceiling was the floor of the Creature's massacre.

The carnage above needed to stop, and Sam Bertrok's cargo was only a few rooms over.

The Creature had run out of crewmen.

Bloodshed and butchery coated *Rita* like rainfall. The masts were damaged from the claws of the Creature as it scaled them up and down, picking its victims off individually from above. The thing was used to the swamps, soil, shrubbery, and the tall and strong bark of neighboring trees of the forest on this island, and many obscure islands like it. It traveled among every terrain and was never slow about it. A collection of adaptive traits from a potpourri of wildlife. Nevertheless, its natural home was the waters below, where it mated and bred with more of its predatory, carnivorous kind.

Captain Archibald Black laid against *Rita*'s railing. As he came back to consciousness, he felt the incredible pain of severe bruising and several cracked ribs. If he were to survive this, a full recovery would be immeasurably far away.

He coughed to his side, without realizing that blood spewed from his mouth when he did so.

The Creature's head turned at the sound. It was atop the opposite railing of the ship, inspecting the corpse of the man who attempted to shoot it. He missed, and only succeeded in further pissing the thing off. Captain Archibald Black possessed no gun nor the strength to wield one, nor even the strength to stand himself upright. All he could do was stay there and wait.

It did not move as fast as it normally did when approaching Archibald. *Rita's* deck was barren of the human life it once had, replaced by whatever type of life that undiscovered Creature was. There were no longer any threats to it, and so it took its time. It crawled on all fours most of the way, but as it got closer to Archibald, the Creature transitioned to only its hind legs, standing itself fully upright once more. The shadow grew exponentially across the bloody floorboards between Archibald and his Creature. It passed Archibald's sword that wedged itself into the deck, and the Creature's tail inadvertently knocked it on its side as it walked by.

The claws on either side widened as it fleshed out its webbed hands. Archibald got a clean view of the true length they could be, and was unfathomably horrified. It massacred his crew with speed like a cannonball and claws like daggers, this draconian abomination that he had planned on defeating. He could not move nor resist. The Creature drew closer and closer, respirating heavily from both lungs and gills as it did so.

Archibald put his hand up instinctively.

The Creature paused at the sight. It cocked its weird head and looked on with its ghastly pair of demonic eyes. Archibald kept his hand in front of his face, then slowly started to move it down.

The Creature raised its own claw, mimicking Archibald's movements.

The doors to the captain's quarters opened up as Iliff emerged with Sam Bertrok's cargo.

The Creature turned and screamed an ungodly screech at what it saw: Another victim. It was a tall, menacing figure clad in black robes and silver chains. Iliff used the key only he had access to, and freed Hoxton, the famed Brute Man, from his chains.

The Creature left Archibald and scuttered quickly towards the mast in the middle of the ship. Hoxton grabbed the thing's hind leg as it attempted to scale the mast that it'd been tactically retreating to, and with the strength of ten men, yanked the Creature down straight into the floorboards. They snapped and splintered, but did not cave in, and the Creature quickly regained its footing and recovered on all fours.

The thing looked at Hoxton and sized him up. The grimace on his face was unyielding, partly due to having been stuck in hellish captivity for endless days. Partly because as Iliff freed him, he'd whispered an opportunity into his ear.

Hoxton despised Archibald and his crew and cared little for their deaths, but was too reasonable of a man not to follow Iliff's idea, and save the one man who could bring them off of this parasitic island.

The Creature launched itself toward Hoxton, who had already formed fists with his hands. The moment before the thing would land on him with those spiky, abhorrent claws, a lightning-fast right cross sent the Creature off-balance. The body flopped from the strike and landed on *Rita's* guardrail, and Hoxton was not one to let up from an attack. Though he moved swiftly toward the Creature, it still managed to wrap its legs and tail around *Rita's* railing, stabilizing itself almost immediately. Hoxton attempted another punch, but the Creature dodged and instead slashed at his abdomen, attempting to draw blood. His clothes tore at the claws of the Creature, but the skin of the Brute Man withstood the strike. Visibly, there were now marks on his hardened skin that the claws had made, but there simply weren't any wounds.

The Creature slashed again, this time with the opposite claw right at Hoxton's face, and though he attempted to block the strike, he knew he was not as quick as the thing he was fighting. Like a brick hitting a wall, the clawed hand of the Creature smacked against his brittle skin and cocked his head to the side, dazing him. Hoxton had never been struck that hard before in his entire life, and any normal man would've been decapitated in that instant. The shockwaves of the hit reverberated down the arm of the Creature, and it, too, felt a strong sense of confusion at the stubbornness of its opponent.

Still reeling from head trauma, Hoxton used both hands and shoved the Creature overboard, staggering backward himself. The Creature flipped over but held on strong by its tail, swinging and pulling itself back onto the side of the ship. It quickly scuttered along the broadside and boarded again, further away from Hoxton. Hoxton shook his head violently and smacked himself, returning awareness to the fight. He scanned for the Creature and saw it now traveling down the railing of the ship at him, clawing its way forward like a cheetah after its prey. Hoxton shifted his footing more defensively, and the Creature did not slow.

Hoxton swung high, and the Creature went low. It dove down and caught the splintered floorboards beneath Hoxton's feet, and before he could look down, the Creature sprung up and straddled his neck. Hoxton grabbed onto the body of the beast with both hands, but as he stumbled backward, the Creature's tail wrapped itself around his right arm. The tail forcibly pulled Hoxton's arm away from the Creature's body, and the Creature's claws planted themselves firmly into Hoxton's collarbones. The Creature opened its jowls as if to bite, and Hoxton reacted with his free arm: He braced the beast's bite with his forearm, and the thing chomped down against hardened blue skin. The Creature kept biting at the arm, and each time those disorganized teeth made contact with Hoxton's brittle body, a weird clanking noise blared out for all to hear.

Iliff ran to his captain. Archibald's body was throbbing heavily from the hit that he took, but his mind was no longer dazed by it. He accepted Iliff's outstretched hand trying to bring him to stand - and hopefully run. As Archibald ascended, Iliff's helpful embrace turned swift and painful as he forced him onto his feet.

"THIS WAS YOUR PLAN?!" Iliff screamed at Archibald, who cringed in pain as he was forcibly brought onto his own two legs.

Archibald put his arm over Iliff's shoulder and the two started moving toward the captain's quarters, steering very clear of the battle of the monsters. Archibald remained silent.

"You wanted us to find this bloody thing, *did you?*" Iliff lashed out at him. *"Well, Cap'n, you got your bloody wish!"*

Though its tail was still wrapped around his arm, Hoxton used his leverage to grab the Creature from two opposite points and hurl it into the nearest mast. The Creature's back *snapped* in half at the impact. Hoxton moved in with determination. The Creature attempted to slash his arm, but Hoxton reached down and lifted it by the neck. All the slashes succeeded in doing was scratching the skin of Hoxton's arm, and shredding the sleeves of his long, black robes.

Hoxton grabbed the open jowls of the Creature with both hands and tore it from its neck, right in half. A satisfying *crunch* accommodated the snapping of its head, followed closely by the pungent slithering of the Creature's spine as Hoxton pulled the completed head out of its body.

Iliff and Archibald stopped and looked as the body of the beast fell to the splintered floorboards, joining the many carcasses already on board. Hoxton did not move, and neither did they. A moment passed as Iliff, Archibald, and Hoxton all breathed the same breath of air: Cold, calm, and full of mist.

The sun was starting to set. If they didn't leave soon, they'd be substantially late to meeting Sam Bertrok.

Hoxton slowly marched over to Archibald, much like the Creature did before the fight. The way he moved exuded a great power and cadence, which was something the Creature lacked. It was almost rhythmic, albeit terrifying.

Iliff set Archibald up to stand on his own, then promptly left his side.

"You."

It was the voice of God himself that came from Hoxton's mouth. A deep, gravely tone that demanded submission from all who heard it.

Hoxton stopped not one foot from the withering Captain Archibald Black, who used what strength he could muster to try and stand upright, lest he anger the being before him. The menacing voice continued:

"You will meet with your client and share news of my death at the hands of this Creature. You will then bring me back to America."

Hoxton suddenly grabbed the injured shoulder of Archibald with his monstrous hand, and squeezed.

"If you do not," Hoxton said as Archibald winced in immense pain, "I will separate your jaw from your mouth as well."

Hoxton was bluffing. He could not stomach the idea of harming another man so gruesomely as he did the predator on board. And Archibald was in no state to test him.

Hoxton released the shoulder of the beaten man, then walked directly inside the captain's quarters. He had turned eighteen almost fifty years ago, and though his natural pain was gone, the life he lived had not become much easier. He had earned his rest and nobody on board would stop him from getting it. Not even Archibald's Creature.

Iliff looked at his captain forebodingly.

"Iliff, that Creature..." Archibald started. "It wasn't violent towards the end. I lifted my hand, and I swear to God in Heaven, he stopped... He *looked* at me, Iliff. It was as if he were-"

"That storm up ahead," said Iliff dismissively. "The one you steered through this island to avoid. It wasn't a real threat, was it, Cap'n?"

Archibald relented.

"It was harsh, but entirely manageable," said Archibald. "Rita would've pulled through safely, and not been a minute late in delivering your Sam Bertrok's cargo."

Iliff desired to strike the man, right in his jaw. But there had been enough bloodshed aboard this cursed ship. And someone had to steer it.

"Best you go now to your helm," Iliff gritted through his teeth. "Rita needs your handlin'."

Archibald departed towards *Rita*'s wheel, but stopped himself.

"What will we tell your Sam Bertrok when we arrive?" Archibald asked Iliff.

Iliff looked down at the corpses around him. His eyes stopped at the one that wasn't human.

"If I know my client well, he's going to be more interested in the Creature from this god damn lagoon."

With that, Iliff Frye headed toward the bloodied mast. He'd need to loosen what sails were left if they were ever to get out of this hellish land. Archibald watched him scale the mast with speed, and knowing the Brute in his captain's quarters wouldn't be of any real help, he headed toward *Rita*'s helm. With the sudden lack of crew, it was going to be a long, long ride.

By the old, rickety dock stood a man with an inappropriately dark trench coat. The sun had set, but the humidity was still blazing hot by the shoreline. Standing by Sam Bertrok's side was a large man with a bland, unemotive expression. This place was Watling's Island, and the man named Sam Bertrok had been checking his pocket watch for the past half hour.

The tides were normal when Captain Archibald Black's ship finally arrived.

The Captain wasn't too terribly late, arriving on the precise *week* that was promised, but not the day as specifically requested by Sam Bertrok. The ship named Rita calmly swayed as its sails caught the warm nighttime winds, and from this distance, Mr. Bertrok could not notice the litany of her damages: The claw marks trailing along the bow, the tattered sails hanging from imperfect masts, and the absence of most of the crew. Even as she approached the dock, Mr. Bertrok's mind was simply too fixated on the time to take heed of any of the ship's numerous irregularities, and once she finally halted and docked promptly near his feet, he looked straight towards the first mate: A disheveled associate of his named Iliff Frye.

And Iliff saw him back.

The disdain in Mr. Bertrok's eyes burned a hole in the man's skull. Iliff felt the wrath of his employer's immeasurable disappointment as he halted the ship and furled its sails. Aside from Captain Archibald Black at the helm, Iliff was the primary, unaided force driving and docking *Rita* by his lonesome.

The ship docked, fitting neatly beside where Mr. Bertrok and the large man stood. Ropes lassoed the structure and held it in place. And once it did, Iliff leapt down from above and stepped out onto the dock.

"Late."

The only word Mr. Bertrok said. The only one he needed to.

Iliff shivered in fear as he stared into his employer's eyes. Mr. Bertrok's gaze was toxic. Though he briefly glanced at the accompanying large man, Iliff found himself drawn to Mr. Bertrok's own eyes as though they were boring right into Iliff. As though they could see into his mind. Invading his thoughts and fears.

"Do go easy on him, Mr. Bertrok," Captain Archibald Black said as he arrived from the helm.

Mr. Bertrok's gaze found Archibald and took him in: A man who looked about as well and shapely as *Rita* herself did right then.

"Where is my cargo?" Mr. Bertrok calmly asked Archibald.

Archibald bowed his head. "Something attacked us on the way. It destroyed your cargo and took most of my men with it."

Iliff added: "It was a lagoon-"

"I asked *Archibald*," said Mr. Bertrok in a stern voice. Iliff quieted instantly, and Archibald became disturbed for a moment.

Mr. Bertrok looked again to Archibald, and nodded for him to continue.

"...Iliff's right," said Archibald. "It was a lagoon we'd passed through. A storm came and..."

Archibald was at a loss for words. He'd rehearsed what was to be said to Mr. Bertrok when he arrived here, but when looking into the man's eyes, he felt an intensity about them. Something was making Archibald's task of lying incredibly difficult.

"...the Creature found us out there," said Archibald.

"It wrecked your ship and slaughtered your crew?" said Mr. Bertrok, now much more curious.

Archibald turned toward the deck, and Mr. Bertrok and the large man followed him. Iliff came after them both until Mr. Bertrok turned around and gave Iliff a stern look. He did not have to tell him to *stay put* right where he was on that dock until they returned.

Archibald showed Mr. Bertrok the Creature's body, along with its severed head about ten feet away. Mr. Bertrok just stood marveling at the Creature's multi-charactered carcass, with traits of at least a dozen aquatic animals that he could spot.

"Iliff had said you'd be more interested in this Creature than the cargo you requested," said Archibald honestly.

"I would be most interested in what I actually asked for," Mr. Bertrok replied.

Archibald stared blankly at Mr. Bertrok looking for a hint of humor or irony, but detected none of it. Mr. Bertrok looked back up at Archibald with that same intensity from before. That same paralyzing energy.

"But," Mr. Bertrok continued, "I can see how much you must have suffered to arrive here at all. You have my deepest sympathies, Captain."

Archibald didn't reply. He couldn't muster the strength to say anything at all.

"I will accept the Creature's body as compensation," said Mr. Bertrok.

"*You will accept the Creature's body as compensation,*" repeated Archibald stoically.

"You will never speak a word of what transpired here."

"*I will never speak a word of what transpired here.*"

Mr. Bertrok nodded to the weak-minded Captain, then left the ship with the large man at his side. Once alone again, Archibald shook off the haze that he'd felt and returned to the ship's helm. Though he could not recall many details of their conversation, he knew he'd lost the desire to discover this creature for the world as intended. Something didn't feel right about it. As if it were taboo to do so. Archibald started freeing *Rita's* ropes from the dock, thinking of how after returning to America and acquiring a new crew and first mate, he would stick strictly to his usual trade routes from here on out.

Once back onto the dock, Mr. Bertrok nodded to Iliff, who had stood perfectly still right where he was. Iliff went right up to the deck and dragged the Creature's carcass onto the dock. Then, he went back for the Creature's head, and brought it right to Mr. Bertrok's feet.

"Good boy," Mr. Bertrok said begrudgingly to Iliff.

Iliff smiled. He pulled a knife from his waistband and held it out to Mr. Bertrok, handle-first. He was waiting for him to grab it. Waiting very patiently.

And Mr. Bertrok relented.

He took Iliff's knife and sliced open his own wrist. Black blood began to pour from the vein, and Iliff dropped to his knees and began ravenously sucking on the open wound. It was though he'd never drank anything in his entire life before. Nothing tasted so succulent or sweet to that man than the blood of his Master on that dock.

The large man looked to Mr. Bertrok with a desire to go back onto the ship. To feed on the flesh of Archibald. Mr. Bertrok shook his head, denying the large man the privilege.

"The man's done well," said Mr. Bertrok to the large man beside him. "He is not a threat to the secrecy of monsters."

Mr. Bertrok was strong in his convictions. He'd spent many years, decades, centuries, even millennia pondering this very idea: Whichever day mankind discovers a monster they fear, that creature's extinction would soon follow. The threat was universal, and had the power to affect vampires, werewolves, or whatever Archibald Black was on the cusp of bringing to the world: This strange, carnivorous Creature from Black's lagoon.

After this passing thought, Mr. Bertrok looked down on Iliff as he fed on his wrist's open wound. Such a desperate creature, indeed. Borderline incompetent without stern leadership. Though he'd had high hopes for Iliff when first turning him long ago, Mr. Bertrok could only see his assistant as an underling, now and forevermore.

"Iliff, you've been terribly kind to me. Terribly kind. But, as it stands, I no longer believe our goals are aligned."

Iliff leapt up from Mr. Bertrok's wrist and wiped the man's black blood from his own mouth. The fear he felt when Archibald first suggested the idea of being *late* now resurfaced stronger than it ever had.

"What do you mean?" Iliff couldn't blurt out the words fast enough.

"I believe you to be unfit for your role," said Mr. Bertrok.

Something broke in Iliff's mind.

"I can do better! Master, I can do so much better than I've done for you. I swear it on all I hold close to my beating heart, I can do-"

"That's enough," said Mr. Bertrok sternly.

Like a loyal dog, Iliff heeded Mr. Bertrok's command. He could feel the large man next to Mr. Bertrok bearing down on him, like a personal bodyguard.

"I care nothing for how much 'better you can do' anymore, Iliff. Many men like yourself have served me for thousands of years, but not all of my needs are met by them. This is the reason I wanted the abomination whose skin could not break. The *wonders* to be accomplished with The Brute Man in my stable... How his blood must taste on my tongue..."

Mr. Bertrok caressed Iliff's head with his hand. Though the wound was now healed, the black blood left on his wrist smeared across Iliff's cheek.

"The Brute Man wouldn't have failed this mission," Mr. Bertrok began. "My Brides wouldn't have failed this mission, individually or otherwise."

Mr. Bertrok rested his hand on the large man's shoulder, finally introducing him.

"My new assistant wouldn't have failed this mission."

Iliff trembled. Pure terror became of the man.

"But Master, I've brought you-"

"Yes, and I'm grateful to Archibald who encountered it. And should I ever head to Black's lagoon and find others that aren't *de-spined,* I might have some use for them one day... But you, Iliff, had a very clear task. And you did not follow through on it."

Mr. Bertrok made a gesture with his hand.

The large man's bones began to break inside his own body. As the transformation took place, Mr. Bertrok looked up at Archibald standing up near the ship's helm, who started to catch a glimpse of the large man's transformation. Mr. Bertrok gazed at Archibald once more, and forced him to turn the other way and continue getting ready to set sail, disregarding whatever it is he might have seen. Iliff stood in horror as the large man, who now became an even larger werewolf, extended its translucent talons from its fingertips.

"You've chosen a monster over me?" Iliff muttered in horror.

"We're all monsters here, Iliff," said Mr. Bertrok with a friendly tone. "Some are just superior to others. And they get to consume those who aren't."

Rita departed from the dock with a lone Captain guiding her away. Through whatever strange sensation he'd recently felt, he was forced to ignore the helpless screams of the man named Iliff Frye as he was torn into many smaller pieces and feasted upon by the Underlord's latest pet.

Below the ship's deck, as Archibald departed for America's embrace and reconciliation so very far away, the Brute Man had tended to his wounds and had his great, long sleep. He'd awoken when they docked, and overheard the above parties' conversations through a piece of floorboard that'd splintered open during the Creature's fight.

This world was home to so many more monsters than himself or the Creature from Black's lagoon: Werewolves were just as legendary, and now carried the same legitimacy. Monstrous beings born from and allegiant only to evil. The Brute Man had sworn on his sister's death that Theia's gift of suspension would not be squandered, and were it not for his intervention aboard *Rita*, neither Archibald nor Iliff would've survived that encounter at all. And even now, as *Rita* departed for America, Hoxton could not intervene as he once did and save Iliff's life. Whatever power Sam Bertrok held over that beast would likely consume him too.

To imagine places where more innocent men than Archibald or Iliff resided. Places where werewolves and swamp creatures were waiting for them with malevolent intentions.

Hoxton made a vow: When Archibald returned him to America, he wouldn't take up his old jobs and obligations, waiting for the next time he'd be captured by some weird entity like Sam Bertrok. He would scour the world's ends in search of the beasts untamed and untold, and give them all that very same fate of the Creature before more innocent blood would be spilled. *This* would be his calling. And he would pursue it without delay.

Most men would call it coincidence, but Hoxton knew better than that. He'd been around too long to try and ignore the Lord's signs.

Hoxton had finally found God's plan.

An Abridged History of Bats and Wolves

I

The Forest

Several millennia before the Bible would be written, the waning ice age's frigid air swept the grassy European plains and made the primitive, tribal men shiver amidst the orange dusk of daylight. Their pelts and furs protected them faintly as they hid among the moist shrubbery, and grasping their spears warmed the palms of their hands. This clan of nine exceedingly brave men knew nothing but the harsh dealings of fate when lesser hunters could not return home with a kill for the coming winter's season. Their leader was named Ta, and he was not this position's keeper by choice. The last season's winter took the life of their previous one.

Muddy paint coated most of their bodies. This was both the group's attempt at camouflage, and one of the earliest forms of warpaint. It did both jobs successfully. Their target emerged through the path they'd been stalking: A thick, hulking brown bear came out from the forests nearby. The men knew this was the path this bear took to hunt and eat, and this ambush was carefully planned around it. All nine of them were prepared to give their lives to take this beast down, so long as some survived to memorialize them, and carry the animal home through the freezing air.

The bear did not stop or take notice of the bushes the men were patiently waiting in. It was a predator, and knew only of lesser prey. It had no reason to assume an attack.

The astonishing cry of Ta first reached the men's ears.

Swifter than air, Ta's spear hurled from the bush into the bear's shoulder blade, several more following its lead. The men went brilliantly fast before the bear had time to resist or run. It took several moments before the beast fell to the ground, sending grand tremors in all directions as it landed. With the combined force of his acolytes, Ta had won the day and fed the stomachs of his tribe for a great deal of time.

The difficult part would now begin.

It took several seconds and the average competency of the Stone Age for these men to bring down the bear where it stood. It would take three days for them to haul their game back to their homeland. The men had called out in celebration as they diced the body up into parts and threw it onto their backs. Ta refocused the rowdy clan and directed them back from the path they'd come. A long, clear path through the knoll they'd come to. One that did not end anytime soon.

Ta carried the beast's head, as was customary, both as a show of triumph and because it was the lightest part they'd severed. This hunt was designed to honor their leader, which Ta strongly disliked. Their previous leader, Korr, was a close personal friend of his, and when he passed it was just assumed that Ta would take his place. He was well-enough equipped to lead them, and only did so to honor his late friend's memory. But this was not the life he desired. And that mattered little to the minds of his followers.

The day's light was at its end as the men walked, revealing a new source of light behind the clouds. One that made itself clearer as the sunset passed. A gorgeous, vibrant full moon illuminated the grassy plains around them, sending tiny rays of white light bouncing off of each plant's blades and leaves. The moon's bright light grew stronger with every passing moment from day to night, as though they were stepping into a new world with each footstep. It was a world that mirrored the one they were accustomed to, but expressed itself very differently. A world which was more fit for a nocturnal creature's gaze than a human's perception.

As Ta's men entered the clearing in the forest, dreading their days-long journey toward the place that they called home, an unexpected noise stopped them where they stood. All nine, like a trained unit of soldiers, froze in place. They lived at the boundary of survival and annihilation, forever and always, and knew never to overlook even the most minute of inconsistencies. This was all they'd done. This was all that Korr had done before Ta, and the previous leader before him. This was nature's truest form, unmitigated by science and culture: A disgusting food chain that never manifested as peaceful.

The noise repeated from an entirely new direction.

The nine men huddled close, their backs to each other. They'd gone far enough into the forest where they no longer saw the valley's clearing, and the moon's bright light barely peered through the trees. Their spears were drawn and their eyes were sharp, capturing everything they could with what little moonlight made it this deep into the looming woods.

A branch snapped on a nearby tree, drawing the attention of the entire clan upwards. Nothing jumped out and attacked them, but something certainly caused it. Something unfriendly. Ta's heart sank. He wasn't sure if his peers would join Korr in the afterlife, telling stories of their failed bear hunt on an unfortunate night like this one. Or perhaps Ta would tell him himself. With the noise of a deep, disgusting growl like a lion's or a jaguar's, fear finally overcame the men and fueled their adrenaline. They looked to its source and saw something larger than them. Larger than the bear before they'd separated its body.

One of Ta's men broke.

Unprompted, the man hurled his spear toward the beast that'd been pestering them. Their strategy was always to wait for their leader's command, but upon sight of this freakish monstrosity, no rules were followed, and no time was wasted. The spear pierced its shoulder, and from the other side of the men, another beast just like it emerged and abducted the man who threw it.

The men panicked, and in all of one instant, Ta was aware that he'd lost all of his control over them. All nine men frantically attacked and stabbed at the beasts, who swatted their pointed sticks away with meaty claws. The arms that swung had lively gray fur, translucent talons, and the muscled frame of Satan himself. The bear's fresh meat fell from some of their backs as they swung their weapons in acts of desperation from the unruly beasts. Ta could not glance at them, for he and three others decided not to stay. Ta called out for his remaining men to follow them, but they either could not hear him, or were already the monsters' food.

The four remaining men, carrying with them only two small portions of the bear's body, sprinted through the woods far and away from the massacre. It would be more valiant of them to stay and defend their allies, but it was simply more practical to attempt to salvage all that they could in the face of unavoidable doom. They ran until the snarls and screams were no longer audible, not because they were sufficiently distant from it, but because there were simply none left to resist the wrath of the two beings of the forest. The silence behind them that soon followed, rather quickly, was replaced by the noise of the creature's pacing and mantling forward. Ta and his men now knew that they did not escape death, but rather prolonged it.

The four men burst from the thick of the forest, and emerged out the other side onto a rocky hillscape leading into a river. There was a stone path the men had built to cross the river without washing asunder, and they always moved over it very carefully. Their path was about to be tested against the pace of men who moved with the aspirational speed of a shadow of jaguars, and felt the piths of terror in their souls.

Four men crossed the river with careful footing, and three made it across safely without falling. The one who slipped had caught onto the rocky path as he did so, preventing himself from being washed away into the river's currents. It was Ta and two others who had successfully crossed, and they all stopped and caught their breath. Now, finally, Ta looked behind him, and through the thickly wooded forests, saw the two beasts come through, vigorously pursuing the man who fell.

They were humanoid, predominantly. Thick, muscular bodies were coated entirely in luscious gray fur, and from those bodies were the heads of two wolves, with long, viscous snouts and tall ears that pointed straight upwards. They worked in tandem, more powerful and effective than entire packs of normal wolves. More hungry than one.

Ta's two other men ran without him, but Ta himself was petrified. As he watched the two beasts tear into the man hanging from the rocky shore, spraying a fair deal of blood into the river's ripples, all traces of defiance had left him. Ta had lived his life the same way, doing the same hunting and gathering practices each time of the year, in this land he'd known tremendously well, and was always successful in spite of the dangers and miscreants that made up mother nature's brood. There existed no being like these two that matched another from his memory. The closest of which was a gray wolf.

The two beasts had finished tearing the man's flesh from his body with unprecedented speed and efficiency. They looked forward at Ta, who no longer attempted to flee, and the two monsters crawled *through* the river, completely ignorant to the rippling currents of the tides. Ta was awestruck at their sight, but took strong solace in the fact that the two men who made it were now far gone, and his own death would continue to stall them a little bit longer. Eventually, he reasoned, these two beasts would have to get full. With an unfathomable hope, this would end here with Ta, and those two men would spread word of what's happened here, safeguarding his homeland from venturing this far for food ever again.

This was the thought that Ta chose to die with.

The werewolves honed in closer to their last target, crossing onto the shore and dripping wet. They didn't need to move quickly. Ta looked up at the sky, now becoming clouded, where he knew Korr was watching him from the afterlife with favorable eyes. *This* was the job of a leader, and Ta knew he would die having honored those who've come before him. The two beasts stopped short of him, opening their jowls and baring their oversized canines.

They stopped.

Something forced them to. Ta paused with confusion, still glad they'd keep spending their attention on him and not the escapees. Their bodies started to jerk and shift violently, as though completely possessed. The werewolves' elbows bent backwards, with fingers breaking into ways they weren't meant to. Their legs snapped, the very bones that propped them up shattering amid a fantastical, unseen force. One of them howled, and the second followed suit, and suddenly their claws hit and tore at the ground beneath them as their bodies continued to transmutate.

In the sky above, a cloud had begun to block out the light of the full moon.

Ta looked around him at what he knew to be a divine intervention. The bodies of the werewolves metamorphosed into *people*. Naked, soaking wet, and shivering in the cold of night. Ta kneeled down towards one of them, his spear once again at the ready. He was given a second chance by the powers that be, and wished to take no more chances with these evil creatures. With the tip of his spear, Ta pulled the creature's head up and saw the man's face: It was Korr himself, who looked not a day removed from when they last met.

Ta dropped the spear out of shock. The stories of those who returned said that it was in this place Korr had been killed during last winter's hunt. What he was witnessing was not only impossible, but it was neither divine nor grand. It was wicked. This cruel trick had taken the lives of most of his men. Ta screamed a confused battle cry at his old friend, forming fists with his hands. Korr could only lay there, completely speechless, with his eyes beaming back at Ta. Innocent, and horrified.

Korr looked past Ta to the night sky again, and pointed. Ta turned around to see the cloud over the full moon start to dissipate. Ta looked back to Korr and his companion, whose bodies started to shift once more in the growing moonlight. As the abhorrent transformations began again, Ta looked to the body of the fallen man in the river. It, too, started to jerk violently in the midst of the moon's pale light.

The beings fully transitioned, and rose majestically. No longer were they Ta's peers and colleagues. Their brains were much more simplistic. One of the very last things Ta saw before being taken by the night's predators was a view of the forest they came from, where five more werewolves emerged, having just transformed for the very first time.

II

Transylvania, Part One

Creighton Talbot had found this place based on rumors: A home, abandoned, isolated by treelines on every end, and only accessible by a long, rocky driveway. It wasn't for sale on the housing market, yet the home's owner lived off the world's grid and never reported taxes or any sources of income. The year was 1974, and the means by which this place had been forgotten by the country's basic laws were mysterious, only fueling the local legends of what lived inside.

Stealthily, Creighton bypassed the door's locks with a pick and creaked it open. It was nighttime, so the interior of this place was difficult to see, but one thing became certain to Creighton as he stepped inside: This place was lived in.

Creighton moved slowly across the hardwood floors, eventually making contact with an old red carpet. He had no weapon in his shaggy overcoat, and no defensive tool in his hand-me-down jeans. It wasn't a fight he'd come here for. As he moved through what must've been the living room, his eyes laid on an old notebook. Creighton picked it up and only had time to skim the first few pages before the noise cut him off:

"*Leave.*"

The sound was indeed ominous, but scarier to hear echoed on the cobwebbed walls. Whoever lived here didn't care to maintain this place, but certainly accepted no intruders. Creighton spun toward the source of the voice and saw a short hallway, which housed the tall figure in it, and apologetically relented.

"I'm sorry," said Creighton to the specter. "I thought this place was abandoned."

"You would not move so carefully if you believed you were alone," spoke the deep voice of the figure.

The source of the voice began to step closer. Creighton stepped back in tandem. His demeanor was disarming, as if to concede the lie he'd been caught in.

"Put that back on the table," the voice commanded. Respectfully, Creighton abided. "Not many know of this place. Those who do are always looking for something."

"I'm only looking for help," Creighton said confidently.

"You'll find no such thing here," scoffed the voice.

"Those notes in that book," said Creighton hastily. "They were written by a scientist. The terminology is academic."

"Leave this place or be removed from where you stand."

"Is it here?" asked Creighton. "The serum?"

The figure paused for a moment. He realized this intruder would not be so easily scared off by theatrics and threats.

"That notebook's owner passed away many years ago," said the figure sternly. "Were she here, she would not approve of intruders meddling through her things."

"Was her name Rebecca Chamberton?"

The figure stepped closer still, revealing a large man with pale, gray skin and an immutable scowl. This was Rebecca's son, a mighty being named Adam Chamberton, who'd changed substantially since his time as a little boy with a broader mentality and a stronger physicality. Adam produced a modest shotgun from beneath his black blazer. He was still in no mood for this stranger's life problems, and his knowledge of Rebecca Chamberton was the final offence in a long list of misdemeanors the stranger was continuously committing.

"I am a man of mercy," said Adam. "Do not force violence."

Creighton, almost petrified, took a moment to weigh his options. After relaxing, he stepped closer to Adam's gun.

"You don't fear death?" Adam asked quizzically.

"I fear it greatly," said Creighton. "My death will not come from a shotgun, nor from my pursuers. If it could, I'd ask you to inflict your mercy."

Creighton continued moving toward Adam, who yielded no ground and stood more still than a tree. Finally, inches from the gun's barrel, Creighton stopped and spoke again.

"That serum was derived from a combination of stem cells, aconitum, scopolamine, and a rare Tibetan plant called mariphasa. The company she worked for was synthesizing it to restore a sickly human back to a sense of wellness."

Creighton looked down at Adam's gun. Seeing as it still wasn't lowered, he continued explaining the situation, rationalizing that a clear communication was the only potential way out of this house with the serum in his hands:

"If that serum exists to any effect, I *must* have it. It's not an option. My pursuers are hunting me for what I am, but they don't know about what I've done. It was I who successfully tested that serum on unwell rats, goats, and dogs, and they *all* reformed. The entire lot of them. We were days away from human trials when Rebecca stole it from our-"

Adam Chamberton used his free hand to grab Creighton by the collar, lifting him promptly into the air, and spun and tossed Creighton's body by the doorway.

Creighton's backside clipped the living room's recliner, knocking it over and bruising the man before his impact with the threshold.

"You created it?!" Adam barked at the intruder.

"I was *on the team* who developed it," said Creighton back at him. On the ground, he recovered quickly. Quicker than a man should.

Adam withdrew the shotgun back into his coat and made his way over to Creighton, who tried to scurry away from him on his back.

"Deformities and defects are unfavorable, aren't they?" spoke Adam with such bravado and spite. "Those hideous little things, like the acne on a young boy's face as he reaches adolescence. Perhaps the stretch marks on a woman's hips don't turn heads in a new bikini."

Creighton's back finally hit the bottom of the door. He had nowhere left to flee.

"Wouldn't it be nice if we could *eradicate* those defects?" Adam pressed sardonically. "Concoct an elixir for the error of our being? Otherwise you'd be left as an ostracized little monster, wouldn't you? Something unworthy of a lover's touch. Deplorable in the eyes of your God."

Adam reached down with both hands and brought Creighton up to his own height. Horrified beyond reason, Creighton whimpered to his aggressor:

"*My defect... is lethal...*"

"I assure you I'll survive," grumbled a crazed Adam with a fire in his eyes. "You cannot say the same."

Creighton grabbed Adam's arms. Instead of fingernails, translucent talons dug through Adam's blazer and straight into his skin. Adam panicked, and again threw Creighton's body: This time, directly out of his house's door. A long, unkempt dirt driveway cut through the thickly settled forest that shrouded Adam's house. Creighton's body tumbled through it, accreting bits of dust and rocks throughout his clothing.

Creighton got to his feet, but was not transformed. Not fully. His nose had begun to elongate and take the form of the wolf's snout, but only partially. His body's bones began to snap in certain places, but Creighton strained himself to not let them reheal in their desired ways. Fur coated his forearms and the sides of his head, but stifled before spreading to the rest of his body. This man had shifted forms many, many times in his life, but could only marginally keep a handle on his lesser half.

From the front door's threshold stepped Adam, who stopped and almost gawked at the being he'd assaulted: A Wolf-Man, now up on its hind legs, snarling at the mouth and shifting back into Creighton Talbot.

This was the dark power of Darwinistic selectivity: A scientific process by way of a deep supernatural influence. In the 1700s, the Underlord - then going by Sam Bertrok - had encountered a werewolf for the very first time. It only took a *small* level of influence for him to break the lunar cycle of the werewolf's transformations. Instead, under a vampire's control, a wolf and all of its kin would transform purely by emotion-induced thought.

Over hundreds of years and countless generations, the Underlord had effectively shifted the werewolf species to all have this inherent quality. The curse of the Full Moon was no more.

The moments of the night passed slowly as Adam watched his intruder shift. The man was normal once more, and his gaze matched the onlooker who'd tossed him away.

Creighton composed himself. His breath deliberately started to slow. In that moment, the beast had briefly met Adam Chamberton, and the carnage of their clash would've left at least one of them dead.

"If I wanted a fight," grumbled Creighton, "I would've *brought* one. You thundering, brutish jackass."

Adam stepped out from his house and moved toward Creighton, who raised his fists and expected a fight. But the pale gray man did not attack. He approached Creighton, stopping directly in front of him with a firm, reserved stance. Creighton matched it in body language, lowering his defenses.

"What are you?" Adam asked coldly.

Creighton began to answer, but cocked his head to the side before he could do so. Something tried to pass by unnoticed. Something only Creighton's animalistic senses could detect.

"I'm a werewolf," said Creighton plainly as he looked around, "and I'm being hunted by something worse. *Raise your gun.*"

Adam paused. These creatures were mythic. Had Adam not seen inklings of the thing his intruder almost became in a fit of rage, he'd have dismissed this claim outright.

But this claim had too much merit.

With speed unseen by a human eye, Adam's throat tore open. The fiend responsible vanished as soon as it struck, for one swift, clean motion put Adam Chamberton on the ground, letting him bleed out onto his own walkway.

Creighton Talbot hadn't even moved. He looked around again, trying to detect where the fiend had fled. It would strike him next, but not kill. He knew very well that he was wanted alive. As Creighton looked over again at where Adam had fallen so ungracefully from the being's strike, he couldn't help but feel a mixture of empathy and disappointment. *You should've raised your gun.*

The weird nightly creature struck with the same speed once more. It knocked Creighton back into the trunk of a tree on the opposite end of Adam's driveway. Creighton's back cracked against the bark, a feeling he knew would again trigger the transformation he tried so valiantly to avoid. He'd been getting sick of being thrown through and into large objects, and yet could not prevent them without shifting into his lesser half. As he again recovered, Creighton pushed himself up and saw the being that'd done this: His pursuer and soon-to-be captor.

A woman with white hair, laced in black silk-like garments.

She walked toward Creighton, having no more need for her supernatural movements. Vampirism gifted this woman almost every ability in the Underworld's grasp, but they still served him and him only. She was an independent, free agent of unholy wrath, who was paradoxically subservient to her Vampire King's will. This woman's name was Verona, and she was the Underlord's Bride.

"I only overheard the most recent part," said Verona in a whispered, gravely tone. "Am I really so much *worse* than a dog like you?"

Creighton stood himself up, his body still shaking. He would not give her the satisfaction of transforming into the monster that she wanted.

Verona walked closer to Creighton, revealing her palm: A small knife with a silver blade. Both of them knew the damage that a weapon like that could do against him. Neither of them knew the damage that was about to unfold.

The loudest noise that Creighton had ever heard sent his body into a fetal position. With no warning, Creighton was covered in the black blood of the Underlord's Bride, as was the tree and the ground around him. Creighton looked up at the source of the noise and saw Verona's chest, now riddled with the holes of a shotgun's deliverance. Verona fell, traumatized by the event, and Creighton sprung out of his position to grab a branch from the tree behind him. As fast as he could possibly move, Creighton snapped the thick twig from the tree and jammed the weapon through Verona's heart, killing the fiend with vitriol.

Verona fell and aged centuries in seconds, and as she did so, Creighton could see the blast's source: Adam Chamberton stood tall, as if unaffected, with the wound on his neck almost completely closed up and shrinking by the moment.

Tonight, for the first time in his entire life, Adam Chamberton caught a ghastly glimpse into a strange new world that housed monstrous beings other than himself. A world of defects and deformities that plagued others in uniquely evil ways.

III

A Tangent in Llanwelly, Wales

Ben stood at the edge of the windowsill, high-up winds whistling in his ears. His heart rate was something he very consciously tried to control. He didn't know what would trigger the shift he wanted, but the only time it had ever happened to him was when his life was in danger, so recreating that fear seemed logical.

The seventeen-year-old boy had used his upper body strength to situate himself out of his wheelchair and in the window's frame, his grip digging deep into the window's threshold. He knew he was clinging too strong to ever risk an actual fall. Even if his legs worked, he wouldn't survive the fall without the shift.

Channeling every ounce of his fleeting willpower, he forced his grip to loosen.

This wasn't a fall of attempted suicide. Benicio Watterson was a boy in relatively high spirits who'd had two very tragic events befall him in recent years: When he was fourteen, a car had struck him and made him paralyzed, destroying his motivation along with his ability to walk. More recently, while coming home from studying in his junior year of high school, the boy had found himself in the crosshairs of a mythical creature of the night.

The unfathomable chasm between him and the rocky earth below set in. His pupils dilated, crystallizing this moment of unadulterated fear into a powerful memory that would linger for years to come. He closed his eyes, shaking in terror, as an inevitable drop became less and less avoidable.

His spine suddenly cracked in half. No outside force caused it. His eyes shot open, as the very thing he'd pursued shocked him into letting go of the ledge.

As he plummeted, the bones in his body continued breaking, re-healing into uncanny forms. He reached terminal velocity as the hand that once shakingly held an old window frame dug itself into the side of the building. Huge claws tore plaster and cement from the infrastructure of the old warehouse, slowing Ben's fall almost enough to stop it. Monstrous features shredded through most of his clothes as his grip solidified this grotesque result to the side of the warehouse.

This was a place Ben knew was abandoned. No one would witness him fall, and no one would tell stories of what didn't hit the ground.

With an ungodly crunching of bones and muscle, his jaw unhinged and shot forward, and his eyes rolled back into ghastly white pits. After the longest ten seconds he'd ever experienced, his massive, muscular build catapulted himself upwards from the building's edge, splinterings of old brick and concrete parting with each Herculean lunge.

As Ben hurtled himself back up to the sill of the window almost as fast as he fell down, he felt an unusual sense of balance.

His whole body shivered as his fur cascaded in the winds. Unable to perch properly, he lobbed himself back inside through the same windowsill and crashed down onto the floor, the claws on his hands planting themselves between the floorboards.

His breath slowed as his predatory eyes scanned the room. Calming himself, his claws slowly retracted from the floorboards with a soft crunch. As he pushed his frame erect, his head whacked against a light dangling from the ceiling, something in his entire life up to this point he'd never known the feeling of.

First he looked down at his hand. He never got a good impression of them the first time it happened. Claws, shaped like human hands with five digits. Translucent talons extruded from the tips, and with just a thought they retracted neatly into his fingers. This sliding of the nails felt so unbelievably natural to him, and fleshing them out once again brought such satisfaction. Finally he looked down, confirming what he didn't want to believe.

His legs were much larger, lying completely limp under his frame. He moved a bit forward with his arms and watched them softly drag on the ground beneath him.

It had been over three years spent in that wheelchair for him. He had long by now accepted his fate, and under no natural circumstance would he let this frustrating sense of depression creep back into his optimistic mind. But this circumstance was *supernatural,* and so he bought into it with the prospect that somehow, if he got lucky, the curse of the werewolf might return his legs.

Tears quickly swelled his nocturnal eyes. Certain animals develop tears to clean out their eye cavities, but this emotional experience of crying was intrinsically human. There was nothing supernatural to be done about his disability.

He felt himself shifting again. He'd controlled himself when jumping out of the window, and he'd controlled himself during the fall, but for all he tried, he was unable to stop the tremendous weeping as his body metamorphosed back into a boy.

"You are too beautiful to cry," said a voice from behind him.

Ben spun around and found himself face-to-face with a woman who wasn't there prior. Not ten seconds ago. The fear in his stomach shot up to his throat and he quickly screamed.

"What?!" Ben cried out, hastily wiping the tears. As if to present himself formally.

"You simply don't deserve to feel the pain you feel," said the woman as she held out his hand to Ben.

"Who are you?" the boy asked. He stared at the stranger, unwilling to accept her help.

The woman smiled, retracting her hand. She knew she'd have to earn Ben's trust.

With a quick flick of the wrist, as though she were a magician at a child's birthday party, the woman summoned a bat through the open window. The bat carefully landed upside-down, dangling from the woman's hand. With a light scurrying, several rats from around the warehouse started to crawl up the woman's body and assemble on her palm, making room where they could along the forearm. With them, legions of insects and tiny little spiders emerged from the crevasses in the floor and moved up her arm as well, conglomerating around her hand. She held her hand forward, and like a crowd of lifeless drones, every critter on her hand stared blankly into Ben's eyes.

"My name is Ilona," said the stranger. "I have a way with animals."

Ben wasn't sure whether to feel the depths of fear or the heights of wonder. His mind was in a freefall between both, mesmerized by the woman's absolute control over her unconventional pets.

"H... How did you know about me?" said Ben, not breaking eye contact with them. They diligently stared right back at him, all in a row, unlike anything he'd ever seen.

"Secrets are second-nature to me," said the woman kindly. "I know that several people died in Llanwelly last month, and you weren't one of them. I know that the beast found an easy target in you because you couldn't run away. I know that the first time you transformed was an accident..."

Ilona glanced at the window, finishing her observation: "But this wasn't."

Ben looked down from Ilona's arm.

"I'm not suicidal," said Ben. "I wanted to-"

"Trigger it, yes. You're a very smart kid," said Ilona. "The curse of the werewolf did not return what you've lost, but in its place, I believe it's given you something *greater*." Then, with a quick non-sequitur: "Did you know that werewolves used to shift only when it was a full moon?"

"Really?" asked the boy, the color returning to his face.

Ilona lowered her hand, allowing the bat to depart back out of the window, and the crawling rats and bugs to scutter back to the crevices that they emerged from. She leaned in close, her eyes peering into Ben's with an electric intensity. It felt warm, almost. Like a weird comfort was cloaking and overtaking the young boy.

When she spoke, it was a request almost like a whisper: "Shapeshift again. Just one more time."

Ben closed his eyes, breaking the contact they'd maintained. This disturbed her, but she showed no signs of it.

"I shouldn't," said Ben dutifully. He began to regret coming to this place and trying what he did.

"If you do," said Ilona, "I know a way to make you whole again. You've seen what I can do with animals, haven't you?" She smiled once more, *hard*: "Have you *imagined* what I could do with you?"

Like mold on old food, the thought began to grow in the boy's mind, overpowering the fears and tribulations he'd been steeped in thus far. What if the woman was right? Those animals were *possessed*. If anybody could change the way he was, it *had* to be this stranger. The thought was too alluring to ignore.

Ilona placed her hand on Ben's cheek. "Let me help you. *Change* for me."

Ben grabbed the woman's hand as though it were his mother's. Then, he rolled his eyes backward and closed them, and imagined the sensation of falling.

His body did exactly as Ilona requested. Ben grew, eclipsing the tall height of Ilona herself, and stood with a gorgeously primal ferocity. The moment he did so, Ilona outreached her hand. Physically, she only touched the air, but unmistakably, the vampire grasped firmly onto the animalistic mind of Benicio Watterson and didn't let go.

Ilona stopped.

Something, suddenly, was *deeply* wrong.

The psychic connection vampires shared was faint. They could not use it to read each other's minds or track each other's location. All it offered them was a shared empathy. At all times, they knew how the other was feeling. But something troubling was happening to one of them. It wasn't sadness, or anger, or even a sense of dread.

It was a large amount of pain, and then it was nothing at all. There was nothing left to sense.

Master had ordered a werewolf's hunt on this night, and his three Brides were following suit in three different parts of the world. Ilona went as fast as she could to Transylvania, where Verona had chosen her prey.

When Benicio Watterson shifted back into a boy and awoke from his trance, he found himself alone in the warehouse's tallest room. He had a vague memory of choosing to fall, and thought he had imagined a visitor.

IV

Transylvania, Part Two

Creighton enjoyed the warmest and sweetest coffee he'd ever tasted, or at least that's how it felt to him. It felt good to enjoy something small like that for a change, sitting in that comfortable chair in Adam's living room as opposed to being thrown through it. This coffee, expectedly, was generic and store-bought, and was not made by the loving embrace of Adam Chamberton. He had none of that to offer his guest.

Right beside where it sat, the small, silver knife reflected a sliver of light in its blade from overhead.

Adam rested his head in his hands as he sat on the couch across from Creighton. Too much was on his mind.

"I'm sorry," said Creighton honestly.

Adam looked up at his guest. An odd state of curiosity washed over him as he struggled with his newfound knowledge.

"Why are they after you?" Adam dissonantly responded.

"The Underlord has been controlling werewolves for a very long time," said Creighton. "His hypnotism grasps those without sentience. Anything non-human falls to his will, and he has a marginal level of influence over the weak-minded."

"And why werewolves?" Adam asked, now more invested.

"The Underlord is millennia old. From what I know, he stopped taking human underlings about two hundred years ago. He manipulated monsters, mutants, sea creatures, and any other beasts he could track down. Werewolves fit his needs best."

This all came like a shock to him, as if every sentence Creighton spoke was a new gospel. But before more questions, a deep-rooted fear had to be alleviated.

"We killed one of them," Adam said, piecing it together. "They will seek their vengeance."

"They are most likely coming and I'm sorry for being the cause," said Creighton politely, "but it moreso forces your hand: Whatever serum flows through your body, I need a sampling of it. If I become human, the Underlord will take no more interest in me."

Adam's state of curiosity was broken, and replaced with the usual anger.

"There is no more solace in being your form of imp than being mine," said Adam.

"You retain your consciousness, yes? At all points in time? That's more than can be said of me," quipped Creighton.

"I will not damn another to my state of-"

"Why did she choose you, anyway?" said Creighton, pressing the issue. "What motivated the Rebecca Chamberton I knew - the most brilliant woman I've ever met - to gift *you* with such a thing? Only an arrogant, ungrateful imbecile would agree to become an ideal form of man and then withhold this power from-"

Adam slammed that massive gray fist onto the table. That was all he did, no longer picking a fight with his guest. He'd been down that path and knew what Creighton's lesser half might do to his house.

The two men glared at each other with the burning fire of a hundred stars.

"Her son was born with Down's syndrome. My name is Adam Chamberton, and I did not agree to the wretched life of an undying lout."

Creighton turned pale.

So much of what he'd already known about Rebecca's theft now fit much more into place. It wasn't greed or selfishness that caused her to steal what they were developing. It was simply love. The purest form of it, in the form of her young little boy.

"You're her son," said Creighton slowly, disbelieving his own words.

"And you are a monster who refuses to embrace it."

Adam finally stood up, now looming over Creighton as he spoke.

"Perhaps my curse could be your cure," said Adam, now ranting. "But if those creatures come to my house seeking a form of retaliation for what *you did* in that very form, you'd be the most idiotic soul I've ever known to get rid of it. It took the strength of a werewolf to tear that branch off of my tree and thrust it into that demon. Have you ever tried to do the same to him? Or do your balls only drop when you become a wolf?"

Creighton paused before responding, as though escaping a trance: "There's no mind in what I become. There's only *his*."

Adam scoffed: "Your beastly powers bleed through to your human form if you demand it. Your senses heightened on command. Your strength was summoned from nowhere."

Adam took Creighton's arm and held up the hand.

"I felt a set of serrated claws dig into my arm. Yet you've remained human since pestering me with your presence. If your better half's qualities can bleed through to this form, why can't your mind bleed through too?"

Creighton pulled his arm free and adjusted his sleeve.

"I *can't*, I just... I can't do it. It's impossible."

Adam squinted when looking deeper into Creighton's eyes. As if seeking something.

"Listen well, stranger," said Adam coldly. "There are things inside of this house that I must protect with more than my life. If and when your Underlord comes, you stand a far better chance as what you are than by haphazardly injecting my blood into your veins."

Creighton became confused: "Is there none left? Is it *all* with you?"

Annoyed, Adam ignored the man's question, though in doing so, revealed the answer.

"Adam, that serum was probably strong enough to reanimate a *corpse* if one wanted to," said Creighton desperately. "It cured Subject 5 with no consequences."

"You overestimate my mother's methods," said Adam. "She was a sociopath and a fool."

"She was much more than that," said Creighton, looking Adam over again. "She didn't know how to..."

There wasn't time to finish that statement.

Creighton looked suddenly to Adam's front door. It was shut and deadbolted. But that wasn't enough.

"He's going to knock." Creighton snapped back to Adam. "I wish we had more time... I didn't know about you, Adam. I'm so sorry."

Adam walked past Creighton and grabbed his gun.

"You need to kill me," Creighton barked. "Right now. Or he *will* take me, and he will use me to kill you and countless more."

Adam ignored him as he loaded up a round.

"That won't work," said Creighton.

"It did last time," said Adam bitterly. "And it's not for you. Though if you insist, I'll kill you however you'd like once this man is dead."

"We only killed the Bride because of *me*," said Creighton, now petrified.

Adam cocked the shotgun and turned to his guest: "Then you'd better do it again. You thundering, brutish jackass."

The knock at the door took neither of them by surprise.

"Leave, or be thrown out like a dog!" Adam bellowed through the door's thick layer of wood.

Adam held the end of the shotgun right up to the door itself. Uneasily, Creighton went quickly to the table and grabbed the silver knife. He thought of how important it would be, for everybody involved, to jam the weapon straight through his own chest. Right then and there. Before things became infinitely worse than they already were.

Silence befell the air around them. Adam stayed transfixed on that door, scanning for even the *slightest* movement.

Still nothing.

Adam turned to Creighton, who since grabbing the knife, hadn't made a noise at all. The Underlord stood where Creighton used to be.

Adam whipped the gun around to shoot the tall figure: A man in a black cassock with pale skin and slicked-back hair. The Underlord fled in front of one of the chairs, near-instantaneously. Adam again repositioned the gun to face the vampire, who put his hands up.

"Where is Creighton?!" Adam yelled at the intruder.

The Underlord, smiling, sat down comfortably in Adam's chair. Adam knew that the monster would probably flee faster than the buckshot if he ever pulled that trigger, but he still never lowered the gun. Not after what happened with the

Bride.

"What have you done with him?" Adam asked the Underlord again.

"You're braver than most, but still too dumb to see the answer to that question," the Underlord said, holding up a shredded piece of Creighton's jacket.

Adam grew furious. As he did so, the Underlord dropped his smile. He'd realized something when angering the man.

"Your will is strong," said the Underlord. "I don't need to try my tricks on that bizarre mind of yours."

"I will not ask again-"

"You won't need to," said the Underlord blankly. "He's close by. A real smart bastard, too. He's been cursed for quite some time."

"I don't care," Adam interrupted.

"You will," said the Underlord.

Adam had been slowly walking closer and closer to the vampire, but where he stood now was close enough: The Underlord glared at Adam, showing a clear awareness of what Adam was trying to do. There was no fighting his way out of this one.

On the table with the silver blade, the Underlord placed a wooden dagger down beside it.

"Look at them," said the Underlord. "The wooden blade was made almost two thousand years ago. The silver one by Creighton. In all this time, our hunters haven't made anything more advanced than daggers and crossbows."

The Underlord could tell by Adam's expression that he wasn't making his point clear. Frustrated, he pocketed both of the weapons, and for a brief glimpse, Adam saw a larger collection of hunter's weaponry beneath the Underlord's cassock, collected almost like sporting trophies.

"Weapons like these don't belong in hands like yours," the Underlord muttered. "You're too weak to live without them, and usually too incompetent to use them properly."

The Underlord moved the table aside, revealing an unconscious Creighton lying dormant underneath, and then discreetly waved his hand, forcing Creighton to regain consciousness. Adam realized the man's current state: Too weak-minded to resist the Underlord's power, even in human form.

"Tell me," said the Underlord, "who killed my Verona?"

"He injured her, and I took her life," said Creighton wearily.

Though satisfactory enough, the Underlord was not done with his interrogation.

"Why have you come to this place?"

Creighton relented to the Underlord's power: "To find my serum, Master."

"And what was your serum for?"

Creighton's head bobbled slightly as he spoke. He was only *partially* aware of this conversation, but his mind was almost lost.

"Genetic engineering. Rebecca and I developed the serum together, Master. When the abortion failed, she stole the serum and used it to benefit our child instead."

Adam almost dropped the gun. The revelation struck him like a hammer: Though accidental, Creighton Talbot was his biological father.

The Underlord shifted his attention to Adam himself: "This *abomination* resulted?"

That question set off something inside of him. Every negative emotion a man could feel ran through his mind, all governed by an overwhelming sense of pure, unadulterated rage. Adam shot at the Underlord, who'd anticipated the attack.

By the time the shotgun's buckshot had traveled across Adam Chamberton's living room, the Underlord was standing tall, holding Creighton's body in the path of the blast: An inhuman shield.

The shotgun particles tore through Creighton's body, creating a fantastic, short-lived agony for him. The Underlord grabbed the silver knife from his cassock and thrust it through Creighton's backside.

"*NO-NO-NO-NO-NO-NO...*" Adam desperately screamed as he furiously cocked the gun.

The Underlord tossed Creighton's body to the side and dashed towards Adam with a bullet's speed, pinning the man against the living room's wall. He held Adam down and vigorously took a bite of his neck, driving those fangs straight inside.

The Underlord gagged.

Adam's artificial blood was toxic to the vampire, who coughed it out with as much force as his lungs could muster. Adam stumbled, catching himself and deciding whether to attack or flee. But he could do neither: The Underlord vanished with his usual speed straight out of Adam's front door, blowing it off the hinges. In the same dirt driveway Creighton had found himself in earlier, the Underlord hunched over the ground and vomited. It was an exceedingly rare experience for the vampire: The grotesque pain and agony of a mortal.

Adam moved quickly, sprinting to tackle the Underlord against the same tree that Creighton had found himself near. A purposeful tactic, this time. Adam now pinned the recovering Underlord against the tree with one hand, and with the other, snapped an adjacent branch off of the trunk. He raised his hand and attempted to stab straight down, just as his unwelcome guest had done to the Underlord's Bride.

Ilona's hand caught Adam's arm.

Adam flung away from the tree at blinding speeds and crashed into the ground, the grass of his front lawn smearing against his face. The two remaining brides swarmed him and pummeling him onto the ground, bashing and breaking everywhere they struck. They punched and kicked and attacked him with formidable speed and furious strength, snapping his bones and tearing his skin apart.

Finally, the Underlord waved his hand and called them off, and Adam's mangled body shivered and twitched amidst his own carnage.

Very, very slowly, the bits and pieces of him tried to reform and reheal. Once

Adam's head grew back the ear that'd been torn off in the scuffle, the Underlord leaned in real close and made every word clear.

"She was my favorite Bride, abomination," the Underlord spoke with care. "If we cannot kill you, then we will do the same to you that you've done to us."

A moment later, all three of them vanished with their usual speed.

The winds of the night howled through the vast assortment of trees, and below them, the artificial man laid broken. Adam's body kept healing and reforming over several agonizing minutes. The pain of it all wasn't the main source of Adam's struggle. It was the Underlord's final words to him.

"The same to you that you've done to us..." The Underlord's sentence rang through his head endlessly. He couldn't mean what Adam feared. It wasn't possible.

Once mostly restored, Adam hobbled over to the threshold of his house, his body trying to keep up. This was the first time all night that he truly felt any fear. And it was a powerful, petrifying possession. In the living room, all of Adam's bones had rehealed. As he ran up the stairs, all of Adam's muscles had put themselves back in their proper places. In the upstairs hallway, all of Adam's skin had slithered itself back into position.

Adam opened the first door on his left, and saw what had been done.

There was only one soul in this world who provided Adam love. This girl had grown into a beautiful woman who had never judged his horrid gray skin at first glance, and could never hear his deep, barbaric voice. Deaf-blind at birth, she had only three of the usual five senses, and for many years as she and Adam matured, had used them to feel his warming touch, smell what roses and daffodils he brought her, and taste his lips on hers. This woman's name was Elsa Chamberton, married two years, and all her husband could see was what remained of her: A woman's corpse, lying flat on her bedside with two puncture wounds in her neck surrounded by her dried-out blood.

Almost every piece of furniture or tapestry had some semblance of Adam's wife's blood spattered over it, alluding to the malignant, arduous extent she'd suffered for. Her clothes were shredded open, revealing cuts and bruises that showed a clear struggle; It was her life at stake, and the last fight for it she'd ever have. This was the retribution of the Underlord's second and third wives for the death of their unholy sister, for although he'd forgone human underlings for the past two centuries, the Underlord consistently sustained three inhuman beings as his succubus mates.

The man stood broken.

Everything he'd valued in life, to this moment, had been subtly or viscerally ripped away from him. Neither the deformed boy nor the mutated man gained love from his mother nor praise from his alleged father. Adam owned nothing of value and could offer nothing of use to this untimely world, and until Elsa, he'd known himself only as a damned, unfit wretch beholden to the toxic malevolence of mankind. His *real* father, through all of this, was nothing more than a lycanthropic corpse in the middle of his living room.

Adam collapsed to Elsa's bedside and lamented in the deepest sorrow how the only person on Earth that had loved him, in waking life or beyond, was taken away for no other reason than being the wife of a monster.

V

Hamilton, Ontario

In shredded clothes, Gwen awoke with her face pressed against the pavement, a pounding headache plaguing her mind.

She'd been dreaming about the week before: Her boss finally stopped tolerating the late arrivals and random no-shows several days prior, making her unemployed for the third time this year. Mere days later, her boyfriend broke things off with her, citing something about "too many secrets between us." In reality, Gwen only really kept the one.

Dazed, Gwen pushed herself up with very little strength, recovering it in pieces, and carefully got to her feet. The nighttime wind rushed by her sensitive ears in a pestilent way, biting at her earlobes with a subtle chill. Her vision started to clear up from the foggy haze once she rubbed her eyes.

The first thing she saw was a police car, parked diagonally, partially up on the sidewalk. The driver's side tire was slashed open in multiple places, the fender above it was torn into several bits, and the spiderwebbed windshield had a man-sized hole in it where the driver was, evidently, torn directly out of it.

Gwen looked around and found the body lodged into the sidewalk. The man's head was missing. She scanned his chest, seeing the empty spot where the bodycam used to be. She felt her stomach, trying to detect the camera's shards and pieces.

Please only one, said the voice in her head. *Please.*

This was the first time in months that Gwen let something like this happen, and it seemed like the worst of the bunch. Getting fired and dumped back-to-back had sent her down a path of insecurity and loneliness, from which only alcohol and attention could pacify. She started to remember last night's endeavor piece by piece, recalling how she'd gone bar-hopping and found the best-looking guy there. Chad, his name was. Maybe *Charlie,* actually. Something with a C...

There he was, too. Looking up the street revealed more bodies, spread into a healthy amount of carnage. Heads, arms, limbs of all kinds were missing, and what was left of them had been slashed and torn open by claws much larger than Gwen's hands. Gwen looked down at her fingernails, ignoring the blood underneath them. They seemed so *small,* harmlessly filed down to a minuscule length. She couldn't even open a can of soda without a little struggle.

And yet, there everybody was, lying around her in putrid chunks.

Gwen looked up to the sides of the buildings. The only camera she could find was aimed at the opposite street. She couldn't chance it.

Quickly, Gwen went over to the camera and leapt up towards it, her hand just barely missing the wiring.

"What happened?!" a distant voice cried.

Gwen leapt up again, her fingers slipping after touching the wiring. If she could only summon those long, translucent talons at will...

"Oh God!!" the voice cried again, probably from further down the street. It was closing in on her.

"Call the police!!" another voice yelled.

Desperately, Gwen jumped as high as she possibly could and grabbed onto the lowest wire of the camera. As she fell, the wire yanked out of the camera and aimed it directly at the ground, a small spark of electricity accompanying the sabotage. Gwen ran as fast as she possibly could in the opposite direction of the voices.

Gwen found her apartment intact, confusing her. The door was still securely locked, and none of the windows were shattered. Her previous apartment was ground zero for her most recent shift before last night, necessitating her finding a new home in the new, faraway town of Hamilton. This time was different. The shift wasn't here, and all evidence of Gwen's presence had either been shredded, dismantled, or were currently digesting away in her stomach.

The thought disgusted her.

Gwen unlocked her door and threw what was left of her clothes in a small pile, ready to be burned at the soonest opportunity. She had another interview today for an entry-level position somewhere down the road. Given the morning she'd just had, that didn't seem like a realistic title on the day's agenda.

A warm shower couldn't remove her stressed-out state of mind. Neither did the TV dinner or reruns of her favorite sitcom.

Eight people.

Gwen found the article online after she fled the scene of the attack: Eight Confirmed Dead in Hamilton, Ontario. Her schizophrenic companion wouldn't leave the subject alone.

We killed eight people, the voice reiterated.

"It's in the single digits," said Gwen to the empty apartment.

The voice was her oldest companion. It existed before her earliest memories of her family, even her parents. It was her most important ally, yet a trustworthy sense of reason whenever she'd done something abominable. Still, it was not always a welcome presence.

We shouldn't have been out, the voice continued.

"I needed to go out," Gwen admitted. "I wouldn't have if I'd known what would..."

Gwen waited for her voice again. It said nothing.

Gwen turned the TV off and threw away her dinner. She didn't realize how full she already was. Washing dishes didn't take her mind off of it either.

The zoologist, said the voice.

"No," said Gwen, scrubbing away at a particular plate.

He says he can help you.

"He's full of shit."

How do we know that?

"We just do."

We don't have reason to-

"*I* do," she corrected.

Gwen dropped the plate into the sink. She'd been scrubbing the exact same spot for the past thirty seconds. It couldn't possibly get any cleaner.

The voice went quiet again.

"This is stupid," Gwen lamented. "We're going to spend more time unemployed, looking into a bunch of nonsense from strangers who say they can help, and I'm just going to turn again. And we start this whole shitshow over again."

Language.

"Fuck you," said Gwen.

She grabbed the sink's edge with both hands and leaned over it, dropping her head down in a deep state of thought. She expected the voice to chime in again, but it didn't. Her frustration was shared with nobody.

Gwen sighed and left the kitchen, grabbing her laptop. Beyond all signs to the contrary, the zoologist from Mexico was her most promising sign of a cure.

With her hypersensitive ears, Gwen heard the faint *drip* of soap into the sink from the dish she'd let go of. It drew her attention away from the screen.

The dishes can wait, said the voice.

Gwen looked back to the laptop, calming down. She never realized how much she missed it when it disappeared. It was only when she found herself alone with her own thoughts that she enjoyed the voice's company.

HER DEATH IN THREE PARTS

I

Before Her Death

Elsa Riemelt felt the knob of her apartment door and twisted the key, accompanied by her date. The two were standing at her apartment's doorway after Adam volunteered to walk her upstairs. She had the route memorized, and didn't need eyes or ears to traverse it from her building's front steps. But he insisted on it. Adam became mesmerized by the entirety of her, not just in appearance but by the very *idea* of who and what she was. And that made it impossible for him to look away from her.

Elsa Riemelt had accepted a date from Adam Chamberton despite being several years his senior. He'd never made a move on anybody before, and after seeing her, never planned to again. She had no sense of sight to see his hideously gray skin, and no sense of sound to hear his deep, ghastly voice.

Standing by her entryway, Elsa cupped her hands in his and said a message in sign language: *Goodbye, Adam.*

Adam said nothing back.

Adam? she asked.

Adam took his hands in her own.

I'm staring at you, he replied.

She blushed at the words, and he did the same, slightly embarrassed at his own confidence. It was a new feeling for him. His eyes became fixated again at her features, following her lips, moving up and down her face to her cheekbones, and back up to her unopened eyes. He imagined what they would look like if they could see him, and how beautiful they must be to get lost in.

Though she had no sense of it, she could still feel him looking at her. It was a purely *powerful* feeling to have, and she so rarely felt it by anybody. Her breath caught in her throat, and he noticed it. Neither of them moved for a moment. Both were unsure of what was going to happen next.

He leaned forward, something bursting inside of him that he couldn't keep locked up any longer. Elsa was stricken, unable at first to react to his forceful, compelling kiss, as a shock of fear was overtaken by her all-consuming desire. She kissed back, returning in droves the passion she'd been dealt, wrapping her arms around his neck as he intuitively grabbed her waist and pulled her body closer to his.

They separated. Neither knew who pulled away first, but it happened, and they met again like magnets unavoidably being drawn to each other; His with his eyes, and hers with her hands on his face. His body. Moving down to his strong, thick chest. She looked a tad shocked, and mostly surprised. This had been on his mind for longer than she realized, and for him, it was a grandiose payoff. Even if Adam had died right there and then by her apartment's door, he still would've been satisfied with the kiss of Elsa Riemelt.

Elsa started to say something.

Adam stopped. He'd never heard her actually speak before. But despite him waiting for more, she did not formulate a sentence. She trailed off staring at him with her palms, peering into his soul without the need of a set of eyes, betwixt by his alluring appearance.

The moment passed, and Adam grew tired of waiting for words that would never come.

He kissed her again, and as she returned it, the two spun and fumbled their way through the threshold. Habitually, Elsa shut the door without breaking the kiss, and her arm snapped back to where she needed it to be. She quickly undid each button with it, top to bottom, of the shirt that was separating the raw passion of Elsa Riemelt from the body of Adam Chamberton. To her, this man was a hulking mass of sensation that she indulged herself in. Once open, she felt his heaving chest and dug her nails into it, scratching at the robust hair coating his strong, stocky figure.

Adam carefully separated her corset's backing, fearing the destruction of her clothing would ruin the moment. A fumble onto the countertop of her kitchen caught and stabilized the two of them. He leaned up against it, Elsa practically forcing his body onto it. Adam grabbed the back of her neck with one hand, reaching into her shirt with the other. This lit a fire inside of her that almost forced her to start stripping, lest she combust from the intensity.

But she suddenly stopped.

"Ahh!" Elsa said sternly as she pushed herself away from him.

Adam wasn't sure how to process what was said.

He cupped his hands in hers: *What's wrong?*

But she broke away from him.

As he watched her turn around and fix her corset, the bold, strong, and mighty confidence that made him kiss her in the first place suddenly dashed away as a world of insecurity flooded his mind.

She turned to face him again and took his hands in her own: *I want to. Very, very much. But not like this.*

Elsa took a long, steady breath.

I need more time, signed Elsa in Adam's hands.

Adam put his hands back in hers: *For you, I would wait an eternity.*

She felt his body again, up and down, his shirt still wide open. Slowly, Elsa moved her hands back onto his face, feeling those features she'd felt before: The coarseness of his skin spread across the strong, shapely details of his face. She could do this for hours. And so could he.

Adam took her hands down slowly, cupping his own in them: *What are you doing tonight?*

Elsa blushed as she answered him: *Isn't this the end of our date?*

Only if you want it to be, he pointed out.

Elsa laughed nervously, then shot him a warm smile.

Put your shirt back on, she told him.

Yes, ma'am, he replied.

Elsa led Adam to her living room, redressing herself in the process. She took a seat at her table, which only had two chairs. Adam took the hint, and sat across from her.

They placed their hands in the table's center.

Why are you in Romania in the first place? she asked, her hands moving in his.

Traveled all over, Adam replied. *Needed a house with no...*

Adam struggled to find the proper word in sign language. "Identity" was what he was after, but not in that context.

A place nobody knows about, he finally said.

Where in Romania?

That'd defeat the purpose, said Adam, making her laugh. He could listen to that laugh all night.

Elsa put her hands in his again, debating what to say next. He quickly threw his hands in hers before she could think of her next question, because something had been on his mind every time he stared at her neck and saw the dangling pendant of a silver crucifix.

Do you believe in God? he asked.

I do.

Why?

I believe in fate, said Elsa. *I believe we're all destined for something... You don't?*

I don't know what I believe, Adam admitted. *I just don't think there's a God.*

Why not?

Because if there is, he's done a terrible job at being one.

Elsa chuckled, making Adam smile. The two sat with this moment for a time. Characteristically, Elsa's smile slowly faded, and she asked Adam a more personal question.

Why do you like me?

Adam hesitated. It was the first question to which he didn't immediately know how to respond.

I just do, he told her.

Elsa withdrew her hands, then put them back in his: *I can't see and I can't hear. Few women are more revolting to boys than somebody like me.*

Adam took his time before saying anything else.

Few men are more revolting to girls than somebody like me, he finally responded.

You're healthy, Elsa pointed out. *You're tall and strong and really smart.*

I wasn't always. I used to be without all of those things... I was changed into who I am.

Elsa turned pale.

You were deformed too?

In different ways, Adam signed.

How did you overcome it?

Adam didn't plan on telling this story on their first date. Still, this date seemed so whimsically unconventional thus far. Perhaps it wasn't really inappropriate.

There's something sinister living within me. It's why my skin is coarse and unpleasant. I plan on taking it to my grave, so none may experience a life similar to my own.

Elsa felt his skin, stroking his palms intimately.

I don't find it unpleasant, she told him.

Adam blushed. He'd never known intimacy like this before. If anybody were to know about who and what he was, it had to be her.

My mother was a doctor, he began.

II

After Her Death

Elsa Chamberton was breathing anew, resting on a newly-bought bed with a fresh set of comforters and pillows. By her side, her husband held her hand warmly. That familiar strength of his let her know he was there. Somehow, she knew he wouldn't leave her side.

Due to her disability, it was impossible for her to see the extent of it, for beyond the bed itself, the entire *room* had been redone: Paint instead of wallpaper, a dresser instead of a bureau, huge black drapes instead of the short white curtains, and a large rug covering the polished hardwood underneath. It had been transformed since when she last knew it, but that mattered very little to her since she had been deaf-blind since birth. Even in resurrection, that affliction did not change.

Adam gracefully touched her arm, taking a great deal of care not to startle her where she lied.

Elsa rose up petrified. Her memories all flooded back into her mind in a horrifying whirlwind: The two assailants giving no warning to their entry, viciously tearing her open and ending her life. She had only three senses in this world, and as Elsa Chamberton spent her dying moments with no way to defend herself, she'd smelled the putrid stench like a cold corpse, felt the pain of a thousand wounds, and tasted her own blood rise up and through her mouth from her innards as her three assailants forced their way inside.

None of that was present now.

Elsa was clean, and felt only faint *remnants* of the attack that'd killed her: Her arms hurt most of all, and so she had them bandaged up in wrappings. Whatever she was wearing felt like a chef's apron or a loose-fitting lab coat, and underneath it all was nothing but a fresh, new change of light clothes. This was not the state in which she'd died, but rather the one she was spending in her second life.

In Adam's cupped hands, Elsa asked him simply through sign language: *How?!*

Adam put his hand in hers, and responded: *Not important. You're safe. That is important.*

I thought I died, she signed back.

Adam put his arms around her and held her close, feeling her shiver. Terrified as she was, being in her husband's presence seemed to overcome all other worries in her world. She never thought she'd have a moment like this again.

A moment passed of pure peace.

The blacked-out memories of her death started to return to her mind, obliterating this feeling of harmony. Details returned in fractured, fuzzy ways, then quickly grew clearer and sharper, until the past felt more like the present.

Elsa pushed Adam away and ran out of the room. Adam put his hands on her shoulders as if to calm her, but she freed herself from it and hurried down the hallway. Adam followed her down and into the living room, where she collapsed into the couch and screamed in anguish. It wasn't from any physical pain, but the *sensation* of it from a time recently passed.

When Adam arrived by her side, she turned to him and signed: *Why am I here, Adam? What happened to me?!*

Solemnly, Adam cupped her hands around his own. This is not how he wanted the news to be broken.

They killed you, Adam signed. *They were trying to hurt me.*

What were they? Elsa signed, envisioning the way those two women moved so quickly and ferociously with their clawed hands and fanged mouths.

Vampires, he admitted.

Her memories were so vivid that they began to replay endlessly: The sensation of the vicious slashing open of her throat plagued her sense of self. The feeling was inescapable.

Elsa frantically ran to the house's patio and threw up over the railing.

Following her out, Adam came quickly through the sliding doors and placed his hands in hers:

I'm sorry-

Elsa swatted them away. She realized what he had done.

Adam tried to place his hands in hers again, but she threw them back at him and followed up by smacking him across the face. Elsa then screamed a guttural cry at him. Disarmingly, Adam stood there and took the punishment.

This is not right, Elsa furiously signed.

"Elsa..." Adam said instinctively. He tried to put his hands in hers to sign to her, but she fought it again. This time, he insisted.

I saved your life, Adam signed.

Elsa stepped back and replied: *It wasn't yours to save.*

Adam came closer, but Elsa turned away and went back inside. He decided not to follow her this time. Perhaps she just needed more time.

Perhaps not.

Adam second-guessed himself and went back inside after her. He found her in her room, feeling the remodeling Adam did since her death. She tore the wallpaper apart and started to overturn the furniture. As soon as she detected Adam's footsteps cross through the doorway, she turned to him furiously and asked: *Why?!*

Because you were dead! he signed back, his hands moving quickly in hers.

I'd already died! I'm not supposed to be alive!

Elsa, I couldn't let you be taken from me-

It wasn't your choice to make!!

Adam was speechless. He watched Elsa's face stream with tears, unable to console her in any real way. He chose to stop trying to convince her that he was right. He chose instead to listen.

You've broken our trust. You never even considered if I've ever wanted this... if perhaps I was meant to die when my time came. And it came *for me, Adam. I belong in the ground, decomposing for the worms and maggots of the world to feast on. You've robbed them of even that, and for what? A bride who relives that moment of her death in such detail? The endless trauma of a fatal pain and experience? Adam, they tore open my throat with their bare hands! I can't escape the feeling of my own blood leaving my neck... I felt it happen. And I can't unfeel it... I can't...*

She trailed off, the blurred outline of Adam becoming visible to her.

Elsa trembled in horror at first, which subsided into deeper curiosity. The outline started to sharpen in front of her. Light penetrated through her slowly-opening eyelids clearer with each passing second. The image of Adam became so bright and vibrant that it seemed almost surreal in form. She saw his body respire, in and out, and watched as the tiny little pores stretched across his gray skin as he did so.

Adam was confused, but not deterred. He'd remembered how much longer it'd taken Rebecca's serum to change his own physiology. It was on a timescale of weeks and months, not *minutes*. Instead of a serum, Adam had transfused his own blood straight into his wife's veins. For him, that was the most convincing reason why.

Elsa reached out and touched Adam's face, feeling all of the coarse bumps and grains in his rigid, symmetrical jawline.

Adam cupped his hands in hers: *I'm sorry. I am unable to imagine a world without you, Elsa.*

Elsa looked down at his hands as he signed to her. It was a foreign experience in every conceivable way, but it was intuitive to learn. Especially with a mind as brilliant as hers now was.

I was fated to die, too, Adam continued. *You and I are living proof that fate has no say in our deaths. Life is only what we make of it... and my mother made this one for me.*

Elsa looked up, seeing her husband's eyes start to swell. He'd broken his vow to take this serum to his grave, and he didn't regret any part of it.

Adam took a step back. He didn't cup his hands around hers.

Loving you is the only part of my life worth living, Adam signed.

Elsa smiled. Not only could she understand what he just signed, but the sleeves of his shirt moved softly with his arms, creating tiny little noises. She heard them clear as day.

And so the two were betwixt, forever crossed to share one another's lifetime. They drew power from each other in true codependence. Adam looked forward to teaching her what noises accommodated each letter, word, and sentence of sign language. Her fast-moving mind would be up for the task.

There would be just one more person who'd play an important part of this codependent relationship, though neither of them knew of his existence at that time. His name was Franklin Chamberton, and he would greet them both less than nine months later.

III

Beyond Her Death

In terms of credentials, Adam found no struggle whatsoever finding his way into and through that retirement home. His immortality would presumably make it exceedingly difficult in the centuries to come, but currently, the year was 2006, and Adam was hardly approaching fifty. The ghastly gray skin sold the idea of an elderly, unhealthy individual. This, in both regards, could not be further from the truth.

Adam found the corresponding room towards the end of the second hallway, passing many thresholds with drawings and letters from loving family members hanging on the doors and signs. He knew the room he was looking for wouldn't have any of those. His hand turned the doorknob slowly, knowing it wouldn't be necessary to knock given her condition.

Coated by long, thin strips of light through the window's blinds, Rebecca Chamberton laid still in her bed.

This was the first time Adam had seen his mother in many, many years. The feeling of being there felt so *alien* to him, like it were from a vision or a dream. This was not at all how he remembered her. Regardless, he knew he was running out of time before her condition would worsen, and her cognitive functions would start to fail. The doctors were surprised that they didn't need to have her on an oxygen tank yet. They feared it would be soon.

The only thing ever on that obsolete television of hers were reruns of current game shows. When she was able to pay attention to them, she loved to play along and cheer out the answers she knew. Most of the time, she strained to focus on it. In her mind, it was oftentimes nothing more than a screen full of static.

"Hello..." Adam asked softly as he approached her bedside. Rebecca turned to him, revealing the half-gray, half-brown hairline and countless wrinkles on her face that'd formed in her son's thirty-year absence. The image of her in his mind was buried beneath all of this. The true face of his mother he once knew. He squinted in trying to recognize it.

"Hello young man," said Rebecca as she grabbed Adam's hand. "You're... so cold."

Adam smirked. It wasn't the greeting he'd expected. Then again, he had no idea what to expect on this visit. Or if she'd even know who he was.

"How have you been?" he asked in a hushed voice.

"Oh... same ol', same ol'. Are we getting dinner early today? It's Friday night," she told him.

"I'm sorry, I..." Adam didn't have it in him to tell her that he wasn't one of her caretakers. "I don't know anything about dinner," he said, playing along.

"That's alright," she said, smiling. "Just get me an extra fruit cup when you bring it."

Adam nodded. He'd heard about the Alzheimer's a few years back, keeping updated on her health and well-being. He knew how the drugs she was on altered her emotional state sometimes. None of this mattered to him since he'd never planned on visiting her directly.

The past thirty years had been a beautiful dream for Adam and Elsa as they raised their child. Approaching his thirties, Franklin Chamberton had chosen to move away and start his own life in America. Without him, Elsa had felt that it was finally her time. Since she was born, Elsa knew that she didn't want to live through eternity, even if it was alongside her soul mate. With Adam's assistance, Elsa ended her own life.

With nobody left, Adam felt the need to see his mother. He needed to talk to her at least one more time before he never could again.

"How... You have a son, right? Named Adam?" he asked nonchalantly.

Her demeanor changed. Hearing the name triggered so many uneasy memories.

"That boy... He... Problem child, you see. We never really got along."

Just as a gross discontent started taking a hold of Adam's mind, discouraging him greatly, Rebecca clasped his arm and slowly pulled him in: "Why, has he *done* something to you?"

"Yes he has," Adam relented.

Rebecca scoffed in her disappointment.

"*Damn* that boy... He'll be the death of me. What's the damage? How much do I owe you?"

"No no no, you don't owe me anything," said Adam frantically.

Adam put her arm back by her side as he leaned back. Rebecca became remarkably sad all at once, as though the entire world's problems now rested on her frail shoulders.

"That boy..." she became emotional the more she spoke. "*God,* that boy o' mine... I failed him. I really feel like I failed him in life."

"How do you mean?" Adam asked, knowing how *he* would answer the question.

"Can you keep a secret?"

"Yes," said Adam with conviction.

"He wasn't my husband's son."

Though Adam was well aware, it felt different hearing it straight from the source.

"He was troubled," she continued. "I wanted to help him..."

"You *changed* him," Adam said.

"I didn't mean to turn him into a *monster.*"

Adam looked away. She was verbalizing all of the thoughts floating around in his own head. There were no surprises on this visit for him. Not until she continued that very thought.

"I wish I'd never done it," said Rebecca sincerely. "I wanted him to have the same chance everybody else did. I wanted him to hold down a job... find a wife... bring me some grandkids. I thought that by changing him, he'd be able to do all of those wonderful little things with his life..."

Her eyes started to tear up, and she stopped trying to suppress it.

"I just hope he's happy," said Rebecca, choking over her words. "I wish I'd given that to him."

Adam froze. He didn't know the first thing to say to her. All he could think to do was reach down and hold onto the silver crucifix on the end of his necklace, and run his thumb along the textured metal. It evoked memories of when he touched it as it laid on Elsa's neck, and brought him straight back to picture-perfect memories and sensations that they'd shared together. It was this one, final time where he needed to draw power from his better half, and tried to imagine what she might tell him to say.

Finally, Adam let it go and instead used his thumb to wipe the tears from his mother's cheek.

"Can you keep a secret, too?" Adam asked. He tried to stay nonchalant, but found it harder and harder not to become emotional like his mother.

Rebecca nodded, and squinted through her watery eyes to try and make out Adam's face. She gave up trying after a few moments.

Adam swallowed hard.

"Your son was... Your son's married now," said Adam. Rebecca's face lit up as he continued: "Her name is Elsa, and you wouldn't believe just how beautiful she is. They live in Romania together. And they have a son... *Franklin Chamberton...* You have a grandson, don't you know. He's the greatest man you'll ever meet.

Sometimes... Adam tells me... your son forgets just how happy he is to be living the life he has. I think he's lost sight of the fact that without his mom, he'd never have met Elsa in the first place. He'd never have gotten to see the way his son looks at him when he's curled up in his arms... Your boy did really well for himself, Rebecca. I guess he just wanted you to know that."

As Adam spoke with a trembling voice, he failed to realize Rebecca's attention having shifted back to her television. Another one of her dissociations. Holding back his own tears, Adam grabbed Rebecca again on her arm.

"Hello young man," said Rebecca.

Adam smiled. "I just came here to let you know that dinner's coming early tonight. Because it's Friday, and all."

"Wonderful," said Rebecca joyfully. She turned again to her television, this time with a big smile on her face. "Thank you so much."

XI
THE HOUSE OF THE MAD POACHER

What do we know? the voice in Gwen's head asked.

Gwen picked out what she could past her cell's gateway: The interiors of the other cells were traceable by the soft, dim light of their televisions. It was *almost darkness* in a holistic way, and trying to solve it was something like a game for her.

Closer.

Gwen rose from the bed and put her head as close to the gateway as possible, without actually touching the poisonous silver. She saw everything but the two most immediate cells to her left and right: The empty one to her left, and the one with Abrem Trosk and his ultraviolet lights. She made it a point to remember what everybody was called: The Brute Man whose name was Hoxton, The Ape-Woman, The "Creature," the gray-skinned person, the Phantom, and the Gargoyle who raved about an impending doomsday. The unseen cell to her right was Abrem Trosk, who cared little for mortal men and women.

And insisted there was a cure for lycanthropy.

Overwhelmed, Gwen spun around and turned on the television, illuminating some of her cell. Amidst all of the live channels and content she skimmed through, none of it interested her. Nothing was satisfactory. She turned the thing to its basic display: The false view of outside, with tropospheric clouds spattering across the daytime sky's vista.

There was something familiar about it.

Gwen squinted, trying to pinpoint whatever it was. The shape of that hill... The way the grass touched the water...

This was the picture hanging on Waylon's living room wall. One of the dozens of them. *What a tool,* she thought. It had to be a grand display of arrogance to consider one's own artwork so gorgeous and charming that it needed to be the baseline for everybody's initial view through a false window. If the real world was not visible, these would *surely* make a superb substitute.

Gwen laid back down on her bed. She could write at her desk, or draw or anything else, but she felt motivation for none of it. What argument could she make to grant her her leave? She was a true menace to the outside world, so much so that she didn't even deserve to see it ever again down here. Only digital photographs, and various old movies and television. Forever and ever, and then some more after that. Suicide wasn't even a viable option. There was no point even in that, for it would just deprave Waylon of one of his trophies... meaning he would simply fetch another in her place.

As if there weren't enough burning questions to ponder, the voice in her head brought a brand new one into her mind, and let it linger there: *Why's everybody so quiet?*

Most of them had spent years, sometimes decades trapped behind these bars, yet until she approached each one of them, they remained completely silent. Even now there couldn't be found one singular word of dialogue among them. They all sat or ate or slept or watched their televisions obediently. Was this all more sorcery? Or did they all truly hate each other, as well as being here?

This could not go untested.

Gwen got up from her bed and walked up to her gateway of silver bars, careful not to touch any of it.

Ask one of them, said the voice pedantically.

"No," Gwen whispered as quietly as possible.

Ask.

She swallowed hard.

"...*Abrem*," Gwen said in a somewhat-hushed voice.

Practically every single one of them turned their creepy, uncanny heads over to her. It was a mass of confusion, as if the very thought of talking to one another was disturbing. Gwen lost her confidence. She bowed her head and turned back to her bed.

"Yes, werewolf?" Abrem Trosk asked in a normal speaking voice, unafraid of the judgment of his peers.

Gwen didn't expect it at all. They were the only two who could not rightly see one another, so Gwen moved closer to the wall separating the adjacent cells. By now, most of the monsters had lost interest in the both of them, and moved on to their usual hobbies.

"Why don't they talk?" Gwen asked.

"There's no reason to," Abrem Trosk said plainly. "Everybody here knows all that they need to know about each other. They asked all those questions when they were first captured."

"And they don't ask any about me?"

"They don't need to," he replied. "They have ears. Most of them, at any rate. You paraded yourself around like a pageant's queen. They all know you're just Waylon's next trophy."

They. Something in how he used that word didn't sit right with her.

"You said there was a cure for what I am," said Gwen.

"I did."

"Where is it?" Gwen persisted.

"Right here in this crypt," he said. "I look at it every day."

Gwen sighed, running out of patience. She had no use for this vampire's riddles. There was no reason to believe anything he said. Or anybody else.

"Why do you want a cure?" a voice called out from across the crypt.

Gwen looked to find the source of it. It was a deep, guttural tone. She couldn't narrow it down.

"*Hey,*" said the Gargoyle, the next cell over from Abrem Trosk and on the very edge of Gwen's view.

"What?" Gwen reflexively asked.

"Why do you want it?" the Gargoyle repeated.

She had no idea how to answer it: "To be... *human,* again?"

"It sounds like you're in denial of what you are," said the Gargoyle.

"I'm not in denial," Gwen said defensively.

"Aren't you?" the Gargoyle continued. "There's never been such a thing as a cure for lycanthropy, for as long as I've existed. And I've been around for almost six centuries."

Abrem Trosk laughed. He couldn't contain it.

"What the hell's your problem?" the Gargoyle asked.

"Nothing," said Abrem Trosk. "*Six centuries,* wow. I bet you're really proud of that."

"High and mighty today, are we?" the Gargoyle snapped. "Funny how among all of your *thousands of years,* you too couldn't evade one mad poacher with a bank account."

"*STOP!!*"

The voice of a million men at once.

Hoxton had awoken from a rather enjoyable dream. He *relished* in pure silence, even in waking life. All of this noise was revolting to him. At his gateway, Hoxton approached with his hands clenched into fists, and spoke through gritted teeth:

"*That's enough.*"

"What, do you have work in the morning?" said the Gargoyle sardonically.

"He's right," said the Phantom in an ethereal voice. "The Brute Man, I mean. Your bickering is frustrating."

"How do you hear without ears?" Gwen asked the Phantom.

Hoxton, the Phantom and the Gargoyle all turned to Gwen inquisitively. She almost didn't realize she even said it, amidst all of the tension in the room. But there was no taking it back anymore.

From where Gwen couldn't see, Abrem Trosk smiled.

"I'm sorry," said Gwen timidly.

"No, she's right," said Abrem Trosk. "Why do you even care? You completely *disappear* most hours of the day."

Gwen interjected: "Actually, that's not what I-"

"You think I'm *gone* when you can't see me?" the Phantom replied. "You really trust your eyes when looking for a ghost?"

Hoxton furrowed his brow. Tonight was going to be a sleepless one.

Far upstairs, accessible by a long, spiral staircase and many locked doors, was an observatory atop Waylon's manor with a large dome-like skylight.

The telescope was rarely used, but the room had been converted into a workroom with many unfinished projects. Large generators powered bizarre machines meant for industrial complexes, like plasma cutters and towering centrifugal pumps. These were purchased, but some had to be stolen for practical purposes: A makeshift MRI machine had been scrapped together by ordering all of the lesser parts. This room was *coated* in machinery like this, and strewn atop several lab tables were bits of iron presses and copper dynamos, salvaged from wherever one wouldn't mind parts like these going missing.

In came Waylon with Jack by his side. They went with purpose right to the centermost table in their unconventional workshop. A large lockbox with a passcode's entry was waiting for them.

"It's just the Gargoyle we need a solution for," remarked Waylon as he sat down and removed his werewolf's hyde.

Jack grabbed Waylon's coat from him and hung it up beside him. Waylon looked on, still not used to the sight of his coat *floating* away like that.

"This would be much easier if I could at least see your face," said Waylon.

Jack ignored him. Contractually, he was under no obligation to reveal himself. That wasn't a requirement of the job.

Waylon entered the lockbox's code. The codes of the manor's secrets were held only by those very two individuals in that room, and those codes governed *everything*. Practically anything connected to electricity had some sort of software installed to be operated remotely. The power lines to Waylon's manor ran underground, as to reduce risk of a tree falling in a brutal storm, and even still there were several generators programmed to rejuvenate the house in a matter of seconds if the electric company's power were ever lost.

The lockbox opened, and Waylon took the device in his hands. He inspected it up and down: "We're all set with silver, iron, rotenone... Do we have more salt?"

"Plenty," Jack said.

Waylon watched as Jack's invisible fingers entered a code into the cabinet door across the room. Inside, dozens of different types of bullets made of all the world's materials ran up and down the shelves and rows of the cabinet. Jack restocked the ones marked *SALT* before sealing the box back up.

Waylon tried the device on.

It was a left hand's glove. Though recently forged by the observatory's machines, Waylon had been working on creating it for many years, designing a number of lower-tech prototypes. This gauntlet was the product of a combination of arcane alchemy and contemporary software and hardware engineering. The material was remarkably thin. Too thin to protect the wearer against any sort of strike from an opponent's weapon. But that was not its purpose at all.

"I have a name for it, Jack," said Waylon confidently.

"Why?"

"All good tools deserve a name," Waylon replied. "You've never named a car in your life?"

"Do I look like I need a car?"

That comment bothered Waylon, who simply wanted to share his pride with somebody.

"You don't look like anything at all," Waylon said dismissively.

Waylon held it out to where he last heard Jack's voice come from. He formed his fingers into a very specific position: As though he were holding a gun.

Tiny little wires and cables sent their signals in a moment's notice and produced the *components* of a gun into Waylon's hand. Impossible by contemporary science, and still impossible by way of alchemy. But unified into one, hybridized force, the components of a gun moved from the gauntlet and assembled themselves together. The pieces moved flawlessly, yet the weapon had no ammunition whatsoever. With his free hand, Waylon spun the cycling metal band running around his forearm like an armlet. Each section had one bullet of distinct origin and making.

Waylon couldn't see it, but Jack remained steady. Unamused. Waylon rotated the band to the very last cartridge: Normal, common bullets.

"I'll just *trust* that you're putting your hands up," Waylon said sardonically.

After a moment, Waylon shifted his attention across the room, where a thin sheet of metal was placed against the wall. It was probably a detached panel for a much larger machinery, from what Waylon could remember about it. Surely a bullet hole through the side wouldn't change much about it.

From the drawer, Waylon grabbed himself a pair of noise-dampening earmuffs. Jack simply didn't care about putting on a pair. He'd been around too many gunshots as to be almost desensitized to it. With as steady of a hand as he could make, the marksman in Waylon pulled the weapon's trigger, and within the gun's chamber, a bullet from the aligned cartridge *appeared* inside of the barrel. A wake of mist briefly appeared in the bullet's wake as it loaded, glowing a vibrant blue.

But the weapon did not fire.

Waylon tried again to no avail. Frustrated, he stripped the gauntlet from his hand and sat back down.

"Every time. This is *every time,* Jack. I don't know why," Waylon fumed.

"Is it an oscillator?" Jack suggested.

"No," said Waylon confidently.

"How do you know?"

"I *just* replaced them, mate," said Waylon.

Waylon opened the gauntlet up to see its innards and sifted through some wiring. Upon doing so, he swore under his breath.

"It's one of the oscillators," Waylon admitted.

Jack sighed audibly.

"You sound frustrated," Waylon said, not taking his eyes off of the gauntlet.

"I'm fine," said Jack.

"I'd glare at you, but I have nowhere to aim it."

Jack relented. He explained: "Why not gather each monster's bullet in its own magazine, and just use a normal handgun?"

"There isn't always time," said Waylon. "Imagine you're in a room with two or three of them. One vampire, one werewolf, and one Mechi. Vampires are fastest, so you load your wooden bullets first. If their speed hasn't gotten to you, you successfully shoot it. The werewolf's traveled twenty feet in the time it's taken you to do that. You've now got to unclip your magazine of wooden bullets, slot it away, reach for your *silver* ones, clip *those* into your gun, rack up a round, *aim* it at the-"

"You've made your point," Jack said in frustration. "You just seem hell-bent on this 'glove' idea."

Waylon finally looked away from his glove to address his assistant, wherever he was.

"I imagine your grandfather put up with similar criticisms before creating that bloody costume," Waylon said candidly.

There was silence between them.

Waylon went back to tinkering with his device. Though his assistant was stealthy, Waylon still heard Jack pass him by and make his way to the exit.

"When you get a chance, send for Hoxton," said Waylon.

Jack didn't reply. Something Waylon was used to.

Now awake, Paula continuously batted her chest the more that everybody spoke. It was an absolute calamity to her, and she was enjoying the stimulation. The floodgates had been thrown open by Gwen's simple curiosities.

"She's confused," said Gwen.

"She's smarter than you know," said the Gargoyle.

"And yet, not smart enough to avoid being trapped in Waylon's basement," Hoxton belligerently replied.

"*Glass houses,* Brute," the Gargoyle fired back. "Haven't you made a career out of hunting things like us? Somewhere buried in all of those skills must've been a way to evade Waylon's capture, no?"

"I can only hunt what I know," said Hoxton. "It is the only reason I am glad to know you."

Abrem Trosk chuckled quietly to himself. Not quietly enough.

"Have you something to add, oh mighty Vampire King?" the Gargoyle taunted. "I'd imagine Hoxton's had you on his ledger for a great number of years."

"Him and many others," said Abrem Trosk.

The crypt's door opened, and all of the room's discourse instantly ceased.

Everybody remained silent and attentive as the inaudible footsteps of the invisible man approached the center of the crypt. Only in pure, perfect silence could the cushioned soles of Jack's shoes be detected as they walked across the ashlar ground. The only caged creature not partaking in this communal lull was Paula, who couldn't reckon why all of the commotion had simply stopped.

Two gateways were opened.

The first was Hoxton's, much to the shock and surprise of many of the crypt's members. This man had been the most problematic of all of Waylon's prisoners, with all trust squandered and all potential bridges burned to ash. He was easily the least likely of the lot to get so much as a passing moment of freedom from his cage. But it wasn't really freedom being offered to him at that moment. And he knew that fact well.

Breaking the group's expectations a second time, the other gateway that opened up was the Gargoyle's. This was not ordered by Waylon. This was a decision on Jack's part, and one he was prepared to defend.

Hoxton and the Gargoyle approached the center of the crypt where they presumed Jack to be standing. They glared at each other, wishing desperately for this to be some weird two-man brawl orchestrated by Waylon. Instead, the invisible man spoke only this into the aether, his voice flowing steadily like the circulated air they were breathing: "Waylon needs you both. Follow me."

Do it, the voice prompted. *Do it now.*

Gwen shook her head.

Jack knew that Hoxton could not attempt a jailbreak without feeling the loyal Gargoyle's wrath. Even if he managed to escape on foot, he could never run faster than the beast could fly. The Gargoyle, concordantly, recognized this fact equally as well, and the two began walking out of the crypt at each other's side, accompanied by an unseen host.

Now, the voice repeated.

"Jack..." Gwen's voice called out.

All three stopped in their stride at Gwen's unexpected holler.

"Let me out," she said calmly.

The tension in the room was salient. So innocent was the idea of just asking to be let out of one's cage. Jack accompanied Waylon whenever he came down, and thus far, Gwen hadn't betrayed any of his trust like certain others of her lot. Gwen could not look Jack in the eye, but stared firmly ahead as though she were talking to an empty void. Her spirit did not break. She did not slouch, nor stand too tall, and in these passing moments she tried to remember how to breathe at a normal, unassuming pace. Not too slow or too fast. She was as carefully, deliberately *normal* as she could possibly be.

After a long silence and consideration, her gateway opened up.

"Back inside when I return," said Jack's voice.

Gwen heard the words, but with the tone he'd taken, inferred their actual meaning: *Try something stupid, and you'll spend a lifetime behind those bars.* The warning was clear and understood.

The voice in her head was finally satiated.

Waylon was puzzled when he watched the door to his observatory open.

He expected only to see Hoxton, aided intangibly by his assistant. Instead, the Gargoyle accompanied them.

"Your gauntlet is composed of science *and* magic," Jack's voice explained, presumably standing somewhere near the open door.

Reasoning it out, Waylon nodded his approval, and said to Hoxton: "You first."

Hoxton had never been inside of Waylon's observatory. As he approached Waylon's work bench, he scanned the surroundings with his analytical mind and saw all of the projects Waylon had tinkered with and abandoned over the years. They seemed to be the unfinished makings of a scatterbrained hobbyist with an intermediate understanding of chemistry and engineering. Less qualified than a mad scientist, but much more effective than one.

"This is a weapon designed to quick-fire a dozen different types of ammunition at a moment's notice. You wear it on one hand like a glove, and use the other to rotate the armband. That aligns the bullet with the barrel," explained Waylon.

"How does it enter the barrel?" asked Hoxton.

"Sorcery," said Waylon. "Pull the trigger, and the chosen type of bullet teleports inside of the gun."

"Then what do you do about the snow?" said the Gargoyle.

Waylon and Hoxton looked over to him. Somewhere in that room, Jack felt quietly vindicated.

"Would you?" Waylon asked, beckoning the Gargoyle over.

The Gargoyle obliged. He walked to the workbench and inspected the gauntlet. Beside him, Hoxton kept looking around the room for any item or piece of information he could use to escape: Burners, surgical tools, glass cylinders, a large box of power tools, and an old pile of books. These and many more useless trinkets all coated the main workbench in some disorganized way. Hoxton didn't bother to look further than this workbench for any answers. The Gargoyle had little restrictions on his movements and actions, whereas Hoxton had attempted two separate escapes over the years. He knew Jack would be monitoring him closely. Anything outside of his arm's reach was akin to a pipe dream.

But he could not snag anything unless he knew Jack wasn't watching him.

"You know that blue mist when the bullet loads?" said the Gargoyle.

Waylon nodded.

"Every form of magic has a byproduct," said the Gargoyle. "Teleportation Spells create snow. A large enough amount generates a localized blizzard. At such a *small* size, the snow from your gauntlet is so minimal that it quickly melts away."

Seeing no opportunity to steal anything, Hoxton made his presence worthwhile.

"The discharge is frying your circuitry," Hoxton pointed out.

"Is there a way to disable it?" Waylon asked.

The Gargoyle shook his head.

"*Circumvent* it, then?" Waylon insisted.

"We could build some type of barrier. Contain the discharge," said Hoxton.

"We *could*," said the Gargoyle. "Or we could modify the spell."

Waylon raised an eyebrow. The Gargoyle noticed.

"How much do you know about magic?" the Gargoyle asked Waylon.

"Very little," Waylon replied. "It's a dead art spoken in a dead language."

"You're not wrong," said the Gargoyle.

"I can wield some of it," said Waylon, "but it's not a system I understand."

"Not yet," the Gargoyle remarked.

"You consider yourself a sorcerer?" asked Waylon.

The Gargoyle became uneasy at the term.

"Sorcerers, wizards, whatever you'd like to call them. They manipulate *spacetime*. They're either rearranging atoms or bypassing fundamental laws of physics," the Gargoyle explained.

"Yes, but that's not something I'll ever be able to... fully *know*, I don't think," said Waylon meekly. "Perhaps nobody will."

The Gargoyle turned all of his attention onto Waylon.

"Brilliant people of the past have made many, many statements about how something is unknowable. Every single one has proven wrong. *None* have been right. The track record is so poor that I have no reason to believe that something is unknowable at all," said the Gargoyle passionately.

Then, the Gargoyle leaned in closer.

"It's one of the reasons I am *here*," said the Gargoyle, "entertaining your idea of a community of hellions. Your experiment *does* have an answer. I trust you to seek it out before the second half of your life goes by, and time finally renders you dead. I will still be here, having lost nothing but a blink of my existence, and I will simply walk out of here with far more knowledge than I came with. The kind of knowledge you can't get from reading all the world's books twice over."

Waylon didn't blink.

Hearing the term, Hoxton looked back to the pile of books on Waylon's desk. *The Notes of Rebecca Chamberton*, with some of the notebook's pages torn out. *An Account of Sigma*, which seemed like a hand-made pastiche of several written documents. An incredibly short manuscript labeled *Drake's Only Chapter* laid towards the bottom.

Hoxton's original journal was beneath them all.

It had been months cooped up inside of that tiny room, looking out through those bars of hers at the many other cells of Waylon's crypt. The image of it was burned into her mind. Finally roaming free, Gwen swiveled her head many times, taking in as much as she possibly could until whenever Jack and the rest returned. She still didn't know if Waylon would approve of his assistant's decision.

Not much time left, cautioned the voice.

Gwen pulled her phone from her pocket and unlocked it quickly. She knew that those LED torches operated off of WiFi, just like any smart device for one's home. There was a reason the torches were only in the crypt, and not in the cells, where they would be shrouded by the faraday cages.

And there was a signal.

Despite living far away from urban towns and cities, Waylon's home WiFi was still password protected. This is information she would need to accrete from somewhere above. Somewhere outside of this crypt. Something like that probably wasn't possible this early on... She'd need to gain more trust.

Perhaps there were another way.

Clockwise, she accounted for who was left: Paula... the Creature... the quiet one with gray skin... the Phantom... and Abrem Trosk, whom she feared the least of all.

"Vampire," said Gwen as she approached his cell.

Abrem Trosk didn't sit, lay down, or do much of anything at all. He only stood upright at the gateway's edge.

"Werewolf," Abrem Trosk affectionately said back.

"Would you have any idea what the WiFi password is?" Gwen asked politely.

Without a physical body, it was impossible for the Phantom to laugh from across the crypt. But he absolutely would've upon hearing something like that.

"No," said Abrem Trosk.

Abrem Trosk became puzzled when looking at Gwen. A werewolf was not *all* that she was. There was something else beneath the surface, like a disease that wasn't harmful. A benign tumor, maybe. It was hard for him to place...

The more he stared at her, the more she struggled to look away from him.

"You're going about this the wrong way," Abrem Trosk added.

His additional comment caught her off-guard. Of all the people in Waylon's crypt, none seemed so eager to help her but *him*. Practically everybody else sitting behind those bars had long since accepted their fate.

"What's the *right* way?" she asked.

"Learn your limits," he said in a whisper. "There will come a time where Waylon's leash on you will loosen. You have to be prepared to strike quickly. Fatally, if need be, but *always* inconspicuously."

"More riddles?" Gwen scoffed.

Abrem Trosk shook his head, all the while maintaining a stare as if he never blinked. Perhaps he never needed to.

Or perhaps he was insane.

"Ghost?" Gwen asked as she spun around. She was eager to talk to the only other creature capable of actual speech in this crypt.

"What do you want from me?" The standoffish Phantom replied.

"Can the Isolation Spell be broken?" Gwen asked.

"Not by any of us," said the Phantom. "Gargoyle, maybe. Though he wouldn't."

"Why not?" Gwen asked.

"It's like you said," the Phantom replied. "He likes it here. Can't fathom why."

"Perhaps he likes your company," said Abrem Trosk sardonically.

The Gargoyle and Waylon tinkered away at the gauntlet.

Hoxton had to be careful. Three other parties were in this room with him. All three were capable of preventing him from leaving or trying to escape, each in their own unique ways. But of course, escaping was exactly what the Brute Man had on his mind. It was the only thing he'd ever thought of since his initial capture.

"Waylon," said Jack's disembodied voice. "I forgot to mention that Gwen asked to be let out."

"Did she, now?" Waylon replied.

"I told her she'd be back inside when I returned," said Jack.

The Gargoyle smiled.

"The girl's a clever one, isn't she?" said the Gargoyle. "She'll probably try to escape. *To no avail*, I'm sure."

And now the thought was in Waylon's mind.

From his work bench, Waylon pulled up a tablet and opened one of the only applications on it. In seconds, he had what Hoxton could only estimate to be *dozens* of cameras inside of that crypt. At least one per cell. Several more adorning the pillars.

This was something Hoxton was unaware of.

"She's fine," said Waylon. "Talking with some of the others. Getting them out of their shells, I hope."

"Conversations quickly turn to arguments down there," said the Gargoyle, now intently focused on the gauntlet. Something specific had to be repaired in a very delicate manner.

"Jack, can you hold this up?" the Gargoyle asked.

And Jack abided.

Hoxton watched the object's movement very closely as it floated into the air. He'd been in the crypt longer than anybody else down there. Jack's invisible movements were well-known to him, down to the finer details. With careful attention, Hoxton took note of how Jack's hand must be grabbing the object for it to move, rotate the way it did in the air, which indicated one very important detail: The way Jack's body was facing.

Away from Hoxton.

With a careful hand, Hoxton swiped his journal off of Waylon's workbench. He'd been planning how to move in such a way that the table wouldn't rock or shake, but he also couldn't lift the books on top, for that would've been much more obvious and taken more time. For those few passing moments, Waylon, the Gargoyle, and a distracted Jack kept their focus entirely on the gauntlet.

Gwen visited the hallway's edge leading up to the stairs, at the exact boundary of Waylon's Isolation Spell. She reached out her hand delicately. The closer her hand got to the invisible boundary, the more powerful the resistance. As she pressed her hand forward into empty air, something moist dripped onto her palm and fingertips from nowhere whatsoever.

It was rainwater, appearing only when she interacted with it. Gwen retracted her hand, and the localized drizzle vanished.

"This spell," said Gwen. "Why does-"

"Do you do anything other than ask questions?" the Phantom snapped.

"She's curious," said Abrem Trosk in her defense. "Most humans are."

"She's no human at all," said the Phantom.

"True, but she conducts herself as one," said Abrem Trosk. "*You* certainly don't."

Gwen came over to the Phantom's cell, visibly insulted. She placed her hands on the steel bars of his gateway.

"They seem useless to a ghost."

"I couldn't leave anyway," said the Phantom. "Not if you tore this cell down with all of your lycanthropic strength. Put it to good use and bash Waylon's head in the next chance you get."

"That wouldn't be smart at all," said Abrem Trosk.

"Wouldn't it?" the Phantom replied. "You were *just advocating* for her to strike him dead."

"Without arising attention," said Abrem Trosk.

"From who?!" the Phantom exclaimed. "His useless assistant?"

"It's idiotic to underestimate humanity at their worst," said Abrem Trosk.

"You *overestimate* them. On the day she was welcomed, you actually had Waylon in your *clutches*... and you threw a tantrum and tossed him aside. You misuse your corporeal body, Underlord. Or whatever you're *going by* these days."

"Police would investigate his death," said Abrem Trosk. "That's a fate far worse than confinement."

And the Phantom laughed.

"*You're* scared of *law enforcement?!*" the Phantom bellowed. "He, who moves with such unbelievable speed and strength. Whose immortal fangs have probably drained more gallons of blood than there are people alive today. Calling the authorities would ward you off more effectively than all the world's Holy Water."

Abrem Trosk's patience finally ran out.

"There were never any Holy Crusades against vampires," Abrem Trosk ranted. "There were never any exterminations of ghosts during the second World War. Men and women have hunted, and tortured, and killed their own kind for tens of thousands of years. They've done this *to their own species.* If they found out that even one, insignificant little werewolf were out there in the real world, they'd treat it with more hostility than any parasite, dictator, terrorist, or pandemic in all the world's history. They'd be endangered within a year. Extinct soon after."

The Phantom responded: "And yet, Waylon-"

"Waylon's a man who pays his taxes and bills on time," Abrem Trosk interrupted. "His death begets questions. Before long, people with judicial power show up on his front step, and it doesn't take them very long to find their way down to this massive crypt below his foyer. Once the men of this world discover that things like you and I exist, they'll *eradicate* us. There isn't a shadow of a doubt in my mind that they would both wage *and* win a war such as that."

The Phantom stayed quiet. He recognized the futility of arguing with a stone wall.

After completion, the Gargoyle handed Waylon the gauntlet.

Waylon stood up and aimed it at the metal plate across the room, spinning the armlet to a silver bullet. He fired, and the blue mist of melting snow formed in a small ring around the gun's barrel... but when he fired the gun, the bullet was able to launch without issue. It tore straight through the plate and buried itself into the observatory's wall behind it.

Waylon couldn't help but let out a childlike laugh.

"You've aided our kidnapper in hunting us more effectively," Hoxton mumbled to the Gargoyle.

Waylon had made his way over to the wall, assessing the damage he'd created. Out of earshot of the two stone-skinned men.

"I did," said the Gargoyle. "But you and I are not species. We're unique. That gauntlet is for vampires, werewolves, creatures from faraway lagoons..."

"That doesn't change anything," said Hoxton.

The Gargoyle looked to Hoxton with a curious eye.

"Be honest with yourself," said the Gargoyle. "If you could hurl a javelin at Waylon, right here and now, you'd take the weapon off his wrist before fleeing."

And Hoxton glared back at the Gargoyle.

"Did you know we were being recorded?" Hoxton asked.

"No," said the Gargoyle. "But I really don't care at all."

Waylon returned from the cabinet with the silver bullet in his hand.

"Barely any damage, Jack," said Waylon.

Jack took the bullet from Waylon's hand. All three of them watched as the bullet floated across the room to one of the large containers, hidden away under a small tarp. Jack removed it and opened the container's lid.

Ancient symbols coated the interior of about ten or twelve boxes in the container, each of which were filled to the brim with a specific variety of hand-fashioned bullets. Jack opened the lid to the silver ones and redeposited it inside.

"That's all I'll be needing you for, gentlemen," said Waylon to the two. "Gargoyle, you may roam freely if you please. Hoxton-"

"I know," Hoxton interrupted.

Waylon nodded. With a wave of his fingers, the components of the gun retracted back inside of the gauntlet on his wrist.

"Jack," said Waylon, "give the Gargoyle and I the room. I'll send him out shortly."

Hoxton glared the Gargoyle's way, then felt a light tap on his shoulder. A silent indication to leave.

The Gargoyle watched Hoxton be escorted out of the observatory. When the door closed, he turned back to Waylon quizzically.

"The only person on the cusp of discovering how magic worked was a man named Drake Tremmond," said Waylon, "and his aspirations sadly died with him."

"Who's Drake Tremmond?" asked the Gargoyle.

"A scientist," said Waylon. "He died alone in a psych ward many years ago. As far as I can tell, he's the only modern man to successfully catalogue the *reason* for magic's existence. He intended to write a book on his findings and share his knowledge with the world... They found him dead in his cell with only one chapter written."

"What'd he die of?" asked the Gargoyle.

"Lack of brain cells," said Waylon.

Waylon clamored through the pile of books on his table, pulling out the smallest one.

He noticed a certain journal's absence, and froze in place.

"Something wrong?" the Gargoyle asked.

Waylon briefly smirked. He quickly recanted it.

"Nope," said Waylon, handing *Drake's Only Chapter* to the Gargoyle. "Skim through it when you have a moment. Maybe you'll be inclined to pick up where he left off."

The crypt's entrance opened back up.

Gwen turned from facing the Phantom's cell to see Hoxton and the Gargoyle re-entering. All thoughts of escaping this place were shuffled to the back of her mind. She steadily controlled her heartbeat, trying to appear calm and normal. Whatever that meant.

"Back inside," said Jack's voice.

Gwen nodded. She re-entered her cell and watched the gateway shut on its own. Curiously, Hoxton and the Gargoyle re-entered their cells at about the same time, and despite the three of them all being several cells away, all of their gateways closed at approximately the same moment.

So Jack wasn't physically moving them.

"I'll return shortly," said Jack.

Gwen nodded.

"You did well," said Jack.

Gwen nodded again.

From nowhere, a small packet appeared in the air and tossed itself through Gwen's gateway, landing at her feet. Gwen reached down and grabbed it, feeling the inside of the packet to be some type of fine powder. On the packet's side was a note, written in marker with shotty penmanship:

Good Job

— W. R.

She opened the packet's seal and took a sniff.
It smelled sweet. Just like Waylon's coffee.
"Thank you," said Gwen to the aether.
And there was no response.
"Jack..."
All she could do was hope that he was listening.
"If I earn my trust... will I be allowed to go free?"
She saw and heard nothing.
But she wasn't really listening.
Closing her eyes, Gwen channeled her lesser half's senses and heard Jack's heart beating several feet in front of her, along with the vivid smell of his body odor masked by several layers of cheap deodorant. Her eyes shot open again, and stared confidently at him, her gaze all but begging for an answer.
"I don't know," Jack muttered. "Were I in your place, I wouldn't ask for it."
"What would you ask for?"
Again, there was silence. Gwen closed her eyes and tried her trick again, but before she could locate him, the door to the crypt's exit audibly opened up again, and closed on its own.
Gwen pocketed the mariphasa. She looked out and gauged the two monsters after their recent departure from their cells: The Gargoyle was the same as he'd always been, sprawled in a comfortable position, turning on the news like always. First worldwide, then localized. He made it a point to shift periodically between several types of news stations, seeing how the political biases affected their coverage. It seemed to be the only thing that captured his interests.
In his hand was a small book, which he periodically looked down on. He didn't seem positive if he actually wanted to read it or not. At least not at that moment.
But Hoxton was decidedly different.
He was frantically looking around the crypt, as if searching for something. Then, upon catching Gwen staring at him, turned away from his gateway and searched *around his own room*.
Unexpectedly, the Gargoyle took notice.
"You've been in this crypt the longest," the Gargoyle said to Hoxton. "You really didn't think it was possible?"
Hoxton knew what the Gargoyle was referencing. But he also knew that *nobody* knew except them. Perhaps, for the time being, that was a good thing. Most creatures inside of Hoxton's neighboring cells were not allies to him. They

were the exact things he'd spent his life hunting down and destroying. Quietly, Hoxton tossed his journal into his bedside drawer. It was impossible to read with Waylon's oversight and omnipresence.

Gwen wanted to ask what the Gargoyle meant, but she didn't want to hear any more complaining from the Phantom about her curiosities. And so, after Gwen's first month among her new neighbors, no more regular conversations occurred inside of that crypt.

She turned around and collapsed onto her bed, face-down. *This place will be the death of us,* the voice muttered in her head.

She made herself laugh with that intrusive thought. Death's reach was eternal, shared by all creatures who lived then, now, and ever shall... but it would never come for her without one of two things: A bullet forged of silver, or an alleged cure for her condition.

This place cannot be the death of us, the voice admitted.

When Jack returned to the observatory, Waylon was nowhere to be found. Along with his new toy.

Jack roamed the halls of the mansion in search of his employer, his skills as a tracker proving useful in mundane life. He stopped at the open door on an adjacent corridor, around the corner from the hallway's end.

The trophy room.

The walls were adorned with glass display cases of all sizes. They encompassed the room, covering everywhere except the entryway, and housed things nobody owned in the world but the mad poacher to whom they belonged: The skull of a vampire, a set of teeth from a Creature, the severed tendril of a Mechimigardion, the preserved skeleton of a werewolf, and countless other victims of Waylon's unprecedented career coated his surroundings.

On each display case was a loose piece of paper with Hoxton's handwriting. Some had Waylon's as well. They were reprinted entries from Hoxton's journal, organized by whichever case housed what Hoxton had already written about.

Waylon stood in the center of it all, his hands folded behind his back. Basking in his own work.

It's where he went to think.

Jack approached his side. This time, Waylon could feel the silent footsteps hitting the ground beside him.

"Did she get it?" Waylon asked.

"She did."

Jack had been around Waylon long enough to recognize when he was distraught. Amidst his assistant's silence, Waylon finally shared what was on his mind.

"The Gargoyle's words bothered me, Jack."

"The Gargoyle is docile," said Jack in a reassuring tone.

"I know..."

Jack studied Waylon's face closely.

"You're still worried," Jack pointed out.

Waylon pondered how to explain it.

"He's... something else," said Waylon. "He's so normal, usually. So nice. But he's interested in the same things that I am, and he has a lot more time to accomplish what he wants. I only have the century that I'm given."

"You're not dying anytime soon," said Jack. "That one just likes to hear himself talk."

Waylon chuckled. "So do I. Nasty habit."

After a lull, Jack raised his only concern: "She wants her freedom."

Waylon turned to the sound of Jack's voice, but looked at the ground. There was no point in trying to establish any eye contact.

"If you were me," Waylon asked, "would you give it to her?"

Jack remained silent, unsure of his answer. But Waylon was patient enough.

"If I had to choose one to release," Jack admitted, "I think it'd be her."

Waylon smiled to himself. He knew his assistant had an affinity for women in need of rescuing, so he took those comments with a grain of salt.

"The vampire and the ghost had their usual debate," Waylon said apathetically. "I don't understand either of them. They fear what others might do to them, yet kill those too weak to escape them... I've treated this crypt of monsters better than they've ever treated each other. Tell me how *I'm* the enemy."

"It happens when they're left alone," said Jack dismissively. "Arguments are all they have behind those bars... Anything else I should know?"

Waylon recalled one last thing, pulling him out of that dreary state of mind.

"Hoxton took his journal," said Waylon, his personality returning.

"Should I retrieve it?"

Waylon looked back to the wall of trophies. He inspected certain details in the taxidermied Creature's head on one of the plaques behind the glass. The eyes never quite looked the same as they did when it was alive.

"Not yet," said Waylon. "He should study my revisions."

XII
A HUNCHBACK'S BANE

The frigid air atop the cathedral's roof made the man shiver, for he had only forlorn, weathered rags to keep him warm. He had a name by birth, but all who saw that twisted spine of his called him *Hunchback* and nothing more, so the man had taken it as his own. Paris never looked so appealing from any gaze other than high, high up in the air as one hung from the gargoyle's body beside the belltower of the cathedral.

There was a therapeutic nature to watching the people move far down below. The hunchback's eyes were astute: They saw incredible distances and picked out surprising detail in the pure darkness of these Paris nights. He lived there unbeknownst to the building's inhabitants, for no place would hire him or provide a home. Oftentimes, he'd overhear the church's ceremonies, and when he could, followed the words of the preachers when they talked of morals and themes from the Bible's many passages. He reflected on them after the hours of congregation, overlooking the vast nighttime skyline of Paris in 1482.

For these reasons and many others, that night seemed like any other night for him. It would prove to be otherwise, beginning with the chill that came about from nowhere.

It was a weird, untimely gall of wind that glid over the hunchback's skin and made the half-man shiver. It was an omen of the theatrics about to brew on the rooftop before him. He could see out onto it and walk across it as though it were a ledge, but *rarely* did since it was in more plain a view of the Parisian citizens far below. This place, however, was where the remarkable event took place.

A quick noise like a thunderbolt accommodated the flash of smoke on the rooftop about twenty feet away. These thick fumes shrouded the figure inside, slowly dissipating to reveal him: A man, tall and healthy, and in the very prime of his life. He had a handsome face and strange, embroidered clothing looking to be custom-tailored, and many garments of jewelry strewn across his hands and wrists.

The hunchback was in awe.

The man, who was known only as legend by a myriad of terms like *wizard* or *sorcerer,* looked out over the very same skyline that the hunchback usually enjoyed. It was marvelous and unmatchable from anywhere else.

"Where did you come from?" asked the hunchback.

The sorcerer spun around defensively. He hadn't expected anybody up here.

"Nowhere of note," said the man. "Who are you?"

"Hunchback," he replied.

The sorcerer didn't know how to respond.

"Your name is Hunchback?"

"It is the only one I know," said the hunchback.

This only stoked the sorcerer's growing confusion.

"How often do you leave this cathedral?" the sorcerer asked, noting the shoddy way the hunchback conducted himself, along with the old, unclean clothes.

The hunchback paused. He was trying to *abridge* something that was very complicated.

"I was a boy the last time I did so," said the hunchback. "It is why the deformities on my face have deep, cutting scars."

The sorcerer looked around the cathedral's rooftop.

"You eat, sleep, shit in and around this place of worship?" the sorcerer asked. "Every single day?"

The hunchback reluctantly nodded. Before the sorcerer could ask anything more, the hunchback interrupted with his own burning curiosities.

"You practice magic," the hunchback pointed out.

The sorcerer became skeptical, and the hunchback noticed it.

"Everybody who asks me about that is *looking* for something," said the sorcerer. "Shall I count you in the community of beggars or of onlookers?"

The hunchback became silent, bowing his head in embarrassment.

The sorcerer looked back over the Parisian city, taking in more of the place's view. Melting away his grievances, his troubles. The beauty of it all acted as a calming agent to his immense, underlying frustrations with the people in this world.

But the night remained silent only for a few passing moments.

"If it's not too much trouble..." the hunchback began.

The sorcerer turned back to the hunchback with an expression colder than the night's air.

"It's just that..."

Where's the ask, thought the sorcerer.

"...I need you to change me," said the hunchback. "My spine, my features. Grant me strength I do not have, a body I do not own. Gift me only that which is gifted to everybody else at birth. Nothing more."

The sorcerer kept glaring at the hunchback with his silent hatred.

"It's a few minutes of your time," said the hunchback, "but a lifetime of fortunes for me."

"They all say that," said the sorcerer.

"But it's true!" the hunchback pleaded.

"You know what else is true?" the sorcerer exclaimed. "Everybody has their problems. Everybody. If you fix one person's problems - just *one* - then all others follow suit with problems of their own. 'My loved one has died.' 'I don't have any money.' 'The one I love doesn't return my feelings.' On and on and on these people whine and complain to me about problems, and if I say no - *God forbid* I say no - they cite the *one time* that I decided to do something generous. As if that means they're *owed* anything from me."

The hunchback watched on marvelously as the sorcerer, full-force, was nowhere near done with his rant.

"And you know what *more*, Hunchback? For those who aren't sorcerers, the problems I solve are like the head of a Hydra. Cut off one, three more appear in its place. I give somebody money. Two days later, that same person comes back to me asking how to get out of his debts, how to get family members off of his back, how to track down the ones who robbed him... Nobody's ever *happy* with their lives, Hunchback, no matter how many problems get solved."

The sorcerer finally cooled down. He looked again at the city scape, and talked more cordially about what was on his mind.

"It's why I'm here, you know," said the sorcerer more solemnly. "I've come to listen only to the slight whistling of the night's wind. It's a grand escape from my daily obligations... An escape from the people who *obligate* me in the first place."

The hunchback approached his side.

"It's the greatest view I've ever known," said the hunchback sincerely.

The sorcerer raised an eyebrow at the hunchback. It was the first thing they'd agreed on thus far.

"Sorcery knows no amateurs," said the sorcerer. "I've spent my time in life studying and honing and *mastering* these practices. You're a beggar who ought to start paying rent to this place. And what do you expect of me, Hunchback? Transmute you into a nobleman to sleep with droves of women? Suspend you to live a million years?"

"*Normalcy*," spoke the hunchback harshly, not taking his eyes away from the city scape. "My spine has made me weak. I can't lament how women scream at my face's sight, because my body, too, is unworthy of their love. Their rage is justified. My existence is an abhorrent mistake, abandoned by parents I know nothing of. I ask of you, sorcerer, for one spell to cast and one only: I don't need your powers or immortalities or anything likewise. I need only what everybody else is already granted at birth. Make me a common man with a common figure, and I will be happier than all who take it for granted like you."

The sorcerer paused. The hunchback's words were audacious, and laden with insults. Much like his own.

"A commoner's luxury is a hunchback's bane," said the hunchback.

The sorcerer shook his head.

"I am indifferent to your problems, Hunchback."

"I'll give you reason not to be."

The sorcerer laughed. If nothing else, his companion atop that cathedral had become an excellent source of entertainment.

"You have something to offer me?"

"Two, actually," said the hunchback. "Wisdom and anonymity."

"How do you mean?"

"You talk as though every time you walk down the street and perform your spells, you're swarmed and mobbed with needy peasants," the hunchback started confidently. "Nobody, ever, for any reason whatsoever, has or will ever mob me for anything. They fear me as though I'm a rodent invading their home. I'm a vermin to this world. If there is somewhere you'd rather not go, something you'd rather not do... I'd be obliged to do it for you."

"But you don't leave this cathedral," said the sorcerer.

"I choose not to," said the hunchback. "That doesn't mean I don't know *how.*"

The sorcerer pondered this deeply. It wasn't difficult to find people who came pleading to him with their wants and desires. After all, a sorcerer's powers were undefined to the outside world, and therefore seemed limitless. But that wasn't the same as one poor, desperate soul, making an ungodly offer.

"This is your anonymity," said the sorcerer. "What of *wisdom?*"

"I'll save that until after you fix my spine."

The sorcerer scoffed. Whether he realized it or not, this hunchback was rapidly growing on him.

"I could cast a spell and force you to tell me," said the sorcerer.

"I could bash your head in with a rock," said the hunchback. "I reckon my way is faster."

The sorcerer shook his head, trying to remove his smile. He couldn't deny that a part of him was actually enjoying this.

"*Anonymity...*" the sorcerer repeated under his breath.

The hunchback turned to him, reading his face.

"You have an idea," said the hunchback.

"How do you know that?"

"It's all I do," said the hunchback. "I watch people think. I've become quite good at it."

The sorcerer conceded, and that ghastly idea came pouring out of him.

"There is another sorcerer like myself who takes solace from the world in times of stress," he began. "He rests not on a cathedral such as this, but atop his own house on the coast of the River Seine. It's not twenty blocks from here. I've wanted him dead for many years, but I cannot expose myself as his would-be-assassin. I can have no connection to it."

The sorcerer opened his jacket, and out came a very strange creature.

It was a goblin, taller than two feet but shorter than three, with long, lanky limbs that bent backward at will. Thick, black skin coated the tiny creature as it moved almost mechanically across the ground. The eyes of the goblin were closed shut and filled with two patches of sand.

In the goblin's hand was a long, jagged stiletto. He held it up to the hunchback by the blade.

"Kill the man named Alfred Louis," said the sorcerer. "Leave no trace of him."

The hunchback took the stiletto and inspected the blade's sharp, irregular edge. No armor in any knight's arsenal would protect against a well-placed strike with it.

"If you see this task to fruition, Hunchback," the sorcerer said as he opened his coat for the goblin to return, "I will repair your spine, remove the deformities from your face, and grant you exceptional strength. If you fail, you will become something even uglier than what you are. Something so repulsive that Satan himself would cower at the sight of you."

The hunchback pocketed the blade, bewildered by the sight of the blinded goblin robotically returning to where he came from.

"With all the magic you wield," said the hunchback, "you arm me with a commoner's weapon?"

The sorcerer smiled.

"Anonymity," he said snidefully.

The hunchback passed through the streets, gutters, and sewers amidst the passing whispers of an oblivious crowd.

The outside walls of the second sorcerer's house were easy to ascend for a creature whose only life was a Parisian vagrant. His hands and feet grappled with flawless dexterity up and onto each ledge, windowsill, grotesque, or chimera strong enough to hold his weight. Everything and anything adorning a building's side were as simple to him as the rungs on a common man's ladder.

In seconds, the hunchback's hand reached the highest part's edge and heaved him up onto the shingles of the second sorcerer's roof.

The view was comparable to the cathedral's. Slightly inferior, if anything.

The hunchback took his rest in this place and leaned his back against the chimney, watching the birds fly in unison above him. *Something* must've governed them to flock together as one. Watching this unknown phenomenon served as the hunchback's pastime until the second sorcerer joined him on this rooftop.

And so he did.

It was not a fanciful portal made of gales and snow. A group of shingles moved up to reveal an unseen hatch, and beneath them, a middle-aged man in a commoner's change of clothes emerged and looked out over the adjacent river. The hunchback hid himself behind the chimney and stood still, careful to steady his breath into a silence.

The second sorcerer, Alfred Louis, sat cross-legged and closed his eyes.

The hunchback peered around the chimney's edge. The shingles around Alfred had a similar set of blood-written symbols in a circular fashion, with Alfred at the center of it. Within moments, Alfred's body began to quietly float, and a cloud of mist emanated from his body, orbiting him slowly.

The hunchback crept out from behind the chimney.

Steady footsteps approached Alfred, whose back was turned and whose eyes weren't open. *This is the perfect time,* thought the hunchback, whose hand creeped closer to the dagger in his waistband.

Alfred's head suddenly turned, motivated by a strange, otherworldly form of detection difficult for the uninitiated to comprehend. It was a byproduct of spending so long in the astral plane.

Alfred saw the hunchback in total fear standing behind him. The orbiting mist dissipated, and his legs met the ground as his body lowered from the hovering meditation. The hunchback dropped to his knees and put his hands in the air, accepting whatever fate this sorcerer had in mind for him.

"Why are you here?" Alfred calmly asked.

The hunchback noted that the sorcerer's tone was *friendly*. No trace of anger whatsoever.

"I..." the hunchback began, puzzled at the fact that he was still alive.

Alfred put his hands up disarmingly.

"It's alright, hunchback," said Alfred. "I'm not going to hurt you."

"Why not?" the hunchback asked.

Alfred didn't understand the question.

"Why *would* I?" Alfred asked.

The hunchback looked around him. He was clearly intruding, and his intentions were far worse than that. But this home's owner didn't seem interested.

"I'm sorry," said the hunchback. "I'll leave, if it's what you prefer-"

"Stay," said Alfred, "and ask the questions that are *really* on your mind."

The hunchback took a breath. He needed a moment to formulate his thoughts, and certainly his plan.

"Where did the mist come from?" The hunchback asked.

"Mist?" Alfred asked.

"When you..." the hunchback started, unsure how to describe it.

Alfred smiled.

"I was in the astral plane," said Alfred. "I go there when I need to think."

"I'm sorry to have interrupted your thinking," said the hunchback.

Alfred laughed.

"Hardly," said Alfred. "I was in there for almost a human lifetime."

The hunchback blinked hard.

"Time works differently there," Alfred explained.

Unexpectedly, Alfred extended his hand to the hunchback.

"Would you like to learn how?" Alfred offered.

The hunchback didn't believe it.

"You've only just met me," said the hunchback.

"You can tell a lot about a person when they come to your house in need," said Alfred. "The world could always use more sorcerers."

In need. This wasn't exactly true, but the hunchback obliged. He took Alfred's hand.

In the hunchback's hand, Alfred placed a book open to a certain page:

ASTROMANCY

Beneath the emboldened letters were dozens of spells, all in Latin, regarding the human soul.

"These spells are for the living," said Alfred, "and can only be *performed* by the living. That means you only have the rest of your life to study them."

The hunchback became possessed by a fascinating idea.

"Do you have a book on transmutation?" the hunchback asked.

Alfred turned pale.

"That magic is *dangerous*," warned Alfred. "There is only one sorcerer I know of who practices Vertomancy, and he *shouldn't...*"

Alfred's passion evolved into skepticism. For the very first time on that roof, he looked back at the hunchback adversarially.

"How do you know about transmutation?" Alfred asked.

The hunchback didn't move.

"I... just assumed," said the hunchback.

"You didn't assume," said Alfred. "There are only several types of magic men can wield. That's one of them, and the only sorcerer I know who wields it also happens to live in Paris."

Alfred scanned the hunchback's body.

Having read people for a very long time, the hunchback knew instantly the types of questions that Alfred was about to ask. *Did you meet him? Did he give you something? Are you only here to kill me?*

Like the rest of his life thus far, the hunchback avoided a fight.

The hunchback turned and tried to run. Alfred grabbed the hunchback's shirt and yanked him back, causing him to stumble.

The dagger fell from the hunchback's waistband.

The hunchback grabbed it instantly, but Alfred grabbed the handle too, and the two of them struggled for a few moments as they almost tossed each other to the ground. Alfred's elbow whacked the hunchback in his temple, causing the hunchback to instinctively push Alfred's body away.

As this happened, the hunchback's dagger plummeted into Alfred's chest, severing multiple arteries.

Alfred reeled in pain and collapsed on the roof, surrounded by the ring of symbols. The hunchback ran up to him in a panic.

"I'm sorry!" the hunchback yelled over and over. "I'm sorry! I'm sorry! I'm sorry!"

The dagger in Alfred's chest disintegrated into sand, which slowly migrated away. It was only then that the hunchback realized that the blade was *cursed* in some way, and probably thirsted for blood.

It was no coincidence that the brief scuffle ended the way that it did.

"*YOU...*" Alfred began, soon unable to speak.

The hunchback snatched up the book and backed out of the ring of symbols.

"I can save you!!" the hunchback yelled, frantically skimming the spells on the page.

Alfred tried to crawl over to him, but his blood was draining out of his body too quickly. His eyes began to close.

The hunchback found a spell designed to save somebody's soul.

Having never spoken Latin, the hunchback did his absolute best in reciting the incantations. He actively ignored the sound of Alfred's final breaths being taken, and didn't dare to look at the sorcerer's body. It would only distract him.

Some of the symbols caught fire, but quickly went out when the hunchback stuttered and choked on his own words.

The hunchback didn't quit. He kept on repeating the incantation, pronouncing certain syllables differently than before.

The symbols went ablaze once again, *all* of them this time, and the flames wavered in the growing winds around the ring. Mist swirled in what seemed like a miniature tornado over Alfred's body.

As the hunchback completed the incantation, the swirling group of mist dissipated throughout the surrounding air.

The spell was complete.

The hunchback inspected Alfred's lifeless body, confused as to why nothing had happened.

"Alfred..." the hunchback said softly.

The corpse did not move.

"He told you my name..."

The ethereal voice came from everywhere, all around the hunchback, but originated only from the thing above Alfred's body.

The hunchback looked up to see the intangible shape of a man hovering over him with a scowl on his translucent face, and all of the fear in the world took hold of the hunchback's frail, timid form. With a controlled descent, the hunchback ran and leapt off of the rooftop before the Phantom could do any harm to him.

The sorcerer at the cathedral watched as the hunchback pulled himself up onto the ledge, and smiled at his return.

"Is it done?" the sorcerer asked.

The hunchback's face was void of any color. The trauma of what had just happened to him was still fresh, gnawing away at his thoughts infectiously.

"I killed Alfred Louis," said the hunchback.

"Wonderful," said the sorcerer. "Stand over there."

The sorcerer gestured to a freshly-painted ring of symbols on the rooftop beside them. He'd painted two: One for himself, and one for the hunchback. The intricacies of how these spells worked were still a mystery to him, but the hunchback continued to have faith. He stood in the empty ring of symbols.

From inside the ring, the hunchback noticed the sorcerer tilt his head back, and suddenly, the sorcerer's eyes went completely white. Wind began to circle the sorcerer's ring of symbols, along with the collection of mist now emanating from the sorcerer's body.

Before the hunchback could say anything, the mist dissipated and the sorcerer's eyes reverted back to how they were.

"He's not dead," said the sorcerer.

"I assure you he is," said the hunchback.

"Don't lie to me," said the sorcerer. "He's not in the astral plane."

The hunchback hung his head in shame.

"I'm not lying," he admitted. "Alfred is dead. Your dagger turned to sand, and his body fell to the ground."

The sorcerer glared at the hunchback.

"Then why can't I see him?"

The hunchback looked back up at him with pain in his eyes.

"I tried to save him..."

"What did you do?!" the sorcerer said, now becoming concerned.

From his waistband, the hunchback pulled out the book of Astromancy.

The sorcerer's eyes widened.

"What spell did you cast?!"

"I attempted to save his soul-"

The sorcerer crossed into the hunchback's ring and grabbed him by the collar. He glared straight into his eyes.

"What - did - you - do?!"

"He's *bound!!*" the hunchback admitted.

The sorcerer released him.

"To his house?"

The hunchback nodded.

"You killed a sorcerer and bound him to his own house for eternity?"

Again, the hunchback nodded.

The sorcerer sat with this for a moment. He turned away, looking out over the night's skyline.

"The blade was cursed, wasn't it?" the hunchback asked.

The sorcerer solemnly walked back over to his own ring.

"Wasn't it?!"

"It was," said the sorcerer without looking back at him. "Those sands will find their way back to their shorelines from whence they were retrieved."

"Why did you have me kill him?"

The sorcerer turned back to him, no longer processing what had transpired. His mind was finally clear: The hunchback followed the task instructed, but didn't accomplish the intent whatsoever.

"He holds a position of power that I seek," said the sorcerer. "His death would've allowed me to take it overnight..."

The sorcerer sighed. This situation was a catastrophe.

"But not with his spirit still roaming our world," said the sorcerer.

The hunchback became enraged.

"He seemed like a good man," said the hunchback.

"He *was* one," said the sorcerer.

Biting his tongue, the hunchback extended his arms, wanting nothing more to do with this sorcerer after he was repaid.

"Cast your spell," said the hunchback. "I took his life. I'm owed my restitution."

"Restitution?!" the sorcerer scoffed. "You've made matters worse than they ever were!"

"*I took his life,*" the hunchback repeated. "That's *all* that was asked of me."

From across the rooftop, the sorcerer eyed down his opponent. *He had a point.*

"I don't know whether to strengthen your body and align your spine for killing him, or have you turned abominable for failing me," said the sorcerer in deliberation.

The hunchback remained exactly how he was, and said nothing, stewing quietly in his own anger.

"As both reward and punishment, it's only fair that you experience both," said the sorcerer, who moved his hands in a purposeful way.

The hunchback watched as the ground's symbols blazed into an inferno, producing a thin wall of smoke in the ring around him. Thicker, deeper black smoke began to emerge from the hunchback's own body.

"*SORCERER!!*" the hunchback screamed.

His hands changed first: The vapors of smoke emanating from them grew painful, more threatening than before. The fingertips caught fire with immutable flames. The hunchback waved and shook his hands as hard as he could, smacking them against his own body, and changing nothing about the combustion. The fire steadily grew and migrated down his fingers and onto his palms, scorching the skin and tissue underneath. The hunchback screamed and tried to escape the circle, but smoke clouded his vision, and the mounting pain quickly caused him to collapse onto all fours.

When he landed, catching himself on the rooftop's tiles, the hunchback noticed the new anatomy of his hands.

The raging fire accelerated in its expansion, consuming the hunchback in a wild inferno localized entirely on his fast-changing body. What was once skin now smoldered and thickened, changing form entirely to a jet-black mineral, and what was once a small, scrawny half-man was now a much larger beast. The hunchback more than tripled in body mass by the end of it, and the end was fast-approaching: The flames subsided amidst the completion of the new creature, whose hulking body simmered in the dissipating smoke.

The hunchback was no more. He'd died a painful death on that cathedral's rooftop. Born from his pain was a Gargoyle.

The sorcerer smiled. He'd cast many spells in his early career of alchemy. Many creations. Many destructions. None had been so rewarding as what he'd just done.

With a pair of eyes only reminiscent of two shiny black orbs, the Gargoyle looked up at his associate and glared. Instead of fingertips, giant claws dug their way into the rooftop's tile, stabilizing his body for the wings on his back to unfurl. Their true length was a remarkable sight for the sorcerer, instilling more awe and wonder than the sight of a thousand Parisian skylines. Quickly, the awe faded. The sorcerer realized what was happening.

The Gargoyle beat its wings and pulled at the ground in unison, launching forward with a blinding speed at the hapless sorcerer. With a few quick hand gestures, the symbols around the sorcerer caught fire, and a chilling breeze orbited the man. With fanged teeth and an outstretched claw, the Gargoyle swiped at the localized snowstorm and hit only the air inside of it.

The sorcerer vanished.

Forcefully, the Gargoyle landed in the center of the sorcerer's ring of symbols. His mighty body tumbled and slid, distorting some of them. The Gargoyle whipped its head around and watched as the snow blew away in the soft nighttime winds.

The Gargoyle screamed.

Years were spent in careful silence and solitude atop that monumental cathedral. Years spent to maintain a level of invisibility and namelessness, such that onlookers would have trouble finding and eradicating the cathedral's unwanted tenant. None of the hunchback's anonymity mattered to the Gargoyle.

The Gargoyle looked down at his own arm. The residue of falling snow from the sorcerer's escape accreted onto his arm's stone-like skin, building up a thin layer. It became more and more opaque with each passing moment. The Gargoyle gave no body heat to melt it. So long as it stayed cold enough, he could keep it there all night.

The sorcerer, with a beard now grayed and a face full of sagging wrinkles, sat alone in his study on the west wing of the old mansion. He'd had it built in the recently-discovered Americas, yet had the power to travel further west than Columbus would ever live to explore and colonize. Every element of this house was upkept to an extreme standard, as though a cult of housekeepers swarmed every room hourly. If one stepped foot through one of the ivory thresholds onto the polished, pristine hardwood floors, they'd never be able to guess that this sorcerer lived alone.

At his desk, the sorcerer's staff was laid out delicately before him while he tinkered away at it. He was holding a sharp needle, which carried one minuscule drop of his own blood.

The winds began to circulate.

The sorcerer turned slowly away from his books. He recognized this spell, this specific form of wizardry. He was only confused as to who ever it could be, porting through straight into his home.

Frost and snowflakes adorned the swirling wind as the thunderous display rampaged on, knocking some of the sorcerer's many books off of the shelves.

The sorcerer didn't stand up from his seat.

A clashing *bang!* accompanied the sudden arrival of a familiar, long-lost soul behind the icy air. A soul made completely of stone.

And the sorcerer's eyes went wide.

As the snow faded, the abominable Gargoyle stepped forward, revealing his full, wicked form to his creator, and the sorcerer marveled at the supernatural beast standing before him.

"I never thought you'd find me," said the sorcerer in a raspy voice.

The Gargoyle took in his surroundings. The walls were painted white - *perfect* white - and carried with them some of the finest portraits and paintings he'd ever seen.

"Is this how a wizard lives?" the Gargoyle asked. "Greedy and alone?"

The sorcerer sighed, preparing himself for this conversation.

"You aren't capable of killing me," said the sorcerer.

The Gargoyle cocked his head to the side, and observed the sorcerer quizzically.

"Don't delay," the sorcerer insisted upon his unwelcome houseguest. "Launch your strongest attack. See if I turn to dust."

"I have no attack in mind."

"Oh, don't you?" the sorcerer scoffed. "Have you come all this way for a conversation?"

The Gargoyle paused at the thought.

"I do like a good conversation," said the Gargoyle. "I haven't been able to have conversations with anybody before you cursed me-"

"It was not a *curse-*"

"Must you interrupt?" the Gargoyle interjected. "I'm well-versed in Defixiomancy. I was speaking hyperbolically."

The sorcerer was stupefied by the Gargoyle's rhetoric.

The Gargoyle shook his head, taking a long, calming breath as he did so.

"You told me that sorcery knows no amateurs," said the Gargoyle. "I wrote and rewrote all of the symbols on that roof over and over again. I thought I'd run out of animal blood after a while. It all brought me *nowhere at all...*"

The Gargoyle stepped closer and closer to the sorcerer as he spoke. Behind him, the sorcerer hovered his hand over the staff on his desk.

"It took years, and years, and *years* of trial and error to replicate your skills," said the Gargoyle. "All day, every *single* day, without sleep, without food, without the slightest *hint* of an amateur's tendency to concede before victory is had. You joked about suspending me... Stone doesn't age the same as flesh. Perhaps I will live to see those million years you spoke of in jest. I can think of *excellent* ways to spend an immortal life..."

The sorcerer grabbed the staff and aimed it at the Gargoyle.

Just as fast, the Gargoyle's tail ensnared the staff and snatched it out of the sorcerer's hand.

The Gargoyle finally came close enough to grab the sorcerer by the neck with his large, coal-black claw, and lift him right up out of his seat.

The sorcerer only had one leg.

The Gargoyle saw this and placed him back onto his chair, taking a small step back in the process. Ashamedly, the sorcerer reached out towards his staff.

After a moment of consideration, the Gargoyle's tail put the staff back into the sorcerer's hands. The sides of the staff were engraved, as the Gargoyle quickly recognized, with symbols conducive to Defixiomancy.

They came from every unseen corner and crevice of the house.

Small, imp-like creatures gathered before them from all directions. Their skin tones were varying shades and hues of green, and their faces were plain and stoic. They used their lanky limbs to scutter across the walls, floor, ceiling, assembling at the sorcerer's location.

The Gargoyle recognized them as goblins, and noticed that all of their eyes were filled with sand.

The group of goblins built themselves into a small pillar beneath the sorcerer, connecting with where his leg began, and the sorcerer stood up on his own.

"You've cursed them all," said the Gargoyle in bewilderment.

In his enemy's presence, the sorcerer had no reason to keep any secrets.

"I didn't stop at Alfred's death," said the sorcerer. "I killed many on my way to the top. Almost got there, too. A mutiny formed under my nose..."

Recalling his past became painful for him.

"They made me *choose*," said the sorcerer.

"Choose what?" The Gargoyle asked.

Unable to stop it, the sorcerer became emotional.

"My arm or my leg," he said, almost choking on his own words.

The Gargoyle stepped forward once again, seeing the sorcerer take a moment to gather himself. The sight of the goblins moving beneath him, masquerading themselves as one of the sorcerer's legs with their eyes blocked out amidst the sentient sand, reminded the Gargoyle of the way the accursed dagger fled the scene of the murder, as Alfred Louis crawled on the ground enduring a torturous pain.

He did not need to reap the vengeance he sought. Time would do it for him. Time had already begun to.

"I am indifferent to your life's problems, sorcerer," said the Gargoyle maliciously.

The sorcerer's eyes lit up in fear.

The Gargoyle didn't strike his opponent, despite the lingering desire to.

"I don't know whether to thank you for the boundless amounts of time your transmutation has given me, or watch you endure an inescapable encounter with death. As both reward and punishment, it's only fair that you experience both."

The Gargoyle shoved him down into his chair with a controlled amount of force. Not too hard to cause serious injury. Not too soft as to have no effect. As this happened, the sorcerer's staff fell out of his hand, snatched up by the

Gargoyle's swift catch.

The group of goblins below the sorcerer dissipated around his body.

"Thank you," said the Gargoyle through gritted teeth.

It was the very last thing the sorcerer heard before losing consciousness.

The Gargoyle watched the sorcerer's body intently, making sure it was still breathing. After Alfred, he'd already vowed to never take another life. Forcing a deep sleep with a small concussion would be the extent of his wrath on this man.

Holding the staff firmly in his hand, the Gargoyle snapped it in half.

The sand fell from the goblin's eyes, no longer motivated by magic. The goblins aggressively rubbed their eyes free of it, and finally caught a sight of their demonic savior with both halves of the staff in his hand.

The Gargoyle nodded to them, and they nodded back. Then, their stoic faces turned into little devilish smiles.

And the Gargoyle left.

Time was the most effective weapon in the Gargoyle's arsenal. No mortal could ever avoid it.

The Gargoyle returned to this place several decades later and found the descendants of the goblins he'd freed, welcoming their legendary hero with praise and glory. They'd claimed complete and total ownership over the house.

The Gargoyle explored the corridors and pathways leading to all of the sorcerer's collected treasures. Swords and daggers of bygone eras adorned certain passageways, and the skeletal fossils of some primordial demons were reassembled behind glass cages with impeccable detail. This place was a monument to the relics and knowledge the sorcerer had accreted throughout his long-gestating lifetime, and the Gargoyle could recognize all of the time and dedication that went into a place like this. The Gargoyle intended on doing the same, one day. Whatever century he got around to it.

After a long, in-depth tour of the sorcerer's former home, facilitated by the more-than-welcoming goblins, the Gargoyle encountered the final room behind a large set of doors.

It was a library.

The Gargoyle lit up like a light when he walked inside and saw it: Long, parallel shelves coated every wall, full to the brim with a near-endless amount of books. More reading material than any one man could ever sift through.

No bane for an immortal to handle.

With the goblin's permission, the Gargoyle strolled to the bookshelf's furthest edge, and grabbed the top-most book on the very left of the shelf. He opened the cover and began to read. It wouldn't be until almost two thousand books later when the Gargoyle would find a book alluding to transmutation, referencing a potential account of it written on a runestone somewhere near Norway.

XIII

SIGMA'S FIVE VISITORS

I

The Castaway in 1896

When the day was young, this stranded seaman had been a cabin boy aboard a minor seafaring vessel. That ship had sunk on account of the Atlantic Ocean's tendency to inhibit man's desire to travel over water, manifesting this primordial wrath in the wicked forms of storms and hurricanes. The Castaway was no stranger to these threatening conditions, but the same could not be said of his inexperienced captain. This was why that ship, and every other soul on board, now rested with Davy Jones at the distant bottom of the roaring sea.

The Castaway wore old rags and a bandana on his head to keep the sweat out of his eyes. He carried nothing more than a knife on one side and a drink of whiskey on his other. This was all that he needed in the world to survive this island.

The island became his salvation whether he wished it or not.

This place was luscious in every meaning; Tall trees and thick shrubbery adorned the inside of the island rather generously, lending itself to be painted onto an astute artist's oil-doused canvas. The flora was prominent and full of wonder. The fauna remained unseen.

In the island's center was a large rocky peak, with a current flowing through it that culminated into a tiny waterfall on its furthest edge.

On the first night of his unwitting exile, the Castaway laid next to a large boulder on the island's shoreline. He planned on recovering his strength with a long, powerful sleep before chopping down trees and attempting to construct something out of it in the morning. That plan did not come to fruition.

The Castaway awoke suddenly to a strange pain in his leg. He looked down at it, struggling to clearly see the area in the faint moonlight. It was near his shin, not far from his calf, and it grew larger than any pimple or blemish ever could. The area was begging to be scratched.

Without a second thought, the Castaway started scratching away at the area, which felt like some weird rash no doctor had ever documented. As he checked his surroundings, finding nothing in the immediate area, the Castaway caught a glimpse of something far-off the size of a bear, crawling away with a litany of many-jointed legs.

Now alert, the Castaway stood up and drew his knife.

Silence coated the air, albeit for the humming of the trees as the insects sang their mating calls and the soft crashing of waves on the island's shore. The Castaway spun around, seeing nothing different as before. He turned forward again and saw the beast that had bitten him.

It was the size of a man but only partially bore a man's likeness. Parts of it were human, like the legs, abdomen, and some of the arms, but the rest of the monster carried traits of a large insect, scaled up even larger to match the beast's body. From the snout, a long, tendrilous appendage dripped with the Castaway's blood.

This monster had a name on that island, for it was the One Who Drains.

The Castaway swung the knife laterally, trying to slice the tendril straight off of the monster's face. He succeeded only in wounding the One Who Drains, and tremendously agitating it. It tackled the Castaway faster than he could react, cracking his back on the boulder's edge as it pinned him down. The One Who Drains plunged its appendage straight into the Castaway's chest, sucking and ingesting the gore out of the man's bloodstream. The Castaway dropped the knife, unable to remain conscious any longer than he had.

The One Who Drains was forcibly torn away from the Castaway's body.

It turned around, the Castaway's blood still dripping from his mouth, and saw the One Who Crawls. A humanoid with a spider's features.

The One Who Drains smacked the One Who Crawls in the head, prompting a brief brawl with legs and tendrils swatting viciously at each other. Swiftly, the One Who Crawls pinned the One Who Drains against a tree, ending the spat unceremoniously. The One Who Crawls released his opponent, glaring at him with all eight of his eyes. Solemnly, the One Who Crawls shook his head to either side.

The two of them looked back to the Castaway's body, blood still oozing from the hole in the corpse's chest. They then looked at each other, mutually recognizing that a meal would *not* be made of this man. The One Who Dwells Below wouldn't want that.

II

The Explorer in 1922

The landing of *The Queen's Legacy* was performed rather smoothly by the Explorer in the shining light of noontime.

The Explorer's ship had ventured and wandered far from the coastline of late 19th-century Europe, with the express intention of stopping only at the first uncharted area. It had taken a great deal of convincing by the Explorer to gain approval from the British Empire for this expedition. They'd only recently received their funding and endorsement, but the Empire still had little to no faith in their journey, fully expecting them to return empty-handed.

Whatever new territory he'd discover had to be named for their beloved Queen Victoria, as would be enforced by her sponsor.

And so it had come about in a rather ceremonious way for him: He'd assembled a modest crew of three - a seaman, the sponsor, and himself - and attempted to chart what remained uncharted in the faroff Atlantic.

Victoria's Island had finally been founded after several weeks at sea.

The Explorer was first off of the boat, tailed closely by his quartermaster. The sponsor elected to stay on board while the more ambitious of the crew attempted to firmly plant an English flag at the island's peak.

Lethargically, the Explorer drudged through the swampy grounds below his heavy sailor's boots, resisting the mucky Earth as it kept sticking to the bottoms. His sword was drawn, used so far for splitting the many types of vines in his way. Mosquitoes and gnats became a growing nuisance the further into the island's woodlands they went.

The quartermaster had been taking detailed notes of the island's qualities as they went along, intending to report back with the trip's sponsor on his findings.

A strange howling caught both men off guard.

The Explorer ran in the direction of the noise, which almost resembled a person's screech of pain, and the quartermaster followed his path. The noise grew louder as they drew near, but remained unrecognizable. Whatever it was, all that was clear was that it was in pain.

The duo arrived at a small river cutting through the island, and laying on its edge was the beast in question.

The fur was orange, but it only covered most of the creature's body, with sporadic patchings of human skin infused over the rest. Its legs were canine in shape and size, yet were adorned with human hands carrying wolf-like talons. This thing was a melding of a man and a fox, and on this island, it was known as the One Who Runs.

The quartermaster froze in place, halted by a strong sense of fear. Unlike his assistant, the Explorer was propelled by empathy and courage, and ran straight up to the One Who Runs. On the sight of the Explorer, the beast panicked and screamed at him, but didn't attack or move away. The Explorer looked down and saw exactly why: The beast's leg had been wounded.

"The kit!" the Explorer called out to the quartermaster.

Reluctantly, the quartermaster abided. He produced a first aid kit from his gear and gave it to the Explorer, who knelt over the One Who Runs with a strip of gauze.

"Easy..." said the Explorer calmly.

The One Who Runs glared at the Explorer ferociously, watching intently as the strip of gauze came closer and closer to the beast's leg.

"Easy..." the Explorer whispered.

Gently, the Explorer tended to the beast's wound. The One Who Runs occasionally twitched, swiping near the Explorer's head with that set of hybridized talons. The Explorer remained still and tempered as he did what he did.

The One Who Runs stood back up onto all fours, which partially resembled a human being hunching over. It scurried away from the Explorer.

It was stopped by the One Who Crawls.

The Explorer and the quartermaster raised their guards. The One Who Crawls drew closer, and as it did, so too did the One Who Hides: A man with green, scaled skin and a large shell on his back.

The One Who Crawls and the One Who Hides looked solemnly towards each other.

The quartermaster drew a gun from his holster, alerting the creatures. The Explorer recognized this instantly and put out his hand, gesturing for his assistant to lower the weapon.

The One Who Hides communicated nonverbally with the One Who Crawls, and the One Who Runs joined in. The three of them continued a conversation told only through strange movements from their hands. Watching this, the quartermaster panicked again, and disobeyed the Explorer's orders, aiming the gun at the head of the One Who Crawls.

The Explorer shoved the quartermaster's hand out of the way, making him fire at a nearby tree.

The One Who Runs pounced on the quartermaster, tearing out his throat with his teeth, and the Explorer leapt back in bewilderment. He kept steady as he watched his assistant meet his fate. With a crazed look, the One Who Runs looked back and eyed down the Explorer.

Again, the One Who Crawls intervened.

The One Who Hides signed something to the One Who Crawls, who relayed the message to the One Who Runs. From what the Explorer could surmise, it seemed like an argument, and it ended with the One Who Runs subsiding its rage.

The One Who Crawls gestured with one of its eight arms, enticing the Explorer to follow.

The three creatures led the Explorer down a specific path through the winding forest, bringing them indirectly to the island's peak, where there stood a constructed pile of rocks at the top.

They were constructed into a throne.

The One Who Hides came to the peak's edge, right beside the throne, and let out a deep, grating cry to the sky above. It was a call loud enough to be heard from every corner of that island.

In moments, they converged.

From all edges of the island's peak, hybridized men climbed and crawled their way over the ledges and up onto the peak. The Explorer saw them with reverence: The One Who Prowls, a lynx's body twisted with a man's, pounced up briskly from the furthest edge. The One Who Swims, which bore more resemblance to a jellyfish than a man, walked up with slimy tendrils and tentacles like a human would use their legs. An insect-hybrid crawled up from the opposite side, for the One Who Drains had only one wing on his back, unable to fly.

All of the island's inhabitants bowed down as the Queen of Sigma stood from her throne and turned away from the overlook of the peak.

The Queen was draped in a cloak made entirely of human skin. She stood from her seat atop the peak's tallest boulder, and descended the handmade steps of her elaborate throne of rocks and stones. The skin-cloak brushed the ground behind her as she walked, brushing the tip of each step as she neared the Explorer. Atop her head was a crown composed solely of disparate types of teeth, one plucked from each of the island's inhabitants. The only human tooth in her crown once belonged to the Castaway.

The One Who Crawls came by the Explorer's side, signing his story to the Queen.

At the end of the story, the Queen looked to the One Who Runs, observing the bandage around the wound on his leg. She signed something back to the One Who Crawls, who gestured to the One Who Runs. The Explorer stayed still and silently observed.

The One Who Runs removed the bandage, revealing the size and shape of the wound to the Queen. The very moment that he did so, the Queen turned to the One Who Prowls with accusing eyes.

The One Who Prowls tried to run.

With a quick movement as though he were in water, the One Who Swims launched a tentacle towards the One Who Prowls, catching his leg and pulling him down to the ground. He sent an immobilizing shockwave through the One Who Prowls' body. Soon after, the One Who Hides came over and used his immense strength to lift and restrain the One Who Prowls before bringing him over to the Queen, where the One Who Crawls ensnared the One Who Prowls with an intricate set of webbing from his abdomen.

The Explorer's eyes went wide at how fast the One Who Crawls was able to move its eight arms.

Completely subdued, the One Who Prowls wriggled on the ground before the Queen, barely able to move any part of his body. The Queen had warned the One Who Prowls what would happen if he ever tried to feed on one of his brothers again, and it was much harsher than the simple submission he'd just received.

The Queen turned her head once again to the Explorer.

The Explorer started to sweat, but didn't show any signs of nervousness. The Queen came directly in front of the Explorer with a wild look in her eyes and sized up the island's intruder. She looked again to the wound on the One Who Runs' leg, weighing her options.

The Queen reached her hand out and lifted the Explorer's head up by his chin. She grabbed his cheeks and squeezed, inspecting the head thoroughly. The eyes of the Explorer glistened in the morning's light in a powerful, genuine way. She could tell that, unlike the quartermaster or the One Who Prowls, this man was no threat at all. He was exactly the opposite.

The Queen made an easy gesture with her free hand. A moment passed as the Explorer became calm in the revelation that he *wasn't* going to be eaten alive. He looked to his sides, seeing the rest of the island's inhabitants approach all around him, starting to bow down to the Explorer and the Queen.

III

The Farmer in 1925

Almost three years prior to the day of his landing, the Farmer had left his duties on his family's ranch to pursue whatever entity caused the mysterious disappearance of *The Queen's Legacy*. Compounding his agricultural skills in those thirty-one months were nautical ones: Rigging sails, maneuvering a roaring tide, even whaling when needed. He dedicated much of his recent life to this very craft with unshaken commitment, and his determination was fantastically repaid when he finally arrived at Sigma.

He chose to travel down the island's leftmost edge, where the rocks grew larger the further one traveled down the shoreline.

The Farmer started to see the makings of the waterfall adorning the edge of the island's peak, the flow cascading onto and through the layer of old bedrock below. The time was dusk, with the thin clouds overhead unable to fully shield what was left of the day's sunlight. This island smelled strange from the moment he got off of his vessel and planted his feet in the sand below, like a stench of some rotten piece of meat, yet not strong enough to be noticeably revolting.

As the sun started to set, the waterfall's tint veered darker and darker, implying some level of depth behind it.

A twig snapped in half by the Farmer's side, turning his head. It at least *sounded* like it, but he wasn't sure what exactly. He only knew what direction it came from. The Farmer stepped back with one foot, hiding his pocket from view as he slowly reached inside of it.

Soon after, the Farmer heard a sloshing of water from the river behind him.

Tentacles rose up from the water and planted themselves into the bedrock by the Farmer's side, making him jump back instinctively. The One Who Swims stopped short of the Farmer, soaking wet and dripping water all over the ground as it adjusted its many limbs.

The Farmer's heart raced, but he deliberately remained calm.

The One Who Crawls came from the other direction, slowly approaching them both. It waved one of its many arms towards the One Who Swims in a disarming manner. The Farmer looked back to the One Who Swims, who moved a bit back and rescinded itself.

The One Who Crawls eyed the Farmer down, using all of its eyes in unison.

From his pocket, the Farmer produced a photograph.

The One Who Crawls studied the image intently, then looked over to the One Who Swims. A moment later, the One Who Swims held up the only one of its tentacles with a human hand on the end of it. The Farmer watched as it used sign language to communicate with the One Who Crawls, starting a brief conversation.

The One Who Crawls nodded to the Farmer.

The pair of them led the Farmer to the other end of the island's peak, where a massive shell was placed at its base. The One Who Crawls nudged the shell carefully, causing two pairs of limbs to dispatch out of it and prop itself up.

The Farmer had trouble believing everything he was witnessing, but he thought it best not to question everything thus far. This place was like a fever dream, and if he dwelled on it a hair too long, it might vanish just as fast as it came.

That shell belonged to the One Who Hides, who had just been awakened. It looked at the picture in the Farmer's hand, then used its turtle-like eyes on its human-like head to scan the Farmer up and down, critically inspecting every inch of the man. The One Who Hides looked up to the skies next and took a step forward, summoning a deep cry into the heavens above that shook the Farmer down to his bones.

Within moments, an ornithological monster descended upon the group.

The being was coated mostly in feathers, allowing for a seamless takeoff at a moment's notice, and it landed with a set of human-like legs adorned with the razor-sharp talons of a hawk on each end. This creature, aptly named, was known to the island's inhabitants as the One Who Dwells Above, and it gazed upon the Farmer with a predator's fearsome scowl.

The photograph in the Farmer's hand was that of the Explorer, many years before he left in search of this island.

The Farmer's eyes widened.

"Do you recognize me?" the Farmer asked.

The One Who Dwells Above twitched slightly. It was a moment of mutual recognition, despite the hybrid being unable to speak. His vocal cords were closer to those of a bird's than a man's, and any attempted verbal communication would be unintelligible.

Deep down behind that furred exterior, the Explorer's face was present in the beast's revolting head, and the Farmer could see it clearer the more he stared at it. The Explorer's hands had turned into powerful wings, and his legs into sharp talons, but the face of the Farmer's brother was unmistakable to his own kin.

With a gesture, the One Who Dwells Above showed the way, keeping close to the steep face of the island's peak.

The Farmer watched as the surrounding inhabitants followed the One Who Dwells Above, traveling at a slow-enough pace that a man would not lose track of. The Farmer took the hint, and followed fast behind them.

The One Who Dwells Above led the Farmer to the bottom of the island's peak from the opposite side, through a thin chasm small enough only for a man to enter through. He stopped at the entrance and watched the confusion grow on the Farmer's face.

"What is this, brother?" asked the Farmer.

The One Who Dwells Above remained silent, gesturing again to the chasm's opening. The Farmer could see that it led somewhere towards the giant rock's center, and that there was some source of light from deep within. It was too faint to determine without getting closer.

The Farmer looked again to the One Who Dwells Above, then to the entrance. Reluctantly, the Farmer entered the chasm.

His chest and back brushed against the grainy walls of the cave's interior, mildly scraping his arms and legs as he wriggled his way through. As the Farmer got closer to the source of light, the walls widened more and more until he was able to turn and face it, walking normally once again. The sound of falling water got louder and louder.

When the Farmer got to the peak's interior, he noticed another entrance to the cave, shielded by a thick waterfall. The cave's light came from a kerosene lamp, resting precariously on a flattened rock like a shelf.

A syringe entered his neck before he could take in too many details of this cave. The Farmer spun and tried to retaliate, but stumbled in pain and confusion, catching himself on the ground before the rocky flooring could lacerate him. Instead, one of his palms split open a bit.

The Farmer crawled away on his back, getting to his feet at the other end of the cave. He examined his palm, wiping away the blood on his tattered shirt.

"You have three minutes," said the assailant.

The Farmer sized the man up: He was elderly, with a beard reaching down to the middle of his chest, and a bald head to complement it. These were the only details he could pick out in the dim light of the cave's lamp.

"Before what?" asked the Farmer.

"Before your life ends," said the old man, "and your next one begins."

The old man sat comfortably down onto a nearby boulder. "Ask away," he said disarmingly.

"What'd you do to me?" the Farmer asked instantly.

"A sedative."

"Why?"

"I'm going to *change* you."

The Farmer felt his muscles weakening with every breath he took. He pressed through it.

"Is that what you did to my brother?" asked the Farmer.

The old man grew curious at that thought.

"Which one was your brother?" asked the old man.

"The... bird... thing..." said the Farmer, finding it harder and harder to speak.

The old man became despondent at the thought. The Explorer was the first and only inhabitant of Sigma that the Queen selected as her mate. It was a painful reminder of the old man's ineptitude.

"The One Who Dwells Above is not your brother anymore, I assure you," said the old man.

"Yes, he..."

The Farmer pivoted, saving his precious time for more important queries: "What will I become?"

"I haven't decided yet," said the old man. "I'm considering a reptile."

"Who are y..."

The Farmer collapsed against the cave's wall before finishing that question, grabbing a crevasse for support. The old man brought out a pocket watch, calculating what little time was left.

"Dr. John Sigmund, in a past life," said the old man. "Here, I am the One Who Dwells Below."

The Farmer conjured all of his willpower to stay awake.

"Wh... Why are you doing this?" the Farmer asked, barely able to whisper it.

The old man stood up from the boulder, closing in on his victim.

"She deserves the world," said the old man. "I can only give her this island."

IV

The Hunter in 1939

In Dr. Sigmund's cave, Paula laid on her back and screeched at the top of her lungs in the rawest form of pain and agony. Stillborns and miscarriages had plagued Paula and her mate for almost two decades, credited solely to their unnatural physiologies; Half of their DNA wasn't compatible with one another. This embryo, which had been gestating for almost ten months, was by far the most viable of all thus far.

Dr. Sigmund had no experience delivering babies, let alone hybridized ones. In his old age, he was eager to discover what natural-born mutant would emerge from his first creation.

On the island's surface, the Hunter approached the forest.

With the evening still young, the Hunter set foot on the island with nothing but a machete in his hand, though he was so large that the machete seemed akin to a modest hunting knife. He held it inverted as he strolled towards the island's center, as if to drive it straight down into an opponent. Any hand-written notes regarding the fate of *The Queen's Legacy* had been virtually lost to time, and found only by this one very curious mind.

Finding this island based on nothing but a partial recovery of Queen Victoria's sponsor's notes and a large amount of hearsay proved almost impossible. Any level-headed man would say it couldn't be done. The Hunter was not so level-headed.

Trees all around him whistled in the fading day's usual galls of wind before the nighttime's storms emerged to upset the calming nature of this place. The island's inhabitants shrouded their sounds in this natural noise, maintaining their element of surprise. Their attack would have to be coordinated to best an opponent this large.

Impulsively, the One Who Drains struck first.

The Hunter turned his head towards the sound of the monster pouncing on him, forcing the Hunter against a tree with thick bark. The One Who Drains plunged its wicked tendril into the Hunter's arm.

It crumpled as it attempted to pierce the Brute Man's skin.

Hoxton looked at the beast infuriated, a fire lighting up in his eyes. He snatched the tendril with his free hand and pressed the machete up to the One Who Drains' neck. Forcibly, Hoxton *yanked* the tendril towards him, slicing off the beast's head against the weapon's serrated edge. The blood of the One Who Drains, which itself belonged to many different victims, splattered all over Hoxton's unbroken scales.

Bushes rustled near him, turning Hoxton's head. He knew that this island's creatures were moving all around him, encircling his position. He could do nothing about it but wait.

Hoxton looked down at the severed head of the One Who Drains. He held it up to the moonlight, inspecting the details. The skull was human, but the eyes were those of an insect, and the entire thing was covered in an exoskeleton adorned with tiny little bristles.

From the trees above, the One Who Crawls quickly traversed through the air across a giant, unseen spiderweb.

The One Who Runs pounced onto Hoxton's back just as the One Who Swims latched onto his legs, the two of them toppling Hoxton over onto the muddy ground. The One Who Runs bit into Hoxton's neck, his teeth clanging against the hardened skin. Hoxton swatted the beast away and looked down at his legs, still wrapped up in the tentacles of the One Who Swims. He sent a shockwave coursing through Hoxton's body.

The One Who Hides started charging towards Hoxton with mounting momentum, letting out a powerful cry for all of the island's inhabitants to hear.

From the cave in the island's peak, Paula and Dr. Sigmund heard the cries of the One Who Hides from afar. Paula was still screaming herself, pushing as hard as she possibly could amidst Dr. Sigmund's guiding voice. Neither of them had the capacity to help their allies.

Hoxton freed his legs from the One Who Swims and rolled out of the way, letting the One Who Hides charge into the nearby air, almost stumbling as he stopped himself. He turned, his face meeting Hoxton's powerful fist, and stepped backward into an ungracious fall.

The One Who Runs pounced onto Hoxton again, but this time Hoxton sprawled, catching the beast's body with one hand and plunging the machete into its head with the other. He sliced deeply into the One Who Runs' throat, opening the neck efficiently.

The One Who Hides charged and tackled Hoxton into the nearest tree, mowing it over with their combined body weights. The trunk snapped against Hoxton's back, and the entire thing came crashing down shortly after them, landing thunderously on the Earth below.

From the cave, Paula felt the tree's tremors emanate through the ground as she continued pushing. Her child was almost born.

The One Who Hides strangled Hoxton's neck vigorously, putting all of his weight and power into doing so. As he squeezed, he felt the scales on Hoxton's neck slowly start to crack.

From his side, Hoxton drove the machete in the cavity between where the shell ended and the One Who Hides' arm began, piercing through the creature's skin with ease. The One Who Hides screamed out in pain and released Hoxton from the pressure, letting him stand up and remove the machete from the side and use it to end the distraught creature's life quickly and powerfully.

The One Who Hides was silent as his lifeless body crashed into the ground right near the fallen tree.

Hoxton ducked as the One Who Swims launched a flurry of tentacles his way, dodging most. Three of them still landed on Hoxton's upper body, and tightened rapidly. They sent what seemed like an endless barrage of electrical currents surging into Hoxton's body, making the Brute Man seize up and cringe in immense agony.

Hoxton thought back to his life prior to his suspension. Every waking moment was pain, and he'd been alleviated of that pain for over two hundred years. A few passing moments of agony was nothing to falter to.

Driven by passion, Hoxton forced his free arm to wrap itself around the extended tentacles of the One Who Swims, increasing the painful sensation, and grabbed ahold of all three of them at once. He stepped backward and forcibly yanked the monster towards him. The One Who Swims stumbled and toppled over towards him, trying to get back to its position as Hoxton adjusted his grip and sliced the tentacles clean off of the creature's body.

The One Who Swims had no mouth at all, so it could not scream.

Hoxton stepped forward and planted his foot into the head of the One Who Swims, pinning it to the ground as the rest of its body floundered. He reached inside with both hands and pulled the body apart, fighting against a powerful tension, until the head of the One Who Swims snapped apart into two, and the rest of the tentacles went completely lifeless.

Hoxton looked to the island's peak, where a massive winged creature had just flown to it and landed. It turned its head Hoxton's way. A strange, simian screeching came from the peak, though it didn't seem to be coming from the winged creature.

Hoxton stepped off of the gushy corpse and started off towards the island's peak, getting close enough to almost be able to climb it before an invisible wall stopped him. He pressed his hands through it, trying to power through the strange membrane, recognizing it now as a thick wall of webbing.

The One Who Crawls abducted him into the sky, pulling him a dozen feet in the air by his legs. Hoxton hung there and felt the creature's eight limbs work briskly all around him, cocooning him into an overhead trap.

From below, the latest inhabitant emerged with venomous fangs: A man crossed gruesomely with a predatory snake. This entity, the One Who Slithers, was an accomplished farmer before landing on this island, just wishing to know what happened to his brother.

Hoxton freed his arm before the One Who Slithers could bite him, but the One Who Crawls quickly tried to mend that arm back into the cocoon with fast-moving webbing. Hoxton resisted, grabbing one of the eight limbs from the One Who Crawls and squeezing so hard as to *crush* it beneath his hand. The One Who Slithers climbed a tree and opened its jowls, lunging and clamping down onto Hoxton's arm.

One of the fangs dulled against Hoxton's scales, chipping a fragment of them away. Hoxton was finally cut.

Enraged, Hoxton forced his other arm out of the webbing, grabbing firmly onto the One Who Crawls with both arms and ripping several lines of webbing apart, dipping all three of them down closer to the ground. The web ultimately held, suspending them several feet off the ground as they continued wrestling. Hoxton's machete fell and stuck itself into the soil just out of reach as the One Who Crawls and the One Who Slithers now swarmed him, attacking furiously. He could only block his head defensively like a boxer surviving an onslaught.

In time with a tree branch snapping, the webbing finally gave way to all of their weights, and all three of these monsters careened straight down into the ground below.

Now nearby, Paula and Dr. Sigmund heard the crash from the cave inside of the island's peak. Paula's baby had finally been delivered, and Dr. Sigmund only had a passing moment to bask in his creation, proceeding cautiously from that point forward. He handed Paula her child and signed to her: *Quiet!*

It was a little girl, having the body of a human, the limbs of a gorilla, the wings of a hawk, and a litany of traits from all three of her native species.

Outside, Hoxton was the first one on his feet. He didn't have time to look for the machete.

The One Who Slithers lunged at him again, forcing him to think fast and catch the slimy monster by the neck and wring it out ferociously, squeezing and snapping the monster's neck with vigor. The One Who Crawls barely got to all eight of its feet as Hoxton tore the sharper fang out of the One Who Slithers' mouth and stabbed it straight into the One Who Crawls, piercing the monster's heart.

Hoxton dropped them both.

The creatures fell to the ground around him, joining their allies in the dirt and mud that coated their graves. Hoxton looked again to the top of the island's peak, seeing nothing. The winged creature was no longer there.

Hoxton climbed the peak, digging his stone-like hands into the peak's rocky edge. He ignored whatever injuries he had thus far and ascended quickly. Feeling the Lord's power in him, Hoxton wouldn't let himself heal until all of Lucifer's progeny were all but extinguished.

At the top, Hoxton found nothing.

Hoxton walked over to the throne of the Queen, studying the hand-placed formation of the rocks. It was a shrine. The monsters of this island worshiped a false idol.

The One Who Dwells Above swooped down and knocked Hoxton off of the cliff's edge.

Hoxton clung to the side of the cliff, dangling over a swift death. He hoisted himself back up and quickly ducked before being attacked by the monster again. Steadily, Hoxton lifted himself upward and looked to the skies, spotting the One Who Dwells Above soaring in the distance. Hoxton got to his feet and readied himself, watching the One Who Dwells Above move craftily through the air. It dipped below the island's peak, completely vanishing from Hoxton's sight.

Hoxton grabbed a rock from the Queen's throne, snapping it off of the armrest.

The One Who Dwells Above came up from the opposite edge, tackling Hoxton backward into the flowing waterfall. Hoxton bashed the creature with the rock, then grabbed onto its leg before it could fly away, pulling them both chaotically down off of the waterfall's edge, tumbling them both down into the bedrock below.

Paula cupped her baby's mouth before it had a chance to start crying. She held it tight with her thick, simian palm.

Leaning over his opponent, Hoxton pounded away at the One Who Dwells Above's head, spilling blood with every crushing punch. The monster's head started to crush bit by bit until life no longer flowed through the body, and Hoxton's hideous abuse could finally end.

Paula and Dr. Sigmund huddled to the cave's edge, avoiding the moonlight peering through the waterfall. They looked towards it, seeing the silhouette of a tall, almighty man who'd just slaughtered her mate with his bare hands. The silhouette scanned the island around him with a careful eye, prying his surroundings for another hybridized demon to inevitably vanquish.

He looked into the waterfall.

Hoxton saw the running water and put his hands into it, washing off the blood of all of the island's inhabitants from his scales. His fingers found the chip in his scales. He knew that if even so much as a drop of the snake's venom found its way inside, he probably would've been immobilized and eaten alive tonight. For this miracle, he was grateful to the Lord and all that He'd done to empower him to carry out His will, this night and a thousand more.

V

The Collector in 2004

The island of these sailors' lost and forgotten notes had proved immensely difficult to find, so of all the journal's entries, he opted to begin with *this* journey. To start with a real challenge would mean that the rest would come so much easier to him. This was his mindset, and he clung to it like a religion. Modern satellite technologies coupled with the approximations from the notes narrowed it down significantly for him, but the process of locating Sigma still took almost two years. Upon discovering it, he took no crew and brought no companions with him on his modestly-sized ship, named *Abraham's Progeny* with pride, and would employ the same tactic for the next species to appropriate.

After four days and three nights at sea, from Mexico's coastlines to the faroff, semi-charted waters of the Atlantic, Waylon Ross had arrived at Sigma.

The island's candor hit him first: Vast, open and lush fields and shrubberies towards the center of it, with a rocky shoreline where the ocean met the island's edge. This place hadn't been visited since Hoxton tracked it down almost a century prior. Hoxton's notes forewarned that any intelligent life had all been extinguished, but Waylon wasn't the type of man to take somebody's word for it. He was all too familiar with monsters who took solace hiding right in plain sight. Even from each other.

Waylon stepped off of *Abraham's Progeny* when it dropped its anchor nearby to the coastline, then leapt overboard and swam towards it like an athlete. He worked out five times a week for about two hours in his personal gym, and never strayed from this formula. It was just enough time to watch a movie as he did so. The escapism helped him forget he was exercising at all. A trick-of-the-mind that led to his tone, strapping shape.

Crawling his way onto the island's coastline, Waylon scanned the environment carefully. Would a sharpened rock hurl into his shoulder from some distant bush? Ideally, the thin layer of kevlar would prevent any long-term harm. He paced through the island's untouched sands and entered the flora, large and small, that now surrounded him.

It wasn't a rock that came for him.

Waylon ducked when seeing the bushes launch a hand-made spear straight at his head. When it missed, the one who threw it quickly emerged.

It was with the speed of an old gunslinger that Waylon pulled the weapon from his waistline, but he couldn't aim it properly before the Ape-Woman came just a little too close to him. Waylon jumped and rolled away as Paula planted her hands into the sand where his feet previously were, gripping the terrain for support and steadying herself. On his back, Waylon held the gun up and shot Paula with the tranquillizer right in her shoulder.

She was the sole inhabitant of Sigma, the Queen of Nobody and Nothing at All, and she did not fall instantly to the powerful sedative in her veins.

Paula came up to Waylon and smacked her hand straight down onto his chest. In that horrifying moment, Waylon could feel that the impact caused at least one of his ribs to crack, though he wasn't sure which. Paula grabbed Waylon by his collarbone and brought him up to her eye level, showing him the face Mr. Walters used to charge exorbitant prices for people to see.

And Waylon marveled.

She was hand-crafted, not with precision but with *passion*. He could recognize the scientist's work in her. Intentionally grotesque, yet impossible to look away from. Waylon watched as the rage in her eyes slowly faded, her eyelids starting to close, mouth hung open in an emerging confusion...

Paula collapsed onto the ground beside him.

The weight of Paula's body was tremendous. It kicked up tufts of sand as it landed onto the beachy shore. As Waylon laid there next to her, partially covered in her sand, he took as much time as he wanted to look up at the beautiful sky and recover from her attack. He dreaded having to get up again, only to throw her body over his shoulder *and* heave it all the way to the island's edge, only to find no practical way to get the Ape-Woman's body onto the *Progeny*.

Perhaps going at this alone was something to reconsider.

Far, far away in the sky up above, Waylon spotted a bird flying away from the island. It was a strange looking one, bearing no resemblance to any recognizable species or breed, and its limbs seemed simian in nature.

XIV
HIS CONCUBINES OF LATE

The man was spattered in blood from head to toe as he stood alone in the dimly-lit cellar. In his hand was her severed finger, and he held it up to his lips. The rest of her was diced up, still fresh from the controlled murder, and those pieces were mostly confined to a large metal bucket by his feet. Slowly, he placed his tongue on the bottom of her severed finger, and licked straight up to the tip.

The taste was sublime.

This is what drove him to do it. The salty texture of a woman's skin, covered in dark, wet blood, danced across the surface of his tongue in an exquisite cacophony of pleasure.

A normal upbringing, middle-class parents, and a local college's scholarship propelled David from Class Nerd to Assistant Finance Officer before he turned 35. An average, normal description of an average, normal man.

David tossed the finger into the bucket with the rest of her body parts. Slowly, *deliberately,* he took a breath. The air he'd filled his lungs with was therapeutic, and only after soaking in every drop of the moment did he let out a serene exhale so soft that even a dog wouldn't have heard it.

An untroubled tranquility filled the room.

But he couldn't stay too long. There was a great deal of work that needed to be done.

David left his cellar and sealed the door like it were a dungeon, with multiple aftermarket locks bolting themselves into the threshold. He walked quickly to the bathroom and washed his hands in the sink. Then his arms. Then his face. Then, and only then, did he strip naked and begin to shower. In the steaming water, troubles and reservations melted away like wax amidst a candle's dwindling wick. It was an equally raw purification of the mind as it was the filth that surrounded his thin, lean body.

Grabbing a towel, David quickly went back to his sink. It was a strong source of sanitation and security for him, and over it, he dried off his body with segmented parts of the folded towel. This way, no wet towel would touch his skin; only the dry little squares and rectangles of it made contact with him. After tying it around his waist, David caught his sight in the steamed-up mirror. He splashed his face with more water, adjusting tiny little details like the shape and uniformity of his thinly-kempt beard. The slight wax in his ears. The two or three tiny nose hairs that've barely passed the threshold of his nostrils.

Though the bloodied body parts of young girls certainly stimulated his desires and cravings, David's favorite subject of fascination, without question, was David.

In the bedroom, after throwing on a long, red-and-white robe, David opened the top drawer of his dresser and picked one of many almost identical black pairs of pants and socks. Opening the middle drawer, he saw about a dozen smartphones all in a line, charged by several cables fed through the drawer's ball bearings. The cable management was spectacular, with zip-ties guiding each wire deliberately where it needed to go, and almost no visible slack.

Unlocking each one - with separate passcodes, each anagrams of each other - brought him to a home screen with only one app each: Various brands and types of dating apps, ranging from long-term relationship goals to casual sex. David checked many, many notifications on each, settling on tonight's entertainment: An app somewhere between the realms of serious and free-spirited.

Tonight's entertainment was Lillian.

David closed the drawer and grabbed his keys, almost forgetting to even wear a shirt. The thrill of it all got the better of him.

The bar was cheap, and the people were mostly older men drinking after a long day's work. David used to try and pick up his fancies at bars on-the-spot, but the mystery and uncertainty of it all made his unusual hobby rather frustrating when it didn't pay off for him. The mere *sight* of a certain girl would have him betwixt, and his mind would think of nothing else until she was his to play with. His desire for domination was, sometimes, insatiable.

Lillian entered in a sparkly red dress.

It was stoned by hand, as though it was made for a beauty pageant, but covered by a short black leather jacket. A marriage of a beauty queen's wardrobe and a casual day off with friends, bewildering on first glance. David's minimalist black blazer couldn't compete with it.

Lillian smiled and sat down next to him. She was excited, but he could tell she was nervous, and the fact that he'd already ordered her a drink quelled those nerves a bit. She felt welcomed. And he felt proud.

The bug didn't know it'd been caught in its dreaded monster's web.

Time passed quickly for them; Minutes became hours over all of the sultry conversation, the both of them playing mental mindgames with one another to make sure their wording wasn't stupid or mistimed. His devilishly charming facade matched her curious, almost innocent glance. They were bewildered with each other from the start, for wildly different goals and reasons.

There finally came a lull in the dialogue, and with it, a moment to think and really breathe for the both of them. David pivoted the conversation:

"So why me? Here and now?"

Lillian smiled, almost laughing, and responded honestly: "You said you were only in town for a little while. I need to get my mind off of some things."

"So that's what I am?" David asked playfully. "A distraction?"

She blushed. He was completely right.

"I'd do a hell of a lot better of a job distracting you at my place," said David with all of the confidence in the world. He didn't possess any fears of rejection.

Lillian looked down at her shoes. It was a rare break in her courage. David's gaze on her was relentless, and he hid his confusion behind his wicked smile. He expected this to be the easiest part of the night.

"Can we come back to mine?" Lillian asked as her head raised again.

Briefly, for no more than a *second* of time, a look of concern came over David. A fraction of a moment where he let himself slip.

"I'm sorry," she continued, "it's just that I usually don't-"

"It's fine," said David in a quick, deliberate tone. He feigned a disarming smile.

"You can grab a seat on the couch," Lillian said to her guest as she shut the door behind him.

"I'm alright for now," said David, looking around her home. He didn't have much trouble adjusting to Lillian's apartment. It was cheap, made up to be warm and inviting, and it carried a strong aroma of store-bought fragrance. There was an electric fireplace near her TV, which David found humorous considering she also had fireplace pokers near it. *As if to stoke the electricity.* The thought made him smile.

"I'm gonna freshen up. Did you want anything? Wine?" Lillian asked him.

"No, thank you," he responded, "You probably shouldn't have driven home."

Lillian scoffed at his comment. The couch that he'd passed on looked firm: He'd become accustomed to his own, which was now worn out from too much use. Hers was much younger and full of strength. Probably less comfortable. On her way to the bathroom, Lillian's finger caressed his chest. This made *him* blush, remarkably. Unplanned revenge for all of the times he'd done it to her at the bar.

He was alone again. His favorite state of being.

David lifted the syringe from his pocket and removed the cover. From a tiny bottle he'd hidden within his palm, David extracted a very specific dosage of semitransparent liquid from it.

"You have some lovely... interior decoration," David said out loud. He rolled his eyes. *Fuck, that was stupid.* With his back still facing the bathroom, David pocketed the bottle and flicked the air out of the syringe.

"Maybe I will take you up on that wine-"

David turned as he spoke, hiding the hypodermic needle behind his back, only to see her standing directly behind him with a lovely, adorable little smile. David smiled in return, adjusting his grip on the hidden syringe. Her doe-eyed, friendly expression doesn't change. David cocked his head slightly, trying to understand. *Did she see me?*

Her smile began to morph, revealing a set of unusual teeth. Her mouth widened, further than imaginable for a girl her size, and as her jaw descended and her head tilted back, those beaming eyes he'd fallen into had rolled backward into her own skull.

Lillian lunged forward and bit David's shoulder with diabolical force.

David cried out in agony, dropping the syringe and stumbling backward over her newly-bought, never-used couch. Without it, Lillian thought, this place wouldn't look like a normal human being lived here.

He collapsed on the ground and held his bleeding shoulder, no longer focused on the syringe at all. Alas, it *did* make a noise when it fell, and Lillian's attention was now on it. Before moving in for her kill, Lillian picked it up from the ground and inspected it. As she did so, David looked around for the only thing suitable to be a weapon: The fireplace poker. It still had the price tag on it, something Lillian forgot to remove when staging this place. Though useless, Lillian still felt that the pokers tied the room together. None of her victims had commented on it so far.

While distracted by the syringe, David got to his feet and plunged the poker through her back. The tip of it burst through her chest coated in the disgusting black blood of what she was.

A moment passed as David caught his breath. He was distressed and in shock, but she seemed frozen in time, not even looking his way. As though Medusa had turned her to stone. The couple simply stood there, lingering in this most significant microcosm of tonight's events.

Lillian took a step backward.

As her body approached David's, her torso brutally slid along the shaft of the poker and made a horrifying noise of flesh grinding against steel. Lillian stopped walking when her body was nearest without contact, almost pushed up against his. Only the withdrawn length of David's arms separated them as he held firm on his grip of the poker. As though it would save him.

David was petrified. Lillian seemed unaffected by his attack, though he could only really see the details of the back of her head. Like a bomb going off, Lillian whipped around at the blinding speed that only her species could exert, and tackled a defenseless David to the ground.

Not a day over nineteen, Lillian was a simple housewife two hundred years ago, who spent most of her days raising her husband's child together. She lobbied for a second one with him, but didn't understand why he never wanted more than one. Not until she'd found out about the twenty-year-old affair in red lipstick and high heels. The Underlord intervened, offering her a similar polygynous relationship, but one where all parties knew and embraced one another. One where all could act as agents of their own independence. It took little convincing for her to cave to his bloodletting and hypnotism.

When wiping her mouth of David's blood, Lillian inspected the syringe one more time, and the cogs in her mind started to turn: *Maybe we should've gone to his... Whatever it looks like ought to be of interest.*

Though betwixingly beautiful, Lillian was always aware that she was no longer the youngest of the Underlord's Brides. Instead, a woman named Hope enjoyed that title.

She had dark skin and long, curly hair, and wore every eye-catching dress that she came across. Some were given to her by Master or her Sisters as gifts, but most were procured independently from the wardrobes of her own victims: Young, thin girls like herself who didn't take drugs but frequented nightlife. It was these people whose veins were unpolluted and rife with rejuvenating blood.

Seeing as it was their fifty-year anniversary, the Underlord found a hotel in Transylvania where they first met, and Hope laid on the bed with a smile. She was blindfolded, stirring in anticipation of just how much better the night was going to get.

"*Sit up*," Master's voice whispered from the end of the room.

Hope did as she was told.

"*Take off the blindfold*," whispered the voice again.

Hope removed the blindfold and saw Master with his arms outstretched, bearing two gifts by his sides: Two women, roughly the same size and weight as her, whose hands and legs were bound behind them. Master smiled, matching Hope's energy, and Hope nearly exploded with joy.

"Here are the rules," said Master as he lowered his arms. "Both are intoxicated with a litany of strawberry daiquiris from the bar downstairs. One of them will wake up in their own bed tomorrow morning, untouched by either of us. The other will stay... and not survive what we do tonight."

Hope grinned from ear to ear. Of all the beverages she gave up when becoming a creature of the night, strawberry daiquiris used to be her absolute favorite. She tried to hide how much she was blushing.

"Choose quickly," said Master with an intoxicating smile.

The decision was difficult. The girl to Master's left had a purple fit and flare dress with ruffles on the collar. The girl on the right had a gray bodycon, skin-tight. Both looked equally gorgeous and divine. His taste was absolutely exceptional.

"Her," Hope said, pointing to the women in purple.

Master bowed gracefully, concluding his grand show.

"Don't start without me," he said to his Bride as he took the woman in gray out of the room.

"I never do," Hope said back in a sultry voice.

As Master left, she stayed fixated on the woman in purple, lying helplessly on the floor. Her head spun in and out of consciousness, induced by a combination of the alcohol that he convinced her to drink, and the powerful sedative of his otherworldly hypnosis.

On the fire escape of David's apartment, Ilona appeared as if from nowhere and entered through the locked window from the outside.

Most of the Underlord's brides never made it much more than a century or two before being staked through the chest, decapitated, cremated, or some twisted combination of all three. Ilona's longevity by Master's side in comparison to most of his concubines highlighted exactly two things: Of all the brides that he'd ever had the luxury of tasting and drinking and spoiling himself with, Ilona was by far the smartest. And of course, the world's hunters had slowly been dwindling as the status of vampires became myth and tall tales. A deliberate choice by her Master.

Ilona made her way through David's apartment and down into the newfound dungeon room, where Lillian had strung the man up by his feet. Lillian sat atop a cooler watching what she'd done, draped head-to-toe in that same blood-spattered dress, and holding a wine glass half-empty from David's blood. From above, David's sliced-open neck dripped slowly into one of the buckets, one minor little drop at a time. Lillian saw Ilona's reaction to her most recent prize.

"You were truthful about this man's hobby," Ilona stated in awe.

Lillian rose from the cooler and faced Ilona, stroking her cheek with her long, painted nails: "I've missed you, Sister. I believe I've encountered my very *favorite* victim."

"His blood looks divine," said Ilona with her eyes lighting up, and a gorgeous, exotic smile forming on her face.

"Does Hope follow you?" asked Lillian.

"Not yet," said Ilona softly.

Ilona lost her smile when she looked down at the glass.

"You've already *tasted,*" said Ilona.

"Only a sip," said Lillian innocently.

Forcefully and suddenly, Ilona smacked Lillian across the face, knocking her down to the cellar's concrete ground. The impact skinned Lillian's elbow and tore her long, red dress.

"Master always gets first bite," said Ilona sternly.

Lillian recovered from the fall, but stayed on the ground. It was out of respect.

"I thought... because they were in Romania tonight..."

Ilona looked down at Lillian, seeing the injury she'd made. Volatile as Ilona could be, she could not stay mad when she saw Lillian's eyes. They beamed at her with an innocence she rarely saw in the world anymore. Ilona shook off her disappointment and extended a hand to Lillian, who hesitantly grabbed it. Carefully, Ilona fed Lillian the rest of David's blood from the wine glass, and as the young woman drank, the laceration on her arm began to close.

"For a man like this," said Ilona, watching Lillian slowly drink, "it would feel wrong to feast without all of us."

Ilona looked again to David's body, swaying very subtly from the ceiling, and Lillian's gaze followed.

She grabbed Lillian's hand as they watched David's blood slowly keep dripping into one of his buckets, and Lillian felt her trepidations melt away. Every time that Ilona held her hand like that, a fulfilling, joyous feeling overtook her. It was the touch of her favorite Sister, whom she'd blissfully follow to the world's ends.

Hope crawled to the foot of the bed and came closer to the woman in purple.

"Who's... Who is that now?" the woman in purple said with a strong slur, her eyes trying to stay open.

Hope's black claw gently stroked the woman's cheek, gliding down to her neck and collarbone. She wasn't starting without Master. She was only playing with her food.

A breeze from the open window took her attention away.

Hope saw nothing at the window's sill. She didn't remember opening it. Leaving the inebriated woman on the floor by her bedside, Hope went over and started to shut the window, but the smell of something present stopped her in place. Somebody was here, and their blood smelled absolutely delicious.

Before turning around, Hope closed her eyes and used her ears: There were two intruders. Adult males. Healthy. Not young, not old. Unexpectedly calm, with a steady blood flow and a knack for trying to remain silent.

These were her last thoughts before losing consciousness.

The woman in purple flinched at the sound of Hope's body hitting the hotel room floor, then dazed back off into her mindspace.

Many hours had passed in David's apartment.

Ilona and Lillian's patience was being tested. Master and Hope, his newest concubine, were supposed to have returned much earlier than this from their fifty-year anniversary in Romania. Hope had been a fourth-runner-up to a high-profile beauty pageant for a populous American state. Master had deduced that if the pageant's winner had gone missing, there would be a great deal of public attention. Although the pageant's many losing contestants were equally as divine in their beauty, much less people would bat an eye at one's disappearance.

Lillian remembered that day vividly: Verona had just been murdered the night before, and a void in their hearts was created. Master found Hope out at a Transylvanian nightclub with her friends in 1974, trying desperately to forget about the pain of losing the pageant. He'd brought her back to a room he'd rented only for the one night, and before any foreplay, began beaming those powerful eyes of his at her, putting many alluring thoughts into her young, not-so-innocent mind. He'd suggested the idea of a relationship where she'd always have the power she desired, and much, much more than that. So much more than any beauty queen would ever have in this world.

"Do you remember our first night together with Hope?" Lillian recalled to

Ilona, sitting across from her beneath David's dripping corpse.

Ilona thought back to it in her more detail-oriented way: Once Hope's will was dominated by Master's, he signaled Lillian and Ilona into the hotel room through the open window. They appeared quickly, taking Hope by surprise. It seemed unwelcoming at first, but Master continued his potent suggestion on her, warming her up to the idea. Lillian placed her careful hand on Hope's shoulders, sparking that sense of seduction that turned hesitancy into desire.

"Yes. You were brilliant," remarked Ilona.

Lillian blushed. Sprawled out on the table between them were all of David's decoy phones with all of his old accounts. Lillian reasoned that if Master wanted a *fourth* bride for whatever reason, his job would be made much simpler with devices like these. Ilona looked up to David's body, then down at the bucket of blood, and the tinge of disappointment started to set in.

"It's not nearly as fresh as it was," said Ilona.

"He's *never* late," said Lillian. "It makes me feel like... I don't know. Should we check on them?"

Something about Lillian's worries triggered whatever compassion was left in Ilona. Though strict, she did love her younger Sisters dearly. Both of them.

"Preserve this psycho's body in one of his coolers. We'll go to Romania together."

Relief washed over Lillian. Ilona stood from her chair and watched her Sister fly with her vampiric speed to untie David's hanging body.

The Romanian hotel was illustrious to walk through. Money was something Master never cared much about, spending centuries having his underlings earn it for him. But even if that weren't the case, he could just as easily rob the world blind in one misfortunate night.

Circumnavigating the globe was something that took humans days or even weeks to accomplish, depending on when which flights would be available in which places. Until a more advanced device than an airliner were invented, the Brides of the Underlord had no desire to wait that long.

Room 304. Ilona got the information from the bellhop who gawked at her when she entered. She didn't need to probe his mind very long to realize just how weak it was. The two brides entered through Room 304's door aided by the master keycard Lillian lifted off of the hotel's manager. If they returned it and left this place in a timely fashion, nobody would ever think this building was being intruded.

The room was in flawless condition. Curtains were adorned neatly on the windows, no longer blocking the sunlight peering its way inside. The furniture was put back in its proper place. Whoever was last here had saved room service a great amount of work.

But the vampires felt a presence in the room. One without the traits of a vampire, but also not *identical* to an actual man. They could hear the intruder's blood being pumped from the shadowed corner beside the bathroom. They knew he was there before spotting his shaded outline.

"Abomination," said Ilona.

And the hidden man stepped forth.

Lillian felt a rage surge through her like no other power ever had. Her talons spread wide as if to slice open the intruder's neck, but Ilona was smarter than to let her fellow Bride try anything like that. She held Lillian back with her hand's passing motion, much how their Master had always done to the both of them. As grateful as Lillian was for discovering Hope, she desired so greatly to destroy the abomination that took her Verona from this world.

Franklin recognized Ilona's mastery over Lillian. He nodded and smirked, as if telling her to *stay in line.*

A spark generated in Lillian at the act. She ignored Ilona's gesture. Lillian dashed over to Franklin and smacked him in the jaw, dislocating it with her incredible strength.

"*Stop!*" Ilona commanded her Sister.

Lillian backed away after her strike. Franklin's ugly head turned to her and glared as his jaw dangled from the side of his face. Carefully, it pulled itself up and back into place, the bones and muscles binding and reorienting themselves into position.

"If you think I'm here looking for conflict," mumbled Franklin through his newly-healed teeth, "you would be even dumber than I know you both to be."

Lillian spoke with hatred: "Abomination, your-"

"*Franklin,*" he grumbled calmly. But Lillian did not care.

"-Your father killed Verona in Transylvania fifty years ago-"

"He shot at an intruder on his property," Franklin clarified. "It was a werewolf that killed her. But you know this already, don't you? Perhaps your prejudice follows only where your Master guides it."

"Let me strike him once more," Lillian pleaded with Ilona.

But Ilona waved dismissively toward Lillian, and asked the only question that mattered to her: "Why are you here?"

"Tragic news," said Franklin without a hint of respect.

Despite Franklin's pacifism, the Brides prepared for another fight. Given the nature of the three people standing in that hotel room, Franklin knew how pointless something like that would actually be.

"There's been an altercation between your Underlord and a human man," said Franklin. "He's been kidnapped, and I think I know where."

"Where did he take the man?" Ilona asked.

Franklin held back a laugh. "The *Underlord,*" he clarified.

The Brides were confused. This news was difficult to fully absorb.

"He's captured my father, too," Franklin continued. "Not that it'd matter to either of you."

"A *human* is abducting vampires and monsters?" Ilona asked.

Franklin nodded.

"To what end?" Ilona asked.

"No idea," said Franklin. "It's good to know you're just as curious about it as I am. That means you're not going to turn down what I'm about to ask you to do."

Franklin had long since left. He was returning to his Romanian home to gather enough food to last several days and whatever unconventional weapons the three of them could agree would actually *work* on the things Waylon had been hunting. The Underlord's two remaining Brides waited alone in the hotel room for him to return. Lillian refused to leave it.

"Rest," said Ilona. "You'll need all of your strength."

"I *cannot*," Lillian insisted.

Ilona paused. She realized she'd been pushing Lillian too hard in the wake of their loss. Lillian remained at the bedside, staring at the bloodstains on the floor. Piecing together how it happened. The angle of the weapon as it must've entered Hope's chest. It was all she could fixate on.

Ilona was about to leave, but empathetically felt Lillian's confusion growing. She turned, seeing her Sister's eyes all over her, scanning Ilona up and down.

"You don't grieve," Lillian pointed out.

"What do you mean?" Ilona said back.

"You don't... You don't feel *anything* for her."

"Of course I do!"

But Lillian wasn't convinced. She could feel Ilona's emotions. They were void of any sorrow.

"Did you even love her?" Lillian asked.

Ilona didn't know how to respond. The fact that she didn't right away told Lillian all she needed to know about the answer.

Ilona left the hotel room.

Lillian turned around in worry. She wanted to chase Ilona down, but couldn't muster the strength to leave the room. This was where she deserved to stay. Somebody like Hope was not to be an afterthought to her. Lillian wouldn't let her be.

And instantly, Ilona returned, carrying the cooler in her hand.

Lillian looked solemnly upon the cooler, reminiscing on how it had made her feel before traveling to Romania and walking into this room. She'd spent the entire trip thinking about David's body and blood being shared amongst her harem and bringing smiles and bliss to the four of them. Now it was nothing more than fuel. Sustenance. A simple means to an end to embolden them with strength to find Master and confront Hope's killer. Though it was the same victim's blood enjoyed by the same pair of vampires, Lillian knew that it couldn't taste the same at all.

XV

THE HOUSE OF THE IMPRISONER

"*Werewolf,*" whispered the affectionate voice of a friend.

Gwen wasn't asleep, but she was attempting to be.

"*Vampire,*" said Gwen, maintaining the whisper.

"*Why do you stare into the darkness most nights?*" Abrem Trosk asked from his adjacent cell. "*Human eyes can't see very well in the dark.*"

Gwen rose from her bed. She had no idea how to explain it to another person, let alone a nocturnal parasite on the other side of a wall.

"*I don't know,*" Gwen whispered. "*I like to look at things when there's only a little bit of light to see. It makes the details stand out. Kind of like an outline.*"

"*I imagine you've been doing it right now?*" Abrem Trosk asked.

Gwen smiled. He was absolutely right... but the smile quickly faded upon her next realization.

"*You can't see me,*" said Gwen.

"*The reflection on Hoxton's screen.*"

Gwen went to her gateway and looked across the crypt. His was the only screen that remained turned off, and it *did* cast some reflections of the rest of the crypt. She tried to peer through at it and see what Abrem Trosk was doing in his cell, but couldn't from her angle. Gwen readjusted her stance. Finally, she saw the bright light of his cell's ultraviolet rays.

The crypt's entrance opened up, and many of them awoke.

In came a slab with two items on top of it: One was a large, wooden box the size of a living room couch. The other was covered by a massive tarp. This entire assembly was being pulled by a large rope, hoisted over the shoulder of Waylon's invisible assistant.

By the crypt's entrance, Waylon came in after the slab. He nodded to Jack, and the floating rope fell to the floor.

Gwen watched her fellow inmates take little notice or attention towards Waylon's latest. Their indifference still confounded her.

Waylon beckoned to Jack, who helped him move the slab towards the cell next to Gwen's. It was the last available cell in the crypt. Unable to be detected by the beast, Jack unfurled the tarp and shoved the animal inside before quickly shutting the cell's gateway.

The monstrosity had the torso of a man, but the characteristics of a black scorpion: Massive claws adorned each hand, though one of them appeared injured. A set of mandibles stood in place of the man's mouth, which sat under what seemed to be a dozen jet-black eyes adorning his head. The plated skin of the creature encased him completely, even so much as the six insect legs holding him up and the long, powerful tail extruding from its lower back. It was curled in a large curve, and hovered comfortably over one of the man's shoulders.

Being adjacent, Gwen was the only one who didn't get a good view of it.

"What about the box?" asked Jack.

Waylon mulled his options.

"Toss it in with him," Waylon finally said. "He seems to care a great deal about it."

And indeed, Jack did so. He opened the gateway for all of five seconds and wheeled the wooden box off of the slab. The beast was still restrained, with each claw shackled and barely able to move. The sight reminded Waylon of a lobster shortly before being boiled alive, with small rubber bands preventing it from attacking the chef. The thought made him uncomfortable.

"The journal's running out of creatures," said Jack casually to Waylon.

"I'm aware," said Waylon, still staring at the beast. "It's exciting, isn't it?"

Uncharacteristically, Hoxton came to the edge of his gateway.

"I've spent three hundred years cataloging them," said Hoxton, "and you've captured almost every last one."

"Not a Mechi," Waylon corrected. "That reminds me, Brute. I'm still making revisions to your journal."

From his furred jacket, Waylon produced Hoxton's disembodied journal and held it up in plain view. Hoxton became despondent at the sight. He was blindsided by the revelation, but soon cursed himself for not assuming that something like this might happen.

"I re-bound your pages on the *left,* and started putting my revisions on the right. It's chronological that way. When we're done, I'd love to publish a finalized copy. It could serve as a definitive bestiary for hunters out there like you and I."

Hoxton went completely quiet. There was no part of his life that Waylon hadn't probed into and taken away from him. Even his last remaining secrets. Hoxton closed his eyes and turned to the Lord for support, quietly hoping he'd get a response.

"You'd be a greater fool than I took you for, Waylon," muttered the Underlord from across the crypt.

As Waylon glared the Underlord's way, Gwen intervened, propelled by her usual curiosity: "Where'd you find this one?"

Waylon smirked as he turned to her. He wasn't just proud of what he'd done or who he'd captured. He relished the idea of showing them off to a curious party. It was his life's joy.

Waylon pocketed the journal and pulled out his phone, taking a picture of the cell next to Gwen's. In seconds, it showed up on Gwen's television.

"This Scorpion Man has no name," said Waylon. "If we find a way to communicate, I'm sure he'll tell us. Maybe share what happened to his claw."

Though it wasn't obvious to anybody, the Scorpion Man was looking straight at Hoxton.

Gwen saw it on her screen. Like usual, the creature was simultaneously revolting and alluring. She was unable to look away from it.

"Where?" Gwen again asked.

Waylon turned to leave. "Egypt," he said before departing.

And the Gargoyle arose.

The Gargoyle had finished *Drake's Only Chapter* several nights ago in a matter of minutes, and yearned for a completed version that ceased to exist. Since then, he'd remained completely silent, pondering what the method of study could've been.

No longer was he steeped in thought.

The Gargoyle went to his gateway and garnered the best look he could at the latest creature behind bars. Gwen watched the stone-skinned demon, a figment of men's nightmares, express a look of fear she'd never known him to produce. It was a fear reserved for the likes of men upon seeing one of Waylon's monsters for the very first time, not at all appropriate for a face so horrifying as his.

And yet, it was there.

"Waylon!!" the Gargoyle called out.

But the crypt's door had already shut. The Gargoyle's yelling had prevented most of the other creatures from returning to a nice, warm sleep. But most of them were never going to, anyway.

When Waylon first mentioned a *Scorpion Man,* the Gargoyle assumed it was another chimera from Dr. John Sigmund's handiwork. He knew better than that now.

"*Please* look away from your TV," the Gargoyle pleaded with the artificial person.

Abrem Trosk laughed.

"Of all the wicked things he's brought down here," said Abrem Trosk, "what makes *this* one so special, Gargoyle? Here and now?"

"That thing is a curse," said the Gargoyle. "Our best hope is to leave this place, and burn it asunder beforehand."

Hoxton joined the conversation: "I'm on board with killing it. Came close once."

"That won't work," said the Gargoyle.

"Seems like it would," Hoxton added. "His claw's broken because of *me.*"

The door to Waylon's mansion opened on its own, carefully moved by Jack's invisible touch.

"Hello?" Waylon said from across the room, his long jacket flowing by his feet as he paced to the doorway. He'd just come up from the backmost hallway, at the end of which was the hidden entrance to the crypt, and Jack was careful not to close it until Waylon's body blocked the view.

The man entered.

"I didn't say you could come in, mate," said Waylon frankly. "What the hell are you doing?"

Undisturbed, the man sat himself right at Waylon's living room table. Right in the chair Waylon had sat in across from Gwen when she'd first arrived. Subtly, Waylon gestured to Jack as if to call him off from an attack. There were protocols Jack was supposed to follow if an intruder refused to leave. Waylon was too fascinated to allow for that.

The man had a large hooded sweatshirt covering much of his face, and had the body of a man who worked out more often than he slept. He was uncanny, and appropriately enough for Waylon's fascinations. But he was unwelcome in almost every other regard.

"*Sit*," said the man situated comfortably in Waylon's chair.

Waylon froze. He wished he'd brought the gauntlet with him. An intruder like this would've made for an excellent excuse to test how each unconventional bullet interacted with living tissue.

Begrudgingly, Waylon took the couch across from the man. He was comforted primarily by the idea that Jack was nearby, and only a beck and call away from crushing the man's windpipe.

"Who are you?" Waylon asked. "There's no point in the hood. That face you got sticks out in a crowd any day of the bloody week."

Waylon was completely right. The man's face was hideous in every way, with coarse skin that had no color whatsoever. He removed his hood and glared daggers at Waylon Ross.

"You've lived quite a life, Waylon," said the intruder.

"I'm living it still," he replied.

"We'll see," the intruder said solemnly.

Again, Waylon gestured for Jack to lay off. This time, the intruder noticed the subtle body language, surmising they were not alone in this cordial meeting. Neither man wanted to let on exactly how much they knew - or assumed - about the other, so for a few short moments, the two sat in nothing but complete silence.

"Get on with it," Waylon prompted.

"With what, exactly?" said the intruder.

"Whyever you're here. I don't have any friends with skin like yours. Or look like they've swallowed a bus."

"You're right," the intruder admitted. "But you've met another like me, haven't you?"

"I don't know what you're talking about," Waylon said dismissively.

The intruder adjusted himself in Waylon's chair. He leaned closer to his opponent across the table, resting his hands on his knees.

"What else are you lying about, if that's how you intend to *start* our dialogue?" the intruder prompted in a cold tone.

Waylon didn't panic. He scanned the finer details of the intruder's appearance: Huge, lingering pores littered the man's heavily lined face and hands. Amidst all of this, not a scar or scab anywhere to be found. Not so much as a pimple. He was abhorrent and revolting, but not at all sickly.

"There are two people trapped inside this place that are of significance to me," said Franklin, unwavering in his conviction.

"And who would these people be?" Waylon said, humoring the intruder.

"One of them is a vampire," said the intruder. "I will have him dead by my own hands."

"A knack for fictional tales *and* intended murder," Waylon scoffed. "The other?"

"The other is someone who looks like me," said the intruder. "Someone who shares my gray skin. And show your *honest* side this time, poacher. It'll factor into my decision."

"And what decision is this?" Waylon asked.

"Whether or not you live."

Though he had no way of sensing him, Waylon knew in his bones that Jack was just itching for the opportunity to intervene and perform his favorite task. The task that'd made him the world's most efficient living assassin.

"I'm going to have to ask you to leave," Waylon said diplomatically. "If you don't-"

"You'll what?" The intruder asked.

There was another silence between them as the intruder called his bluff. Waylon glanced around the room, unsure where his assistant was, and the intruder's eyes followed.

"You can't banish a creature like me," the intruder continued. "Not after spending your life collecting us like stamps."

"You're mad," said Waylon.

"Where would my head reside in your display case, Waylon? Somewhere towards the top shelf, I hope."

Waylon started: "That's enough-"

But as Waylon stood up, the intruder reached into the pocket of his sweatshirt. Jack grabbed the intruder's arm suddenly, revealing himself to the unwelcome houseguest.

"Stop," Waylon said to his assistant.

There you are, the intruder discovered.

Like a panther, the intruder snatched Jack's invisible arm. With his other, the intruder swiped for somewhere, *anywhere* on Jack's body - happening upon the side of Jack's torso - and plummeted the invisible man into Waylon's chair as he quickly shot up, standing tall. The chair crashed to the ground, one of the legs snapping from the sudden force as Jack's body tumbled down. The intruder had no guns or weapons on his person at all. He only had his unnaturally brilliant mind and the physical strength to reinforce it.

Now on his feet, Waylon panicked for the first time. The intruder turned his gaze to him, his eyes warning him not to move.

Waylon abided.

Gwen's heightened senses detected the struggle happening several layers of concrete above Waylon's crypt. There was some form of altercation happening with Waylon's new guest. This was something she would've shared with the group if they hadn't been so adversarial to her presence. Perhaps Abrem Trosk could be informed after the Gargoyle finished his ranting.

The Scorpion Man held his restraints up to his head. Slowly, he used the giant mandibles in his jawline to gnaw away at them. This process was laborious, but it would *eventually* work.

"That thing, trying to chew through its own restraints, is the harbinger of something stronger, *deadlier* than any of us," said the Gargoyle. "Even you, Underlord."

"Why the concern?" Abrem Trosk asked.

"It was never supposed to be here," the Gargoyle yelled. "This thing belongs in the desert. Let the East deal with the consequences. We'd all be protected by Waylon's Isolation Spell. But the damn thing is *in here now,* you ignorant parasite."

The Scorpion Man cocked its head, looking at the room around him in eight different ways. Then, it proceeded to continue gnawing at the restraints.

"He wasn't a threat back in Cairo," said Hoxton.

But the Gargoyle didn't care what Hoxton thought was threatening. He figured that nobody inside of that crypt would believe him. In here, he was nothing short of a lunatic raving at the sight of a monster no more grotesque than any other behind these gateways.

The Gargoyle watched the Scorpion Man's mandibles finally shred through the last connection of his restraints, and wriggle his gigantic clawed hands free of them, letting the two pieces fall to the floor of his cell. The Scorpion Man turned around and faced the wooden box. He watched over it like a statue.

"Are there any more?" the intruder asked.

Waylon shook his head. The intruder didn't trust the response.

"You'll be paying for the chair and his medical bills," said Waylon sternly.

The intruder walked closer to Waylon, who stood his ground firmly. Neither of them were the type to be put over by the other. They both had exorbitant amounts of power, and they both knew how to wield it.

"Where is he?" the intruder prompted.

"Where's who?" Waylon said innocently.

With only one hand, the intruder grabbed Waylon by his furred collar and lifted him high up into the air, matching their eyelines eight feet off the ground.

"Toy with me again, poacher..."

"That chair was one of a very limited set," said Waylon without fear, "and my assistant is truly one-of-a-kind. The damage you've done to me is incredibly difficult to replace. Because I'm a better man than you, I'm only going to do damage that's incredibly *easy* for you to replace."

Waylon whipped a small knife from his sleeve and jammed it into the intruder's neck, straight into the jugular. The intruder dropped Waylon, who yanked the knife out and brought the blade straight down into the intruder's chest, piercing the man's heart. Waylon pulled the blade out one more time, and channeling all of his strength, shoved the intruder's body onto the floor. Withering on the ground, the intruder choked on his own blood for a few moments as the severed arteries in his heart and neck put themselves back together beneath his rapidly-healing gray skin.

Waylon ran over to wherever Jack fell and tried to help him up onto his feet. Only by feeling around did he discover that Jack wasn't there at all.

Thank God, thought Waylon.

The intruder stood back up to see Waylon produce a handgun from his coat. One of many, on standby. The intruder coughed out a final spurt of blood, clearing his throat from the previous moment's hemorrhage. Waylon winced at where it landed.

"You wouldn't have any idea how frustrating it's been to keep this goddamn carpet clean," Waylon grumbled.

The intruder deliberately calmed himself. He hadn't been beaten, but he hadn't accomplished much beyond incapacitating Waylon's assistant.

"I can't kill you," said Waylon, "but I can give you a world of pain with every bullet that comes out of this gun, Franklin Renwick Chamberton."

A noise was heard far behind both of them, sounding something like a door moving along its hinge. Franklin looked to the spot where Jack's body presumably laid, then back to Waylon. With a slow pace, Franklin started moving towards Waylon's gun.

"Test me to my limits, poacher, and tire yourself in boredom from it," Franklin said as he widened his arms, embracing Waylon's threat to the fullest. "I will not leave your home until I have him back."

Waylon took several steps back, preparing to fire as the gap between him and Franklin kept closing. Franklin sped up, and so did Waylon. Finally, Waylon shot twice: Once for each of Franklin's kneecaps. Franklin stumbled, then stood back up as the bones in his legs formed themselves back into place. Waylon watched as the bullets slowly pushed their way out of Franklin's body, tingling on the ground as though they were loose change fallen from one's pockets.

"Headshot, next. That's your best bet," Franklin advised.

Waylon had no reason not to heed Franklin's words: He executed Franklin straight through his forehead, watching as his brains blasted out behind him. This, and only this, managed to stop Franklin where he stood. The hole in Franklin's head reformed, the cavity filling with the gray matter and skull tissue that belonged there. The layers of muscle and skin reformed over the whole thing with a slithering quality Waylon could almost *hear* happening as he watched.

Franklin grabbed his temple and furrowed his brow. Decades worth of memories all flooded back into his mind rapidly, and he shook his head to power through all of the fog and haze. He fine-tuned this bounty of information down to the most recent year, then month, then week, then *day...*

Recalling the past hour's events, and what exactly he was doing there, Franklin continued toward Waylon in his deliberately slow pace.

"*Alright!*" Waylon surrendered, holding the gun in the air like a white flag.

Franklin stopped not three feet from where Waylon was standing. There were more bullets in his gun, but Waylon realized that they would only be wasted rounds.

"Your father's alive," said Waylon.

"Well aware," Franklin snapped. "That's not what I asked."

Waylon took a moment before speaking again.

"There is a room in this house where he sits down and watches his television, all day, every day. Though he's exquisite in every way, his personality doesn't fit well with the community I'm trying to foster and build," said Waylon.

"And what community is that?" asked Franklin.

Waylon holstered his gun, putting his hands behind his back in a cordial way.

"A haven," he replied. "A place to protect people like you from hunters and murderers, and to protect innocent people from monsters and nightmares."

Franklin stepped even closer: "Has he done anything more despicable than what you've been doing to us? You kidnap and imprison us against our will, hoping to *force* a community to form? By what, your own sheer willpower?"

"I would consider my actions far more ethical than what the Underlord did to your mother," said Waylon. "Perhaps it wouldn't have happened if I were around back then."

Franklin became uneasy. He was losing control of both the situation and his own temper.

"Define a monster, Waylon. Right now. What qualities does my father share with a vampire or a werewolf?"

"They're inhuman," Waylon quickly said. "They're dangerous. They cannot die. And most sound-minded men would try and put you down like a pack of rabid animals... But not *here*. This is the haven I'm creating, Franklin, and I'll protect it just as well as you would your own family."

Franklin prepared another question, but Waylon had stalled just long enough. Jack had returned, and using Waylon's body to block the view, placed the gauntlet in Waylon's hands.

Calm down, said the voice.

Gwen had been ignoring the bullets going off in Waylon's chateau. It was nauseating. The stress increased with every gunshot. Trauma of innocent men and women firing weapons at her as a werewolf rang in her head. It was one of the only parts of that half of her life that bled through into her human memories.

Waylon had been feeding her normal, healthy meals since her time down there. Her lesser half hadn't yet shown her face.

Open the mariphasa, said the voice sternly. *Right now.*

Ignoring the rest of the Gargoyle's ravings and rhapsodies, Gwen sat alone at her bed with the packet of mariphasa in her hand. She'd felt tidings of a coming transformation. Maybe it wasn't connected to the gunshots firing off above, she wasn't sure. Sometimes her shifts were completely random. Murphy's Law had led her to believe that it would happen at the worst possible time.

Waylon had cautioned against using the substance flagrantly. It was addictive, and its effects became less and less effective with further use.

Forget Waylon, said the voice. *Do it.*

"Shut up," Gwen whispered as quietly as possible.

Gwen put the packet into her nightstand's drawer and held her head in her hands. She was searching for the power within her to resist what she would become. Conjuring willpower was one of the most difficult tasks any person with a disease could attempt. So very few of them could pull it off without assistance.

And she had absolutely no assistance in that crypt.

Trying to distract herself, Gwen listened in on the crypt's conversations:

"How do you even know?" the Phantom prompted from the Gargoyle.

"It was *foretold*," said the Gargoyle. "The runestone-"

"*Every* culture foretells an apocalypse!" Hoxton yelled. "How many actually come true?"

Paula went ballistic on her cell's gateway. Never before was this crypt so passionately divided.

"I don't care if you believe me," said the Gargoyle. "I care that I see the outside of this crypt. This *country*. Stay here steeped in your ignorance and you'll find yourselves *dead*."

"*Death* will come for us?!" Abrem Trosk taunted. "That'd be a first for most present. Is the wooden box full of stakes and silver bullets, Gargoyle?"

Another gunshot from up in Waylon's chateau rang through Gwen's hypersensitive ears, claiming all of her attention. This one wasn't a conventional bullet.

Her heart began to beat faster.

Waylon pulled the gauntlet over his hand and took a step back, rotating the armlet and selecting a vile of red liquid as his ammunition. Franklin instinctively put his hand up to block Waylon's shot. It impacted him, spreading the weird substance over Franklin's palm and fingers, and dripping little globs down to his wrist. Like a corrosive acid, the liquid began disintegrating Franklin's right hand down to the very bones underneath. Franklin watched as the skeletal structure of his hand no longer heeded to his will. The fingers could no longer bend. The segments of bone in each finger, one by one, fell down to the ground, and after a few passing moments in this state of searing, unbridled pain, Franklin's hand did not grow back at all.

"It's a solution, reverse-engineered from Rebecca's notes," said Waylon. "Instead of restoration, it *degenerates* inhuman cells."

Franklin could not speak. He didn't have time to feel the emotion of anger. The fascination with his own physiology overtook all else in his mind for the time being. The pain was irrelevant... His body had always grown back, no matter what tore it apart. This substance, whatever *solution* it was, had been weaponized by the man who'd taken Adam captive.

There was nothing else for Franklin to do.

"Are you still here to negotiate his freedom?" Waylon asked.

Slowly, the long-delayed rage began to manifest in Franklin's heart. And it wasn't going anywhere.

"No," said Franklin, shifting his tone. "I'm here to let them reign blood from the imprisoner's throat."

Waylon became confused. *Them?*

With his remaining hand, Franklin reached into his pocket and pressed on the device unheard by human ears.

The first noise *heard* by Waylon was the sound of the large overhead window bashing in as the women arrived, landing almost gracefully amidst the splintered shards of glass falling to the living room floor. Even in such a violent entrance, the Underlord's two remaining Brides commanded their surroundings with divinity.

They were diverse in their beauty, but looked identical in age: The zenith of existence. The primes of their lives were now and always, with a powerful grace and artistry in their figures that most women would murder for.

Waylon turned the armlet to the wooden bullets. He got so far as to raise his weapon before Lillian had him by the throat.

"Calm yourself," Ilona ordered from Lillian.

Lillian stayed still for a moment, her blood boiling with rage. With her other hand, Lillian suddenly grabbed the gauntlet and aimed it at Waylon's own head. The vampire's strength was impossible for Waylon to match.

Lillian's thumb hovered over Waylon's trigger finger.

Ilona nodded to Franklin, who nodded back.

"I imagine she was getting a bit restless out there," said Franklin.

"We tried your way," said Ilona dismissively.

Lillian smirked, never breaking eye contact with Waylon.

Ilona smelled something strange. Something about the room wasn't right. Something nearby was unaccounted for.

Franklin watched Ilona's vampiric eyes scan the room, finding nothing. She closed them. It was her ears that had to track him down, honing in carefully on the man's blood flowing steadily through his veins. He was a calm one.

Finally, Ilona's eyes opened wide at a fixed position in the room.

Jack turned and ran down the hallway, his speed leaving audible footsteps. Franklin followed after him.

At the end of Waylon's chateau, one of the books on a huge, wooden bookshelf withdrew as if pulled by a human hand. Franklin stopped, watching the entire bookshelf revolve to its side, revealing a long, winding entryway made of stone and mortar illuminated by an array of artificial torches.

The bookshelf started to close.

Franklin sprinted towards it, just barely slipping past the hidden entryway before it sealed shut.

Bursting through the crypt's entryway, Franklin tackled the unseen body to the ground with his only hand. The two of them tumbled down the stairwell and landed not several feet from the crypt's main entrance. In a desperate attempt at freedom, Jack shoved his thumbs into Franklin's eyes, crushing his corneas and completely blinding him.

Rampaging without vision, Franklin tried to swipe at where he estimated the man's head to be, but instead only managed to grab a hold of Jack's mask, quickly peeling it off of his face. Jack looked on at Franklin, not through the lens of his invisible mask but with his own two eyes, and watched, with the artificial blood still dripping, as Franklin's empty corneas manifested new eyeballs from their sockets. Those newborn eyes peered straight into Jack's soul.

For all of the hideous, grotesque, twisted, disgustingly horrifying monsters that Jack had spent over a decade helping Waylon assemble in his crypt, no sight was truly so horrifying for him to witness. This, beyond all logic and reason, was his antithesis of well-being.

Franklin stood up slowly, not losing sight of Jack's disembodied head. It was the only visible part of him. Jack was petrified in his state of fear, and Franklin knew it well.

"Free my father," said Franklin, recovering from the pain, "or I'll do the same to you. *And yours won't grow back.*"

Like a whipped dog, Jack sprawled to his feet and ran off for Adam's cell. Franklin stepped into the crypt and observed them all in true fashion, reasoning that God himself wouldn't have allowed such demons to reign in Hell.

Jack arrived at Adam's entryway. The commotion had drawn his attention away from the television, and beyond Jack's floating head, he saw his son at the crypt's entrance.

It was a face he never thought he'd see again.

Try as he might, Franklin did not maintain eye contact with his father for terribly long. He was distraught by two things: The first was the peculiar source of what appeared to be sunlight from overhead, which he found to be nothing more than a television screen adorning the very center of the crypt's ceiling.

The second was standing inside one of the cells.

It was a quintessential answer to a lot of open-ended questions that'd drawn Franklin's attention, coated in ultraviolet light three cells to his right. Franklin's trigger finger started twitching at the sight of him, something completely involuntary on his part. Though visually human, so sinister was his visage, and so slender his wicked form.

Jack knew that there was only one definitive way out of this situation: To regain his anonymity and quickly flee. The tried-and-true tactic of an invisible man. He placed his hand not on the gateway to Adam's cell, but on the keypad beneath the suit on his wrist, and typed in a passcode only him and Waylon had access to. What Jack was about to enact was the proposed catalyst to Waylon's eventual utopia, available primarily as a tool for benevolence and harmony when the time would come.

But that time was not now.

In this moment, Jack activated it defensively. It was the last weapon he had against a full-on siege of Waylon's manor. The last hope at evading a feared torture or death by Franklin and his father.

And as an added benefit, whether Jack wanted to admit how he cared or not, this action would also bring Gwen a much better chance at her freedom.

For only a fraction of a moment, Jack and Franklin locked eyes again before Jack's head completely vanished.

Franklin held up his hand - the one that'd been holding Jack's mask - and felt only the grainy texture of his own skin. As he would find out, this revelation was the least important of his problems at that very moment.

The noise was universal, coming from every corner of the crypt at the same time: Metal clanking against itself. It echoed off every wall and slowly died down into a soft lull. Franklin watched as the failsafe on Jack's wrist silently triggered, simultaneously opening every single gateway in Waylon's crypt.

Many of the inhabitants stood in disbelief, and for a passing moment, nobody moved from their spots. Adam promptly grabbed his cell's gateway and sealed it shut, holding it firmly in place. He was the only one who did so.

The first ones out were the more animalistic of the lot: Perturbed by Paula's bashing, the Creature raced itself to freedom, splashing the water of its tank everywhere with its serpentine movements and frantic body language. It approached the source of the noise as the Ape-Woman charged out of her cell and tackled the Creature down, tumbling towards the center of the crypt.

This violent dispute set much else into motion.

Hoxton and the Gargoyle emerged simultaneously, both stone-skinned brutes cautiously assessing the situation... and their eyes met in an estranged fog. Without speaking, both of them acknowledged the tension brewing in the room, and a silent, uneasy alliance was formed. Their conflict with one another could only be resolved once this place was tranquillized.

Gwen stepped out and clutched the gateway's threshold as she began to shift in an anxiety-induced reaction to the oncoming meeting.

The Ape-Woman caught the Creature by its neck as it lunged for her, but the momentum was too strong: The Creature grappled the Ape-Woman, bringing her down and desperately trying to bite at her head. She rolled and thrashed with the serpent, eventually looking around for something, *anything* to help her - and snatched one of the artificial torches off of the pillar nearest to her.

The Ape-Woman shoved the object straight into the gullet of the Creature as it bit down, causing it to gag amidst the shards of shattered plastic. She kicked the sea beast off of her and got back onto all fours, her massive arms now cut up from its assault, and roared in a mighty way while batting her chest. The Creature spat the torch out and roared back at her, mimicking her deep, guttural tone, and pounded the ground with its tail.

The Scorpion Man's claw clamped down around the Ape-Woman's neck, and the Creature scuttered away at the sight of a much larger, more ferocious monster than itself. Hoxton's fist came crashing towards the Scorpion Man, only managing a glancing blow. He wound up another, but the Scorpion Man's tail ensnared the Brute Man's arm before the second punch could land.

It was chaos incarnate. A brawl manifested that would only end when the prisoners of that crypt reduced themselves down to a sole, bloodied victor standing over a pile of torn-up corpses. This is the vision all of them shared and aggressively pursued with their fullest, most vicious intentions. The crypt was the board for a grand game of chess with a dozen kings, and the threat of checkmate loomed over all of them at once.

Franklin scanned the growing crowd of monsters for his father, and saw him voluntarily locked away. He gritted his teeth. His job was being made far more difficult than he'd intended.

The Gargoyle avoided this struggle by batting his wings and launching himself straight for the hallway's exit. He saw Franklin near it and decided to avoid another potential fight, maneuvering straight over him and out of the dungeon. Acting out of instinct and fear, the Gargoyle absentmindedly *slammed* into thin air at the hallway's entrance as though it were a wall, feeling the moisture of rainwater on his rocky skin.

The Phantom, to his misfortune, was not involved in this scuffle. The soil beneath him limited his reach to the 7-square-foot cell floor, and nowhere beyond it in any direction.

Hoxton freed his arm from the Scorpion Man's tail, only for it to whip around and swat him away, launching him into one of the dungeon's pillars. Both the pillar and Hoxton's skin cracked upon the devastating impact. As Hoxton stood up, he noticed the Phantom to his right: This pillar was conjoined with the Phantom's cell, separating it from its neighbor.

"Step onto the dirt, Brute Man," said the Phantom in a voice hushed like a whisper.

Hoxton shot the Phantom a disgusted look before heading back to the Scorpion Man.

Near the dungeon's entrance, Franklin finally saw the Underlord standing and watching this all from his cell. Before he could decide whether or not to pursue the Underlord at that moment, he heard a scuffle from the wall near him. He turned and saw the Creature scuttering along the pillar to his right and tried to defend himself.

Like a moving car, the Gargoyle pinned Franklin up against the pillar of the nearest cell, bashing him into the artificial torch and shattering it. This weird noise caused the Creature to flee, scurrying somewhere else for a new encounter.

"Bring me Waylon," the Gargoyle demanded.

Franklin took one of the Gargoyle's forearms and freed himself from its grasp, feeling the incredible resistance of the Gargoyle's rocky skin. Near them, the Ape-Woman's body tumbled to the Gargoyle and Franklin's feet. Protectively, the Gargoyle panicked for Paula's safety for only a fraction of a moment. It was all Franklin needed.

Franklin kicked the Gargoyle's leg, then punched the stumbling Gargoyle square across the jaw, his knuckles splitting open when making contact with the Gargoyle's disgustingly thick cheekbone. Franklin winced in pain, but freed himself temporarily.

"Stay down, demon," Franklin yelled.

The Gargoyle's tail wrapped around Franklin's leg and squeezed firmly. His wings fleshed out to their fullest length and flapped only once, propelling them both straight into the air. Neither of them stayed airborne for too long, since something neither of them saw headed straight for the flying beast.

Crawling on the wall was a demon of a different breed: A feral beast with a mouth full of fangs and murderous intent. The voice in her head had gone dormant, replaced now with the Wolf-Woman's untamed ferocity.

Gwen's much lesser half leapt up and latched herself onto the Gargoyle's body. All three of them tumbled down together towards the center of the crypt, not far from the Scorpion Man's ongoing debacle. With his leg now freed, Franklin stood up and came face-to-face with the snarling werewolf.

The beast charged Franklin with a veracity that Gwen had no chance of holding back anymore. It lunged high, about to crash down on Franklin with both claws, but every move the werewolf made was carefully sensed and felt by the fast-reacting mutate. The moment it got close - the *instant* - Franklin caught the neck of the werewolf with his left hand, and wound up a punch with his right.

Franklin turned, seeing his right arm end at the wrist.

The Wolf-Woman snarled and hissed and clawed at Franklin's throat with disorienting strength, delaying his attack. One of its hind legs straddled the ground for support, forcing the two to hold this position. Finally, the werewolf's claw gripped firmly onto the neck of the artificial progeny, timed perfectly with Franklin's long-delayed strike: The severed nub at the end of his arm crashed into the werewolf's temple.

As the Gargoyle landed nearby, Hoxton delivered a devastating assault on the Scorpion Man, who blocked with his two massive claws. Bruises and cracks started to form on them. The Scorpion Man's poisonous tail *smashed* down onto Hoxton, then lifted up for another strike.

Hoxton dodged before the second hit. The tail instead collided into the Gargoyle's wings of stone. Neither the Scorpion Man's tail nor the Gargoyle's wings broke from the strike, but both of them felt the devastating impact's effects ripple through them. The Gargoyle stood up from the Scorpion Man's strike and glared at it with the unbridled rage and energy of the monster he knew himself to be.

The Scorpion Man retreated its tail in pain, backing up defensively. With escape ruled out as an option, the Gargoyle again took flight and charged at the Scorpion Man, and the two clashed in an ugly power struggle, their tails tactically trying to ensnare the other, and neither succeeding.

Hoxton held his fists up, instinctively protecting himself, but Franklin's unconventional attack had sent the Wolf-Woman careening towards him, and the two collided violently.

The recovering Ape-Woman batted her chest at the group of them with ferocious, uncontrollable anger. She looked to Franklin, who recognized her as, at least *partly*, a gorilla. As the Ape-Woman made her attempt at Franklin's life, Franklin held up his hand in a non-violent way. Without his other hand, he was forced to spell some of it out, letter by letter:

I'm not an enemy, Franklin quickly signed to her. *I'm a friend.*

The Ape-Woman froze, wide-eyed and distraught while still seething in primal rage. Many emotions wrestled in her mind at once.

Hoxton withstood the Wolf-Woman's ferocious attack of sharpened fangs and translucent claws, battering him with the feral power of an untamed beast. Tactically, Hoxton finally landed a punch to her chest, sending her some small distance away. She quickly sprawled to her feet as all four of her claws planted themselves firmly into the ground, startling Paula and taking her out of that trance-like moment with Franklin. Paula turned to her, and Gwen saw her back.

From a cell left alone at the dungeon's edge, the very patient Underlord had been quietly resting after the deactivation of the ultraviolet restraints. He felt that *now* would be the optimal time for his involvement. Nothing held back his sinister powers anymore.

The battle had escalated to insanity, with the entire crypt now filled with the sounds of ripping flesh and crunching bones. In a crazed state, Gwen tackled Paula and pinned her body to the ground, preparing a strike on her simian throat.

The Underlord held out his hand.

All fighting ceased instantly. Most of the beasts went stiff, freezing firmly in place. The Scorpion Man, the Ape-Woman, the Creature, and the Wolf-Woman dutifully directed their attention right to the Underlord. It was only Hoxton, the Gargoyle, and Franklin Chamberton who resisted the suggestive powers of the vampire, who held his dominion over all that his hypnotism could reach.

Calmly, Adam opened his cell's gateway and rejoiced with his son.

XVI

WAYLON'S GAME

Hoxton awoke to the sight of the bars of his gateway, seeing only pure darkness beyond them. He buzzed for a moment with the most throbbing headache he'd ever experienced in all three hundred years of his lifetime, since being suspended. His memory was foggy; He recalled fragmental details of what he was doing beforehand. Some forest somewhere, chasing a vampire down... That conflict had a definitive ending.

He killed it.

Turned it to ash with a wooden stake. Hoxton checked his side, finding it missing. *Where was this place?* The entire room was foreign to him, having more in common with a jail cell than a hotel room. Adrenaline hit his system as his reality started setting in. He rose from the bed he'd never seen before and ran straight to the gateway, clenching his hands into huge, destructive fists.

"Where am I?!" he shouted in the usual deep pitch of his voice.

The darkness became illuminated, and Waylon Ross stood right in the crypt's center.

Hoxton looked around: Empty cells ran across Waylon's background in a circular fashion, all facing him. Waylon started toward Hoxton's cell and stopped short of him, then slowly reached into his pocket and pulled out a journal. Hoxton recognized it instantly.

"You've done more research than any scientist who's ever lived," said Waylon. "A benefit of being alive for three centuries."

Hoxton slammed on the bars of his cage's gateway.

"Let me out!!" he screamed at his captor.

"I'm all in favor of it, but trust like *that* doesn't come for free. You'll have to earn it."

Hoxton shouted again: "Where am I?!"

"A crypt," Waylon explained, "where my father's enemies would rot from the inside. I have a more noble intention with it."

Hoxton seemed confused. Waylon smirked, and whispered: "We're a long way from East Freetown, Brute Man."

East Freetown. That was the place he last remembered. It was that faraway feeling of the rubber bullet bouncing off of his cranium. That sensation came from a biting, unfriendly synapse that reminded him of everything rather quickly:

Hoxton had followed the vampire to Massachusetts, caught up to it and destroyed it, when out of *nowhere* came a man putting a round in his forehead. *This* man in front of him.

"You shot me," said Hoxton.

"I could've done much worse," said Waylon. "I'm still not sure if an actual bullet would've pierced your skin or not, but I knew I didn't want you dead... I just knew I wanted you."

"Why?" Hoxton asked.

Waylon paused, thinking carefully before trying to explain it. Finally, when the answer came to him, he smiled and took a breath.

"You and I agree on our initiative. Evil should *certainly* be hunted. Where we disagree is whether or not it should be vanquished," Waylon reasoned.

Hoxton looked around his cell. He spotted many of his own personal belongings, most of which were not on his person when he lost consciousness.

"You broke into my home," said Hoxton.

"I purchased the property," said Waylon. "That's not breaking in."

Enraged, Hoxton bashed the gateway of his cell, clanking the metal against his unbreakable skin and shouted: *"RELEASE ME!"*

"I'm going to carry on with what you started," Waylon continued, "and take them away from their deadly environments."

"RELEASE ME!!!" Hoxton kept shouting, bashing over and over again on the gateway's bars.

"Vampires and ghouls and werewolves and everything else you've hunted with all of your blind, poisonous rage... They're going to be your neighbors. Whether it takes one year or a hundred."

For all of his furious, unbridled animosity, powering his unmatched strength and vigor, Hoxton couldn't break the binding force of the gateway's bars.

East Freetown was over 2,500 miles away from this manor previously owned by the late Abraham Ross. Once knocking the Brute Man unconscious with the rubber bullet, Waylon kept him sedated and cared after him for the eight days it took to transport them both, and everything in Waylon's log cabin home, down to Mexico. The only inhabitants of Waylon's old East Freetown home were the endangered animals he'd collected in childhood, which were no longer confined to the patio. They were now free to roam the entire breadth of the cabin.

Hoxton was Waylon's first capture, and after visiting Sigma, Paula had been his second. Presently, Waylon was venturing out towards his third.

Abraham's Progeny approached the lagoon's entrance with Waylon's steady hand at the helm. His other held the journal, rereading the highlights: *Predatory. Carnivorous. Claws, scales, spikes. Only known weakness: Beheading.*

Seven or eight months had passed since capturing Paula, Waylon wasn't sure. He hadn't been keeping track anymore. No activity he'd ever experienced made him feel so rewarded or so blissful. Still, he read words like "beheading" and realized that this book was written by a narrow-minded hunter. Its sole purpose was to answer two simplistic questions: *What is it and how do I kill it?*

Hoxton's journal was *almost* the godsend Waylon initially imagined it to be. The beginnings of the very secrets of the universe were in his hands, and yet they were incomplete and imperfect. They demanded many revisions.

The lagoon's entrance smelled revolting. Waylon actively ignored it, anticipating to stay here for longer than planned should anything go horribly wrong. The Creature - and that was indeed its very name, as the Brute Man first wrote - resided in the unnamed lagoon that Archibald Black wandered into in the 1700s. This species despised visitors. As all predators did. Whatever the case might've been, Waylon's harpoon gun would correct any mistakes in judgment.

Waylon's careful eye caught something moving quickly in the water, like a shark's fin or crocodile's spine, and it vanished almost instantly. Were it not for the wake created, Waylon might've doubted it happened at all. He pocketed Hoxton's journal and grabbed the harpoon gun leaning against the boat's rail. It was large and clunky and awkward to wield, especially for his second time using it. The first was on a whaling trip his father brought him on, though he only fired the thing with Abraham holding his hands where they ought to be, like a father teaching his son how to swing a golf club. Waylon hoped those very basic skills would serve him well on this trip. If not, he had several contingencies, like the tranquillizer gun in his waistband.

At this point, Waylon figured that he had to be deep enough into the lagoon's maze-like structure to encounter it. Any further, and one would most likely be heading out instead of in. If that was even possible in a place like this. The journal reported as much, but that was no guarantee at all. As was clearly evident to him, Hoxton's notes already needed many revisions.

Waylon saw it move across his eyeline at the same exact moment that he'd heard it scutter across the ship's deck.

The fact that it even *landed* on board in such a stealthy way was a guttural shock. The fact that it moved so wildly faster and meaner than Hoxton and the Ape-Woman combined... *This* was what disturbed Waylon the very most. His slow draw on this unconventional gun would need to outmatch the Creature's brisk motions. Waylon fired the harpoon straight where the Creature was, but wasn't able to lead the shot at all. The Creature continued its motion, scuttering up the stairs on the exterior and onto the bay where Waylon was near.

Reloading was unattainable.

Waylon reached for his waistband when the Creature came for him. Learning from his encounter with the Ape-Woman, Waylon actually managed to aim his shot when drawing. The Creature's slick, slimy scales snapped the tip of his shot before it tumbled onto the deck, rendered completely useless. What's more, the shot itself didn't even slow the Creature in its rampage.

There was only one more trick for Waylon to try. But he had no time left to try it.

Waylon's kevlar vest prevented the Creature's claws from penetrating into his skin, but didn't prevent the massive relapse in pain from where Paula fractured his ribs less than one year prior. Waylon fell backwards, letting the Creature land over him and pin him down with its clawed feet. Having moved like a panther, the Creature now stood bipedally, flexing the full extent of its dexterous body, and letting that massive tail slither along the floorboards beneath them both. Waylon pulled one of his last remaining weapons and jammed it into the beast's leg, bracing for any further pain.

It was a knife, aimed between the Creature's scales, and laced with a poisonous chemical called rotenone.

The Creature removed its foot from Waylon's chest, shaking instinctively to free itself from the pain. The blade had already started damaging the Creature's cells, killing it little by little. Cringing in an almost brutal agony, Waylon came to his feet and pulled the last item, this time from the inner pocket of his coat. He fired the police-issued taser at the Creature and stunned it, letting the extreme voltage course its way through that large, protean body.

The Creature slumped to the ground, seizing mildly. Some sick, petty part of Waylon took pleasure in the sight of it. He admired creatures like the one he'd just beaten, but resented the fact that his chest pain had returned. *Occupational hazard,* he figured. The thought made him laugh. And laughing brought him pain.

Waylon returned to the helm of *Abraham's Progeny.* Before turning the ship around, he noticed another Creature just like it in the swamp's marshy wilderness.

It was a third the size of the one he'd just caught. A third the size of what was described in Hoxton's journal. One became two, then four, then... There had to be dozens of them, flocking around him and staring at his ship. Staring at Waylon.

Offspring.

Scanning the Creature's stunned body, Waylon found traits of a parthenogenetic animal. One that probably laid its eggs underwater, judging by how defensive it became when a ship passed through this approximate area. Theoretically, a mother protecting her young would be the most likely cause for a beast to attempt to slaughter an entire crew of dozens of non-confrontational people...

Many, many revisions.

Unlike the previous logs in Hoxton's journal, Waylon's next target didn't reside on the obscure waters of some strange, uncolonized island. The Mechi were more audacious than that.

Waylon arrived in Chicago's inner city when the weather had cleared, allowing for a nice view of the city's inhabitants from the hotel he planned to stay in. Crime rates had begun to plummet in this section of the town to a near-zero rate. It was either an unlikely miracle for the city, or a byproduct of something much larger.

He'd done a lionshare of research on an Officer Kerry Blake, a local policeman who moonlighted as an esteemed member of the Ku Klux Klan. Decades of this man's life had been spent harassing minorities and acting aggressively, at worst serving a one-week suspension for excessive force. Officer Blake, as of the past year and a half, hadn't done anything like that. He'd also stopped visiting his favorite coffee shop in the morning. Favorite fast food restaurant. *Any* restaurant.

It just so happened that Officer Blake had rented a room at this hotel tonight.

Waylon's room was three floors removed from where Officer Blake was staying. He'd waited until Officer Blake's car pulled into the lot, only to see through his window that Officer Blake wasn't alone. He had a little boy, no more than twelve or thirteen, accompanying him inside. Waylon did find records of a son when investigating him, but he would be in his thirties by now, and had moved out of Chicago many years prior. Even more remarkable was the apparent fact that, inconceivably, the boy at Officer Blake's side was black.

Racists and pedophiles, by anyone's standard, were absolutely monsters. But these were not the kind that Waylon was interested in hunting.

Waylon ascended the stairs in the maintenance section of the hotel, arriving at Officer Blake's floor. He casually walked down the entire hallway, over and over, until the elevator doors opened and Officer Blake and his companion exited. Waylon carefully tracked them both to their room and watched carefully as they entered. He waited several moments before preparing to break the door down. His handgun, carefully-chosen to be of lower caliber ammunition with a strong silencer attached, was drawn from his side and aimed straight at the door's bolt.

Waylon fired and kicked the door down, coming face-to-face with two of them.

Mechimigardions, or *Mechi* as Hoxton had described in his journal, were nothing more than a mass of bright-red tendrils stemming from some unseen central point. These creatures ranged from seven to eight feet, but there were no torsos or brains to speak of. They moved and slithered with unbelievable speed in such a mesmerizing way to a spectator, and such a horrifying way to a target. This was the Mechimigardion poised beside Officer Blake and the little boy: A twisted web of disgusting red tendrils. Blake, still in disguise, made a weird, blank expression toward Waylon. An expression that decomposed into the slithering tendrils underneath.

The Mechimigardion that used to be Officer Blake moved quickly toward Waylon, latching onto the floor, walls, ceiling, furniture, and anything else around it with the litany of tendrils that made up its form, and moved like a millipede on stimulants.

Waylon shot at the center of the mass, piercing the body of the disgusting thing. This slowed it down substantially. Waylon ran past it and shot several times at the second one before it could ensnare the little boy and feast on him. He only wanted *one* for his crypt, and in all good conscience, decided to kill the one about to consume the child. This act of heroism, though subservient to his own agenda, was agreeable to a man like Waylon Ross.

The Mechimigardion went limp on the king-size hotel bed, flopping its tendrils all over it and sprawling out everywhere. The one formerly known as Officer Blake recovered from the gunshot and ensnared Waylon's wrist, yanking the gun out of his hand. With his other, Waylon produced a knife and jabbed at the tendril, causing it to recede. Faster than one could even think, the Mechimigardion dashed out of the hotel room.

Waylon ran after the monster, turning the corner to see Officer Blake running down the hallway. The thing had changed appearance and began running for the elevator. Waylon produced his secondary rifle from deep in his coat pocket, and for several seconds, maintained a perfect shot on the monster's body.

He couldn't pull the trigger.

They looked indistinguishable from people in every capacity, duplicating anybody they consumed with stunning accuracy, including finer details like clothes and hair. The shift between forms took seconds, unlike the horrid, painful transformation of a werewolf. This, combined with their incredible speed, made them predatory to all life forms on this planet, common or monstrous. It also made them extremely difficult to track.

After today's events, the Mechi would undoubtedly leave the city as fast as they'd come. A year and a half of planning for absolutely nothing. To kill Officer Blake would restart the hunt for another one of them. To let him run, at least long enough to track him, would keep that hope alive for just a little while longer.

Before the hotel's staff could ever come and intervene, Waylon ran back into the room and severed a tendril off of the Mechimigardion's corpse. He looked over to the little boy, shellshocked in the corner and unable to speak, and sighed deeply. There wasn't time to apologize or explain anything that'd happened. The Mechimigardion that killed the real Officer Blake probably realized that a position of power could procure and lure victims much easier than an average citizen ever could.

After torching the rest of the dead Mechimigardion's body, Waylon notified the front desk about the missing child in one of the rooms. When far enough away as to be finally clear of local authorities - Mechi or human - Waylon reread Hoxton's notes and added this alarming fact to them: A benefit of their seamless autobiological control was the ability to completely avoid capture. Even with his skills and vast financial resources, Waylon knew that a creature like this wasn't something he could capture on his own.

He needed assistance.

The apartment was dark. The man who lived there had been out all day, and kept Waylon waiting in the chair in his living room. He'd passed the time watching videos on his phone, seeing no need to go through the inhabitant's belongings. Waylon knew all there was to know about this man. Even how to break inside the home of the stealthiest man alive.

The front door opened wide.

And then closed.

"Keep the lights off, Jack. There's no need for them."

At the sound of Waylon's voice, the light switch flipped itself on, revealing nobody. Waylon faced the spot where he approximated the man to be standing, and remained untroubled by the fact that the invisible man had completely ignored his initial request.

"I'm not here for trouble," said Waylon cautiously.

Waylon felt those footsteps making their way toward him. Preemptively, Waylon drew a gun from his waist before the inhabitant got too far. The footsteps stopped, and the room was returned to its state of silence and insensibility.

"Just take the damn mask off, at least," Waylon grumbled. "This is becoming strange."

After a moment, the inhabitant pulled the stretchy visage off of his head and revealed a pale, sweaty face underneath. Thick, curly black hair covered half of it, matted together in many parts.

"Do you ever wash that thing?" Waylon remarked, just noticing the man's body odor.

Waylon kept scanning Jack's head for more details. It was the only part of him now visible, and it simply floated in the middle of the living room, unresponsive to anything Waylon asked.

"Jack, this isn't going to work if you remain silent."

"You know too much," said Jack in a gravelly voice. He rarely used it.

"Assume I know everything," replied Waylon.

Jack walked over to the bathroom to remove the rest of his suit, completely ignoring Waylon's gun or threats. Not wanting to be rude, Waylon allowed it.

"You gonna kill me?" Jack yelled from behind the closed door.

"No," Waylon yelled back. "I'd be doing a terrible job of it."

"Then what do you want?" Jack yelled. "The suit?"

Waylon could hear the faucet turn on. He also heard the magazine *clip* into the pistol, something Jack just tried to drown out with the noise.

"No," yelled Waylon. "And you can hold that gun over your head when you come back out here."

The faucet turned off.

Out stepped Jack from the bathroom doing exactly as Waylon said. His wardrobe had been reduced to sporting pants and socks, unwashed for several days.

"You don't take it off very often, do you?"

Jack glared at his intruder.

"How often do you get a contract, Jack?"

"About once a month," said Jack. "Twice is a *good* month."

"And yet, a man with this incredible, unique gift still lives in a shithole like this?"

Jack said nothing.

Waylon could see it in his eyes. It was clear that Jack wasn't motivated by money at all. Something passionate inside him *drove* him to do what he did, and live this holistic sort of way. Jack wished he'd never taken off that damn suit when he walked inside.

Waylon rose from his seat, and with his free hand, reached into his pocket. "You're not happy like this, mate. You don't have to admit it."

"What do you want from me?"

"*You.*"

Waylon produced a card from his pocket. He placed it on the armrest of the chair.

"You're doing God's work with nothing to show for it," Waylon went on. "Day in and day out. You *like* doing it, don't you?"

Waylon took the gun from Jack's hand, letting his arms fall back down.

"I can give you a better deal, Jack. A steady paycheck doing legal work. Off-the-record, out of the country. You'd channel your violent tendencies into something more productive."

Jack eyed Waylon down. His rage was subsiding, but it lingered like a stench.

"Doing what?" he asked.

Waylon smiled. He couldn't help himself.

"Hunting."

Adam Chamberton awoke into bondage and darkness. He could not move despite his strength, and he could barely focus amidst the strong, painful haze in his mind. Enough tranquillizer to kill a horse flowed through his veins, and for a period of time, actually *did* sedate the artificial man. The immune system of Zeus himself was a difficult thing to try to combat.

The muffled voices weren't audible at first. Then, with Adam intently focused, he began to hear their conversations:

"We need better weapons," said a man in an Australian accent.

"I thought that went *swimmingly*," said another. American, this time.

"We got lucky," said the Australian. "His son had already left by the time we arrived. He might track us down when he finds out... We'll need a way to combat the boy's healing factor if he comes for revenge."

"You didn't expect him?" the American asked.

"The journal didn't say anything about him having a son," said the Australian. "Probably checking up on him."

Adam thought back to last night: He'd invited Franklin over to celebrate his father's birthday. They only spoke on birthdays and Christmases, though neither of them really liked holidays, and it was never more than a few hours at a time.

The Australian was only half-right. It was hard to keep in touch with a boy who wanted little to do with his father.

"I'll need to read the rest of this journal if we're going to continue," said the

American.

"When we get back to Mexico, if you're so curious," said the Australian.

So we're traveling, thought Adam. *In what vehicle?*

"Curiosity, sure," said the American, "but also *preparation.*"

"I've already made the preparations for our *next,* Jack," said the Australian.

And we have a name, Adam reasoned.

"Where to?" Jack asked.

"Paris," said the Australian. "We're after a ghost. Or ghoul, spirit. Whatever the verbiage."

The conversation ceased. In the meantime, Adam had deduced several details: Their vehicle was a car, not one built for off-roading. Probably something expensive, which detected every minor imperfection in an unsmooth road. The jostling of Adam's confinement suggested it, combined with the slight shift in weight when turning.

"Your exit's up here," said the Australian.

Highway. That coming from the Australian meant that the American was driving, assuming there was nobody else in the vehicle.

Adam's left thumb had slipped free from the restraints.

Feeling around with the tip of his thumb, Adam found that these restraints were nothing more than several layers of firmly-placed duct tape, probably encasing more of his body than could be felt at the moment. Adam's range of motion was so limited, and he had no field of view at all. He only had his thoughts. And his left thumb.

"I like the new jacket," commented Jack.

"You do?" the Australian responded. "Figured I'd need something stronger than my usual one. It's a werewolf's hide, woven over double-layered kevlar."

"For all of those broken ribs you're going to get," Jack pointed out.

So a trophy hunter, Adam thought. *And I'm just the prize.*

The Australian changed the subject: "All Hoxton's notes detail about them are the value of iron and salt."

Adam could feel a way to free his full hand from the restraint. He could burst out at any moment.

"They don't seem like ideal materials for building a ghost's trap," said Jack. "If there even is such a thing."

"There *isn't* such a thing," said the Australian happily. "I admire the way your mind works. Always pragmatic. Analytical. But hunting is more than logic and reasoning."

It seemed that every moment spent revealed more and more information about these two strange men. Whoever they were, death wasn't a factor to consider, so Adam felt no fear or uneasiness about his own kidnapping. If anything, it would be best to absorb as much information as possible until a firm plan of escape could be manifested.

Channeling all of the world's patience, Adam returned his hand to the bondage, pretending to be unconscious.

"I'm pretty sure you did tell me about this creature once," said Jack. "It was the opera house that burned to the ground. The one they built a restaurant on top of."

"That's the one," said the Australian.

"Waylon, you can't just barge in, guns blazing - sorry, *iron and salt blazing* - and expect to capture a ghost," said Jack.

And just like that, Adam had both of their names.

"As entertaining as all of that sounds," said Waylon, "I have a better idea."

"All ears," said Jack sardonically.

"I bought the restaurant," said Waylon.

Waylon Ross was on his way home with a large bin of dirt.

It was all of the dirt, as measured by some of Waylon's amateur spellcasting, that the Phantom remained irrevocably bound to. Every particle and speck that could be accreted. Jack opened the front door and let Waylon in, as his hands were full. Though the box easily must've weighed fifty or so pounds, Waylon hadn't broken a sweat from carrying it all the way from the car in his garage up that long walkway to his front steps. Jack had offered to carry it, but Waylon enjoyed the exercise. His ribs had been fully healed for several years now. Daily workouts were back in full swing.

"How do we coat the cell's floor if we can't open the bin?" Jack asked as the pair made their way downstairs.

"Very quickly," said Waylon. "I'm thinking we get down there, pull the lid and *dump* the whole bloody thing out. He shouldn't be able to possess us unless we're in direct contact with it."

"Good a plan as any," Jack replied.

Jack opened the passageway that led to the crypt, letting Waylon first down the stairs. That's when the noise became more prominent. It was a banging sound, like two pieces of steel smacking into each other. Waylon passed the bin to Jack and sprinted down to the crypt, drawing the gun from his coat. The rounds were lethal. He would consciously try to *maim* one if he had to. Nothing more severe than that.

He found Hoxton having bent the gateway to his cell.

Half of the bars had broken open. Given Hoxton's tremendously tall form, he needed more than that to break through and attempt to run free. Waylon's presence froze Hoxton for just a moment, and the two men locked their sights on each other. A mutual understanding of conflict, soon to breed chaos.

"Stop it!" Waylon yelled as he aimed the gun.

Hoxton eyed him down. Almost casually, he resumed pounding the gateway open.

His knuckles had cracked and begun to weaken against the repeated pressure. But that didn't matter. Hoxton's mind fixated on only one goal in the entire world: Break free from this place and kill every living thing inside of this mansion.

Waylon fired into Hoxton's cell. A warning shot. It bounced off of the cell's wall and landed into the television's screen, shattering it into a spider-web. Hoxton screamed, putting everything he had into one final strike through the broken bars, and threw his entire body through what was left of the gateway. He tumbled onto the ashlar floor, his foot getting caught on one of the gateway's bent bars, which caused Waylon to miss him when firing the second shot.

Both Waylon and Hoxton were hunters. They'd spent most of their lives learning how to hunt, shoot, and efficiently kill their targets. They both knew that the specific gun in Waylon's hand had a standard capacity of ten rounds. Hoxton had no choice but to brace for eight more shots and hope he'd survive.

Waylon shot a third time. Hoxton threw up his arm to block it, and the bullet cracked one of the scales on his forearm. Hoxton ran at Waylon, who shot for a fourth time, this time into Hoxton's chest. Two scales on Hoxton's pectoral muscle splintered, but remained in place. This area of his skin was some of the thickest on his body. Before the fifth shot, Hoxton was finally close enough for a righteous smack to Waylon's body, sending him near the Ape-Woman's gateway. The gun fell, allowing Hoxton to snatch it ungracefully. He immediately opened the magazine and took a look.

Six rounds. Waylon hadn't used it at all today when hunting his next prisoner.

Hoxton held the gun with his mighty hands, barely fitting his finger through the guard. He swiveled in circles for a moment. His breath was too loud and quick to try and detect wherever Jack was roaming. Finding Waylon's assistant was impossible.

So it was time to run.

Instinctively, Hoxton sprinted for the crypt's exit, bolting up the stairwell. He burst through the door at the top of the steps, almost tripping over Waylon's bin.

Bin? *What the hell's that doing there?* He had no time to think about it. Scanning the room, Hoxton finally located the front door. His only objective. He had no time to take notice of the bin's lid opening itself up, guided by Jack's invisible hand, and scooping itself into the bin of dirt.

It was only a small handful of dirt that the bin's lid flung onto Hoxton.

Like a magnet to steel, the Phantom flew into the Brute Man's body, seizing control of him. The Phantom *screamed* in Hoxton's voice, unleashing an incredible, deafening noise that shook almost every room in Waylon's mansion.

"*I'M FREE!!*" Hoxton's voice bellowed out. Paradoxically, Hoxton himself was far from free. He was bound by the spirit's ethereal grip on its magnificently strong vessel.

"No you're not," said a disembodied voice.

The Phantom looked around through Hoxton's eyes. Nobody had made that comment.

"*Show yourself!*"

"You of all creatures know the value of being unseen."

"*Where am I?*"

"You're in the body of a very *dangerous* individual," Jack explained to the

Phantom. "This is my gift to you. Repay this favor, and walk it back down that stairwell. You'll be rewarded."

"The exit is right there... I could just as easily run away."

"And go where? You're on the other side of the world from where we found you, and you're perpetually bound to the dirt in this box. As soon as that vessel dies, you'll be transported right back inside of it, and when that happens, Waylon and I will not look so favorably upon your presence."

The Phantom used Hoxton's sight to analyze the home. This huge, lavish place. It was fit for absolute royalty. A serious improvement from the ashy remains of his Parisian opera house. Whatever waited for him down that stairwell must only pale in comparison to the world he could see.

"Stay here," Jack continued. "Earn your trust. And when the day finally comes, Waylon will be more than happy to let you out. I'm sure he'd welcome his home being haunted by another invisible ally."

The Phantom waited before responding. Everything this mysterious voice said to him made a great deal of logical sense.

But it was not the same as freedom.

Hoxton's body ran for the front door, swiping the chateau's furniture out of his way. He braced with his elbow and *bashed* open the front doors, charging through them with unstoppable momentum. The Phantom opened Hoxton's eyes and saw the daylight above, shining down on his mutated body. He saw the forest ahead, and the undulating driveway that cut through it. A path to freedom. A path to wherever he wanted to go.

And he ran. He ran using a pair of legs stronger and swifter than any body he'd ever inhabited, even his own before death. The disembodied voice's threat would never come to fruition, because this body was too strong to die. Too powerful. It was made solely to be enjoyed by its user, free of any worries of harm or defeat. Free of everything at all.

A bullet drove itself into Hoxton's shoulder blade.

The body fell down to the grassy field just before it'd made it to the forest's edge. It wasn't a bullet from Waylon's sidearm that lodged itself through the armored skin and into Hoxton's upper back, but the insuppressible round of a sniper rifle. As the Brute Man's body fell, the Phantom saw the view of the rifle that'd shot him: Floating by the front door, suspended in the air.

Perhaps the most confusing aspect of all was the fact that the Phantom felt no pain whatsoever from the gunshot, as if he were only lightly pushed or shoved over. The Phantom could clearly feel the damage to his upper back, the armored scales crinkling as he tried to move. But it was only that: A faint feeling that something was broken. Nothing more.

The evanescent daylight fell upon Waylon's furred collar as he knocked back a nip of vodka. The tall building in front of him seemed insurmountable, given the lingering pain in his chest.

Waylon had spent six weeks recovering from Hoxton's mighty swing, and minor doses of alcohol often quelled the pain. Nothing fractured internally this time, his chest having been cushioned by the kevlar in his jacket. At this point, Waylon had become used to this process of recuperation: Six weeks recovery meant that he had his mornings to himself, not needing to wake up early or exercise most days. He even abstained from watching his usual movies when he awoke. There was no need to break the Pavlovian technique he'd been married to. It was a self-induced reprieve.

At the start of the seventh week, where Waylon could finally stand up and breathe without a gut-wrenching pain shooting through his chest, he'd asked Jack to select the next target and "surprise him." Analyzing Hoxton's journal was fun for him. These targets were so much more interesting than the clients he'd been used to before being hired by Waylon's estate. Despite any monetary power, those clients were always human. Nothing like Waylon's usual fancies.

After a short while of consideration, Jack had settled on their next creature. He'd never been to Paris before.

Hoxton's notes regarding this "Gargoyle" described an unfortunate encounter between them: They met inside of this cathedral, clashed briefly, and neither emerged victorious. Hoxton detailed in his notes that the skin of the creature was likened unto to his own, although probably stronger and denser. No way to kill it had been discovered yet.

But of course, Waylon wasn't interested in killing it. This Gargoyle was the only one of its kind. In fact, he didn't bring any weapons. He didn't even bring Jack.

Waylon's only plan was to *reason* with the creature in such a way that the Gargoyle would, voluntarily, wish to join his community. All of the evidence pointed to this being possible: Hoxton described the Gargoyle as "loving to hear himself talk" and "sophisticated to the point of nausea." Being a man of culture and wealth, there existed no reason in the world for the Gargoyle not to voluntarily join Waylon's new community. If anything, he'd be the least problematic of the inhabitants.

This cathedral was in Paris, making Waylon feel like a fool for not considering *this* creature's capture when acquiring the Phantom. A double-excursion had never been attempted, and from the disparate locations of the remaining creatures, was looking unlikely. Perhaps it was for the better. Waylon's body could only take so much damage at a time.

Day was slowly becoming dusk. Waylon wanted to visit this place when it was bright and sunny, but didn't have the patience left in him. The Gargoyle was unique. None in this *world* were like it at all. He couldn't wait to meet such a divine species. After throwing the bottle away, Waylon scaled the cathedral's walls and entered through one of the windows. In his notes, Hoxton described going straight through the front doors and into the nave, passing by the empty aisles. Waylon wasn't so careless. His skin wasn't made of stone.

Waylon arrived at the octagonal bell tower. Carefully, he searched around the room, which didn't look lived in at all. It was cold and empty; Any bell-ringer would need a nice jacket and a little bit of food to stay here overnight.

"How did you find me?" said a voice from the walls.

Waylon spun around. The dimming sunlight was just enough to scan the surrounding architecture: He saw only dust, cobwebs, and the bell itself.

And gargoyles at all eight corners of the room.

"Hoxton," said Waylon unwavering. "His journal-"

"The Brute Man?!" yelled the voice.

Waylon spun again, looking closely at all eight of them. None appeared to be moving. Not even to breathe.

Because none of them were.

The Gargoyle landed behind Waylon with such force as to send him backward onto his hands and knees, tumbling across the old floor of rotting wood.

"Do you serve him?" yelled the Gargoyle.

Waylon looked up: The hulking mass of the creature was all he could see towering over him. No double-woven jacket would stand up against one swipe from the monster's massive arms. Waylon knew that his destruction would be just as painful as it would be swift.

"I've put an end to the Brute Man's crusade," said Waylon. "He made an attempt at your life in 1926, did he not?"

The Gargoyle leaned forward, using its front arms to support itself like a jaguar inspecting its freshly-caught prey. Waylon, terrified unreasonably, maintained his composure as usual. He'd seen beasts more sinister, creatures more bloodthirsty. Allegedly, this one was fond of conversation.

"How did you kill him?" asked the Gargoyle.

Though he didn't smile, Waylon did widen his eyes at the question. His charm was bleeding through in a way noticeable by the stone-skinned beast.

"I didn't," said Waylon.

The Gargoyle leaned back.

"I brought him somewhere *better*," Waylon continued, standing up. "A place removed from the perils of man's bloodthirst, where creatures like him can live out their lives without harming one another."

The Gargoyle thought back to the castle with no doors he'd constructed for his goblins. It served the very same function.

Waylon swiped the dirt off of his clothes. He coughed during the process.

"I'd like to invite you there," said Waylon. "I had to *capture* Hoxton and cage him up. That's not my intent with you."

The Gargoyle became skeptical. This was one of the bravest men he'd ever met, teetering on the edge of stupidity.

"Why isn't it?" the Gargoyle asked.

"Because you're smarter than that," said Waylon.

And the beast's attention was no longer divided.

Not a week after this encounter, Waylon found the Gargoyle at his doorstep.

Seeing the crypt's setup and design, the winged creature became fully on board with Waylon's vision of this unconventional community. He even showed Waylon how to cast an Isolation Spell around it, with a caveat that only *humans* may cross between the barrier. Keeping himself confined with the rest of them would yield more objective data when the experiment concluded.

Waylon read the passage in Hoxton's journal over and over:

Wooden stake through the chest turn them to ash. Holy water (catholic) burns them on contact. Lack of bloodletting for ~50 years would allow them to die of old age/natural causes... — Sunlight??

It was all of the data that Hoxton had gathered on their weaknesses. It was more than enough for the Brute Man to track them down and hunt them like he had for many, many years. But Waylon had been doing the same for a different purpose: He'd realized that they all had some singular, enigmatic leader. A Vampire King that, allegedly, owned and bound every vampire in the world.

An entity called the Underlord.

Through the express torture of his last vampire victim, Waylon became aware of an event: On the fifty-year anniversary of his youngest Bride, the Underlord and his concubine would elope in Romania. Repeating the tactic used for the Mechi, he'd booked a reservation at the very same hotel they were staying at. He'd learned from the failures of his last version of this plan, and decided that this time would be different for two very important reasons: Waylon didn't plan on breaking the door down and shooting everybody like a madman. And he wouldn't be alone in this attack.

Per Jack's reconnaissance, Waylon knew that there were three entities in that room: The Underlord, his latest bride, and two semi-conscious hostages. Whether or not they were still alive was of no concern to him. That's not what the initiative was for.

Finally, after an hour of waiting, Jack reported back to Waylon that the Underlord - going now by "Abrem Trosk" - had brought one of the hostages out of the room: A beautiful woman in a gray dress. By Jack's account, that meant there was one hostage and one vampire left in that room.

Abrem Trosk returned to the room not three minutes later, ready to enjoy a wonderful night with Hope and the other hostage. She was the one dressed lavishly in red, who'd been dipping in and out of consciousness when he'd last left. He'd told Hope not to start without him. He wouldn't blame her if she had. Powerful, delicious young blood coursed through the woman's veins, carrying pure happiness wherever it flowed.

Upon opening the door, Abrem Trosk instead saw only an open window. It was strange for several reasons, not the least of which being that these windows were never designed to open up. Abrem Trosk closed his eyes and listened. His hypersensitive hearing found many heartbeats closeby. Many more than there should be. One hiding in the room's closet. One passed out on the floor beside the bed. And a third, more steady heartbeat. The beat of a man without fear at all.

A man standing directly in front of him.

Though Abrem Trosk opened his eyes and saw nothing at all, he reached forward into the air and snatched at the throat of the invisible man.

The room's threshold lit up with blazing purple lights. The entire doorway had become illuminated. Abrem Trosk knew the sensation too well, and dropped Jack from his grasp.

Ultraviolet lights.

They bore down on him, keeping his body harmlessly human. From the closet, Waylon emerged as if he'd successfully remained hidden. As if the Underlord only trusted his eyes when dealing with a situation like this. Waylon didn't need to raise the crossbow for Abrem Trosk to know he'd been beaten, and couldn't dream of turning around or running away. But Waylon did it anyway, and showed a clear view of the thinly-fashioned stake holstered in the crossbow's center.

"Vengeance?" Abrem Trosk asked.

Waylon hadn't expected to be the one who talked second.

"For what?" Waylon asked.

Abrem Trosk rolled his eyes. "Did I not kill somebody you care for? A wife, parent, sibling…"

"No."

"Well I don't think it was your child," said Abrem Trosk. "I rarely take children."

Waylon nodded to his assistant. Jack lifted up the body of the woman in the red dress and brought her to the bed, placing her down gently.

"Were you going to turn her?" Waylon asked.

Abrem Trosk didn't respond.

"Was Hope going to?" Waylon continued.

Abrem Trosk cocked his head. He couldn't scan Waylon's mind so easily with those purple lights beaming down on him. He could only use his charisma. And he'd spent several millennia perfecting it.

"Your runt is human," said Abrem Trosk. "Not a ghost or some unseen demon. There's a man hiding under that disguise. No different in biology from you."

"Oh, he's very different from me," said Waylon.

"Hardly," said Abrem Trosk. "Men like you are all the same. Sapient bags of blood thinking they're in control of their own lives."

With Waylon maintaining the crossbow, Jack stepped past Abrem Trosk and out into the hallway. Shielded by those lights, Abrem Trosk couldn't have drawn blood from Jack's veins even if he wanted to. Only then, as the invisible man passed him by, did Abrem Trosk stumble upon a curious thought: The amount of heartbeats in that room never added up, and he hadn't sensed his lover since walking into this room.

"Where is Hope?" Abrem Trosk asked.

"Somewhere far," said Waylon cryptically.

Abrem Trosk looked again at the doorway he'd been caught in: The lights blasting him had been installed quickly and efficiently, from the moment he left the room, with surgical speed and precision. Hope had become a formidable fighter after she'd been bitten by him, so the fact that these two simpletons entered this room *so very quickly* to incapacitate her and ensnare the Vampire King confounded everything he knew. Very, very few humans were this smart, and the ones that were usually weren't so strong or so fast. Perhaps this is why the pair worked in tandem with one another.

But all of this was far too much work for a simple attempted murder.

"What are you going to do with me?" Abrem Trosk asked Waylon, never breaking his confidence.

"There is a place for you," said Waylon. "I've built it right beneath my home. There, no one will ever be able to track you down and shove a crossbow in your face."

"You're offering me protection?" Abrem Trosk asked. "By *force?*"

Just then, Jack had returned, carrying a large coffin over his head.

"It goes both ways, mate," said Waylon. "Out in the world, men will always try and hunt you down, and you'll always feed on them to survive. It's a toxic cycle... Why deal with it at all?"

Jack entered the room and shut the door. He laid the coffin down in front of Abrem Trosk, revealing the ultraviolet lights shining inside of it.

"Now law down," Waylon explained. "When that lid opens, you'll wake up in a community of people like you. Monsters and creatures shunned from society. Hunted for being who they really are... Your years of running and hiding are finally over."

Abrem Trosk laughed.

Waylon didn't understand. It wasn't funny. Not one joke had left his lips.

Leaning against the door for support, Abrem Trosk held himself from all of the laughter he'd generated, letting it flow through and out of him. Waylon waved off Jack from intervening. After a long while, when Abrem Trosk finally caught his breath, he looked back up at Waylon with a genuine smile stuck to his devilishly handsome face.

"I admire your attempts to play God," said Abrem Trosk. "It may well be one of our only similarities."

The home belonging to Officer Kerry Blake resided in a high-end planned community somewhere in rural Illinois. Waylon ordered Jack to park about a mile away in the edge of a parking lot shared by three businesses. He reasoned that a parking lot for only one business would be watched more closely, whereas with multiple, the others could reasonably assume the car's driver was visiting one of the others, and be less likely to tow it.

They'd located the house with some difficulty, seeing as every home on this cul-de-sac was identical to every neighbor's home. The only distinguishing features were the numbers on the mailboxes and the types of cars in the driveways. With approval from Waylon, Jack walked straight up to one of the front windows in broad daylight, completely unseen in his usual uniform, and peered inside. Seeing nobody, he quietly slid the window open and let himself in.

Waylon looked to the neighbor's yards while waiting for his companion to return.

This was the sort of place operating as if it were several hundred years prior. Every family in every house was whiter than the Sun. Most of these families were wealthy enough to afford a housemaid, if not two. For as far as Waylon could spot, whether they were inside doing housework or outside working on their gardens, every single housemaid had much darker skin than the owner's.

But something was even stranger than this archaic system.

Nobody smiled. Nobody frowned. Nobody so much as looked down at their phones, checking any of their notifications. Waylon had been hiding for several minutes now behind this house's shrubbery while waiting for his assistant's return, and spent the entire duration *studying* this neighborhood like it were a novel. The very sight of this entire neighborhood induced careful analysis, reflection, and a tinge of pure fear.

The window slid open again, and soon shut itself.

"He's upstairs on his laptop in an online chat room. I saw his wife in her true form, crawling through the spare room like an octopus. Shoving its tendrils into old boxes and bins of memorabilia. Probably learning as much as it can," Jack diligently reported.

"Jack, I need you to do something for me," said Waylon.

"What's that?"

"Follow as I move. Protect me if anything happens, but *do not strike first,*" Waylon ordered.

"Waylon, I don't think-"

But Waylon had already started walking away. Jack clenched his fist and swallowed before following Waylon into Officer Blake's neighbor's driveway. It was at the street's edge where the housemaid was getting the mail.

Waylon grabbed her arm suddenly, letting the envelopes fall to the ground. He produced his knife from his side and held it up to her throat, looking not at her, but at the neighboring houses.

Through every single window, every single entryway, and every single area where one could see, all of the people in Waylon's sight turned and looked straight at him. Dozens of them, amidst many homes, gardens and driveways all turned in unison to Waylon's position. Only now did Waylon turn and look back at the housemaid he'd ensnared. Her gaze was cold and emotionless, just like all the rest.

"What is your purpose?" Waylon said to the housemaid.

At Waylon's voice, the housemaid's head briefly shifted, only for a split second, into its tendrilous form. If Waylon weren't watching closely, he might not have noticed the slithering and re-camouflaging of her otherwise *normal* appearance.

Finally, she answered him.

"To exist," she whispered, still showing no signs of emotion.

Officer Blake's front door opened up, and out walked the couple. It was him and his wife, whom Jack saw crawling in her true form earlier. The two of them were unmistakably human in their appearances now. And they all shared that housemaid's blank, lifeless stare.

"How often do you feed?" Waylon asked, now talking directly to him.

Officer Blake paused before answering. "Once every few months to function properly."

Waylon looked around him again, seeing the neighborhood stoically staring back at him. *Each one of them... every single month...*

"You eat children?" Waylon asked.

"Age, gender, and ethnicities don't cloud our unbiased judgment. We look first for the isolated. Ones of low profile. We don't harm without purpose, and we don't take more than we need," said Officer Blake.

Waylon knew that at the flick of his knife, he could eradicate the Mechimigardion posing as the neighbor's housemaid, and Jack would soon follow on by killing Officer Blake and his wife. Even if the rest of the community transformed into their natural states, they wouldn't dare try to attack or outrun Waylon and Jack as they fled for safety. But this was not the plan Waylon wanted to execute.

"The man you killed. The real Officer Blake. Do you retain his memories?" asked Waylon.

Officer Blake nodded.

"What was he like?"

"Him and several others from this community organized supremacist rallies every Sunday. One of the last thoughts in his mind was regarding a plot to attack the human version of the person you're holding," said Officer Blake.

Waylon let go of the housemaid's arm.

"He harmed without purpose," Officer Blake added.

Waylon saw the community around him. No country's military was ever so united. They saw, heard, breathed, and felt everything as one mind, and it showed clearer the more that one watched them. It was a surreal orchestra, with all members playing their part in perfect synchronicity.

"How many of you are there?" Waylon asked.

"Between two and three percent," said Officer Blake.

"Of what?"

"Your population," said Officer Blake.

Waylon took this in. He'd already lowered the knife from the housemaid's neck. A brawl was seeming less and less likely.

"Will it ever be lower than that?" Waylon asked.

Officer Blake shook his head.

"Will it ever be *higher?*" Waylon asked.

Again, Officer Blake shook his head.

With that, Waylon made an important decision.

"So long as you leave me alone, I'll do the same to all of you," said Waylon.

Officer Blake, and his entire surrounding neighborhood, seemed confused by this compromise.

"You're not troubled by our presence in your world?" Officer Blake asked.

"I *am,*" said Waylon, "but I have no further interest in hunting you."

Jack was shocked. He wanted to say something, but despised the idea of revealing his location to this group of people. If they could even be considered that.

"Of all of the ones who discover what we are," said Officer Blake, "none have ever said anything like that to us."

"I imagine they don't really say *anything,* do they?" Waylon replied.

For the final time, Officer Blake shook his head.

With Jack following him, Waylon departed the planned community just the way he'd come into it, and with everyone's eyes on him as he did so. When the two of them arrived at their car in the large parking lot, Jack paid careful attention to the people inside of the three businesses.

"Waylon-" Jack said quietly.

"I know," said Waylon, who didn't even bother to look at their stoic faces watching their every move.

A mile's walk ago, Waylon had learned rather shockingly that the Mechi were all hive-minded. One shared consciousness cataloged every victim's thoughts and memories as they became assimilated. And that meant he could never capture one of them without the others knowing about it.

XVII

DRAKE'S ONLY CHAPTER

FOREWORD

WHY THEY CAN'T BE STUDIED

Magic is a real, tangible concept. It's always existed, accessible by every culture in the world since the dawn of civilization. And much further before that. This basic knowledge has fallen out of favor by way of technological sciences, and fallen out of popular belief by way of contemporary skepticism.

It is that last element of skepticism mentioned that I am trying to change, and it is nigh-impossible.

In the world of science and discovery, the burden of proof is - understandably - quite high. It takes more than eyewitness testimony to push the boundaries of our own ignorance. Even though there have been historical documentations of magic which predate modern data-taking tools and methods, this information is not verifiable or falsifiable by any real metric. All that is true, objectively, is that our ancient ancestors *believed* it, and wrote about their experiences attempting to harness its breadth.

It is in this book that I will attempt to explain some of my findings.

I cannot describe the means by which I've accreted this information, for fear of somebody repeating what I've done. I can only share the findings. The following will serve as an eyewitness testimony regarding, arguably, the single most important discovery that mankind may never make. I log my findings only to advance our scientific understandings, bypassing testable methods for the safety of those attempting them. Mine has already been compromised, and it will soon kill me.

Do with this information whatever you can. Write articles, teach at universities, win Nobel Prizes. This world is more useful to us if we know that it is there, and it is not leaving us. But for your own life, and the lives of the people around you, do not become curious. Do not desire to know more.

CHAPTER ONE

WHAT THEY ARE

In a time before time, the form of our universe was wicked and desolate.

All of existence coalesced to a singular point, equidistant to nothing and everything. Rules and laws that govern the physical world conflicted with one another at this scale, and once the quantum and the gargantuan broke apart, a passionate, unbridled chaos was let free. This was the form our universe then took: An abstract vitality consisting of a cross between gaseous matter and cosmological energy, unrelenting in its expansion. Unrelenting ad infinitum.

Remnants of this colossal event discharged in all spatial directions, and the very same forces that bind our existence today kept these remnants from wandering too far. Materials grew denser. Atoms and molecules conglomerated into planets and other wanderers across our night sky. Forged in the heart of the uproar were new stars, whose size and composition would determine how many billions of years they'd brighten up the blackness of space.

It is among these stellar origins that their time begins.

Massive gaseous beings of all states of matter sway and flow through the endlessness of interstellar space. These sapient, ethereal beasts have no limbs nor heads. Particles of all natures oftentimes get wrapped up in their essence, gaining the same sentience as the rest of its physique, but much like gravity, are irrevocably bound together.

They do not think in the conventional sense, as understood by intelligent life, but they do feel. They glide through the bleak nothingness amidst solar systems and the galaxies they comprise with energies that rival those of the largest stars in the universe.

They are immortal by default. Visually, their anatomy is reminiscent of the tail end of a comet. An intangible mind possesses each composited body. Extromytes, of course, are composed almost entirely of cosmic stardust, but this term is inherently broad. Fractions of matter lost from the Extromyte lose this property and return to their inanimate state, boundlessly adrift in the expanse. Their particles are disparate, detached, free-flowing in their essence yet cohesive in their motions. Thus, no impact could harm them, and depending on their contents, no extreme temperature could destroy them.

What is incredibly rare across almost all of these beings, is if two of these delicate, indescribably dazzling creatures were ever to meet each other.

When a phenomenon like this astonishes the lonesomeness of space - for a fraction of a second - a blinding flash of light reigns through the cosmos. Not unlike a strike of lightning, but radial. The kind of burst to fill one's sight were it to be witnessed by somebody, which it never has been. The two bodies slowly bind souls into one organism, inheriting the other's components in a divine, magnificent matrimony of body and being, and the moment they fuse that tight flicker of pure, unsolar light races away from the new, singular Extromyte.

Throughout their journeys they are drawn to and settle in the habitable zones of stars. The sunlight sustains them, seemingly forever, and its presence typically gives way to a planet or moon's genesis of life. This life they naturally generate keeps them healthy, recycling their air via the metabolic processes of terrestrial organisms.

The Extromyte that encompasses Earth has never met another like itself.

It is several billions of years old, and migrated to our sun's habitable zone about a billion years after Earth first formed. The Extromyte found this place, scorching and desolate, and took refuge among its primordial surface. This being, whose essence is that of several layers of gases and cosmic stardust and whose age almost eclipses our universe's, is the source of all worldly magic.

Sentient life on Earth can only manipulate the physical world around them by conjuring the innate interstellar essence of the Extromyte around them. The Extromyte they know primarily as the air that they breathe. This is the same air that's kept birds and planes from falling once they achieve lift. This is the same air that manifests clouds, infinitely cycling our world's water skyward as ethereal mist, and back downward as rainfall's precipitation. This is the same air that conjures sporadic strikes of lightning, giving rise to the mythic nature of Gods and Heavens above.

This air, and everything in it, is still that same cosmological entity which unwittingly navigated to our world billions of years before life ever stepped out of the ocean and began to industrialize.

Our atmosphere is predominantly nitrogen and oxygen, with traces of other gases and particles all over our periodic tables. Beyond these trace elements lies a consciousness unknowable by our minds. The books written by early Man deal with ways and abilities of using the atmosphere for their advantage, serving the ones they love with protection spells and cursing the ones they hate with voodoo dolls. Symbols and talismans and sacrifice and blood are common components for activation. Cultures who've practiced Voodoo, Witchcraft, Sorcery, Black Magic, Maleficium have used all of these different words across our ancestor's languages to describe the same basic concept: The manipulation of our natural world through supernatural forces.

No book ever written, by anybody over the entirety of human history, has ever described how this being works, since all who feel the need to understand it only become more and more enamored by it. This desire tears them down. Something inside the Extromyte causes the cells of the curious man's brain to unravel and deteriorate amidst the growing lust of learning the inner machinations of the Extromyte. This is a biological feature of the Extromytes, safeguarding themselves from intelligent creatures in our universe who could use this information to destroy them. Not unlike the spikes of a cactus, dissuading hungry predators.

This is happening to me.

It has torn my marriage apart, alienated me from my family, my brothers and sisters, my own children. I no longer feel love for any of them, and I don't feel remorse in my heart. These things are objectively true, and to most, subjectively immoral. Studying our Extromyte has been eating away at my mental well-being, causing a sickness for which there is no cure. My mind is beginning to fail me as well: I've lost control of certain metabolic processes, like breathing or digestion. My methods proved their composition, which will comprise the following several chapters, but most recently I've discovered more than I set out to: By analyzing their anatomy and the processes by which they operate, I've caught a glimpse into our potential future.

Our universe is in a superposition of particles, each of which are heading in their own directions and interact with each other in ways that will occur. If one had all of this information, and knew the superposition of every single particle in our universe, observable or otherwise, then the following is all very easily calculable:

Billions of years from now when our sun expands, and when life no longer propagates beneath it, the Extromyte will do what is natural and leave us in search of another habitable zone. Its life as our atmosphere will have concluded.

Immeasurably further into the future, in the waning millennia of our universe's lifespan, our Extromyte will have long since left our cluster of galaxies and encountered another habitable zone of a new star system. One that does not exist yet. This will be a place so unfathomably distant that we could not dream of a way to understand it. When it reaches this place, traveling further than any other life ever will, the Extromyte will no longer be alone. Another will already be there. Another just like itself.

In a cataclysmic event equidistant both in space and in time, the two will merge, and for no more than an *instant,* our dark, expansive cosmos will be greeted with a vibrant interstellar blaze. A raw, orbicular blast of unbridled power will flash across the essence and existence of spacetime, lighting up our universe with the strength of a billion suns and the gravitational impact of a black hole, closing quickly into one culmination of a new Extromyte.

Do not become possessed by a desire for this type of knowledge. It is inevitably fatal. In the following chapters, I will elaborate more on their physiology, diets, life cycles, and the reason they seek planets habitable to carbon-based life like ours. All of this is exclusionary of *how* I discovered this, which I must forcibly take to my grave. You breathe in our Extromyte every moment of every day, waking and sleeping. It knows your own thoughts better than you do. It can *feel* them. As you inhale and it enters your lungs, oxygenating those blood cells of yours, the Extromyte is unprejudiced in its toxic dominion over you. It senses when your mind becomes too keen on discovering something it never should. It will rule unseen with breaths ever-taken so long as men need their brains and lungs to survive.

XVIII
THE HOUSE OF THE MORTAL ALCHEMIST

The Underlord gestured with his wrist, and in unison, the Scorpion Man, the Ape-Woman, the Creature, and the Wolf-Woman all lined up by his sides. Adam broke away from the hug, and met the illusive gaze of Elsa's murderer.

"Hello again, abomination," said the Underlord.

Hoxton and the Gargoyle both looked over to the artificial man and his son, confused on how to proceed. These four were the only ones in that crypt with minds strong enough not to succumb to the Underlord's suggestion, but that didn't mean they were well-equipped for whatever was about to follow.

Hoxton and Franklin readied for another bout, raising their fists. Adam held out his hand and shook his head, as if calling them both off.

"Brute Man," said the Underlord. "We almost met many years ago. I'd heard word of your death at the hands of a Creature like this one."

The Underlord looked to the Creature from Black's lagoon, but Hoxton wasn't impressed.

"I know you're Sam Bertrok," said Hoxton, having deduced the man's identity long ago.

The Underlord smiled. It was a compliment to him. He then turned to Franklin, and majestically gave him a nod.

"You have my gratitude," said the Underlord. "It is not an easy thing to attain."

Franklin seethed quietly in his own hatred as his trigger finger started twitching again.

Unaccounted for, the Underlord turned his gaze finally to the Gargoyle.

"You're a beauty," said the Underlord in admiration. "I've rarely actually *seen* you, Gargoyle. Mostly just heard you bitch."

The Gargoyle was in no mood for a discussion.

At the crypt's entrance, Ilona and Lillian arrived with Waylon's body, bringing it directly up to the Isolation Spell's barrier. Lillian pulled Waylon's head up by his hair, making him audibly cringe.

"Break the enchantment," Lillian barked at him.

With no assistant closeby and no way to resist, Waylon abided. He held his hand high and chanted something in another language, causing the markings of blood on the crypt's pillars to catch fire and a building wind to generate from within the crypt's walls. With a feeling not heard or seen but *felt* by all in that room, a strange wave of energy struck each and every one of them.

The Isolation Spell was lifted.

The Underlord's Brides dragged Waylon right to the center of the crypt. Adam, Franklin, Hoxton, and the Gargoyle did not move or speak as they entered, carefully assessing the situation individually. Their desires were manifold: Adam's being the safety of Franklin, the Gargoyle's being escape, and Hoxton's being the death of almost everything walking or crawling in this twisted home of captured nightmares.

Franklin's mind was elsewhere entirely. He was still processing the fact that he walked straight into this crypt before the Isolation Spell was lifted. On some level, no matter how small, he was considered human. At least by the semantics of millennia-old magic.

The Brides dropped Waylon at the Underlord's feet, and saw the many monsters behind him. They felt the dominion he held over them, for it was that familiar bind over their many wills. It brought a sense of pleasure and a tinge of excitement to Lillian, who dreamed of the many-faceted possibilities to be had with all of these new minds and bodies.

Lillian again held Waylon's head up by his long, curly hair as he forcibly kneeled down.

The Underlord took a step closer to his prey, then graced Lillian's cheek with his pointed nail, caressing it slowly down to her chin. He was proud. Now being the youngest Bride, she had the most to prove to him. The Underlord looked over to the four monstrous men unbound by his dark forces, and glanced at his Brides.

Faster than one could think, both Brides charged Hoxton. Each of them twisted one of his arms behind his back, forcing the Brute Man down onto his knees in an inescapable bind. Franklin was the only one shocked by this maneuver. Adam and the Gargoyle had expected something like it, but were surprised that the Underlord had been so lenient.

"Abomination," said the Underlord, "it's my understanding that your son aligned himself with my Brides to perform this extraction."

Adam looked to his son. Franklin nodded.

"In exchange for freeing you," said Adam, "you will allow my son and I to abandon this wretched place, and leave you to your ways."

"My *ways?*" the Underlord scoffed.

Franklin stared at his father. This is not what he wanted.

"Whatever it is you, and your vampire horde, wish to do with your lives," Adam clarified. "We will not interfere in any of it. Now and forevermore."

"Yes we will-" Franklin began to speak until Adam grabbed his son's arm.

"Be quiet," said Adam.

The Underlord smiled. It was admiration, primarily. Of all his victims in recent years, Adam's will was the strongest he'd ever known.

Franklin was furious. He would've spoken his mind some more were it not for the look on his father's face. It was a look that told him, without any words, that there was always a plan in place.

"We will take these two as well," Adam said confidently.

The Underlord lost his smile.

"You negotiate a deal after it's already taken place," said the Underlord.

Adam continued: "The Gargoyle is harmless, and the Brute Man has hunted your kind for centuries. Neither have bent to your mind's will. If they stay here with you, you'll probably kill them anyway."

"But they are not owed to you," insisted the Underlord. "Nor to your abomination son."

Adam took a step closer, sparked by a newfound rage.

"You beat me to a bloody puddle of broken bones and spattered blood, and ordered your Brides to do the same to my innocent wife. And yet without my son, born *from* that woman you slaughtered, you'd still be rotting away under Waylon's ultraviolet lights like a sad little lobster in a fisherman's pot. You owe me *everything,* you disgusting serpent, and I will settle for nothing less than what I ask you to give."

Franklin's fury subsided.

Ilona and Lillian looked to their Master, fearful of another battle. Not wanting to delay tonight's plans any further, the Underlord relented with a sour taste in his mouth.

"Take them and never return," the Underlord said sternly.

The Brides released Hoxton. Briefly, the Gargoyle looked to Paula, seeing no life behind her cold, blank stare. It killed him inside to know that the Underlord had that hypnotic hold over her. She deserved so much more than the life of a vampire's lackey.

Adam and Franklin started to leave. Before following them, Hoxton glanced over to the Phantom's cell, accounting for the crypt's last inhabitant. The cell was quiet and empty.

The Gargoyle turned to follow Hoxton, Adam, and Franklin out of the crypt, leaving everybody else in Waylon's mansion to the vampire's maleficent will. In the Gargoyle's hundreds of years spent on this Earth, he'd become accustomed to accepting the things he could not change.

After ascending many steps, Adam, Franklin, Hoxton, and the Gargoyle reached the hallway leading to the manor's entryway. When they reached the chateau, the Gargoyle stopped them all before they could open Waylon's grand entryway doors.

"Listen well, as you'll *very much* want to hear this," cautioned the Gargoyle. "When the sky goes black tonight, this side of the world will be eradicated."

"What?" Franklin blurted out.

"Let him finish," Adam said with conviction.

"Thank you," said the Gargoyle. "We cannot stop it. It's impossible. But if you allow me to teleport us, I can bring you all to the safest place I know."

"Enough with your *doomsday* nonsense," grumbled Hoxton.

"It's all true," said Adam.

Franklin turned to his father with skepticism.

"Dad, the Brute Man is right," said Franklin. "This Gargoyle is insane."

With an apologetic look, Franklin nodded to the Gargoyle: "I mean no disrespect."

"Belief isn't easy at first," said the Gargoyle. "Regardless, it's *still* in your best interests to let me transport you: The Underlord never lets a loose end walk away from him. Wherever we travel on foot, those hellions will follow."

This quieted Franklin, who had known very well the efficient brutality of the Underlord. The vampires would track and monitor him and his father's every movement thereon, waiting patiently on a timescale of centuries until a vulnerability emerged.

"Alright," Franklin relented.

The Gargoyle nodded knowingly, then turned to Hoxton.

"Keep your witchcraft away from me," Hoxton clarified.

"I don't care if you come," the Gargoyle replied. "But you need to give me your blood."

"What?" Hoxton said reflexively.

"Theirs is artificial, and I am only stone," said the Gargoyle. "You are the only real blood available."

It all clicked in Franklin's mind. *This* was why he brought them. He needed them both, and *only* them both.

"Do what he says or we'll take it from you," said Adam boldly.

Hoxton read the room: Two men who couldn't be broken, and a duo who could never die. After the crypt's most recent events, another fight would be reductive, painful, and last a very, very long time.

Compliant, Hoxton reached into his own mouth, where his skin had no scales at all. He jabbed his coarse, claw-like thumbnail into the roof above his tongue and sliced a jagged wound. Blood began to pour, which the Gargoyle caught with cupped hands of talons and stone.

"More," said the Gargoyle.

Hoxton shot the Gargoyle a nasty look. He dug deeper into the incision, slicing into his mouth's sensitive veins. With an overflowing amount of Hoxton's blood in his hands, the Gargoyle knelt down and painted symbols on the floor below them. The symbols encircled them tightly, causing Adam and Franklin to step closer together, and Hoxton to step out of the ring completely. When the Gargoyle was finished, he spoke in the same language Waylon did earlier.

A powerful wind formed in the room from nowhere. The four of them watched as the Gargoyle's symbols started catching fire.

Hoxton had rarely witnessed any magic since he became suspended. He despised the concept. The flames of the symbols on the floor wavered and shook in the fierce winds, now building stronger and stronger. He looked to the front doors of Waylon's mansion, then back to the three of them standing in the portal. He'd thought of all of his sleepless nights in Waylon's crypt, and how the Phantom's escape attempt left a spiderwebbed pattern in his right shoulder blade from Waylon's sniper rifle. The bruise had healed, but the cracked scales of his skin never looked the same since.

Before the snowstorm blasted out of existence, Hoxton stepped inside and instantaneously vanished with them.

Waylon looked around him and saw the uncaged beasts taken by the Underlord's control.

The poacher was not bound like most victims of kidnapping would be. He was allowed full, unchecked movement of his entire body as he stood in the crypt's exact center. The Underlord loomed over him and placed the sharp, vampiric fingernail under Waylon's chin, lifting his head up slowly.

"There are many questions that we'd like answered," said the Underlord.

Instinctively, Waylon felt the pockets of his coat. Though he was subtle about it, the Underlord scoffed at what he was doing.

Ilona came from behind Waylon and held the bottle of holy water over his head. As Waylon turned around, she poured it all over his face and hair, drenching every square inch of the man's scalp with it. Lillian giggled, making Ilona giggle at it herself with that same infectious humor they often shared. She tossed the empty bottle to Waylon's feet.

"To be human, rid of the fear of sacred water and wooden stakes," the Underlord mused. "How *calming* it must be for a mortal alchemist."

"My species is also vulnerable to a wooden stake through the chest," replied Waylon defiantly.

The Underlord ignored him. He walked to the beasts under his control, starting at the leftmost one: The Creature from Black's lagoon.

"Three hundred years ago, I did my best to *hide* this sort of Creature from any curious man's grasp," said the Underlord.

"Don't beat yourself up over it," snapped Waylon.

"How did you discover it?" the Underlord asked. "I doubt you *happened* upon it as Captain Black once did."

"He didn't happen upon it," said Waylon. "He was deliberately searching for it. It's why you executed Iliff Frye."

His words struck the Underlord like a bullet from a gun. The Underlord turned to Waylon, his eyes shifted, and possessed by something unsettling.

"How do you know about that?" asked the Underlord.

Waylon, stone-faced, kept his mouth shut. The Underlord maintained his cold, otherworldly gaze on his victim.

"How do you know about that?" the Underlord repeated.

Again, Waylon remained silent. The man trembled as he held in the truth, prompted by the Vampire King's wicked sense of suggestion. Then, with a steady pace, the Underlord said it one more time: "How... do... you... *know*... about that?"

Waylon was sweating now. Though he struggled to close his eyes, Waylon finally *forced* them shut. He made his mind go blank. Void of all thought. Void of all feeling. Just one man's pure conviction and resilience. Nothing inside for the Underlord to try and latch onto.

Finally, the Underlord released Waylon's mind. Waylon collapsed to all fours, breathing heavily.

"Your will is strong," the Underlord remarked.

With bloodshot eyes and a face turned almost red, Waylon looked up at the Underlord without any cowardice: "Stronger than Archibald Black's."

The Underlord felt a whisper from his side. It wasn't audible to human ears. It was barely audible to his.

He turned to the only cell still inhabited.

Raging winds enforced the air's frigid, unlivable temperatures outside, viewable through the only window in the entire home. A window reinforced with many, many layers of insulated glass.

It wasn't a localized snowstorm brought on by a sorcerer's teleportation. It was the view outside.

The view was an icy landscape, stretching farther than normal eyes could ever see. Nothing in any direction indicated any form of civilization, or anything beyond endless plains of permafrost. The home's interior, despite this hellish environment, was rather cozy and comfortable. It was patterned after castles of the Middle Ages, with two notable exceptions: There were no other rooms but this one, making it resemble more of a *fort* than an actual castle, and there existed no door whatsoever. If not for the window, there would be no openings or entryways inside or out of this place at all.

Hoxton had a look around: Fine, expensive furniture adorned one, glorified living room, and weapons and artifacts coated every surface of the surrounding walls. Nothing else was present.

"You've decided against witnessing the world's end firsthand, Brute?" the Gargoyle remarked.

Hoxton was aghast. This place was so far from what was expected that it left him confused. He knew of the Gargoyle's Parisian roots, and his deep affinity with Nordic culture, but he'd never anticipated a place like *this* to be his preferred home.

"Where are we?" Franklin asked.

"I'd rather not say," said the Gargoyle. "I don't need curious souls like you hunting this place down."

"What kind of castle has no doorway?" Hoxton pointed out.

"Mine," said the Gargoyle dismissively.

Franklin turned to his father, a chip still on his shoulder.

"Why'd you let him off so easily?" Franklin asked.

"The Underlord?" Adam asked, sensing his son's rage. "That was a very long time ago. Holding that grudge only brings pain and heartache."

"He *killed* mom!" Franklin pointed out.

"And if he hadn't, I'd never have brought her back, and we'd never have had you."

"So he's forgiven? Just like that?"

"Is *this* why you broke me out?" Adam asked. "Your own, personal revenge?"

"*Our* revenge," Franklin barked. "You were there that day. He killed her *and* my grandfather. How is this... not..."

Franklin shook his head in frustration. He couldn't tolerate too long of a conversation with his father before the subject of Elsa came up. It's why he rarely visited.

"There are more important things in life than your hatred," Adam said.

Adam finally noticed Franklin's arm, and grabbed where his hand used to be.

"What happened to you?" Adam asked cautiously.

"Waylon," said Franklin, pulling his arm away.

"Why isn't it returning?" he asked, feeling over the grooves of the nub.

"He's inverted the serum," said Franklin. "It won't grow back."

Adam was silent. The careful, calculating cogs in his head began to spin in his usual way when some new thought possessed him. The serum had seemed so *immutable* up to this point. The very idea of a counter-agent for it felt absurd to ever consider.

As the stress began to wear off, Hoxton still had some trouble processing the Gargoyle's mystical abilities. This monstrosity, though allegedly an ally, didn't seem at all friendly.

"What contact have you two had?" Hoxton asked Adam.

"Enough to plan an escape, should the opportunity ever arise," Adam admitted. "He's fluent in sign language. Him and Paula."

"Paula?" Franklin asked.

"The Ape-Woman, whose cell I never faced," said Adam. "Her and I were adjacent. Only *he* could maintain contact with her."

Franklin looked back to the Gargoyle, sizing him up with a newfound respect. The Gargoyle recognized this, and nodded.

"Romania, was it?" the Gargoyle asked Adam as he went over to the many drawers of his dresser.

"Yes," said Adam. "The house we discussed."

The Gargoyle opened the dresser's third drawer. It was the largest dresser any of them had ever seen, and it held no threads of laundry. At least a dozen jars sat in that third drawer, filled to their brims with the blood of many species: Human, animal, vampire, werewolf, and everything in between relevant to magic. The Gargoyle took the jar of goat's blood, the way the old witches of Salem used to do it. It was optimal for teleportation, in his experience. Human blood had a longer delay.

"If you follow news cycles, there are going to be endless reports about it, and Mexico's going to be Ground Zero. Ignore it if you don't want to feel so ill inside," said the Gargoyle as he began drawing symbols in the castle's center.

Hoxton watched him do so. Every symbol was being drawn onto a pre-placed stone, fashioned in a large circle in the middle of the floor. Nearby, a towel and a bottle of bleach caught Hoxton's eye, with the coloring of the towel having faded from white to pink from too many uses. This house was nothing more than a conduit for the Gargoyle's many travels. A rest stop on the long highway of the ever-moving magician.

"He's bringing us home?" Franklin asked, coming to his father's side.

"He is," said Adam. "This is the deal we struck should a breakout ever occur. And we knew one would once he'd captured the Underlord."

"I offer the same to you, Brute," said the Gargoyle. "A show of gratitude for sharing your blood with us."

Hoxton cringed at the idea of teleporting again, but he didn't have much of a choice.

"Massachusetts," said Hoxton. "East Freetown."

Something didn't sit right with Franklin. He turned again to Adam, almost in disbelief at what he was about to say. But it was how he truly felt.

"We need to go back," said Franklin.

Hoxton and the Gargoyle shot daggers at him.

"To Waylon's manor?" said the Gargoyle.

Franklin persisted: "There are a dozen people trapped in Waylon's dungeons. The vampires have control over them. What do you think they intend to do with all of that power? Rebuild the Seven Wonders?"

Hoxton remained silent, though very much engaged in their conversation. If a conflict between anybody were to become physical, he would have no part in it, and instead only deal with the fight's victor. For his own sake, he'd hoped it would be the Gargoyle. He was the only one with any ability to bring somebody out of this place.

Franklin turned to his father, pleading: "Our blood is *toxic* to vampires, so they'd have trouble trying to stop us."

Adam shook his head, realizing what exactly his son intended to do.

"There's no guarantee that it would work," said Adam.

Franklin looked at him with those artificial eyes of his own progeny. They carried Elsa's likeness more than his own. With all else uncertain, Adam knew that Franklin had to *try.*

And so did the Gargoyle.

"You can't save them all," said the Gargoyle as he finished painting the symbols. "If you endure the Underlord and his company, it'll be the God-King who destroys you. You and all else in his way."

Hoxton scoffed. He couldn't endure another of the Gargoyle's apocalyptic rants.

"Oh, *do chime in, Brute*," said the Gargoyle venomously.

Hoxton took a moment. Truly, with every fiber of his being, he *hated* that Gargoyle.

"If you have any sense in you, you'll *kill* them all," said Hoxton to Franklin. "Find every weapon they're weak to and plunge them straight into their chests. Waylon used my journal to kidnap a bunch of immortal predators and make a *zoo* out of them. The entire building deserves to burn right down to the foundation."

"Aren't you *one* of those predators?" Franklin asked.

Hoxton came right over to Franklin until Adam stepped in his way. Still, he could not stop Hoxton from speaking his mind: "Everybody *standing here* is one of them. We're all monsters holding extraordinary power, and we spend our lifetimes taking innocent lives with it. When the day comes that I've run out of things like ghosts and werewolves to hunt down, I'll end my years upon this Earth with a smile on my face. And that includes things like *you*."

"Why delay? I'm standing right here," said Franklin. "Throw that punch and split my head open. See if I stay down."

"*Shut your mouth*," Adam grumbled as he turned to his son.

And all became quiet.

"Your plan is insane," Adam yelled at his son. "The only reason I'm even *entertaining* it is because we cannot die. But we won't save so much as an *ant* if you pick battles with idiots like this one."

Hoxton became offended: "*I am no idiot-*"

But Adam cut the Brute Man off: "A man with unbreakable skin who flees to East Freetown when his life's biggest targets are all in the same place at the same time? That's the biggest idiot I've ever heard of. If you are so hell-bent on killing them, then *follow us there and prove yourself a genius!*"

Franklin stormed off from both of them. He went over to the window and stared out into the flowing tundra of the blizzard, escaping into an endless vista of empty noise.

The Phantom loomed with an ethereal quality as he hovered in his cell, beckoning to the vampire. He'd chosen to be visible at that moment. He felt that it made him more approachable. Waylon himself even noticed the Phantom's display, and it further cemented that day as the worst Waylon had ever experienced in his entire lifetime. Murphy's law hadn't applied to him for a very, very long time, and was just now catching up in spades.

"You want freedom, is that it?" said the Underlord.

"Of course I do," said the Phantom. "But you can't give it to me."

"Then *what?*"

"Give me a vessel," the Phantom suggested. "Something with strength."

The Underlord looked behind him: The Creature, the Ape-Woman, the Scorpion Man and the Wolf-Woman. All tantalizing options to a soul without a body.

"And what will you provide for me?" the Underlord asked.

The Phantom paused. Whatever it was he'd come up with, it had to be something worthwhile to one of the most powerful beings on the planet.

"There is a plane of existence only a wandering soul may inhabit," said the Phantom. "Choose someone unable to pass into the afterlife. I'll grant you one conversation."

The Underlord was familiar with mediumship. It was popular before the advent of modern sciences and skepticisms. The issue for him was that he never cared for lost souls in any sort of way. Death was the destiny of an unsullied mortal life. To mourn the dead was only sentiment. When the Phantom suggested this offer, however, the Underlord *did* think of somebody held dear to his heart whom he'd never considered speaking to again.

"Take any except the werewolf," said the Underlord.

The Phantom pointed to the Ape-Woman. With a wave of his hand, the Underlord commanded her to enter the Phantom's cell. The very *instant* Paula stepped her large, sapien foot onto the soil in that cell, the Phantom wasted no time and entered her body. The Underlord felt his grip on her mind completely slip away. He'd traded it off to another.

"Hope," said the Underlord.

The Ape-Woman cringed slightly, but quickly rose to her hind legs and walked out of the cell. It was the first time the Phantom was able to move off of the soil he was bound to in a very, very long time. The Ape-Woman's eyes rolled backward for a half-second as the Phantom scanned the entirety of the astral plane for the Underlord's recently-departed Bride.

"*She is not here,*" said the Ape-Woman, no longer herself.

The Underlord blinked twice.

"She's not dead?" the Underlord asked.

The Ape-Woman shook her head. *How odd,* the Underlord mused. *No matter.*

With that, the Underlord turned to the Wolf-Woman.

His devilish eyes scanned her from top to bottom. He turned his wrist, never breaking his sight on her, and forced her body to move and change with only his gaze. The Wolf-Woman collapsed to the ground in agonizing pain, bones snapping, breaking, re-healing, until moments later there was only the human in tattered clothes named Gwen Siodmak.

Gwen stood up in total fear.

"What'd you do to me?!" she screamed at the vampire.

"It took patience and several centuries to master a werewolf's mind," said the Underlord. "Luckily, I had both. And many, many werewolves."

"You *changed* me," she said.

The Underlord nodded.

"Is this the cure you meant?" Gwen carefully asked.

This made the Underlord smile, if only for a moment. It was a flattering thought to him. He then turned to Lillian and whispered something into her ear, the only words of which Gwen could make out were "observatory."

Lillian dashed out of the crypt, vanishing from everyone's sight instantly. Seconds later, she returned with something in her hand.

The Underlord nodded in approval. Lillian handed it to him: A small vial with a label that Waylon recognized.

"You went through my-" Waylon started to say, before Ilona smacked him across the face.

"You've spent most of your life taking things that aren't yours, Waylon," the Underlord scoffed. "I figured you'd be familiar with the concept."

The serum inside that vial was no different than the one Rebecca Chamberton injected into her son some sixty years prior. The serum that healed and restored the adorable dog named Henry. The one proven to work flawlessly on canines. Surely, the Underlord could've forced Adam or Franklin to stay and extracted something similar from one of them. But a debt was owed, and a debt was paid in full. Waylon's observatory housed anything else that they needed.

"You are *beautiful,* Gwen Siodmak. In one form or the other," said the Underlord as he held the vial up in the air, inspecting every detail of it. "Drink this, and never transform into the werewolf again so long as you live and breathe."

The Underlord lowered the vial and met Gwen's gaze.

"But there is a stipulation," he added.

Gwen became lost in the Underlord's eyes as he spoke. Something was odd about them, and she kept trying to place what. She found herself perplexingly drawn to them. It was an intense feeling of... warmth, somehow. Like a comforting aura that induced a trance-like state. Ilona and Lillian approached her sides without her even noticing, but once Gwen did, it was not unwelcome to her.

"Take it," said the Underlord, "and become exactly what I am. Carry the strength of ten men with the grace of a Queen. Move faster than the sound of your own voice. Become my Bride, Gwen Siodmak, and know nothing but pleasure and grace."

Gwen looked over to Ilona and Lillian, and saw them as more gorgeous than any childhood crush she'd ever had. This moment transcended physical attraction for her... It was as if she were seeing their true personalities all at once, all three of them in that moment: The stern, malicious Underlord, the sadistically charming Ilona, and the playful, jubilant Lillian. She could feel their eyes on her, seeing her back: A woman without a home nor family to go back to, with so much of her life having been spent managing this curse...

How can we trust him? the voice in her head asked.

"Because we're the same," the Underlord replied.

Gwen almost fell over from the shock. Her eyes went wide, and her hair practically stood up from the goosebumps. That was *impossible.* That couldn't have happened. She looked to her sides, seeing Lillian and Ilona with welcoming expressions. They, too, were at ease with the fact that Master's mind was further-reaching than it led on.

Gwen took the vial from the Underlord and drank from it.

She seized briefly, then collapsed onto the floor in a withering mess. Ilona and Lillian forced her body back up in full view of the Underlord as she transgressed: Her bestial form showed inklings of itself, fur growing and shedding rapidly as the two identities warred with one another. Moments passed, and the inhabitants of Waylon's crypt stood watch as Gwen's body was finally rid of the werewolf's curse. The Underlord smiled. He'd theorized that it would work so quickly and effectively as it had just done. Shivering in her tattered clothes, Gwen freed herself from Ilona and Lillian's grasp and covered herself where she could. Her body dripped with sweat and shedded fur, most of it forming into a pile below her feet. Some of it still clung to her body in patches.

Finally, she looked back up at the Underlord with beaming, innocent eyes. Lillian spread her fangs and lunged for Gwen's neck, but Ilona stopped her cold. They both knew well that *he* always had the first bite.

The Underlord grabbed Gwen's arms with his clawed fingers and steadied her as he injected his fangs slowly into her throat. Gwen could not breathe or scream but wanted to do both. Instead, she only *stood* there, possessed by the insatiable bloodlust of her new Master... and felt only bliss. The Vampire King's dominion was as soothing on her mind as it was potent. Ilona and Lillian followed suit, feasting on her as the Underlord backed away and wiped his mouth clean of her succulent red blood.

At the castle's only window, Franklin watched the galls of wind dance their way across the icy tundra. His first guess would be Antarctica, but that was based off of nothing. It may just as well have been Siberia, Greenland, or some elaborate simulation brought on by spells and illusions.

Or just somewhere in Canada.

Something didn't align in his mind about the Gargoyle's story. Franklin believed in his intentions, and respected his indifference about the supposed "end of the world." But something else wasn't adding up for him. The Gargoyle either knew far too little or far too much.

"Have you made a decision?" the Gargoyle asked Hoxton, realizing the artificial family needed some more time.

But Hoxton, too, was indecisive.

"Your son retains your qualities?" Hoxton asked Adam.

"In a manner of speaking," Adam replied, still looking over to where Franklin wandered off to.

"Shame," Hoxton grumbled.

Adam turned to the Brute Man, remaining perfectly calm. He used that flawless memory to recall every conversation Waylon ever had about Hoxton, and in seconds, pieced together his entire backstory off of an abundance of anecdotal information.

"Your sister did the right thing suspending you," said Adam.

Hoxton froze. It was as if time itself froze with him.

"Why did you say that?" Hoxton asked.

"She gave you a good life," said Adam.

An overwhelming stupefaction governed over Hoxton in that moment, the painful thoughts of his past now flooding his mind. This past was meant only to be forgotten.

"I've... spent my life destroying evil like you-"

"You spent your life however you wanted to spend it," said Adam. "She gave you that power. You might not have believed her, but it was an act of love."

Hoxton looked at the ground. He was trying to understand how somebody so evil, so *monstrous* in God's eyes, could be so much wiser than he looked. Still, the question lingered in Hoxton's mind as to *how*. It was so blatant that Adam didn't need to be asked about it.

"You'd be surprised what people reveal within earshot of a man watching his television," Adam revealed.

Before either of them could continue this conversation, Franklin stepped away from the window.

"Why do you believe the world is going to end?" Franklin asked the Gargoyle.

The other three shot weird looks in Franklin's direction. For all of the time that those monsters had spent trapped together in Waylon's dungeons, not one soul had indulged the Gargoyle's eschatological rantings and ravings. *This* was what had been bugging Franklin for the past several minutes: The minutiae of what he believed, and why he believed it, was still a complete mystery.

"Have you ever discovered something?" the Gargoyle asked. "Like *really* discovered something. Been the *first* one to find something out..."

Hoxton could sense another rant from the Gargoyle, but felt differently about it this time. Something in the way the Gargoyle spoke captivated his attention.

"Most men never discover anything," the Gargoyle continued. "They just stumble upon something that's been known for years and pass it off as their own... Well, I *discovered* something. A warning etched in stone written a thousand years ago. All I've been trying to do was avoid the fallout from when it happens. Waylon's crypt was the perfect place to stay for a human lifetime while it happened in the *middle-east*... Of course Waylon had to bring the threat right in the same room as us."

"You believe, to your very core, that everybody in that house is going to die at the hands of a monster hiding in that big wooden box in the Scorpion Man's cell?" Franklin asked.

The Gargoyle nodded.

"Then why do you stay so calm?" Franklin asked. "Won't you die all the same in this apocalypse?"

"Probably not," said the Gargoyle. "Within the hour, the God-King will awaken, and the dead will follow him. In reality, he comes from a time where man's greatest weapons were bows and arrows. Him and his acolytes will begin their rampage, probably take out a billion or so people, and get every country's nuclear warheads fired in their direction before the day's over. He'll be eradicated by nightfall, and most of the North American continent will be uninhabitable."

The room became dead silent. For the first time, Hoxton felt an odd feeling of fear at the Gargoyle's words.

"But I'm nowhere near the blast radius," said the Gargoyle. "Neither's Romania."

The Gargoyle moved his hands in methodical ways, conjuring up a small tinge of frost between them. Tiny particles of snow appeared and slowly dissipated, accompanying the brief breeze that passed everybody by.

"You going home, or on your suicide mission?" the Gargoyle impatiently asked.

Franklin looked to his father for the support that he needed, knowing full well that if rejected, he'd pursue it anyway. They both did.

"I can't let you be an idiot on your lonesome," said Adam sincerely.

Franklin turned to Hoxton.

"Come with us to kill the God-King," said Franklin. "Afterwards, the Underlord. *Nobody else.*"

"You cherry-pick your evil," said Hoxton. "You reek of bias and hypocrisy."

"And you, of ignorance and lunacy," Franklin replied. "Massachusetts is *in* North America. You'll have no home to return to."

Hoxton wanted to refute Franklin. He really did. But something had started changing in his worldview after staying in this place with these three men. He couldn't pinpoint if it was the way the Gargoyle described the coming conflict or if it'd been Adam's words, all of which still lingered freshly in his mind.

It has to be done, Hoxton thought. *Regardless of how.* In what was not the first time for him, Hoxton gave in to his innate call to heroism.

"If we get there, and there is no God-King of any sort," said Hoxton, "then I will turn my attention to the monsters we *do* find in Waylon's crypt."

Swallowing his pride, Franklin nodded approval.

The Gargoyle watched this alliance as it was forged. An unexpected thought entered his mind. Adam read him like a book, and signed to him only one word: *Paula.*

The Gargoyle replied: *Keep her safe.*

Come with us, Adam pleaded.

The Gargoyle shook his head. *Too dangerous,* he signed back.

But Franklin had been following along with their conversation.

She has nobody, Franklin signed to him. *Only us. You can't just let her die.*

The Gargoyle had no response. He thought back to the sorcerer's home, and how he had freed the goblins from the man's curse. *This* was why the Gargoyle had gone with Waylon Ross so willingly to that crypt. Those goblins had asked the Gargoyle for a place to live without the constant persecution and tyranny of mankind, whether from sorcerers with cursed magic, or by hunters like Hoxton, who'd encountered their mansion a century prior in the Americas.

The Gargoyle created this place, divorced from civilization, where they all could live peacefully. They were hiding in every corner and every crevice of the doorless castle they all stood inside of. The Gargoyle believed in Waylon's idea because he'd already had it himself.

Not paying attention to their silent conversation, Hoxton looked to the room around him, scanning the area for something inexplicable. Before saying another word to anybody, Hoxton went over to the Gargoyle's wall of treasures and grabbed a spear from the display.

"If we're going to do this," Hoxton clarified, "then we would be better suited with a weapon."

"Not *that* one," said Franklin. "A gun would be-"

Hoxton threw the spear with such tremendous, incredible force as to make everybody react at once. Though Adam and Franklin instinctively ducked, and the Gargoyle's wing quickly shielded him, the spear was aiming for nobody. Hoxton had spent so many years stuck inside of that tiny cell of his that regardless of how the suit worked or how stealthily the man moved, he'd unwittingly learned the slight pressure of air as he quickly passed.

The spear stuck right into the building's far wall, and with it, blood dripped from its handle.

Hoxton held that secret since arriving in this strange place. He'd hoped the assistant would follow him to Massachusetts when he fled. A small amount of torture would've given him all of Waylon's most personal secrets. Franklin's plan was a smarter alternative, given the circumstances. He just needed something more efficient than a box of stakes.

Lightly spattered with Jack's blood, Waylon's prototypical gauntlet tumbled onto the ground below the spear.

The Underlord sliced a dollop of blood from Waylon's cheek with his talon-like nail, and dripped it onto his latest Bride's tongue.

She'd never known divinity could come in the form of a droplet.

"*It tastes... so...*" Gwen said, barely able to create the words amidst her new, bloodsoaked fangs. She'd been using her tongue to coat them with the droplet, as to suck every ounce of flavor out of it. The blood of Waylon Ross tasted better than any meal she'd ever eaten, or even tried to taste. This included every meal her parents had ever cooked for her, any cheap case of ramen she'd been living off of, and every innocent man, woman, or child she'd consumed when prowling in her recently-retired werewolf form.

The blood of a strong, healthy adult delivered *insatiable* pleasure. All-powerful, all-encompassing. Everlasting and divine.

All in this room were watching the Underlord's latest Bride come into existence.

All except for Lillian.

Lillian had become distracted ever since the Underlord first fed Gwen.

Something across the crypt had caught her eye, and it was so much more extraordinary than what was happening that she couldn't look away from it. In the Scorpion Man's cell, right near the bedside, the wooden box subtly began to tremble and shake. It wasn't the noticeable tremors of an earthquake, but it was a quality that immobile objects did not typically produce on their own. She looked closer, watching the particles of dust actually *elevate* from the surface of it, levitating in the air like moons orbiting their planet.

"Ilona..." Lillian said, tugging on the arm of Ilona.

Ilona was prepared to say *'Not now!'* but couldn't. Upon turning her attention, she, too, became mesmerized by this bizarre, unruly phenomenon.

The light from the overhead sun began to fade.

The Underlord looked up, anticipating nothing more than a cloud crossing the sun's path. But the real-time image of the overhead screen was much darker, more opaque. It was like watching day turn to night in mere seconds.

A solar eclipse.

The Underlord looked to his Brides, seeing what they were seeing, and watched as the wooden box in the Scorpion Man's cage broke apart, board by board. They deteriorated as though their nails and screws had no integrity whatsoever.

A sarcophagus lay inside, the seal cracking apart.

The tomb effigy on the lid split from where it met the coffin underneath, and through these cracks, a dim, golden light shined through. Many more followed suit through the cracking limestone. These scattered rays shined stronger and brighter with every passing moment, as though a spotlight were beaming through a funhouse of mirrors. With this, a surrounding torrent of wind began circling inside of that crypt independent of any tangible source. Whatever power was brewing, it was now about to burst.

Quickly, the Underlord reacted and clenched his fist. Like puppets dangling from their strings, every monster in that crypt beckoned to the Underlord's sides as a pack of trained hounds would. All of them kept attentive focus on what exactly was waiting for them inside of the Scorpion Man's cell.

From the ceiling of the cell, lightning struck the casket.

Surrounding the coffin was a flame caught on nothing, ignited by nobody, and burning nothing at all. Then, without any realistic reason, this flame vanished entirely. The orbiting dust quickly fell to the ground, once again obeying the natural laws of physics.

The lid of the sarcophagus slowly slid aside against the millennia-old surface. It was being pushed by a set of gnarled fingers, prying their way out with inexplicable strength.

NIVALTHNESSER, THE GOD-KING

XIX

Nivalthnesser, High Priest of the Temple of the Summit Karnak, reigned over a portion of Egypt with his devoted acolytes over a thousand years before the birth of Christ. They served his wishes and catered to his every whim. None of it truly satisfied him.

Nivalthnesser hated his mortal life and everything it entailed. He fundamentally resented the idea that every day - every *single day* - he needed to eat food and drink water to survive. Every passing moment of every passing day he had to breathe in a healthy amount of air, lest he die in a matter of seconds. He was wholly dependent on the mortal world's sustenance. It couldn't be more revolting to him.

Godliness was the cure.

Gods didn't require anything. They reigned in their Heavens and Underworlds for all of eternity, judging the pestilent souls of dying men and women, while the living worshiped them with all that they had to offer. *This* was his goal, his deepest desire in every conceivable way. He wished to ascend with his own deification, and chose his strongest acolyte to come with him and protect his tomb for eternity.

Nivalthnesser would become a God-King through mummification.

After a seemingly-endless time at sea, the family of three had finally spotted land in the form of a desert coastline. Even at a distance, this incredible place filled their visions and inspired their minds and souls with purpose.

Pillaging to their hearts' content.

Hailing from Langbarðaland, the Viking's ship named *Naglfari* planted itself firmly on the shorelines of Cairo, and out from it, three seafaring pirates emerged looking for conquest and settlement in the names of their deities. The Mediterranean Sea had been mostly explored and invaded by Vikings long gone, but Tryg Ulfsson was adamant on continuing the expansion and plundering of new lands with his brother and son.

They quested in the name of exploration during the tail end of the Viking Expansion, but their minds were set on something more personal. More selfish.

Their past generations invaded England, pillaged their shorelines, claimed their wives for their own, and had their sagas immortalized by legend. In AD 1024, this glory was long-lost for Tryg's tightly-knit family. The three of them sought desperately to reclaim it.

This land was Egypt, and it seemed primed for invasion before they landed.

Tryg's brash, audacious counterpart was his brother Gjaller, who carried only swords and daggers on his person. Hjalmar was Tryg's only son, who fancied the pen far more than a blade. Where Gjaller would plunge his finest saber into the heart of an enemy during a marvelous raid, Hjalmar would keep his at the ready but hold his shield close to his chest. A preventative measure in case his enemies were anything like his uncle Gjaller. Tryg himself, agnostic in the weaponry and attitudes of his family, carried only a large, mighty ax with a sharper blade than any vampire's fang or werewolf's claw.

They had no map nor guidance. They went on foot across the vast sands of the Middle East, their weapons staying holstered and their water supplies dwindling.

Gjaller was the first to see something of significance in this strange place.

"There!" Gjaller yelled, drawing his ax and running off for it.

It resembled a small sand dune, but with a sharper, almost pointed top.

Tryg didn't stop his brother from exploring it. Gjaller was either right, or would be mocked extensively for being wrong.

"Father," asked Hjalmar, "must we follow his lead?"

"At our own pace," Tryg calmly responded.

The structure only resembled a dune due to the copious amounts of sand covering the structure's exterior. Beneath this, one could make it out up close as being shaped like a pyramid.

Tryg and Hjalmar arrived after Gjaller, seeing him standing atop it.

"How old?" Hjalmar asked his father.

Tryg had no answer. He looked the thing up and down, trying to find out anything more he could about it.

"Has to be hundreds, thousands..." Hjalmar continued, placing his hand on the side of the structure. He only felt sand run through his fingers.

"Is there a way inside?" Gjaller yelled from the top.

"Not up *there*," Tryg yelled back.

Gjaller descended the structure's side. He skidded against the dormant sand, now flowing beneath his footwear like water. Gjaller's foot snagged a sizable rock on the way down and proceeded to tumble the rest of the way. Hjalmar laughed at his foolish uncle.

Tryg parted the sand centermost from the sides. If there were an entrance, it would most likely have been placed at the most practical area, symmetrical with the structure's design. Gjaller and Hjalmar helped in the sand's removal, ignoring just how hot it all was due to the blazing sun overhead.

"This is no *raid*, brother," said Gjaller.

"Your perception knows no equal," Tryg replied.

Gjaller bit his tongue from then on. He longed for battle ever since landing in this humid, desolate place. He'd only found a pile of rocks and what felt like an endless amount of digging.

Before the parting sun turned daytime to night, Tryg had finally found the structure's surface. He ran his fingers down the side of it, feeling a strong, flat stone behind the sand dune.

Gjaller and Hjalmar came to the area and saw it too. They no longer lacked motivation.

The three of them increased their speeds and had freed the entrance from its sandy exterior when the sky was fully dark, illuminated only by the glistening array of stars and the overhead glow of Khonsu's omnipresent moon. Hjalmar's eyes went wide.

"What secrets they must keep," said Hjalmar.

Tryg placed his hand on his son's shoulder, recognizing that quizzical look on his curious child.

"After," said Tryg in a stern voice.

Hjalmar nodded. Tryg and Gjaller situated themselves as if to force the tomb's seal open, as Hjalmar took a moment to log some of them down in a notebook. A puzzle to be solved at another time. As Gjaller passed his nephew, he jabbed Hjalmar in the side with his elbow. Hjalmar cursed him back, instigating Gjaller's taunting laugh.

The three of them all working together barely managed to force the entrance open, which slid like granite across the cold, engraved flooring.

The stench of millennia-old dirt and dust came through prominently, but did not grow into a foul stench as one would assume. It was instead indicative of an absence of scent, as though they were able to smell or detect nothing at all.

Gjaller was the first one inside, as expected by the other two, and struck a small torch ablaze before going too far.

The interior lit up and revealed a place completely lost to time: The preserved essence of a pharaoh's tomb, with large, perfectly-aligned pillars coated in glyphs upholding the steep angular roofing above. Treasures of all cultures and materials hung from every wall, adorned every pedestal, and coated every walkway in sight.

The Vikings ceremoniously began their mission.

The family of three took as much as they could possibly stuff onto their persons and returned to their ship, depositing them and returning to the structure as fast as they possibly could. Withinside an hour, the ancient tomb was depleted of all valuable artifacts.

All but one.

It was a casket on the far side of the tomb. A sarcophagus adorned with Latin and Sumerian symbols rested beneath the dim light of the golden ceiling above him, catching the outside sun only partially from the open door. Gjaller's torch flickered wildly against it, illuminating random parts of the sarcophagus. Revealing finer details.

Tryg and Gjaller got on opposite ends of the sarcophagus, preparing to lift it into the air. Hjalmar, meanwhile, recognized the hieroglyphs from his notebook.

They laid in accordance with the Latin and Sumerian symbols. They correlated.

"It's a message," said Hjalmar to his father.

"Make yourself useful, boy!" Tryg said, straining to lift it with his brother.

But Hjalmar was possessed by the idea of translating it. He couldn't help it. These symbols on the ancient one's tomb were begging to be decoded.

Quickly, Hjalmar opened the notebook and began deciphering the tomb's message, correlating the sarcophagus' symbols with the hieroglyphs on the tomb's exterior. It wasn't a difficult project to solve, since in its heyday, that message was intended as a clear and obvious warning.

Tryg and Gjaller gave up trying to relocate the tomb. Gjaller looked to his brother and traded the torch for Tryg's mighty ax. He used the blunt end to pound away at the sarcophagus' seal, cracking the aged, derelict putty and stone holding it in its place.

Hjalmar spoke the translation out loud:

"DEATH AND ETERNAL PUNISHMENT FOR ANYONE WHO OPENS THIS CASKET IN THE NAME OF AMUN-RA, THE KING OF THE GODS."

Gjaller finally cracked through the sarcophagus' seal, launching shards of rock in a storm around him. He raised the ax again, but noticed the look of shock on Tryg's face at whatever was behind Gjaller.

A scorpion's claw the size of a sword impaled itself through Gjaller's chest before he had time to spin around, spattering Tryg in the blood.

The claw belonged to a man with the head, claws, legs, and lurking tail of a black scorpion, sized up to his own proportions, and dressed in the ceremonial trappings of the tomb's royal guard. Beside him, Hjalmar was frozen in fear, allowing that tail to whack the boy away from the sarcophagus.

Tryg let out a rageful scream.

Without thinking, Tryg snatched the ax as it fell and swung it at the Scorpion Man in a blind fit of vengeance. It clashed loudly against the Scorpion Man's claws. Tryg pressed the attack with all of the world's fury motivating him, never letting the Scorpion Man have a moment to respond, and eventually landed a killing blow at the Scorpion Man's neck.

The Scorpion Man collapsed onto the floor.

Hjalmar stood back up, recovering from the strike to his stomach, and saw his father unleashing his assault onto the body. Tryg kept slamming the ax down into the Scorpion Man's throat, each strike splitting it further and further apart. Finally, when the Scorpion Man's head tumbled away from his body, Tryg stopped himself from striking it again, his ax hovering in the air with intent to clash down.

Tryg dropped the ax, and he and Hjalmar ran to Gjaller's body.

Gjaller coughed up a heavy amount of blood, trying to speak some words but failing to do so.

From the seal on the sarcophagus, a loose pile of rocks wriggled apart from each other, startling the group. The fingers of an undead hand poked through the top and grabbed a hold of the tomb's edge, pulling the body out of the casket, and revealing the owner of this now-forsaken place as God-King Nivalthnesser, High

Priest of the Temple of the Summit Karnak, whose body only vaguely *resembled* that of a mummified man.

Tryg grabbed his ax and swung. Nivalthnesser caught the handle.

Like a predator lunging for prey, Nivalthnesser's hand grabbed Tryg by the throat and lifted him up into the air, eyeing him down with a set of glowing green eyes. The torch in his hand came closer to the tomb's inhabitant, and here, instead of trying to save his father, Hjalmar was petrified by the starkly detailed sight of the tomb's rightful host.

The outer layer was constructed of loosely-overlayed ceremonial wrappings of cloth, visibly aged by several thousand years. Beneath these, the skin of the monster was only a continuous mass of flowing *sand*. Amidst the sand crawled a small army of scarab beetles throughout, flowing as part of the inorganic structure, crawling under and over the exterior of cloth. Defixiomancy at its absolute worst, performing at its absolute best.

"Let him go!!" Hjalmar pleaded.

The Mummy heard the pleas of the boy. He dropped Tryg to the ground, and instead directed all of his attention to Hjalmar. Omnilingual by witchcraft, he responded.

"*This is no afterlife,*" said Nivalthnesser with a grainy whisper. His voice was ethereal like a ghost's, but carried more weight, as if somehow amplified twice over. Every whisper was as loud as speaking volume. Everything at speaking volume was like a scream.

Hjalmar looked to Tryg, whose confused expression had nothing to offer his son.

The Mummy recognized his own breath. The very fact that he was breathing was infuriating. Mummification was a *sacred* process, meant to prepare a dead body to carry the soul through the afterlife. In no circumstance was it designed for being reincarnated and living again on Earth. This was not the Godliness that his burial should've led to.

He looked at Gjaller's body near his casket, recognizing the wounds on his chest. Beside him, his Scorpion Man laid decapitated. The Mummy's hands clenched into fists.

Eternity had forsaken him yet again.

"We'll return what we stole!" Hjalmar said desperately. "Let us live, and we'll bring back everything. And then we'll never see you again."

The Mummy held back his mounting frustrations. He grappled with this pestilent fact of his continued existence in the mortal world, brought on singularly by the human race. This was the very same race he was still forced to be a part of.

And the Mummy spoke.

"*You've entered my city, broken into my place of eternal rest, and executed my tomb's guardian. Returning what was almost stolen does not satisfy the God-King you've disgraced.*"

Hjalmar looked again to his father, who could not take his eyes off of Gjaller's body. The weight of it was hitting them both, but particularly affecting *him*. So much so that he could not contribute anything to this conversation.

Hjalmar was on his own.

The Mummy closed his eyes, using the Extromyte's vast array of knowledge to calculate his own past.

Near-infinite particles in the known and unknown universe were always in motion, influencing each other *ad infinitum...* He calculated their trajectories, their logical paths, and where they've all been in the intervening millennium, all the way back to the day he was buried, and saw the vast desert plain beside the Temple of the Summit Karnak, harshly lit by the sweltering sun overhead.

The answer for his predicament became clear.

All but one of his acolytes were zealously loyal to him. The one that wasn't had altered the tomb's curse while Nivalthnesser was casting it. Instead of becoming a God-King, he was destined to never ascend to an afterlife, and reincarnate as a mortal whenever awoken, fueled by his own connection to the Extromyte. If and when Nivalthnesser were to die, the sand would return to the casket until he were awoken again.

To be entombed in a world of curious souls chasing their greed until their extinction... Nivalthnesser could think of no more horrifying a curse. Godliness was unattainable.

The mortal world continued to disturb him in death. Perhaps he should disturb it back.

"What do you propose?" Hjalmar asked in total fear.

The Mummy's eyes shot open, and he spoke his desire.

"Your extinction."

Hjalmar and his father exchanged a look. Neither of them had an answer.

"You wish to kill *everyone?*" Hjalmar asked. "The women, too? The children?"

"I would purge the world of its mortality," said the Mummy. *"Only then may my slumber be eternal."*

Again, Hjalmar looked to Tryg in desperation. He found nothing but his father blankly staring at Gjaller's corpse.

"Bring me the stolen goods aboard your ship and add them to my riches. Once this is done, choose one amongst yourselves to sacrifice as retribution. In exchange, I will delay my vengeance until your task is done."

The Mummy took a long, deep breath, feeling the disgusting aspects of being corporeal. He felt his sand-based fingers scrape against each other as he wiggled them, detesting the experience.

"Begin," said the Mummy impatiently.

The Vikings complied. Hjalmar helped his father off of the ground, practically forcing him up onto his feet, and the two of them began their laborious task.

Hjalmar and Tryg spent twice as much time as they spent raiding the tomb returning everything where it belonged. Beyond that, the two of them took every stolen treasure on board the *Naglfari* and deposited every one of them inside of the Mummy's tomb. All the while, neither of them spoke one word to each other. Hjalmar watched his father's trauma-stricken gaze stare endlessly at the ground in front of him, his shoulders slouching to a scared man's posture. All traces of his father's unyielding confidence were completely gone.

While the Mummy waited alone in his tomb, he used the blood from Gjaller's body to paint symbols around his sarcophagus and toyed with what magic he still knew how to cast. Nivalthnesser moved his hands with purpose, conjuring up a new spell in the name of Osiris: A curse designed to raise the dead from below to be infinitely replenished with man's own corpses.

In the cooling desert, as the sun had almost set over the horizon, the Vikings' task was finally completed. Hjalmar and Tryg returned to the Mummy's sarcophagus and saw the symbols of blood beginning to catch fire. Hjalmar recognized those symbols that the Mummy used as being the same ones from the beginning of the tomb, only in a different order.

As soon as the Mummy noticed them, he waved his hand and the fire went out. His spellcasting would have to wait.

The Vikings kneeled at the base of the sarcophagus, acknowledging the God-King's presence.

"*Proceed.*"

Hjalmar and Tryg stood up and looked at one another, sharing a long, forlorn silence.

Tryg drew his ax.

Hjalmar panicked, but found no strength within him to stop his father from doing what he was about to do. He tried to calm himself, lest they both meet Gjaller's fate.

Calmly, Tryg flipped the weapon around. He handed it to his son.

Hjalmar froze.

"Take it," Tryg ordered from his son.

Hjalmar looked again to the Mummy, who stood stoically in front of them.

"Please..." said Hjalmar.

"*Take it!*" Tryg insisted with a harsh whisper.

Hjalmar's hand hovered over the ax's handle, then quickly withdrew.

"Please, my son, take the ax," Tryg insisted. "I've already lived my life. You're so young... Please take the ax. *Please.* I could not live if I walked out of this tomb alone. You are all of the family I have left."

"*You* are all of the family I have left," said Hjalmar.

"I know," Tryg said, his eyes swelling with tears.

Hjalmar lashed out: "I don't want to do this!! I'm not like you, father!"

"I know."

"I'm not as brave-"

"Hjalmar-"

"I'm not as strong, I don't know how to-"

"*Hjalmar!*" Tryg almost yelled.

Hjalmar fell silent. His father took a breath, and spoke with newfound determination.

"Take - the - ax," Tryg said solemnly.

Hjalmar looked at Gjaller's body. He saw how the Scorpion Man's claws had entered through the torso so smoothly, as though the armor weren't there at all. He thought back to how the Mummy had effortlessly caught Tryg's ax before he struck him, not a passing thought about it. It was either this, or a plain and simple death for both of them.

Hjalmar took his father's ax.

Tryg bowed down. Hjalmar readied the swing down, having practiced how *fastest* to end one's life with it. One straight-shot, right down the center.

"I love you," Tryg said. "You've made me proud."

Hjalmar's eyes swelled up. He looked to the Mummy, as if pleading.

The Mummy nodded. He was indifferent to Hjalmar's pain. Plenty of better men than these three thieves had given their lives for far nobler causes, not the least of which was that tomb's chimeric guardian.

Hjalmar could only produce a whisper: "...Why?"

Callously, the Mummy responded in the most honest way he could.

"*I hate this world,*" said the Mummy, "*and you've brought me back into it.*"

Hjalmar looked down at his father, trying to accept his inevitable decision.

"*Death is not your father's end,*" said the Mummy.

Hjalmar swung the ax.

Tryg's body fell to the ground, marking the third lifeless body surrounding Hjalmar. Two of which were his family.

Hjalmar collapsed to his knees, and screamed desperately at nobody. His voice echoed harshly in the narrow walls of Nivalthnesser's tomb. He was truly, desperately alone.

The Mummy raised his hand over the sarcophagus, casting a new curse.

The symbols surrounding the sarcophagus caught fire once again, and the droves of loose sand from every corner of the tomb coalesced onto the Mummy's location. They worked to rebuild the casket, defying all natural laws of entropy to reform it into what it once was. Not a crack or scrape anywhere on it.

Hjalmar watched this magic happen. He had no time to fear it. The horror of mourning was still setting in. When the casket was rebuilt, the open lid awaiting Nivalthnesser's return to his death-like sleep, the Mummy turned to Hjalmar and placed his hand on the boy's shoulder in a comforting way.

"*Which one was stronger?*"

Hjalmar couldn't take his eyes off of Tryg's body.

"Why?" Hjalmar asked.

"*I will restore them.*"

Hjalmar's eyes went wide. He broke under the pressure.

"My father," said Hjalmar. "He's the strongest man I've ever known... Ever *will* know."

The Mummy looked at Tryg's body, eyeing the details of it. The muscles, the physicality. He recalled the swift and sudden way he moved that blood-thirsted ax.

Gracefully, the Mummy moved his hand.

Hjalmar watched the Scorpion Man's body transpose back into a human body, decapitated all the same. It was Nivalthnesser's closest acolyte, who'd been selected to watch over his tomb in death. He'd failed spectacularly.

After this, Tryg's eyes shot open, reinvigorated with life.

"Father!!" Hjalmar screamed, running over to him.

Tryg violently pushed Hjalmar away. He could feel what was happening to him from the inside out. Tryg stood tall, his hands growing longer into large, black claws. The eyes on his head split into four, then *eight,* and migrated all across his head.

"Hjalmar..." Tryg said to his boy, straining under the coming metamorphosis. "*Run.*"

His set of legs became six, and from the bottom of his spine, a large, armored tail shot out and anchored into the ground beside him, stabilizing his body during the shift. In place of his mouth, mandibles grew out and clamped together, and his head resembled more of an insect's than a man's.

The Scorpion Man was born anew.

Hjalmar's breath caught in his throat as the Scorpion Man took several steps forward, cycling through the litany of insectoid legs keeping him up. The Mummy turned to his acolyte, his glowing eyes stopping Hjalmar's father where he stood.

With a slow turn of his head, the Mummy then looked to Hjalmar.

"*Would you like to turn as well?*"

Hjalmar was speechless. He watched his father breathe, the exoskeleton of the Scorpion Man's chest slowly expanding and shrinking as it happened. Everything had happened so quickly that it was impossible to fully comprehend.

"*You may avoid your own extinction by pledging yourself to my honor,*" the Mummy continued.

Hjalmar looked again at the symbols on the tomb, then back to the Scorpion Man.

"You're going to cast a new spell," Hjalmar deduced.

The Mummy was impressed. He recognized the innate brilliance in the boy. It was a mind conducive to magic.

"*Do you wield magic?*"

Hjalmar looked into the Mummy's eyes, feeling the suggestive power behind them. It was not unlike a vampire's, only much more potent.

"I'd like to," said Hjalmar honestly.

"*Why?*"

"Because I am powerless," said Hjalmar robotically. "I'm scared. I don't want to be inadequate anymore."

The Mummy freed Hjalmar from the trance. The most devoted acolytes always started from a place of fear.

"Aren't you... going to kill me?"

"*Not if you are of use to me.*"

The Mummy turned to his sarcophagus and moved his hands in methodical ways. As the symbols caught fire, Hjalmar watched the Mummy's fingers move through the air, making specific gestures towards certain symbols at the right times. He could feel the currents of wind shifting and changing with each little intricacy.

"May my body lay rest, while my soul ascends to Godliness..."

The winds increased in speed, generating a cyclical sandstorm. Hjalmar covered his eyes.

"May the dead plague the living as I finish this curse..."

Hjalmar realized that the Mummy was casting the curse in his native language. He was being groomed to join his father's side in protecting this tomb for eternity.

The raging fires on the symbols reached an apex. The curse was finalizing.

"May my heart never beat again-"

"Until you've slept for a thousand years," Hjalmar said, casting his hands in the same motions as the Mummy.

The Mummy turned his head, only to see Hjalmar swing his ax and hit him in the face, the blade dulling against the thick layer of sand.

With speed, the Scorpion Man's tail crashed into the ground in front of Hjalmar. Hjalmar leapt out of the way, watching intently as the Scorpion Man's claw opened wide. In the monster's mind, Tryg could only watch as his body was *compelled,* beyond all reason, to attempt to murder his own son. It was too much for his mind to bear, and he had no way of stopping it.

The claw ensnared Hjalmar's hand, severing it at the wrist.

Hjalmar's hand fell to the ground, and all of the boy's screams returned in totality as he stumbled backwards. Scrambling desperately, Hjalmar made it to his feet properly and bolted away from the thing that used to be his father.

The Mummy's hand gestured to the tomb's open door.

Hjalmar watched the door slowly begin to close. He sprinted as fast as he possibly could, his boots smacking firmly against the dirty, uneven flooring of the tomb. He looked down and saw the particles of sand still coalescing back towards the Mummy's sarcophagus, nearly tripping each step he took.

He could only look back for a fraction of a second, catching a glimpse of the Mummy's body incrementally disintegrating into sand, with every grain and particle heading towards that sarcophagus.

The tomb's door sealed shut immediately after Hjalmar's body was able to wriggle through.

Hjalmar tumbled into the desert's wide-open valleys of sand. The weight of the tomb's door shook a large heap of sand above the structure and sent it showering down, encasing the door from an onlooker's view, and almost burying the boy as it did so. Hjalmar frantically ran from the structure, looking back only to see the large dune of sand that had greeted them when they'd first arrived. The image of it haunted him.

Naglfari was waiting for him at the coastline, barren of any collected treasures. Hjalmar had no idea how to run a ship all by his lonesome. He couldn't even manage to push the thing off of the beach's sands without his family's help. Aside from food, rations, and an exorbitant amount of weapons, Hjalmar was stranded in this strange, deserted land.

He had nobody.

Hjalmar collapsed by the stern of his ship and broke down into tears. Everything he'd set out to accomplish with his family was shattered. Gone as fast as it first manifested. They'd left Italy hoping to return with tales of greatness, and instead, Tryg's orphaned son would return with an empty ship and a heart full of pain.

He had nothing to show for his journey. Nothing but the haunting image of his father's metamorphosis into a monster, eternally bound to an accursed place.

He had nothing. Nothing in this world to show for what he'd been through. Nothing to retaliate with. Nothing, and nobody at all.

...

No.

This would not be his family's legacy. Tryg and Gjaller intended to erect a runestone in this place to commemorate their adventures into a Saga of Biblical proportions. They'd already lost their lives in their reckless endeavors, but whether or not they'd be *remembered* was still up to fate. Whether or not their names left the lips of men not born yet was still to be determined.

Hjalmar Trygson, last of his family name, stood up from the ship's stern with an unyielding confidence. He would not erect a runestone of simple commemoration or celebration, as Tryg had intended. He would erect one far more elaborate than that. Not here, in this godforsaken place where pharaohs of antiquity still held dominion, but back in Norland from whence his Viking heritage originated. It would be a grand runestone that told of this day, and the sacrifices therein.

It would be everlasting, both in its stature and its purpose.

Fortifying his stance, Hjalmar put all of his worldly energy into pushing that ship back out to sea. He could not find his way home, but he could find somewhere, *anywhere* other than here, to create his runestone, and secure the legacy of what atrocities transpired in the endless sands of the Egyptian desert.

It would take a long-gestating journey through the Mediterranean Sea for Hjalmar to find land again, and even longer still to return to Norland, where the mightiest heroes placed their runestones of victory and memorialization. Hjalmar would find his *own* land in the area to plant his father's story, ideally untouched by other runestones. A nearby island would do.

The House of the Greatest Game

Part One

The exposed bones and muscles of the hand pushed that tomb's cracked lid aside, which shattered further when it slammed onto the ground below. That undead hand now grabbed the tomb's edge, and the being inside hoisted itself up onto its feet, stepping out of the tomb for the first time in a thousand years. In the dimly-diffused sunlight around the overhead eclipse, one could only make out the being half-wrapped in ancient linen cloths to be the mummified figure foretold only by the Gargoyle.

He was God-King Nivalthnesser, High Priest of the Temple of the Summit Karnak, and he was owed the world's annihilation.

The Underlord cocked his head curiously. *The Gargoyle was right.*

"*This is not my tomb,*" said the Mummy with an old, gravely voice.

Waylon tried to stand, but Ilona's forceful hand brought him down again. The Underlord saw this, and indicated towards the nearest cell. As the Underlord spoke to the Mummy, Ilona brought Waylon into the cell and locked the gateway.

"A human man has abducted you," said the Underlord. "Abducted all of us here. Shortly before you awoke, we became free."

The Mummy looked around the crypt, quickly becoming acquainted with the environment. *Vampires. Phantoms. A werewolf's scent... No longer present.*

"You are a long way from Egypt, my friend," the Underlord said with an inviting tone.

But the Mummy saw through this veneer of goodwill.

The Mummy scanned the Underlord's mind. It was the first time in his entire existence that the Underlord felt the same hypnotic probing on his own mind, performed with much greater potence. The Underlord tried to do the same to the Mummy, who forced him out of it.

"*Your hypnosis is mediocre,*" said the Mummy. "*You wreak with ineptitude. The stench of it surrounds you.*"

Waylon watched this happen from his tiny cell, recognizing it as Hoxton's. He had very little time to manage. His arms were bound behind his hand by small bits of rope, scrounged up from his own workstation in the observatory. He recognized the material. The edge of Hoxton's bedpost might be able to shimmy them apart.

Through the Underlord's consciousness, the Mummy learned of his companion's presence. The Mummy broke the Underlord's hold over the Scorpion Man without so much as a struggle. With sophistication, the Scorpion Man calmly walked over to the Mummy without any sense of urgency.

Petrified by this, none of the Underlord's Brides tried to stop the Mummy. They all had places in their own minds that they wanted nobody to see. They could only observe: The Mummy's eyes glowed with a weird green tinge. From around him, particles of sand began to slowly orbit the Mummy with a mesmerizing, ethereal quality. Though he was becoming aware of the entire room's presence, those glowing eyes found their sight locked only onto one: The Underlord, who kept revealing new information without trying to.

"You're afraid..." said the Mummy as he curiously pried the Underlord's mind. "You're terrified of what I'm going to do to the world of men. The vengeance I'm owed..."

Finally, the Mummy arrived at a fascinating thought: "You wish to prevent it, vampire."

And with that, the Mummy let go of the Underlord's mind. The Underlord breathed heavily for a moment, regaining his composure.

The vampires all saw it: The Mummy and his Scorpion Man, aligned with one another after a thousand years apart, were completely intent on their worldwide vendetta, by proxy unveiling the existence of monsters to the entire world. That was an unacceptable proposition.

"You're going to die," said the Underlord.

"You're incapable," said the Mummy.

"Not by me," the Underlord replied. "If the world knew of mummies and vampires, we'd both be endangered within a year. Extinct soon after."

"It's the parasite's plea to keep the host alive," the Mummy responded.

"And men have a monopoly on blood?" the Underlord scoffed. "If vampires fed on idiocy, perhaps mankind would have a purpose. No, what I'm saying is true, you disgusting thing: If you trigger this war, you won't make it to the end of the week. Mankind's weapons have advanced so far beyond all of your most powerful spells."

The Mummy stayed silent. He shared a contemplative look with the Scorpion Man.

"Though you both play by the same rules," the Underlord added, "you and them are not playing the same game."

"Do they wield magic?" the Mummy asked.

"They don't believe in it," said the Underlord. "The few who do are fooled by ouija boards and tarot cards."

"Then they're primed for an attack," said the Ape-Woman.

All parties involved looked to Paula, puppeteered by the Phantom's will.

"Phantom, don't..." cautioned the Underlord.

"And why not?" the Phantom said through Paula's voice. "You fear that which you feed on from the shadows. Look where it's gotten you. Gotten all of us. Tracked down and captured by one man with a trust fund and a lot of spare time.

We deserve so much better than to stay hidden. Men have no fangs, no claws, not even *sorcery* anymore. They create weapons because they're *helpless.*"

"And we will die because of that very hubris," the Underlord snapped. "Be clear on this, Phantom: We are not Gods. We cannot smite them. Kinds like ours have been burned, cursed, stabbed, decapitated, staked through the heart and cut off at the head. That is the doing of *man,* not beast, and to suggest otherwise is to deny your own history."

After countless nights spent arguing in Waylon's crypt, the Phantom finally decided not to concede.

"You speak as someone who fears sacred water and wooden stakes," said the Phantom condescendingly. "You're no different than a mortal."

The Underlord sensed the tension. There was no more return to civility.

"Monsters and alchemists have been exiled to the lands of fictions and nightmares," said the Underlord. "I will sooner die than become public knowledge again."

"You will either way," muttered the Phantom.

And the Underlord realized what that meant.

Mist started to emanate from the Mummy's body, circling around him by unseen winds. He'd detected the Phantom's presence in that body instantly, and was about to bypass the coming fight in lieu of a simple conversation. Nobody took notice amidst the building pressure between the Underlord and the Phantom.

The Underlord nodded to his Brides, and in an instant, all four vampires swarmed Paula with fangs and fists.

It was as though all four vampires *stopped* in the middle of the air as the Mummy brought the Phantom into the astral plane.

The astral plane ran *parallel* to the observable universe, with different properties and laws of physics than our world's. When it was accessed, time appeared not to advance at all to whichever spirit entered it. Indescribably, this was not a plane of existence observable by the five basic senses of the human body. It only required the participation of one's mind.

"Why do you stand by me?" the Mummy asked honestly, unbound by his corporeal form.

The Phantom recognized this intangible place. He knew it well.

"We're immortals," said the Phantom. "To hide from men is insanity. The Underlord holds so much more power than he knows."

"He does, but I don't believe he will live to experience it," said the Mummy.

"Will that be *our* doing?" the Phantom asked.

The Mummy paused before answering.

"It could be," said the Mummy.

The Phantom waited patiently for a moment. In this void of everything and nothing abound, the tinge of the ethereal washed over them both in a soothing, blissful manner.

"It's nice here," said the Mummy.

"It is," said the Phantom.

Another moment passed. Both of them knew that they had to return to the mortal world. Neither of them wanted to admit that they'd rather just stay there.

"Reconvene here when the fight is won," said the Mummy.

The Phantom felt the Mummy's power bringing them both out of the astral plane, back into their own bodies. Sensations like gravity, blood flow, and air pressure all returned vexatiously to both of them.

And the vampires swarmed the Ape-Woman.

Controlling the monster, the Phantom crouched down and moved quickly out of the way. The Underlord and his brides just barely missed the Ape-Woman, who jumped on top of the docile Creature from Black's lagoon.

The Phantom switched vessels.

Now possessed, the Creature saw an incoming Bride and spun around, whacking Ilona with its powerful tail across the crypt's floor. It leapt up and swiped at Lillian, and the two landed a slash onto each other. The Creature caught itself on one of the crypt's pillars and scuttered up onto the ceiling, crawling quickly over the rest of them and landing on the opposite end.

The Creature landed right near the Mummy.

Gwen panicked. This sort of stress wasn't healthy for her. She cringed, instinctively grabbing her chest, and hunched over as if to vomit.

There was no change. No feeling of rage or primality.

Gwen stood up straight, taking a deep breath. *So this is what it's like,* she mused. It was a feeling she was happy to get used to.

Parallel to all of the crypt's commotion, the man stuck inside Hoxton's cell was making progress. The binds on Waylon's hands finally broke apart. And nobody was looking his way.

The Ape-Woman was freed from the Phantom's control. The Underlord tried to retake her mind, but Paula's blinding rage amounted to a certain level of willpower she hadn't had before. She'd had her own body taken away from her by a deceptive poltergeist. She would never let it happen again so long as there was still a fight left inside of her.

Paula batted her chest and screamed the Creature's way. The Creature roared back at her from across the crypt.

The Underlord raised his hand to the Creature, intending to wrestle with the Phantom for the beast's mind.

Gwen grabbed the Underlord's arm and pulled it down.

She stepped forward, before the Ape-Woman could unleash all of her rage onto the Creature, and raised her own hand not as a vampire with vindictive control, but with a sense of elegance and charm, careful not to move too quickly or aggressively.

The Creature froze. Something inside of the Creature battled within itself; some grand struggle invisible to the rest of Waylon's prisoners, who sought only to fight and massacre. The Creature wasn't some brooding beast without a mind of its own. Waylon had spoken of the Creature's timeless existence, far exceeding the age of even the Underlord himself. It was wiser than its animalistic nature would lead on.

The Creature's webbed claw responded to Gwen's hand, mimicking it in the air.

From inside Hoxton's cell, Waylon watched as Gwen repeated the interactive motions Waylon used when introducing her to the Creature all those months ago. For the tiniest moment, he smiled. It faded away as he continued searching Hoxton's cell for any chance of an escape.

Gwen moved her hand slowly to her side, and the Creature did the same.

The Creature's claw twitched. These were not the commands of the poltergeist inside of it. These were the inklings of the Creature's own soul, whose willpower had been too weak to withstand the other beasts' influence. With a combination of vampiric hypnotism and trust, Gwen had reached into the Creature's mind without intention of ruling it at all. She sought only to free it from the Phantom's ethereal bindings.

Paula watched intently, subsiding her rage. She recognized how the exact same thing that had happened to her was now happening to her opponent. Her fists relaxed into palms, which she placed on the floor to steady herself.

Like a banshee in the depths of Ireland, the Creature shrieked an unrecognizable roar. It was unequivocal to any worldly animal's wailing, yet was reminiscent of many of the most mighty among them. The Creature went onto all fours and scuttered across the crypt's floor, leaping now onto the Scorpion Man so the Phantom could escape to its next vessel.

The Scorpion Man, now possessed, swatted the Creature away with its massive claw.

Gwen came to the Creature's aid with her newfound vampiric speed, pulling it away from the attack. The Creature did not speak nor communicate in any meaningful way like Paula, but the vampiric mind of the Underlord's latest Bride was equipped with more than the five basic senses of humans. Gwen formed a meaningful connection with the Creature, something the Underlord never considered doing in the first place.

The Mummy recognized the Phantom's presence in his guardian's body. He raised his ghastly hand and his eyes glowed bright as he channeled the wickedest forms of necromancy into his acolyte, and as the Phantom looked down at his clawed hand, the injury Hoxton had given him *repaired* itself before his many eyes. The Scorpion Man's pincer was restored.

Speaking through the astral plane, the Mummy instantaneously conveyed a simple message to the spirit inside of his defender: *"Kill them all, or I'll rip you out of that body myself."*

Piloted by the Phantom, the Scorpion Man nodded to his superior, and looked with all of its eyes at the rest of Waylon's crypt, scanning all of the monsters present. All of its imminent targets.

Across the crypt, the Underlord placed his hand on Gwen's shoulder. He didn't expect to be so approving of her unconventional tactics. He was self-aware; The Underlord lacked a certain level of empathy for the ones around him. He'd known from all of those late-night crypt conversations that there would be an irreplaceable benefit in having somebody like Gwen operating under his allegiance.

And Gwen felt the approval of Master.

It was warm. Comforting like a hot shower on a cold morning. It melted away all of her insecurities, reservations, and any other sources of anxiety or mental stress. She'd been rewired to serve and make him happy. Just feeling his touch was a surreal experience.

Gwen looked again to the Creature and made a fist with her hand in the air. The Creature did the same, minding its long, unnerving talons in doing so.

Paula first recognized that the Scorpion Man was about to attack. Knowing nobody present spoke sign language, the Ape-Woman screamed with her simian roar and attracted everybody's attention. She slammed her fists aggressively against the ground. The Underlord looked back to the Mummy, wrapped in layers of sand and cloth wrappings, with tiny scarab beetles crawling and undulating between them. His body was its own unnatural ecosystem.

The Mummy formed a fist, prompting the Underlord to take a defensive stance. That fist expanded with tiny droves of sand coating it, hardening into a densely-packed exterior. In turn, the Underlord's claws fleshed out to their full extent. Even with Paula and the Creature no longer possessed, the Underlord knew very well that this coming battle would be incredibly one-sided in the Mummy's favor.

It was the bitter, effervescent chill of the growing winds that stopped them both.

The air in the crypt circulated with mounting speed, emanating a tinge of crystallized air, producing tiny little droplets of ice. The winds swirled with power on the level of a coming cyclone. All parties in the crypt became coated in a thin layer of the substance, which reached everywhere from the cold, ashlar floor to the interior of the crypt's cells, mounting and building from winds that originated from nowhere at all.

The Mummy recognized this magic, and shielded his eyes from the coming snow.

With an audible *crash,* a miniature blizzard appeared straight in the middle of the house's crypt. Droves of snow flung out in all directions, coating a thicker layer onto them all as the storm silenced down to a calming lull. In the center of the crypt was a fading tornado of snow not ten feet wide, slowly shrinking and dying out.

Removing his hand, the Mummy looked on with his glowing eyes, projecting a tinge of green onto the slow-fading snow. There came a time where an outline of a person was visible to him. Two, maybe three...

Franklin's fist came crashing through the icy veneer. It was a *goblin,* crouched into position where his hand used to be, firmly holding onto the artificial arm with all four of its tiny claws. This unconventional monstrosity of a weapon collided with the Mummy's left eye, tilting his body slightly.

This fascinating specimen was gifted with the Gargoyle's blessing, whom Franklin affectionately named Handrew.

After this, Hoxton's gauntlet fired three consecutive rounds: Rebecca's antiserum, the Creature's rotenone, and a werewolf's silver bullet. They were chosen at random, as no specific round was designed to combat such an evil. The Mummy staggered back, confused at the strange acidic substances coating his body.

The snow completely parted when the Gargoyle batted its wings into the air, rocketing himself forward towards the Mummy, and spinning in such a way as to whack the monster into the nearest cell with its monstrous tail. The Gargoyle sealed the room shut after landing.

Ilona looked to her Master, searching for an answer. A command, maybe. But the Underlord could only watch as the majestic synergy was in full force.

The Mummy arose in his cell and prepared his retaliation. It was puzzling to him why these creatures thought a simple gateway would be able to hold him back. He could phase through the bars in the form of sand, or tear it open with brute strength...

Something wasn't right.

The Mummy looked down.

In blood, symbols were drawing themselves on the floor.

The Mummy reached forward as if to touch the invisible figure. Shielded by Jack's suit, Adam's unseen kick knocked the Mummy off-center, giving him mere moments to bend back down and finish the ring of symbols. Before the Mummy could get back to his feet, Hoxton opened the gateway quickly and released Adam from the cell.

Since the assault began, the Gargoyle had begun moving his hands in a purposeful way. Only when the symbols were drawn and the gateway shut did the spell take hold.

It was a spell they all recognized.

The newly-drawn symbols formed a ring around the Mummy's cell. The Gargoyle used them to enact his own Isolation Spell with only one stipulation: Only the God-King himself could not cross through the spell's boundary. All others were permitted.

Waylon was shocked. He'd gotten to his feet inside of Hoxton's cell, but had only barely spent the time to look around for any weapons. He was too focused on what was happening right before his eyes, just past the cell's gateway. But he'd dwelled on it long enough. He spun around and scanned every feature of Hoxton's cell, searching for something to help him.

The Mummy regained his footing, only to look around the crypt and see the ring of symbols he'd found himself trapped by. Despite the beating, he was quite patient. Time was meaningless. There was no sense in winning this battle if he could never leave this cell again. The world of men was *owed* to him, after all. The world outside of this man-made dungeon.

Slowly, the Mummy began moving his arms in a manner similar to the Gargoyle's. Decoding the spell. Finding a way to break it.

"That should buy us a few minutes," said the Gargoyle to the others.

In the calm of the storm, Hoxton and the Underlord locked eyes.

The Underlord and his Brides didn't act violently towards the ones who'd just helped them. That was not how they conducted themselves, and Hoxton knew that well. He approached the Underlord directly, his hand ready to lift and fire the gauntlet at a moment's notice.

"I've spent three hundred years hunting you," said Hoxton.

"You've done terribly," said the Underlord. "At a certain point, you ought to throw in the towe-"

Hoxton grabbed the Underlord by the throat, pinning him against one of the pillars of the crypt. And the Underlord let him do so. Subtly, he called off his Brides from intervening.

After a moment, Hoxton released him.

The Underlord adjusted his clothing. "Thank you," he said without meaning it.

Nearby, Franklin heard his father's voice in his ear: *"This is your revenge on him, isn't it?"*

"Hardly," Franklin mumbled, his eyes glued to the Underlord. "He deserves worse than something like this."

"You need to let it go-"

"There's a ghost in this crypt," Franklin snapped. "There *really is* an afterlife, dad. If she's watching us from wherever she is, I'm going to make her proud. You're not going to stop me."

Adam said absolutely nothing.

Inside Hoxton's cell, Waylon shuffled through the Brute Man's personal belongings, stumbling upon all of the stolen books from the observatory. A fact he'd already deduced earlier. Beyond them, hidden away in the corner of the drawer, was a very tiny handmade blade.

Waylon turned to the gateway of Hoxton's cell, careful that nobody was watching. He paid close attention to the gateway's bars, searching with his eyes and the steady tips of his fingers for any imperfections. At the very bottom, two and a half of the gateway's bars had been filed away. *Clever bastard,* Waylon thought. But even that wasn't enough to help him.

Paula saw the Gargoyle and signed: *Why did you return?*

You, the Gargoyle signed back.

She didn't know how to react to such a response.

You came for me? she asked.

Franklin approached the Gargoyle's side.

We both did, Franklin signed. *Gargoyle was scared. Needed convincing.*

Paula howled like a chimpanzee, making Franklin crack a smile. The Gargoyle stood there and took it.

I told you, Franklin signed. *I'm not an enemy.*

Curiously, Paula noticed how Franklin had still been using one hand to sign, leading her to finally look at his other one: The goblin met her gaze, and became defensive.

"It's alright," Franklin whispered to his companion. "She's a friend."

Paula read his lips, emboldened by the idea. Franklin took the goblin with his one remaining hand, forming a small platform out of his palm for it to stand on, and held it out to Paula.

Nice to meet you, Handrew signed to Paula.

Paula's eyes went wide. She'd never seen a creature so hideous, so fierce in appearance, be so affable and affectionate. It reminded her of the much larger creature who'd been far more hostile towards her.

Turning around, Paula approached Gwen and the Creature, who were interacting with mimetic movements; Gwen would move one hand, emphasizing a specific finger, and the Creature would do the same with its own webbed digits, articulating each corresponding talon. Curiosity overtook Paula, in place of the anger she once felt towards Black's Creature. Gwen looked her way, and without saying a word, nodded for Paula to try as well.

Paula moved her hand. The Creature copied it.

With a strong sense of compassion and a minimal amount of hypnotic suggestion, Gwen had prompted the Creature to act as an ally, and now Paula was filling her role.

Franklin turned his attention to more pressing matters. Handrew crawled up onto his shoulder as Franklin turned to face the Underlord.

"We intend on killing you," said Franklin.

"Fantastic," said the Underlord sardonically.

"That being said, the Gargoyle tells me that this entity can destroy the strongest among us with a passing thought. Everything that this Gargoyle says apparently comes to pass, so we're intent on believing him."

"I'm intent on believing him as well," the Underlord mocked.

"Then we act in unison," said Adam's voice.

The Underlord scoffed, unable to see where the artificial man's voice was coming from.

"A bit of a tight fit, I imagine?" the Underlord said out loud.

The Mummy made progress in cracking the Gargoyle's spell. Every time he chipped away at it with his own magic, strong vibrations briefly emanated along the crypt. All of the crypt's monsters took notice of it, for it was impossible to ignore. Paula now watched the group speaking to each other, and the Creature's gaze followed hers like a dutiful pet.

"Could you put up another one?" Adam asked the Gargoyle. "Reactivate the one Waylon had around the crypt?"

"It won't matter," said the Gargoyle. "He'll know how to break it now."

"Do you ever speechify good news?" Hoxton asked.

"The onus is on you to *give me some,*" said the Gargoyle.

Beneath Hoxton's bed, Waylon had used the bladed weapon to slice off a long chunk of the wood, and was currently in the process of sharpening it. A makeshift wooden stake. When being kidnapped by the Underlord's Brides, almost all of the guns and miscellaneous weapons on Waylon's person were taken away. The only one left was a small, gas-powered pistol stowed deep inside one of his boots. If the stake were thin enough, it could fit right into that pistol's barrel.

Another vibration came from the Mummy's dwindling confinement. Quickly, Hoxton turned back to the Underlord, who knew exactly what was going to be proposed.

"Until he is defeated," Hoxton said.

The Underlord nodded, holding back a smile.

"Until he is defeated," the Underlord repeated.

The Brides looked to Adam and Franklin with mutual understanding. This truce wasn't born out of want or desire. It was forged from necessity. Without it, there would be graver consequences than any one of them could ever inflict on each other.

A low hum emanated throughout the confines of the crypt.

The Isolation Spell was broken, horrifying the Gargoyle. That was barely *one* minute, let alone what he'd anticipated.

Franklin looked to Paula, who looked back with the same understanding. Having read their lips, she repeated in sign language: *Until he is defeated.* Beside her, the Creature repeated her hand movements, albeit without understanding what they meant.

But the rest of them did. It rang through their minds like a battle cry.

The Scorpion Man stood by the Mummy's side as he exited the cell, testing his own claws over and over again. The Phantom was enjoying his newfound alacrity.

Hoxton spun the gauntlet to a random round of ammunition. He didn't care which. Franklin smiled, and tore one of the plastic torches off of a pillar. He tossed it to the Ape-Woman, who instinctively caught it, and howled like a chimpanzee.

Waylon finished shaving the stake down to the ideal size. He primed it into his handheld cannon. Carefully, he aimed it with his usual precision right at the Underlord's backside, intending to blast it straight through his chest. Some of the crypt's inhabitants would try to kill Waylon for doing this, namely the Brides and their allies. Others would be grateful that Waylon did what they'd always intended on doing.

But before Waylon could fire, he saw something he'd never seen before. Something he'd only envisioned in his mind's eye as a faraway prospect. It was materializing in front of him.

And so they came forth.

The Brute Man marched straight up to the Mummy, stopping right in the crypt's center. He held the line between the Mummy and the crypt's exit, knowing he would not have to perform this hunt alone. Approaching his side, Franklin let Handrew crawl down his arm and crouch into position on his wrist, still gauging the weight behind the strikes he intended to deliver several more times to the Mummy's head. He was aided by his father, whose footsteps were much louder and clearer than Jack's ever were. Franklin looked over to nobody, and knowingly nodded.

The Ape-Woman's roar was absolutely primal. It incorporated the noise of a feral beast just waiting to be unleashed, and it accompanied her arrival by Hoxton's other side. She slammed her free hand onto the ground, then again onto her own chest in a threat display about to be enforced in blood. With a swift gesture, the Queen of Sigma summoned her ally from the ceiling.

The Creature fell from above, landing methodically on all fours by the Ape-Woman's heel. It stood up, offsetting its weight with the pull and sway of its massive tail, and snarled aggressively on its hind legs. The Creature's front claws lengthened and fleshed out to their true, maximum length amidst the thin webbing between them. It breathed slowly through both sets of lungs and gills in the process, keeping its draconian eye on the duo of enemies across from it.

From above, powerful gusts of wind accompanied the Gargoyle's mighty descent like a helicopter landing down onto a platform. His arrival accented Hoxton's imposing figure, and his wings spread as wide as possible before retracting, almost covering the entire group of them. His lifeless eyes peered straight towards the Mummy, and behind Hoxton, his claws sharpened themselves on the crypt's stony ground.

After them, one by one, Ilona, Lillian, and Gwen dashed to the sides of Hoxton with speeds unseeable by the human eye. Their fangs were prominent and their claws were mercilessly sharp, but above all of this, all levels of seduction were gone from these three wicked creatures. It was a pure, potent rage that drove them. The Mummy had attacked their Master. That crime was punishable only by a permanent death.

And finally, the Underlord appeared midway between Hoxton and the Mummy with his vampiric speed. A provoking move on his part. Amidst this, undercutting all of the tension in the room, the Vampire King did what he'd always done in times of conflict, and *smirked* toward his enemy. He was more than ready for the coming fray. He embraced it with drive and ambition.

Waylon lowered the weapon. He'd formed a community, reliant on one another to work synergistically. One ecosystem. One natural harmony of the world's rarest species, predator and prey alike, coexisting alongside one another. It was everything he'd been building to, in his own unorthodox way, for most of his natural-born life up to this very moment.

They had achieved equilibrium in their environment.

Brilliant minds of the past had killed their own kind for a fraction of this group's power and wickedness. None had arrived anywhere near it. Nothing like it existed until Waylon's Game aligned, right there and then, in the newfound home of the Devil's League.

Piloted by the Phantom, the Scorpion Man adjusted his stance as if to lunge, but to which target was unknown given the amount of eyes on his head peering in all of those many directions. Franklin and the Ape-Woman briefly exchanged signals with their hands, implying a level of coordination to the rest of the group. The Ape-Woman nodded, and turned to the Creature, moving her hands methodically. The Creature mimicked the movement, then looked to the Scorpion Man and went down onto its four legs, slithering both defensively and offensively. It was impossible to tell which.

Keeping his eyes locked on the Mummy, the Underlord gestured with a subtle wrist movement for his Brides to begin the assault. Knowingly, this instigated the rest behind him to follow suit with their attack.

The Mummy didn't have to gesture to the Scorpion Man. The Mummy simply *thought*. And it was so.

The group of them charged in unison, prompting the Mummy and his possessed Scorpion Man to meet their numbers with unlimited power and fury of their own making. Claws, fangs, and fists alike bashed into one another in the most repugnant ways: The massive pincer of the Scorpion Man lunged for Franklin's head and pierced through his skin, stopping part-way by Adam's invisible catch. The Gargoyle's clawed hand smacked the Scorpion Man so hard that the Phantom briefly lost control of his orientation, letting the Ape-Woman swing the torch like a bat and bash him back into the Creature's tail, which whacked the Scorpion Man's body off-kilter.

As the Scorpion Man fell down, battered by the endless barrage of that tactical squad of killers, the Brute Man shot whatever round of ammunition happened to be selected.

A silver bullet drove itself through one of the Scorpion Man's eyes, partially blinding it.

More selective now, Hoxton spun the armlet to a new round of ammunition. As he did so, the Scorpion Man's claw reached out and clamped itself down onto Hoxton's forearm, and in an instant, the Phantom switched vessels, once again overtaking the Brute Man's body.

But the vampires were unconcerned with the larger battle against the Mummy's acolyte. They were focused on its superior.

The vampires attacked like bolts of lightning striking the same place three, four, five times in a row: One would dash forward towards their enemy with a crushing blow somewhere carefully-targeted on the body, then dash back before any counterattack could even be considered, one after another in rapid succession. Anyone with the reaction time of a normal person would be deceased before they realized they were ever being attacked in the first place.

But not the God-King.

The Mummy moved with speed almost equivalent to that of a vampire, leaving a smeared trail of sand in his path. He drew on similar Black Magic as the Underlord's nasty brood. To the Mummy and his four vampiric opponents, the rest of the crypt's inhabitants were moving incredibly slow. To the rest of the crypt's inhabitants, the vampire's entire brawl endured on the timescale of only a few seconds.

The Mummy sustained several blows to his sides and arms, enduring the barrage with a focused mind. Every fourth or fifth blow, dodged or withstood, the Mummy would methodically *block* the oncoming assault and counterstrike the vampire in the gut.

The first victim of this was Ilona.

After the Underlord's attack at the head, Ilona had gone for the Mummy's abdomen a fraction of a second later, not realizing that he'd already spun to avoid it. Instead, the Mummy caught Ilona's attempt at a slice with her vampiric nails and used his opposite hand to strike her in the ribs, knocking the wind out of her as she flew off in the opposite direction.

From there, the Mummy didn't let up.

Lillian dashed after the Mummy, only to crash into the cloud of sand where he used to be. He'd slid sideways, and when she passed him, grabbed Lillian's hair and *halted* her in the air, tearing out a few of her roots in the process. The Mummy yanked her head back to face him and placed his hand on her face, sending a swarm of scarab beetles crawling up, inside of, and all over her face and neck.

Lillian gagged and pushed away from him, coughing up the scarab beetles that attempted to make their way down her throat.

At blinding speeds, the Underlord came next in an attempt to grab the Mummy by his neck, aiming his talons straight ahead for a strangle. The Mummy caught the Underlord's arms and spread them apart, meeting the Underlord's sudden attack with a devastating headbutt. The Underlord flew down onto his backside from the impact.

Gwen was not used to wielding such concentrated speed. Still, the Underlord's latest and most inexperienced Bride prepared her next attack.

Nearby in Hoxton's body, the Phantom grabbed the incoming Gargoyle by the legs and pulled him down out of the air. The Ape-Woman followed the Gargoyle's path, landing a blow on Hoxton's head before being swatted away. The Phantom rotated Hoxton's armlet to rotenone before the Creature could lunge at him upon Paula's command. He fired and hit the Creature in one of its hind legs. It landed near Hoxton, scrambling on the ground near the Gargoyle and trying to deal with its newfound pain. The Phantom then primed Hoxton's gauntlet with antiserum and aimed it at Franklin.

Nothing stood in his way.

Adam grabbed Hoxton's gauntlet and redirected it towards the crypt's faraway ceiling, splattering it with the dripping red antiserum. Hoxton grabbed where he estimated Adam's head to be and shot the next round straight forward, engulfing the chest of the invisible suit.

"*Dad!!*" Franklin screamed as he ran over.

The splotch of antiserum floated in the middle of the air, adhesed to Adam's invisible chest. It fell to the ground all the same, and an audible *thud* accompanied Adam's body hitting the crypt's floor.

Franklin dodged the next shot from Hoxton's gauntlet, letting the round of antiserum fly by him, and leapt onto the Gargoyle's back from down on the ground. Franklin propelled himself high into the air and delivered a devastating punch with his goblin-fist to the side of Hoxton's face. Hoxton fell backward before firing again, collapsing onto the ground with the rest of the monsters he'd beaten.

Franklin went to where his father's body had fallen, but despite his best efforts, could not find it at all.

Gwen launched towards the Mummy at ultraspeeds with an outstretched claw aimed at his leg. All of the others went for more obvious areas, like the monster's head, arms, or somewhere on the torso. She figured that perhaps he wouldn't be as prepared to block this sort of strike.

She figured incorrectly.

The Mummy *caught* Gwen by the throat before she landed the blow. He held her right in front of him and watched as she clawed at the Mummy's wrist, desperately gasping for air beneath his clutches. The Underlord recovered, getting up and locking eyes with the Mummy's powerful green gaze.

"Of all the weaknesses your species has," said the Mummy, *"is this one of them?"*

Without breaking eye contact with the Underlord, the Mummy crushed Gwen's windpipe.

His gnarled fingers forced their way inside of her throat, ripping through her pale flesh. A torrent of sand and scarab beetles poured inside, filling her gullet, forcing their way through her esophagus and down into her lungs and stomach.

The other two Brides froze in a panic.

The sand now coursed through Gwen's bloodstream and started bursting out of her pores, letting dozens of scarab beetles flow out of her disintegrating body in waves. Gwen's blood dripped down onto the Mummy's hand and forearm, which all got sent back inside of her as it clung to and traveled along the monster's flowing mass of sand. Every cell in her body slowly tore away from its neighboring ones by the onslaught of beetles and sand propelled through her by the Mummy's relentless, painful mysticism. She had no capacity to even scream. She could only feel it happen.

A disgusting, putrid, gelatinous slime of blood and muck fell to the crypt's floor. It had the same mass as Gwen once did, shaped into a small pile of diffusing gunk. A nuclear warhead would've treated her body kinder.

Lillian shrieked, channeling her pain into blinding rage.

The Underlord tried to hold her back with his hypnosis, failing instantly. She was unstoppable.

She rushed the Mummy with the unbelievable fury of a widow just scorned and struck him with unyielding claws and fists. The Mummy withstood the first of her assaults, then slid to the side with the same speed and smacked her down onto the crypt's cold, dense ashlar floor, scuffing the exposed skin on her face and arms.

The Underlord looked over to his Ilona, immensely disappointed. No Bride of theirs had ever lasted this shortly. Ilona looked back at him with a tinge of rage, then dashed over to Lillian to help her up.

And the fight between the vampires and the Mummy, which couldn't have lasted more than one minute in totality, was completely over, with nothing to show for it but a pile of disintegrated sludge where Gwen used to stand.

THE HOUSE OF THE GREATEST GAME

XXI

PART TWO

The Phantom kept toying with the rest of the beasts in Waylon's crypt, possessing them rapidly and turning them on each other with discoordinated violence. Unchallenged, the Mummy used the crypt's symbols to cast the spell he'd been waiting a thousand years to conjure, and his eyes glowed brighter than ever before.

From the ground below them, undead hands burst from the ashlar floor and pulled themselves up, a litany of corpses now coming into view. This infectious disease had the potential to overrun the brave and cowardly alike, sparking an endless war to forever be fought on the brink of an apocalypse. An endless war between men and monsters.

In his many, many years spent roaming this world, the Underlord very rarely lost his temper. Tonight was one of those nights.

To a man, a small horde of the undead was nigh-unstoppable. To a vampire, this type of necromancy was not so formidable.

Just as soon as they'd shown up, the zombie horde disintegrated on contact from the bullet-like Underlord shredding through them like tattered paper, his demonic claws tearing through their skulls and vaporising their brains on contact, which painted the surrounding crypt in a tsunami of guts and gray matter.

The Underlord stopped as fast as he'd moved, as though frozen in time, and glared at the Mummy with guts still dripping from his claws. The Mummy looked back at him in time to see his formidable army of the dead finally fall to the ground in a filthy pile of bones and blood.

The Mummy could see, hear, and feel exactly where the Phantom had moved, and admired his latest choice.

From above, the possessed Gargoyle tackled the Underlord to the ground.

Pinned by the Gargoyle's Herculean weight, the Underlord felt the Phantom's spirit trying to overtake him, and fought it with all of his psychic ability. This pestilent Phantom had kept this group divided, fighting one another instead of the larger threat. His latest Bride was dead because they were no longer working as one.

The Underlord landed several blows on the Gargoyle's head, cracking one of the horns off of his forehead.

The impact caused the Gargoyle, just for a fraction of a moment, to come to his senses once again, and this lull in time is all that the vampire needed: The Underlord flipped the Gargoyle's body off of him, pushed him over his shoulder, and *launched* into the nearest pillar, the Gargoyle's back crashing through it.

"Enough of you!!" the Underlord screamed.

The Gargoyle rose up after crashing into the pillar, but had no time to retaliate: Ilona and Lillian pummeled him with an endless barrage of open claws and enclosed fists. They backed away as Franklin entered the fray, grabbing the Gargoyle and bashing his head into the pillar once more.

And the Phantom swapped once again.

The Gargoyle fell to the ground, dazed from all of the attacks. Franklin was the monster's host, and forcefully grabbed Lillian by the neck. He readied his opposite fist with a blow to her head.

Handrew knew that his host wasn't *himself* anymore.

Instinctively, Handrew bit into Franklin's arm, causing the shocked Phantom to let Lillian go. Handrew crawled up onto Franklin's face and violently tore away at his skin, shredding away his nose, lips, eyelids, and any other defining features of his.

Paula kept track of the Phantom's constant shifting and commanded the Creature to target Franklin in a coordinated attack: They lunged from opposite sides simultaneously, clawing into Franklin's arms and chest with fury.

The Phantom swapped again, possessing only one of them. It was impossible to tell which anymore. All of the monsters involved were too busy constantly fighting each other to properly attack the intangible, ever-shifting spirit inside of them.

Coming to his senses, the Gargoyle stood up and locked eyes with the Underlord. He felt the horn on his head, rubbing the chipped-away nub.

The Underlord shrugged.

Turning to all of the in-fighting, the fed-up Gargoyle screamed a new tactic at the group: "Get him out of the crypt!!"

Franklin nodded, his face having healed back into place. Handrew crawled back down onto his wrist, and Franklin could tell by the tiny smile that Handrew had confidence in him once again. Quickly, Franklin signed a message to the Ape-Woman. In turn, she signaled the Creature.

Those three forces together swarmed Lillian - now the Phantom's vessel - with a series of light strikes, careful not to maintain physical contact for more than a passing moment. Doing this, they began to force Lillian backward, step by step, until Ilona dashed forward with the powerful, striking blow that sent her Sister hurtling into the crypt's hallway past the entrance.

The Gargoyle recast the Isolation Spell on Waylon's crypt using the already-present symbols on all of the pillars, and stipulated his caveat: *The Phantom may not leave.*

Lillian soared backward and passed through the crypt's barrier unimpeded, tumbling onto the hallway floor. The Phantom, in turn, was torn out of her body after slamming straight into the Isolation Spell.

The Phantom vanished and apparated back into his own cell, hovering ominously over the pile of ashy dirt he was bound to.

The rest of them looked over to him, recovering from their injuries. Per Jack's earlier command, the Phantom's gateway remained wide open.

Ilona went to Lillian and helped her up out of the hallway.

"A good drink of blood will fix everything," Ilona reassured her.

But Lillian was just happy that her and Ilona had made it out, putting that nuisance of a ghost in his proper place.

The Mummy eyed the Gargoyle from across the crypt. The Gargoyle met his gaze.

And the Gargoyle inhaled.

The Mummy's hands coated themselves in the biomass-like sand, forming thick fists akin to small wrecking balls. He moved towards the Gargoyle with a spark in his eyes and the dexterity of Adonis himself. His body twisted, about to crash down a thunderous strike onto the Gargoyle's head.

With his eyes locked on to his target, the Gargoyle forcefully exhaled, and with his breath came a vigorous inferno that tore straight through the air between them. It engulfed the airborne Mummy and swatted him back down to the ground, pummeling him with turbulence from the fire-breathing demon of Lucifer's imagination. The Mummy's body smacked into the floor, sending bits of sand and charred beetles in all directions, some of his wrappings now burning into crisp flakes of ash.

Franklin and the Ape-Woman quickly signed something between each other.

Before the Gargoyle could do it again, the Mummy got to his feet, flames still emanating from his cloth-wrapped skin, and dashed over to the Gargoyle as fast as he possibly could. He struck the Gargoyle's head, then knocked him into the nearest pillar, rendering him out of commission.

Franklin dauntlessly approached the Mummy.

Turning away from the Gargoyle, the now-burning Mummy moved eagerly and struck Franklin straight through the chest. Franklin's upper body burst open on impact, and the two of them looked down at the Mummy's arm. All of the sand in the world couldn't stop Franklin's chest from closing back up.

Speedily, Franklin grabbed the Mummy's arm, ripped it out of his own chest, and landed a punch on the Mummy's abdomen with Handrew's backside. Beneath the bandages, Franklin felt the bodies of several scarab beetles suddenly crush into paste against the goblin's thick skin.

Handrew left Franklin's wrist and hopped onto the Mummy's chest, digging deeper into his abdominal wounds. Distraught by this, the Mummy wasn't able to stop Franklin from continuing his assault, fists and elbows flying from every which way. Franklin grabbed the Mummy's collarbone with his only hand as Handrew burst out of the wrappings, stabilizing the Mummy's body as he connected Handrew back onto his severed wrist, retracted him, and jabbed the Mummy straight down the middle of his face.

Before the Mummy could react, a large stone crashed into the back of his head. He spun around and saw the Ape-Woman, who had found a loose piece of ashlar flooring and torn it out of the ground. Another piece of it was in her hand, ready to launch.

Distracted, the Mummy couldn't stop Franklin from restraining his arms behind his back. The Mummy briefly broke free but Hoxton intervened, picking up on their coordinated plan rather quickly. Hoxton and Franklin each held one of the Mummy's arms and forced him down onto his knees, and the second of the Ape-Woman's projectiles crashed into the Mummy's forehead.

The Ape-Woman signaled to the Creature, who joined her by her side in a feral attack.

Unable to move, the Mummy struggled to endure the Ape-Woman's fists and the Creature's claws relentlessly tearing into him, removing almost all of the charred, tattered wrappings from his exterior. They pummeled the undead man until he was nothing more than a humanoid mass of sand and beetles, with a fading pair of green eyes looking back at his oppressors.

Hoxton watched closely as this attack continued. Paula's hands and the Creature's talons had something in common: They were starting to become coated in blood. Not sand, not beetles. Real, human blood. They were farming it from beneath the monster's smoking skin.

The Mummy's patience had completely expired.

Possessed with unfathomable rage, the Mummy violently wriggled out of Franklin and Hoxton's bind. He dashed through the entire group of them at speeds they couldn't register and struck each and every one of them in what he estimated to be the most *vulnerable* parts of their bodies. He no longer burned, but remained charred and injured from the group's coordinated attack.

The Underlord flew at his enemy once again.

The two impossibly-fast opponents launched hands, claws, fists at each other in rapid succession, parrying each other's attacks faster and faster with each passing moment. After three seconds and a hundred strikes, the Mummy finally caught the Underlord by the throat.

He was enraged; Both of the Mummy's allies had been beaten by this group of ugly aberrations, and in that very moment, almost destroyed him with nothing more than coordinated fury. The Underlord wriggled free of the Mummy's clutches and retaliated with all of his vampiric strength and speed. Jagged black talons slashed from every angle as the Underlord pressed his attack, but this time, each and every blow was blocked with what seemed like effortless speed.

Enduring all of this, the Mummy grabbed onto the Underlord's neck once again.

Ilona dashed over to the Mummy, getting smacked away by the Mummy's free hand. So did Lillian shortly thereafter.

Sand began to pour from the Mummy's arm and wrist, accompanied by a small army of scarab beetles emanating from beneath the flowing sands of his skin.

The Underlord used his hypnotism to stave off the coming scarab beetles from crawling anywhere near him.

The Mummy concentrated, meeting his opponent's prowess with his own.

The scarab beetles proceeded towards the Underlord's mouth. For the first time in all of his unnatural life, the Vampire King had been beaten at his own game, and the rest of the crypt's inhabitants were either reeling from the pain, or could only watch the horrid thing happen to their strongest, most powerful ally.

Not very far across the crypt where nobody was paying any mind to, the sand-infested pile of sludge began to twitch.

Even in death, a version of Rebecca's serum coursed through her body at the cellular and molecular level. Combined with the undead form of the vampire, and the repressed lycanthropic beast she'd tried to cure, all of these factors brought forth something abominable.

Each little element of the bloody ooze clung to each other and reformed very, very slowly into the shape of Gwen's corpse, fighting against the remnants of sand that had disintegrated her down to her current state. Once humanoid, the gashes on her body began to close. Gwen's outward appearance shifted form drastically. What used to be cold, undead skin turned starkly into the horrid gray of the artificial, yet retained their unbreakable strength and wicked form. Her body *stood up* without her being fully conscious at all. It was purely instinctive. This new form needed to be upright.

And upright it was.

Her bones began to break and re-heal in new fashions. Her size shifted, making her height anywhere between five and seven feet, it was impossible to follow along. She hunched over and slammed her open claw into the ground, driving those vampiric talons into it. Those talons began turning translucent.

The Mummy became distracted by this prospect, allowing the Underlord to again break free of his hold and violently cough out the sand and beetles from his throat.

From her back, gray fur wriggled its way out of Gwen's undead skin.

The fur coursed its way down her chest, expanding to all of her limbs. The sides of her face became coated in it as well, spiking backward and revealing a set of animalistic eyes that nobody in that crypt had ever seen before. Those eyes scanned everything, combining the heightened senses of vampires, werewolves, and artificial humanoids. Rebecca's serum was driving every iota of energy to the forefront of her form, channeling traits of all three monstrous entities governing her body and mind.

She roared with the power of a million bats and an army of wolves. The first vampiric, artificial, lycanthropic nightmare was equal parts godly and devilish. A triumvirate of terror, born from the worst traits of magic and science. An atrocity like no other.

Both the Underlord and the Mummy held out their hands toward her. They focused all of their energies into controlling this creature, hoping to destroy the other with her.

She caved to neither of them.

Rebecca's serum fortified her animalistic mind. She retained the strengths of all three species she'd become afflicted with. They worked synergistically with one another, disallowing hypnosis from other beings. She would never bow again.

Her magnificent mind moved just as quickly as her body: She looked at the Mummy's burned, sliced-up skin, watching the sand migrate around the man's shape. Gwen quickly scanned the rest of the crypt, seeing splatters of blood and sand adorning the hands of Paula and the Creature. She saw how they'd punctured through the skin, not with devil's magic or man's science. They did it with nothing but a healthy amount of brute force.

No force was more brutal than her.

Gwen glared at the Mummy, the digits of her claws fleshing out to their peaks. This group of monsters could battle the God-King from now until the end of time, but there was only one way to reset the Mummy's curse.

There was no warning for what happened in that crypt.

Like a sledgehammer through drywall, Gwen's claw crashed through the Mummy's chest with the strength of a vampire, tearing through it with the untamed fury of a werewolf. Sand, bugs, and charred wrappings burst out of the other side of the Mummy. Gwen pulled her arm back out of the Mummy's body, and held a part of him up as a trophy.

The Mummy's heart.

Amidst the droves of sand, it oozed with human blood.

Just as a tinge of mist began to leave the Mummy's body, Gwen used her free claw to grab a hold of the Mummy's neck and force him to the ground. She pinned him down like he meant nothing at all.

Gwen leaned over the Mummy and locked eyes with him. She ate the Mummy's heart in one massive bite.

And time slowed down to a stop.

With the last bit of fleeting willpower and energy, the Mummy's soul pulled the Phantom's into the astral plane one final time. The pain of experiencing his own death was no longer present, but what was left of his life force was gradually draining.

"Why?" the Phantom asked.

The Mummy said nothing.

"Why bring us here?" the Phantom asked again. "I failed your task. Your death is imminent. It's completely unstoppable."

Again, the Mummy said nothing.

But the Phantom had eternity to wait for a response. The Mummy did not. Gwen's teeth were driving themselves into his own severed heart, breaking the curse and ending his life.

"I don't want to die again," said the Mummy.

The Phantom paused. That wasn't what he assumed.

"I thought I would join Osiris in the Underworld," said the Mummy, "and reign for eternity as a deity... I had no intention of returning to the world of men. Undead or otherwise. I can never ascend like this. The curse will only reset."

The Phantom saw a side of the Mummy he hadn't shown anybody in over three thousand years.

"You won't make it much longer," said the Phantom.

"I know," said the Mummy.

And neither of them said anything else for a time.

Over six years passed in the astral plane as the Mummy's final seconds of life expired. The two of them talked about everything, from their previous lives as mortals, to their favorite colors when they were children, to their preferred foods and styles of making them, to their history of lovers they'd taken and bonded with, and absolutely anything and everything in between.

Alfred learned of Nivalthnesser's original burial. He wished to never yield his title as the Summit Karnak's High Priest, and elected to carry it with him in eternity. Eternity was all Nivalthnesser ever dreamed about before he was buried. To be immortalized as a god, worshiped by generations to come... It was his only goal. It blinded him to his acolyte's betrayal.

Nivalthnesser learned of Alfred's life of solitude at the time of his murder. In spite of being abandoned by his family for practicing sorcery, Alfred took solace in his recreational visits to the astral plane. They cleared his mind in dire times of stress, and kept his outlook on life optimistic. His focus and commitment to the craft let him become heavily promoted among his clan of sorcerers, and made him the target of a dear friend's envy. Becoming a phantom was never his goal, but he still had access to this extraordinary place, and that kept him from going mad.

Both of them had spent their entire lives dreaming of a better place than their own world. Only here and now could they share this dream together.

Finally, after the six-year hiatus from the plight of living in the real world's dictation of time, the two of them knew that it was time to go. Alfred stuck by his friend's side - the greatest friend he'd ever known - for the entire duration of Nivalthnesser's swift, painful death.

Alfred and Nivalthnesser departed from the astral plane, and the moment returned in real-time as though nothing had changed at all.

Gwen's jagged, wolf-like teeth, form-fitted to a perfect symmetrical alignment by the serum, gnawed away at the heart like it were made of clay. The Mummy watched as it disintegrated away, with bloodied bits of sand and veins falling from her mouth onto his face.

The rest of the creatures watched the unraveling beneath Gwen's immutable claw: The Mummy's body crumbled into a loose pile of sand adorned with whatever wrappings were left. The green lights of his eyes dimmed to a faint glow, then went out for eternity.

The loose sand began to move.

It migrated slowly away from beneath Gwen's pin, slithering along the floor of the crypt, and accreted at the Mummy's sarcophagus.

The sarcophagus sealed itself. All cracks in the coffin were made whole and unbroken once again.

And all became quiet.

It felt like the first true semblance of peace any of them had since first entering that accursed crypt. The bliss of freedom had been lost for so long amidst their harrowed lives in these cells. They'd finally achieved a level of well-deserved serenity.

The Gargoyle loomed over the Scorpion Man's body and watched it transform: The Scorpion Man's skin began to smoke, followed soon by inextinguishable flames, and transmutated back into a human body upon the defeat of the pharaoh's curse.

Tryg Ulfsson, brother of Gjaller and father of Hjalmar, laid naked and bloodied on the ashlar floor.

The Gargoyle moved quickly with his spell: He used the symbols on the crypt's pillars and generated sudden winds, catching each one ablaze in the process, and caused a powerful bolt of lightning to crash down on Tryg's body as though the ceiling weren't even there.

He was suspended.

Looking up, Tryg saw the world through a dying man's eyes for only a few moments: Blood blotched out the arena-like crypt's finer details, but revealed his monstrous opponents standing all around him. His memory was fogged like a dream, only revealing itself in sparse flashes from time to time.

Tryg passed out, forever stuck in his final moments of life. The Gargoyle planned to explain *everything* to him when more important affairs were settled. But for now, the Gargoyle had saved his life. It was the first time that he'd *saved* a life by casting a spell.

But it still did not bring him a sense of closure.

The Underlord waved his hand and commanded dozens, then hundreds of insects and little critters to swarm the Phantom's cell. Ten, twenty, fifty at a time, they coated their bodies entirely in the ashy floor and marched out of Waylon's crypt. He'd remembered there being an urn on one of Waylon's mantletops.

Locking eyes with the Underlord, the Gargoyle nodded amiably.

The Underlord nodded back.

The Gargoyle approached the Phantom's wide-open cell and came as close as he possibly could, so close to the dirt's edge that only a caterpillar could cross the gap. He stood perfectly still as the Underlord's army of bugs and critters kept moving little tufts of ash, migrating them all slowly out of the crypt. They avoided the Gargoyle's path.

The Phantom glared at the Gargoyle, continuously looking down at the monster's feet. *Just one step, you demon.*

"It was me," said the Gargoyle calmly.

The Phantom didn't know what he meant.

"I drove that dagger through your heart in Paris," the Gargoyle continued, "and bound you to your own house for eternity."

And it hit the Phantom with a tremendous amount of shock.

"*Hunchback...*" the Phantom whispered venomously.

"I've spent six hundred years with an ill heart," said the Gargoyle. "Taking your life filled me with trauma and regret that's lingered incessantly for all of these centuries... After what you've done today, Phantom, I feel no *semblance* of sympathy. I feel *nothing* for the life I took from you anymore. I refuse to carry that guilt around with me any longer, and I hope that you spend another eternity bound to this pile of ash."

The Phantom processed everything he'd just heard. Repressing his budding anger, the Phantom chose not to lash out at his murderer, because of everybody left alive in that room, only the Gargoyle knew how to free him from that immutable spell.

"Release me from the enchantment," said the Phantom. "You owe me much more than that."

The Gargoyle stepped forward into the cell.

The Phantom looked down at his feet, seeing that the Underlord's bugs were almost done with their transportation, and his breadth of space shrank faster and faster with each passing moment.

"I will break the enchantment when Saturn's rings completely dissolve," the Gargoyle promised his Phantom.

The Phantom began to fade as the pile of ash dwindled and reduced down to the empty cell's cold, tangible floor. The Gargoyle watched as every last piece of ash was carried away on the backs of countless little insects purposely avoiding his legs like they were boulders in a river's current. There was a method and organization among them unmatched by any army or cult of acolytes. The Phantom's very last semblance had finally vanished from view, now on his way to the inside of the empty urn to spend an unclear amount of time.

No matter how long he spent in the astral plane, the Phantom had no way of knowing that, by the best estimates of the world's smartest scientists, the rings of Saturn would dissolve in a little less than one hundred million years.

Paula nudged Franklin's shoulder, pointing to a pillar at the opposite end of the crypt. It was coated in a small splotch of blood, separate from where the bulk of the battle had taken place. There was no apparent source.

Franklin and Paula made their way over to it. When nearing the pillar, Franklin's foot hit something unseen.

Franklin bent down and pulled off the mask, revealing his father's lifeless eyes looking back at him. He had no pulse. Trying to make sense of it, Franklin looked down at a floating section of blood coated around Adam's invisible finger. The blood was his own, taken from his abdomen where the Phantom had shot him dead with the antiserum.

On the pillar, Franklin looked where Adam had written with his dying moments:

Proud.

For all of the bravado he typically hid behind, Adam's only son let it all melt away and became emotional, closing his eyes hard to fight the oncoming moisture. He thought back to every single time his father said he was proud of him, replaying those memories in great detail. It was rare. It made the times that he'd heard it that much more potent.

Paula placed her hand on Franklin's shoulder. From his other shoulder, Handrew wiped the moisture off of Franklin's cheek.

The Gargoyle turned his attention across the crypt. Gwen shifted form seamlessly into her human one, something only a vampire was capable of doing. Werewolves took half a minute, and artificial men couldn't shift at all.

Much like Franklin with his father, Gwen thought back to her memories with near-perfect recall. The incident in Hamilton, Ontario was no longer a fuzzy, blocked-out event. Then, she revisited every incident she'd ever had. All 37 of them. She recalled exactly how long they all lasted, how many lives were lost in the carnage each time, and the traumatizing images of their faces as they stared into the beast's snarling face for half a moment.

Her family's final moments on the night of her seminal transformation were vividly crystallized in her mind's eye. It was an event she'd always known happened, but was happy to repress with drugs or alcohol, or simply enough time passing so as to not feel the painful guilt and regret. The image of her mother screaming for mercy as her razor-sharp talons tore through her chest was no longer blocked out. This, and everything else, was destined to haunt Gwen for the rest of her immortal life.

She waited for the voice in her head to say something. It'd been silent for a little too long.

"It'll be another thousand years," said the Gargoyle, gesturing to the sarcophagus.

Gwen snapped out of it. She shook the feeling away and blinked twice, welcoming the distraction: The thought of the Mummy's return was unsettling for her, because she recognized that she might actually *live to see* those thousand years.

"We should keep watch over it," said Gwen.

When Gwen looked back at the Gargoyle, she could tell simply by the stern look on his weird, grotesque face what exactly he was thinking. Even before he had to say it.

"It will remain with me alone," the Gargoyle affirmed.

The Gargoyle trusted no other with the task. Even the one who'd torn the monster's heart out and reset the Mummy's curse for another millennium. The Mummy had been his passion for the past several centuries. He would let nobody else bear the task of managing Nivalthnesser's tomb. At the very least, he would be the most partial *candidate* to keep a watchful eye on it.

Hoxton's cell opened up.

Having reinforced Hoxton's gateway himself, Waylon had been waiting for the room's conflict to resolve before using the blade to pick the gateway's physical lock and disarm the digital one with his passcode. Waylon held his hands high, disarmingly, and bowed his head out of respect.

"*Never again* will those cells be locked," said Waylon.

The crew of monsters looked at him quizzically.

"You've all earned your freedoms," Waylon continued. "You may roam my manor as you please, uninhibited by any confines or restraints. This day is one of *celebration...*"

Waylon was not done with his speech. He had several more sentences planned before the Underlord dashed over to him and held him up by his furred collar. There were no ultraviolet rays to save him anymore.

Like all men, Waylon could not resist the alluring quality of the Underlord's demonic gaze.

An incredible, unbelievable wrath possessed the Vampire King, and it was all channeled straight into his captor. The emotional effect that the vampire had on Waylon was not one of lust or desire, but of a potent, almighty fear. The sort of fear children are instilled with at a very young age when alone in a dark room for the very first time. The sort of fear usually not felt by grown men who've already conquered the worst monsters they'd ever known. This fear, beyond all other means of description, was primal, and felt in the very pith of whoever experienced it.

"What did you call us again?" the Underlord raved. "I remember your musings about us: *They are the Devil's league, and they're the greatest game in the world.* It's an appropriate title. It may well be the only brilliancy that's left your lips."

Clutching the man now by his throat and painfully *squeezing* the airways, the Underlord channeled the wicked will of all that was evil into his prey, and spoke these words carefully as his fangs became prominent:

"We are the Devil's League, and to us, men like you are the Greatest Game in the World."

The Underlord tore into Waylon's throat like a lion, spattering the man's blood onto the nearby Ilona. She celebrated the red showering her. Waylon couldn't even scream as he instinctively gasped for air that would not come, and squirmed in the Underlord's grasp in his final moments. Every creature in that manor that had their lives ripped away from them were dutifully avenged in one astonishing motion: The Underlord's unbelievable act of bloodshed and deliverance.

And the Underlord looked up from Waylon's corpse, wiping the blood away from his mouth. After a moment, he moved his wrist in such a way as to indicate to Ilona and Lillian to *frenzy* the rest of Waylon's body. It was theirs for the taking.

But the Devil's work was not done.

"The man who took us captive was possessed by a most fascinating idea," said the Underlord to the group. "It would appear I've been possessed by one similar."

Hoxton wanted to shoot him dead, or at least try to. Perceptively, the Gargoyle waved his hand Hoxton's way, shaking his head. *Now's not the time.*

The Underlord continued: "For all present, this house has been the source of your captivity, interfighting, and copious amounts of bloodshed. The way I've interpreted that man's twisted crusade was not to make a safe haven for us, but to protect his fellow man from us. Henceforth, this place will be a better version of what he envisioned."

The Underlord walked over to the crypt's center. His Brides ceased their feasting and took notice.

"All of you will hear me now, for I will only speak this once," said the Underlord. "There are many luxurious rooms spread across this mansion. Take them, all of you, as you please and live freely. No dungeons or cages. Not even locks on the doors, lest you wish for one. By day, come here to my home and lay rest. Feast upon your glories among allies of your own kind. By night, leave as you wish and fulfill your every desire. So long as you act in the interest of the inhabitants of this home, our doors will always be open to you."

Most of the creatures and beasts looked to one another, considering their options. Some strongly opposed the Underlord's proposal. Others needed something *exactly like* what was being offered.

"Waylon Ross may have created this place for your imprisonment," said the Underlord, "but it is irreversibly *mine*. I offer it to you as nothing more than a home."

Franklin stood up. He looked down at Handrew, thinking back to the Gargoyle's story: The Gargoyle had shared an experience he'd had where this goblin's ancestors were *cursed* to serve an old, merciless sorcerer for the remainder of his life. It was a cruel reality that should never be repeated.

"And why should we stay with you, he who controls minds with a thought?" Franklin objected.

"If I wanted to *force* you all to stay, I wouldn't have to ask you to," the Underlord replied. "Rest assured my brides and I will live very happily on our own within the confines of this place. All we're offering is the opportunity to share our safeguard and protection from men like Waylon Ross, who spend all of their time and money hunting you down like little fawns."

There was a moment that passed where nobody did anything at all but think. Then, the Gargoyle walked over to the sarcophagus, and hurled it over his shoulder with immense strength.

"Gargoyle," said Hoxton in shock. "You *can't*."

"It is the smartest decision," said the Gargoyle, carrying it out of the crypt. "I hope you make the same one."

Hoxton clenched his fist, encroaching his finger over the gauntlet's trigger. Franklin and Paula exchanged a glance.

The Gargoyle gritted his teeth.

"Alright," said the Gargoyle. "If I'm being honest, I hope you *don't*. Continue your grand hunt. Write another book that'll damn a new crew of monsters to somebody's crypt when you're captured. But never come back to this place again."

The Gargoyle had much nastier words for Hoxton in mind. Out of gratitude for Hoxton's efforts in combating the Mummy, he held them in.

By the Gargoyle's side, Franklin approached confidently, Handrew crawling back up onto his shoulder and getting comfortable. Paula came after him, bringing the Creature by her side like a pet. The Gargoyle nodded to Franklin, who went over to Tryg and threw his unconscious body over his shoulder.

Their alliance with Hoxton was ended.

The Underlord nodded to all of them. "Any room you wish," he reiterated.

The Gargoyle carried the Mummy's sarcophagus over his shoulder as he walked down the crypt's hallway, with Franklin coming ahead to open the door for him. Paula followed closeby, accompanied by the Creature. She signed something to Franklin, making the man briefly smile. She'd given him a warming thought to dwell on during his grief. It was only the Gargoyle that interpreted what was being said between them, and he thought it best not to share it with anybody else.

The four of them entered the ground floor of Waylon's manor, with Paula having almost forgotten what the world really looked like outside of this underground chamber. They mused amongst themselves about what luxurious rooms Waylon's mansion had to offer them. Though Franklin and Paula were still undecided, the Gargoyle had his mind set on the observatory.

"You are alone, Brute Man," said the Underlord to Hoxton.

But that was not at all true.

Gwen had been looking down at her normal, human hand for some time now. She concentrated and shifted *only her hand* into its beast-like nature, seeing the gray skin beneath the thick fur, and the combined talons of multiple predators.

Full molecular control.

She used her nail to slice her other arm open, straight down from the wrist to the elbow. It sealed back up before losing a drop of blood. Her healing was even faster than Adam or Franklin's, enhanced by the other species she now belonged to. Her hand shifted back into a human's, and she clenched it into a fist. She felt no difference between now and before she was ever bitten by a wolf.

The Underlord came up to her, marveling at her powers along with her. He placed his clawed hand on her cheek, aiming her head towards his.

"You have never been more beautiful," said the Underlord.

Gwen's beaming eyes fell into his again. She saw, with a new sense of awareness, his wicked abilities in action. She felt them on her consciously. Her eyes saw beyond the visible spectrum of light, beyond ultraviolet or infrared. Her ears picked up more than simple soundwaves.

Her mind was ungodly.

"You never gave me a choice," said Gwen.

The Underlord didn't understand.

Gwen looked to Ilona and Lillian, standing closeby, and concentrated.

The Underlord's hold over them shattered.

"*No!!*" yelled the Underlord, who wound up his hand for a smack across her face.

She caught it.

With the opposite hand, Gwen grabbed the Vampire King by his throat and held him up into the air. She produced those unbelievable claws again.

"I've broken your hold over them," said Gwen venomously. "Let them choose to live by your side, or spend their days hunting you. Or neither, if that's what they truly wish."

Dismissively, Gwen tossed the Underlord to the ground. He scrambled back to his feet, maintaining his appearance and dignity.

Ilona shrieked.

Ilona had been the longest-serving Bride of her Master, and never had a rebellious bone in her body after being bitten. That control maintained over her for a consistent eight hundred years. It broke not a moment ago.

Beside her, Lillian became confused. She loved Master, and she loved Ilona just as much. Even still to this very moment. The Underlord's hold over her wasn't what dictated it. It was always innate since the day she was recruited by him.

"Sister," Lillian pleaded with Ilona as she extended a comforting hand.

"*GET OFF ME!!*" Ilona screamed, smacking Lillian's hand away. She felt repulsed by Lillian's very sight.

Ilona looked to the Underlord.

"Ilona," said the Underlord in a hypnotic voice. He wanted her back *desperately.* He'd relied on her for so very long that he couldn't imagine what life was like without her by his side.

Feeling the Underlord's hypnotic gaze on her again, Ilona hunched over and threw up. She screamed once again before scanning the crypt and everyone in it. Blindingly, Ilona dashed over to Hoxton and stole Waylon's gauntlet from him. She switched the armlet to the wooden ammunition and aimed it at her own head.

"*NO!!!*" Lillian yelled, dashing over to catch Ilona's body.

Gwen intervened.

Ilona snapped out of it, bound once more by the Underlord's Satanic abilities. Gwen had restored the Underlord's hold over Ilona and Lillian just as quickly as she'd tore it apart. Ilona shook her head for a moment, shaking off the nasty headache she'd procured. It felt strong enough as if to linger and fester for days on end.

By Ilona's side, Lillian held her arm. She slowly slid the gauntlet off of Ilona's hand. Lillian's eyes produced tears for the first time since Hope's death. *This* one would have been far more impactful on her. She'd never wanted to know what life was like without Ilona. The thought horrified her more than anything.

"Sister..." Lillian said affectionately.

"I..." Ilona began. But she could not finish whatever thought she'd just had. She couldn't even remember it anymore.

The Underlord approached Ilona. He placed his hand delicately on her shoulder.

Gwen reversed her defiant decision before Ilona's life could be lost. She reasoned, with not a moment to spare, that perhaps it was better for the Underlord's concubines to live their eternal lives of ignorance and subjugation, than to burden them with the awareness that their Master stole away from them. There was no positive way out of this landscape. There was only the grave decision of morality which Gwen was forced to make a determination on.

Gwen waited for her voice to return. She needed to hear it say something. It always had some suggestion to be considered, or some perspective to dwell on.

The voice in her head was gone.

The Underlord glared back at her for what she'd just done, and all he found were Gwen's unsympathetic eyes looking back at him. She cared deeply for Ilona and Lillian's predicament, but nothing at all for her former Master.

And then, suddenly, Gwen fled from the crypt - and Waylon's entire estate - in the blink of an eye.

From across the crypt, Hoxton eyed the Underlord carefully. The threat was neutralized. That prophesied Mummy had been defeated...

Something inside of Hoxton wouldn't let him attack. He wasn't worried about the potential pushback from monsters allied with the Vampire King, for the two most powerful ones in that crypt had either died or disappeared moments ago. No, it wouldn't have been much of a struggle to make an attempt on the Underlord's life...

The Underlord met his gaze, knowing he couldn't sway the persistent mind of the Brute Man. This critical choice was Hoxton's to make.

With a steady pace, the Underlord walked over to Waylon's body, slicing his own wrist right over Waylon's head with that razor-sharp talon. Hoxton bent down and took the gauntlet off of the crypt's cold floor, removing it from the thin layer of slush left behind by the brief snowstorm, and caught a glimpse of the engraving on its side: *GRIFFIN, Named for the Greatest Assistant the World's Never Seen.*

"You won't let him die, will you?" Hoxton asked, coming to the Underlord's side.

The Underlord shook his head.

"Good," said Hoxton. "He deserves far worse."

The black blood of the Vampire King dripped down and flowed into Waylon's lifeless mouth. The tongue of the corpse began to twitch.

"We'll give him far worse," said the Underlord.

The Underlord noticed the weapon in Hoxton's hand. It was the only thing of Waylon's that Hoxton had ever enjoyed.

"Why do you still hunt us?" the Underlord asked genuinely.

Hoxton hesitated before answering.

"Because we're evil."

"We?"

"I am unhallowed," said Hoxton. "I deserve death, like all monsters do. But God gave me this purpose, and I will not allow myself to die until I see it through."

The Underlord took this in. He recognized a man in pain when he saw one.

"Keep it," said the Underlord, nodding to the gauntlet. "A parting gift. Hunt whomever you'd like outside of these walls, but consider this house exempt from your tyranny."

Hoxton nodded to the Underlord, then left the crypt. He would've kept Waylon's gauntlet regardless, and he hadn't made up his mind as to whether or not he'd follow his enemy's instructions.

And the Underlord was alone.

Ilona and Lillian came to his sides. The Underlord scanned Ilona's face, mind, body... She was her usual self. The Ilona he'd always known.

He turned to Lillian, seeing her powerful, beaming eyes look back at him. The soul of a woman truly grateful for what she'd almost lost.

"I've always loved you," said Lillian to her Master. "Vampire or not."

"I know," said the Underlord, who placed his hand on her waist. "We will find another to fill Gwen's place. And we will do so *together.*"

Lillian collapsed into the Underlord's arms, beginning to heal. The Underlord held her close. She dared not to ask him if he actually loved her back. She feared the answer he'd give. His arms and embrace were much more comforting than learning that sort of truth would ever be.

The Underlord let out his hand to Ilona for her to embrace him as well.

Ilona hesitated.

Having exited the crypt, the Gargoyle led Franklin, Handrew, Paula, and the Creature all down the many corridors of the manor to one very specific room in the house's east wing. He had Waylon's express trust from the very beginning, and had a full working knowledge of Waylon's manor from all of the times he'd decided to roam about freely.

There was *one* room he had in mind before heading to the observatory.

The Gargoyle approached the doorway of one of the living rooms on the very first floor of the mansion, secluded at the very end of one of the more obscure hallways. This room was poised on the opposite side of the building from the crypt, and it had no dungeons or secret passageways.

Paula and Franklin saw the many locks on the living room's door, all of which were quickly and easily broken by the Gargoyle's grip.

What is this? Paula signed to the Gargoyle.

See for yourself, the Gargoyle responded.

Paula looked to Franklin. She had to be absolutely *sure.*

Franklin nodded.

Paula reached for the knob and turned it, revealing the living room's interior, and her eyes widened tremendously.

Every type of creature and critter Waylon had ever known, found or touched with his bare hands coexisted in this room at once. It was a carryover from Waylon's East Freetown cabin, with a few newer additions from whatever endangered Mexican wildlife Waylon could track down himself. This room - one of the largest in the entire mansion - was on the first floor for an important reason: It had an in-ground pool acting as a river basin, and several trees growing out of the hardwood floor, whose branches housed everything from squirrels and birds to small vines and tiny little bugs.

This door will never be locked again, signed the Gargoyle.

Paula howled with the excited screams of an ape. It was the type of howling that made Franklin's sensitive ears *ring* a little. Blithely, Paula entered the room and interacted with all of the adjacent critters, letting some of them interact back. A large spider crawled up her arm, fascinating Paula as it wove its legs through her thick black fur like it were tall grass to an explorer.

Franklin was in love with the sight of it, but it didn't do anything to soothe his pain.

When entering this room, the Creature quickly dove down into the river where it felt the most comfortable, and habitually swam straight to the bottom.

Before the crypt's most recent events, Waylon and Jack would periodically sedate the Creature, enter the tank and remove its eggs when they were laid. Upon reawakening, the Creature never truly processed why and how the eggs disappeared.

But the eggs were not there at the bottom of that river. Only the remnants of their shells.

Franklin and the Gargoyle watched as the Creature returned to the room's surface, where Paula was now interacting with the Creature's many, many babies. They crawled up and down Paula's massive arms with their tiny little claws and chomped each other playfully, one of them slipping and rolling off of her body. Paula instinctively caught it in her massive hand and protectively held it against her chest.

The Creature approached Paula, and the babies flocked to their mother, several at a time. Their mother screeched loudly, disturbing Franklin from across the room, and the Creature's children screeched back for the very first time.

It landed from above.

A beast larger than Paula crashed down in front of them, batting its massive, angelic set of wings as it stabilized itself. The body was a twisted mirror of Paula's, but without the strange seams between body parts that lingered from Dr. Sigmund's handiwork. This creature was a natural birth from two unnatural monsters, and for the first time in twenty years, finally laid eyes on its mother again.

In Waylon's chateau, Hoxton walked past the demolished pieces of furniture, avoiding the stains on the carpet as he did so. He sidestepped the ring of symbols the Gargoyle first used to teleport them far and away, painted in his very own blood. The sight of it was toxic.

Before leaving, Hoxton turned to the strange noise coming from the other side of the chateau.

On the mantle adorning the back wall, the empty urn was almost entirely filled up with ash by a countless amount of tiny insects doing the Underlord's bidding. When the urn was full, the Underlord's critters sealed the top of it and migrated away, all going back to their own corners of Waylon's manor. They crawled through little unseen holes in the house's trim, beneath the carpets, between a loose floorboard or two.

In moments, they were all gone.

At the front door, Hoxton turned the knob and pushed it open, seeing the blacked-out sky of the overhead eclipse slowly become brighter as the moon moved onward. Two decades of his life were lost in the confines of this terrible place. He would need to make up for all of the lost time, and that started right then with the long-awaited promise of his freedom.

Hoxton stopped himself.

He knew there'd be consequences to the intrusive thought in his mind. It conflicted with his mission, and to an extent, his sense of self-worth. He'd never have even *entertained* this one, horrible idea before being held captive in this house of nightmares for so terribly long.

When the Underlord finally exited the crypt, he took a gander at the chateau's mantle to see where he'd trapped that pestilent villain. All that he saw was the empty spot where the Phantom's urn used to be.

His father could have no tombstone.

Franklin had chosen to disintegrate his father's body with more of the antiserum, then incinerate what was left in the house's furnace. It was the only way to ensure that Rebecca's serum would never be spread to any other life forms that wished to feed on Adam's body. Those flakes of ash and dust were sprinkled over Rebecca Chamberton's grave, and the necklace with the silver crucifix hung from the tombstone's edge.

To the best of his knowledge, it was what his father would've wanted.

With Handrew hidden away under his coat, Franklin visited the cemetery where his grandmother had been buried for many years. He'd met her on several occasions: After his father visited her in the nursing home on his own, subsequent visits involved Franklin. With near-perfect recall, Franklin cherished those moments with her, despite her condition worsening every visit they had.

It was here at her grave that Franklin could mourn his father.

Franklin adorned his grandmother's grave with roses on each end. He'd learned to utilize skin make-up when walking in public, resembling a cross between a bodybuilder and a drug addict. He was not beautiful, but for the most part, he was able to blend in.

"I miss you," he whispered under his breath. "I keep replaying those conversations in my head, the ones during birthdays or Christmases... We never talked much about mom. I realize now: *I* always avoided it. I wish I knew how badly you wanted to just... *talk* to somebody about it. I should've..."

Franklin breathed slowly.

"Paula's been helping me," he continued. "She knows how it feels to lose your only family. People say they 'know how it feels' to me a lot. I want to tell them that they don't, but I know they're just trying to be understanding. She seems to be the only one who actually *does*... and I know that's not really true, but that's how it feels sometimes. I don't know... I'm sorry..."

Franklin knew that he lacked skill with words when expressing how he felt. Still, he knelt down over Rebecca's grave, silently mourning them both. He drew on those fondest memories and stayed with them, reliving them all in the vivid daydreams of an artificial man. He escaped into his own mind like nobody else ever could. Nobody but his own family.

Quietly, Franklin took a deep breath.

"I love you, dad," he whispered.

Having always been nearby, the Underlord finally revealed himself.

Franklin spun around, his rage under reasonable control. That was something *else* Paula had been working on with him. Handrew popped out of the jacket and leapt onto Franklin's arm, forming into a curled-up ball in place of a brawler's fist.

But the Underlord was solemn, and carried no trace of his usual temperament.

Though Handrew was more than ready for an altercation, Franklin stayed still, visibly stewing in his own hatred. His trigger finger twitched passively by his other side.

"Let it out before your skin starts boiling," the Underlord remarked.

"You killed my mother."

They both waited. Both of them expected the other to talk first. Though this lull only lasted a passing moment, it felt like an eternity for both of them. Franklin looked down at Rebecca's tombstone, almost dissociating from this conversation. His trigger finger finally relaxed.

"Your father killed my wife," the Underlord started.

Like a magnet to steel, Franklin's attention came straight back.

"We were hunting somebody," the vampire continued. "He found his way into your father's protection. Verona's death didn't sit well with us... so we retaliated."

Franklin didn't say a word. He could feel Handrew itching for an attack.

"Life is unpredictable," the Underlord continued. "Take it from someone who's lived this much of it. You can't predict that when you kill somebody, they'll be brought back to life and have a child... Every year I do a hundred things that come back to bite me, and all I can do is keep fending them off until I run out of blood to drain."

"Then why do you persist?" Franklin asked. "If it's all so pointless, why don't you just shove a stake through your own chest and spare the rest of us who actually *value* our lives?"

"I didn't say life was futile. It's *unpredictable*. Even at my lowest: Captured by a mortal and humiliated... In walks Franklin Chamberton. The son of my wife's murderer had aligned with my Brides to plan our escape. I'm only reminded of why I do what I do when people like you walk into my life, and prove to me that there *is* something worth fighting for beyond ourselves."

This wasn't enough for Franklin. He rubbed his temple with his free hand, really trying to process what the Underlord meant.

"Your finger doesn't twitch when you're thinking," said the Underlord.

Distraught, Franklin popped up again, now self-conscious about his hand.

"You're a perfect index of memory, aren't you?" the Underlord asked. "Think back to every single time your forefinger's twitched like that."

Confused, Franklin closed his eyes for a moment.

"Seven hundred and twenty-two times," said Franklin.

"When does it occur?"

Franklin thought hard, then opened them: "Whenever I think about you."

The Underlord nodded.

"I'm sorry. I do what I do because I feel it's right, or justified in some way. But what I did to your mother traumatized your family. And for that, I'm truly sorry."

In the Underlord's eyes, where most men see only power and authority, Franklin took a hard look and saw desperation.

It was genuine.

"Why do you care?" Franklin said bitterly. "After everything you've done - you *continue* to do - why do you care about how I feel?"

With esteem, the Underlord replied: "Every time that I take a life and leave a survivor, I'm always hunted down. They spend years channeling all of their hatred and forge a hunter out of themselves, chasing after a myth with sticks and water. And they *all* do it. Every *single time* that I reveal myself, humans hunt me down. All except two."

From the inside of his cassock, the Underlord pulled out something sharp and slender. Franklin looked down and saw a wooden dagger, fashioned with an ergonomic grip.

"The first died a month ago," said the Underlord, "fighting by our side to protect who we are."

The Underlord handed it to him.

"The second was his son."

Franklin looked the weapon over. It was hand-made by somebody who'd fantasized about bloodshed, putting time and care into every serrated groove. He held the blade of Galerius Augustus Domitius, whose legacy had been cut short in a cave outside of Rome.

"You'd move out of the way before my hand ever started raising," said Franklin.

"Everything turns its back," he said passively. "We don't all have a goblin watching ours."

Franklin handed the weapon to Handrew as he walked away, who stowed it away in the linings of his jacket. With reverence, the Underlord looked on at Rebecca Chamberton's tombstone. He knew that he wasn't forgiven by any member of her family, whether they were living, dead, or somewhere vaguely in between. Perhaps he'd never be. Instead, Franklin had given him his trust, and that was enough for him.

As Franklin walked away, he felt something strange attached to his palm, though looked down at his hand and saw nothing. With Handrew's help, they unfurled a long, invisible piece of fabric wrapped around the weapon's handle.

XXII

Plaxton's Journal

As Revised By Waylon Ross

By Grace are ye saved through faith...
Not of works.

Ephesians 2:8-9

Creatures from Black's Lagoon

Piscine Reptilian humanoid

Killed: |

First Encountered: 1762 Originated sometime during Devonian Age

Location: Caribbean Sea

Description: — Webbed claws

serrated dorsal spines

— Head resembling an anglerfish (illicium)

— Dragon-like snout

— Long, unkempt teeth/underbite

— Powerful tail for stability/offence

— Small webbed spikes from spine/limbs

Abilities: — Agile; faster than one would assume, given their size

have mammalian lungs

— Able to breathe in air/water and aquatic gills

— Tail can strike with enough force to incapacitate most enemies

Weaknesses: — Beheading

Creatures from Black's lagoon are predatory, carnivorous ~~amphibians~~ Reptilian? possessing ~~traits~~ of dozens of wildlife, mostly land- and sea-based. The creature displays characteristics from many different organisms; most visibly and notably it's thick elasmoid scales similar to those found on prehistoric bony-tongued fish, such as the arapaima. The creature also displays an anterior spiny dorsal fin, and depicts high mobility in the spines and webbing which allows the structure to lay flat against it's body or stand erect. The creature can use these serrated spines as a sail in the water for speed.

visible textured scale structure

embedded under the skin makes impenetrable to most means of attack

Revisiting Black's lagoon confirmed an earlier
theory regarding the Creature's aggression. Following
other reptilian organisms, the creatures are
Parthenogenetic and can asexually reproduce,
meaning the Creature has been protecting her
valuable egg masses from any potential threat
including passing ships. These eggs are
unlike any I've ever seen, and develop through a bizarre
metamorphic cycle revolving around spinal development, as
if the creature is "blossoming" from the egg.

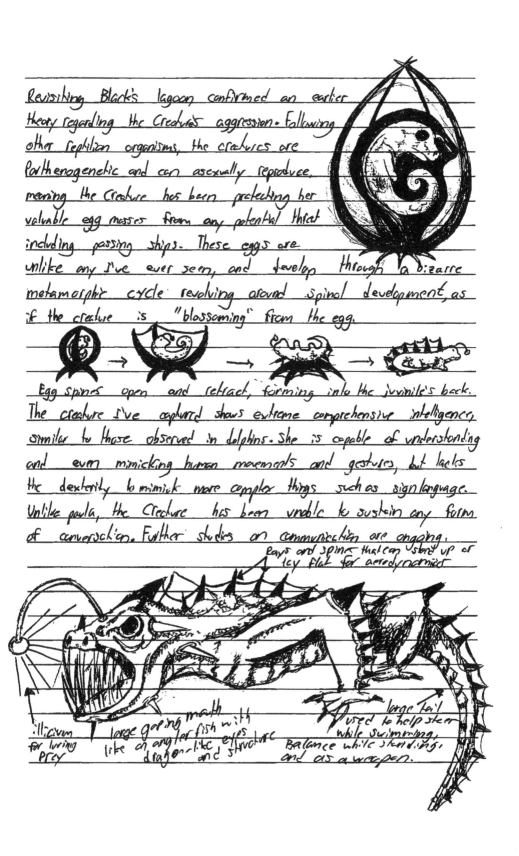

 Egg spines open and retract, forming into the juvenile's back.
The creature I've captured shows extreme comprehensive intelligence,
similar to those observed in dolphins. She is capable of understanding
and even mimicking human movements and gestures, but lacks
the dexterity to mimick more complex things such as sign language.
Unlike paula, the Creature has been unable to sustain any form
of conversation. Further studies on communication are ongoing.

Rays and spines that can stand up or
lay flat for aerodynamics

Illicium
for luring
prey

large gaping mouth
like an angler fish with
dragon-like eyes
and structure

large tail
used to help steer
while swimming,
Balance while standing,
and as a weapon.

Vampires

Homo vespertilo

Killed:

First Encountered: 1762   Year of origin: indeterminate; earliest
Known Location: Worldwide   evidence dates back almost
Description: — Unknown visual age   two thousand years
    black — Pale, white skin — appears mid-20's after feeding.
    nails — Nails (black) extend several inches - slight curve
        — Fangs extend about an inch or so; retractable
        — Has a "human form" and can switch at will;
        stuck in "human form" in ~~sunlight~~ any form of UV
Abilities: — Low-Level Hypnosis (suggestion) radiation
    "The strength of twenty men" as described
    by one of his underlings
    Able to move faster than the eye can register
    Immortality
    Bloodletting
Weaknesses: — Wooden stake through the chest is fatal
        — Holy water burns them on contact
        — Lack of bloodletting for ~50 yrs would
        allow them to die of natural causes/age
    Bite marks — UV Radiation

All vampires are governed by an entity called THE
UNDERLORD. The Underlord always secures three
"Brides" of varying backgrounds and ethnicities. They
are always young women targeted for two factors:
Beauty and insecurity. They share all of his strengths,
and as far as one can tell, all of his weaknesses.

The Three Brides

While it is true that they share many of the Underlord's traits, it's worth noting that, just like the rest of his underlings, the Brides are his victims first and foremost. When breaking into the Romanian hotel room and capturing the Vampire king beneath a set of ultraviolet lights, Jack and I encountered one of his Brides, Hope, and injected her with the same antiserum derived from Rebecca Chambatar's notes, knowing it would outright kill her, or potentially heal her.

Further research on the matter is needed. When the crypt is filled and I'm forced to build new cells, I'll be sending Jack to her bone at an unknown presence to stay updated on her whereabouts in the coming weeks.

THE UNDERLORD'S RULE

The Underlord

The Brides
1. Ilona
2. Lillian
3. ~~Hope~~

Vampire underlings
(no longer used as of ~1700's)
Werewolves (serve as henchmen)

Werewolves

Canis lycanthrope

Killed: ||| ||| ||| ||| ||| ||| ||| |||

First Encountered: 1762   Year of origin: ~200,000 BC

Location: Worldwide

Description - ANCIENT: - 6'-9' tall
- Translucent talons
- Wolf-like head/snout
- Shifts only during Full Moon

an age-old image

MODERN: - Humanoid head with fur down the sides, and a large brow protruding from the head, conjoining with the nose in a canine-esque way.
Translucent talons
- Animalistic body, but still mostly humanoid in appearance.
- Shifts purely based on mood or emotional state

I never took Hexton for an amateur archaeologist. the wonders that three hundred years of spare time can give a man...

Abilities: - Enhanced strength/speed
- Heightened senses for hunting (typically human)

Weaknesses: - Silver (bullets preferred)

Mariposa-native plant in Tibet -
- Animalistic minds are often susceptible to hypnotic suggestion

Prevents transformation upon ingesting (shortens impact over time)

Regarding ANCIENT - Though reports of this extinct species are mostly anecdotal/legendary, this information is compiled based on fossilized evidence as matched with descriptions from cultures across the world.

<u>Regarding MODERN</u> – Present-day werewolves are a Darwinian offshoot of the werewolves that existed in Upper Paleolithic Europe. They've shrunken in height down to approximately match the height of their human bodies, when historically they've been described as almost twice as tall upon transformation.

Despite adhering to evolution, werewolves must have originated as a supernatural. Moonlight is just reflected sunlight, so the light of a "full moon" has no more effect than sunlight would on an average day. Furthermore, it's unclear if an ancient werewolf who subscribes to a full Moon's light would transform in an enclosed room with no windows just instinctively. All of this to say that the transformation must have originated with magic, and not our conventional understanding of biology. Perhaps they are more impacted by the gravitational or tidal influences of the full moon, the way many marine animals are?

Modern werewolves have been influenced by the Underlord's rule through Hypnosis's. Over dozens of generations, He has selectively bred werewolves to have traits favorable to Him – and He's successfully broken the millenia-old link between a werewolf and the Full Moon, shrunk their size to be almost equivalent to humans, and simplified their wolf-like heads into predominantly human ones, only showing select traits of a werewolf, breeding leaner, more submissive monsters optimized to be the underlord's perfect pets

werewolf claw, taken from a corpse found while leaving Hexlens massacre. Claw is sharpened on one side, like a knife.

Mechimigardians

mechimigardians

Killed: ~~HHT~~ ~~HHT~~ ~~HHT~~ ~~HHT~~ ~~HHT~~ |||

First Encountered: 1892   Originated ~10,000 B.C.?

Location: Worldwide

Description: - Completely ~~human~~ exterior, indistinguishable
(simulate all life, not just humans) in every way including false clothes and hair.
- TRUE FORM: A mass of large, red tendrils
They are everywhere with no apparent body, all converging
they are unstoppable   somewhere towards the center.

Abilities - Flawless cloaking   cells contain chromatophores
similar to cephalopods that'd help their cloaking abilities
- Enhanced speed
- Seemingly enhanced strength...

Weaknesses - Their tendrils are made of flesh,
unique muscle-like tendrils form   which is vulnerable to most weapons:
together to make whatever   Guns, Knives, corrosive acid, etc.
shape desired!   uncloaked, organic structure looks like muscle fibers

Their strength is greater than a human's, but
that may only seem that way because of their
amazing speed: One of them struck me in
the chest and sent me flying through a window.
I'm almost positive that perceived "strength" is due to
the fact that, while lightweight, those tendrils move
wildly fast through the air, and end up providing a
devastating impact to their prey upon contact.

   I have no further interest in capturing one.
Mechimigardians are all extensions of the same hive-minded parasitic
individual of indeterminate source. Composed of traits found in many
Earthly life forms, however strongly alienistic in nature.

Each mechi captures and consumes one
human at random per month. There is no
personal bias when selecting their
victim; the only criteria being selecting
those who would raise the least eyebrows
if they suddenly went missing. Diseases
aren't bias in selecting a victim, either.
I hope I live long enough to see things
like cancer or AIDs cured one day,
but these things aren't personified
as "villains" and neither should
the Mechi. Instead, I recognize
it as a natural phenomenon, like
hurricanes and tsunamis that
wipe out innocent villages.
Nobody's waging war on
   the weather, are they?
I frequently consider Officer
Kerry Blake- if the Mechi didn't
get to him when they did, he would
have gone through with his hate crimes
and killed and innocent person. Now, he's
lived a more normal life than he ever would have.
The Mechi are a nasty part of life and a grim reality to consider. But
they are not worth hunting. Capturing or killing one instantly alerts the rest
of them. If I had the power to destroy them I absolutely would.
But until then...

Phantoms

Ghosts, spirits, spectres

Killed: 1 (indeterminate)

First Encountered: 1910

Location: France (most likely worldwide)

Description: -Transparent, spectral image of the top-half of a person; bottom-half tapers down to a faded point somewhere below.

human form:

Raw form as a spectre: also can be invisibly a human as Houston described

Abilities: -Possession
- Intangibility
- Access to the Astral Plane

Raw form: deep black center that fades around the edges; organically shaped; no distinctive edges or body; distinctive eyes.

Weaknesses: -IRON: When contacting the substance, a phantom is compelled to vanish.

almost static looking in raw form

-SALT: Constructing a ring made of salt on the ground will form an invisible boundary which phantoms cannot cross.

- Burning the body's remains

Upon meeting my first phantom in the Leonidas Opera House in 1910, it became apparent that he was bound to the opera house itself. He kept repeating how the opera house was "built on his home's remains," or something to that extent. With neither iron nor salt being lethal, I reasoned that the only viable way to destroy him would be to burn the building asinder. I escaped undetected, though I'd burned most of my suit off of my body. Frustrating to replace.

I should've assumed that the arson was Huxton's doing.

Alfred Louis is an irritable, intolerant guest among my crypt. I've been keeping him anyway, in the hopes that he'd finally warm up to his peers, though thus far he's only been combative or silent. Regardless, the phantom will receive an indelible lesson in the value of community. He is a member of this fellowship, all the same as the rest of them. He _is_ going to learn how to behave as one.

THE LAND WHERE ALFRED IS BOUND

1500   1600   1680   1910   1986   present

a commoner's home

Home removed, businesses built

Leonida's opera house

opera house burns down; various proposed construction deals.

Baron's Burgers (under new ownership)

2013

Goblins

Killed: two or three, can't remember
First Encountered: 1924
Description: —Small, green-skinned feral creatures
      —Anywhere between 6"-2' tall
      —Four humanoid arms, no legs; Moves like a large spider
      —Sadistic/Machiavellian
Abilities: —Strong for their size
      —Thick skin, can withstand anything short of a bullet
Weaknesses: —Bullets (shotgun preferred)

I've only ever encountered them once.

It was an American mansion, kept in pristine condition despite the rural setting and the perceived lack of ownership. I approached slowly, forcing through the steel padlock on the back door, and was swarmed with the vermin from all angles. Their tiny teeth weren't able to penetrate my skin, but they proved frustrating to combat without larger weaponry, like bombs or poisonous gas. Need to revisit these ideas.

Finding this place led me to their winged leader in Paris, France.

Location: Western America

Fascinating, particularly because of the lack of research done on Hoxton's part. Not that murder is the most scholarly way to approach studying a new species...

The monster Hoxton described was completely void of Goblins when I arrived, with all evidence of their existence seemingly removed or destroyed. There are no leads. It stands to reason that these creatures intentionally avoid hunters and trackers wherever they can, hence why Hoxton hasn't been able to get a look on one since.

I visited the monster before recruiting Jacks. The next time I'm able to locate one, he'll be sent after it before I ever arrive. Perhaps Vlad could be convinced into allowing me to coat the exterior of a gun in the same fabric that his suit is made out of...

I doubt such an ask will be accepted

Artists Rendition of Goblins

pig-ish snout

wrinkled furrowed brow

unusually fat fingers

Flat, deflated looking faces

long pointed ears, drooped lobes

underbite

The Gargoyle

Human (formerly)

Killed: Not yet.

First encountered: 1926   Year of Origin: Unknown, allegedly 600

Location: Paris, France

Description: — Visually reminiscent of a gargoyle.

Not simply able to live forever like the undead or the woman, but completely unable to die. The Gargoyle requires no sustenance whatsoever, so a lack of basic needs like food, water, or oxygen has no effect on his body. this is due to the oddly specific spell placed on him, the origin of which he still refuses to divulge

— 6'-7' tall, though often hunched over.

— Deep grey skin, with properties/texture of concrete

— Massive bat-like wings

— Long, powerful tail

— Exaggerated features like a grotesque: Spiked chin, extended brow, protruding temples/cheekbones

— Reflective black orbs instead of eyes

Abilities: — Made of stone, providing incredible strength and durability

— ~~an extension of~~ (Immortal)

Weaknesses: — Forceful impacts damage him — ~~possibly fat~~ curse reversal?

The Gargoyle is more interested in hearing himself talk than taking lives. He's a self-described pacifist. Though at the moment I'm inclined to take him at his word, I will not hesitate to find and exploit more weaknesses if any become apparent. It makes more sense to focus my resources on hunting the many varieties of LETHAL monsters first.

The Gargoyle is the only member of the crypt whom I brought along with conversation rather than capture tactics. It's the reason that he has complete privilege to roam my manor unchecked, and the original writer of this journal does not. By my estimation, the genocidal Brute Man is a far greater threat than any Gargoyle ever was.

MAGIC CHEAT SHEET

Rain - isolation spell - Cohibeomancy

Snow/blizzard - Teleportation - Telemancy

Fire/smoke - Transmutation - vectomancy

Sandstorm - Curse - Defixomancy

Mist - Astral projection - Astromancy

Lightning - time manipulation - Khronomancy

Home Cathedral _____ in Paris

Rather than spying or illustrating from memory, the Gargoyle simply posed for me to draw him in the way he would want to be depicted to the world — Somber and non-threatening.

With his main interest being in the realm of astrophysics, the Gargoyle has expanded on some fleeting fantasies of being jettisoned into space, spending the rest of eternity exploring deep space. When prompted for the reason he's chosen not to, the Gargoyle replied:

"I could only ever pick one direction."

Sigmans

Homo sapien; mutates

Killed: ||||| ||

First Encountered: 1939

Location: Sigma, Atlantic Ocean

all hybrid creatures made
by Dr. John Sigmund, AKA
The One Who Dwells Below

Description: Human bodies, each with unique traits
of a particular animal:

- Gorilla — Mosquito — one who drains
- Queen of Sigma — Fox — one who runs
- AKA Paula — Jellyfish — one who swims
- Turtle — one who hides
- Spider — one who crawls
- Snake — one who dwells above
- ~~Bird~~ Bald eagle

Abilities: — Intelligence eclipses that of a below-
all fluent in   average human; Exhibits basic skills like
Sign language
cannot age   hunting, protecting, forming communities, etc.

Weaknesses: — Anything conventionally lethal to
human-sized mammals, provided their
hybridized traits don't counteract it.

Sigmans are what appear to be the result of
deceased human bodies fused with random animal
carcasses. So far, they are the first and only creatures
which I have completely eradicated, though since some
can fly/swim, the possibility that they're expanded
beyond their island is something to be accounted for.

Paula's shared the details of her origin only in passing, but I've gathered these facts: she and her community of peers were all made by an entity called "The One Who Dwells Below" some long period of time before Haxton ever landed on that island. She's stayed in her relative time from what I can tell, indicating that whatever process she underwent had an un-intended byproduct of immortality. Must return to Sigma for further analysis.

Paula does not know that Haxton killed her family. When and if she learns, it may be detrimental to any relationship they may have in this community I am trying to create.

Paula spends much of her time in the crypt drawing on the walls with a set of crayons I've given her. Her style is that of a toddler's: people and animals fused together as a happy colony.

I feel her creativity is important in understanding her intelligence, and therefore important to share.

<u>Sigmans: Cont.</u>

Some of Sigmund's creatures were simple cut-and-paste fusions of human and beast. The spinal cord of the one Who Hides was fused through bone grafting to a large turtle carapace, with scarring on the inside of its fingers, fusing together the fingers side-by-side to create one webbed unit, appearing like a baseball mitt.

The beak was merely attached to the nose and mouth area with screws, leaving the human nose and mouth (including the teeth) underneath

From Dr. Sigmund's notes

more screws, directly into the lower order bone.

/ nasal cavity left open in the back. must have severely restricted oxygen flow.

large screws boring into the natural human jaw

The One Who Dwells Above sported a large set of wings, protruding from its shoulder blades like a hellish archangel. He also had a large eagle-like beak implanted to the front of its face to formulate a new mouth and nasal structure.

on the opposite spectrum, some of
these beasts had a lot more genetic
alterations. The One Who Swims's skin
was paper thin and almost
transluscent, appearing like a
plastic coating over a thin muscular
structure with no bones underneath. this
gave it an almost tentacle-like arm with
boneless fingers adorning the end. After further
analysis, cnidocytes were found in place
of hair folicles in its pores.

double ended →
cnidocyte

more
stingers

↑ 1 Pore

Inside the cave in which the One who Dwells
Below resides remains piles of
dried decaying remnants
of human and animal
Scraps, presumably,
to be used in
future projects

Hundreds of
anatomical drawings littered
the walls in the style of cave paintings,
laying out the projected structure
of his creations. Several of these
I recognized as the creature's that
Hoxton described, and of those I saw
decaying. Others appeared to be
planned or failed experiments

Envus Ichtlinessa

Leviathan

Killed: 0

First Encountered: 1954   year of origin: middle/lower

Location: Deep Sea   Cretaceous period

Description: — Length is indeterminate; Rivals the length of the average river.

— Armored skin showing a deep green like an alligator's; each plate is the size of a city block

— Gigantic, serpent-shaped body

Abilities: — Can change Earth's tides with sudden, erratic movements; Rarely ever does

Weaknesses: — Envus Ichtlinessa experiences time on a much slower scale than the rest of Earth's life, and therefore has a far slower reaction time than its usual prey of entire schools (gams) of whales.

if Jack and I could get our hands on a scale sample, perhaps we could attempt to properly age a leviathan, if they retain any fish like characteristics. their scales should have date rings, like those used to age ancient trees and forests.

Envus Ichtlinessa is a product of deep-sea gigantism left unchecked by mankind's resources of destruction. Described numerous times by sailors of virtually every culture throughout time. Believed to be myth, but more likely serving as inspiration for it.

There is no fishing net nor aquarium strong enough or large enough for me to take any interest in pursuing this sea demon. Furthermore, the goal of my crypt is to protect these unique creatures from man's wrath and vice versa. Though I cannot speak to the number of lives lost to this creature's mere existence, I can certainly say man-kind poses no threat to this leviathan. They have lived in seperate environments and ecosystems for Earth's entire history, with merely a seamans tale or two to come from any rare encounter. These beasts have been marked on all voyagers maps from all over the world, and have been called serpents, snakes, dragons, and everything in between. It's unclear if there are multiple leviathan, since its nearly impossible to see it mouth to tail at once.

With the world's oceans rapidly changing from human rubbish, glaciers melting, habitat destruction, ocean acidification, off-shore building, and every other unnatural human caused instance, the discovery of a leviathan may be closer than we think. But then what happens? The only weapon capable of killing such a thing would wreak havoc on society too.

common map depictions from viking times

dragon-like face with no limbs

often depicted with a serpent body

Artificial Men

Homo simulacrum (AkA: Adam + Franklin Chamberton)

Killed: none

First Encountered: 1974

Location: Transylvania, Romania

Description: — Grey, wretched skin
— Almost 7' at the head
— Bulky, stocky body type
— No biological flaws whatsoever: Perfect teeth, eyesight, no cuts or scrapes

Abilities: — Near-Perfect Recall: Remembers almost everything about his lifetime.
— Can heal from virtually all wounds in a matter of seconds/minutes
— Strength of an average bodybuilder
— Ages slower than most; an eventual death of old age is indeterminate, but hypothesized.

Weaknesses: — Able to be wounded the same as anyone, but rapid healing prevents any fatality
— Lack of basic needs, like food or oxygen, is fatal

I encountered Adam Chamberton whilst tracking the Underlord in the summer of 1974. After learning that he wasn't violent and was incapable of breeding, I left after a lengthy conversation in his living room.

Adam Chamberton is relatively docile. Once capturing him, I was more interested to learn of his background:

His mother experimented on him at a very young age, apparently as a way to "fix" his physical defects. He's taken a wife, converted her into the same type of creature as himself and had a child with her as well.

Given his innate resentment of himself, I have no idea why he'd want to afflict another person with his condition, let alone procreate... In any case, he's here now with the rest, though I've considered letting him go free as Adam represents a strange crossroad between Man and monster – He doesn't equate to something like a vampire, yet does pose a threat to humanity, and there are definitely those who wish him dead. Simply put; He's not aberrant enough to belong here but not human enough to be integrated into society.

Haematopic stem and Progenitor gene therapy to combat physical and mental genetic disorders

H_2N

NH

O dipratin A inhibitor for renewal of cell structures

OH

Adam not only instinc lied to Horton about his infertility, but done so convincingly enough to stave off the Brute Men without attempting violence.

I'm envious of his skills in communication.

dad and franklin;
fall 1983

The Ape-Men

Gigantopithecus erectus

Killed: 1

First Encountered: 1967

Description: — Humanoid simian approx. 8-10 ft tall at a local library, lifted *can also be white, maybe changes fur in artic climates like fox/rabbit?* Black or brown fur, coating everything except unidentified beings the hands, feet, and face.

Abilities: — Able to move quickly in thickly-wooded *can use and craft wooden tools like stakes - maybe they should aid Haxton in his vampire hunt...* areas, moving up and through the branches of large, secluded trees in order to evade capture/detection *Good at tracking* — Strength comparable to a bear

Weaknesses: — Most forms of tranquilizers/darts

Hunting Ape-Men is difficult and time-consuming. I've done it only once, and it almost came at the cost of one of my arms. These creatures are ferocious if threatened, but are herbivores, and self-isolate in uninhabited woods. The amount of time and effort necessary to hunt one isn't worth it for the time being. Much like the Gargoyle, their death will come when larger threats to mankind are first eradicated.

Known Location: *Haxton's claim that these two creatures of folklore* Humboldt county? California, NA — "Sasquatch" *are the same species from different locations with different adaptations is absolutely correct. Autopsies have revealed* Tibet, Asia — "Yeti" that the DNA from both specimen appear nearly identical from the Genuses Gigantopithecus and Homo. It seems like some in-between human-ape hybrid species

Tracking and killing one from each continent took about six months with Jack's help, including prep-time and execution. Hayden never had a companion on his journey, let alone an invisible one, so it's understanding how frustrating it is to try and hunt one of these beasts down. Jacob and I have located another in Humboldt county California, and we plan on assimilating it into our community. Information unattainable by death will be aquired from studying in captivity.

While the creature is estimated to have been quadrupedal, the most common sightings of them signify bipedal maements. Assumptively, the case regarding these cryptids identities is a result of convergent evolution. However, these two specimen studied have vastly similar DNA nucleotide profiles, indicating that they at the least shared a common ancestor.

Descriptions of Ape-like creatures in different countries could possibly share the same origin (Australia - Yowie)

Hoxton

Homo sapien

Description: — Deep blue scales on every inch
of the skin
- 8' tall, approx.
- Acromegaly has made nose/hands/ears
grow larger than they should

Abilities: — Hardened skin
- Great strength
- Suspended in time (unable to age)
- Several lifetimes of experience in
hand-to-hand combat

Weaknesses: — Though the skin is tough enough to
withstand bullets, it's not impenetrable,
and would be susceptible to enough force.
- Certain parts of the body, like through
the mouth or eyes, are not scaled or
protected, and should be considered
potential vulnerabilities.

When first revising the journal, I was taken aback at the fact that Hoxton
had actually added himself. Moreso curiously, the description's minimalist
and "notes" are completely void. Hoxton is driven by a strong sense of
morality, twisted to fit his mind's own definition: He's spent the
predominant amount of his lifetime hunting down monsters with such
non-negotiable passion in the name of the Christian God. While I'm not
here to comment on God's existence (Holy water as a viable defense for
vampirs is the strangest evidence) I find it particularly fascinating that some
of the acolytes of an all-powered, all-loving deity are willing to commit Genocide.

On the rare nights that I can get him talking, Hoxton and I have had conversations lasting into the hours about this. I'll tell him that their right to live is a birthright, simply by being born on the same Earth as the rest of us, and that humans should have no more or less of the very same birthright, hence why I've spent my life advocating for such a strong separation of the two. Hoxton rebuts by comparing creatures like vampires or werewolves to a common mosquito, and to an extent he's absolutely right; one wouldn't hesitate to swat one out of the air and crush it to oblivion before it bites your skin and leaves a nasty mark.

But, the earliest humans can be traced back to Africa somewhere in the hundreds of thousands of years ago. The earliest mosquitos can be traced to the Late Cambrian era, somewhere in the hundreds of millions of years ago. They may be parasitic and carry a plethora of disease, but they're far more entitled to this planet than humans ever were.

The Scorpion Man

undead curse

Killed:

First Encountered: 2002   year of origin: ~1,000-2000 BC

Known Location: Cairo, Egypt

Description: - Humanoid body
- Head of a scorpion, with several sets of eyes
- Giant black scorpion claws instead of hands
- Large scorpion tail from the lower waist

Abilities: - Immortality
- Supernatural Strength   Broken claw?

Weaknesses: - ?   pedipalp fused to claw,
much like an unset
Broken bone
healing

The first and only encounter I've had lasted about two minutes. Neither of us won. However, when I backed away from the dune of sand where it was residing, it stopped acting with violence... Whatever motivates it is beneath that dune. Must return with stronger weaponry.

stronger weaponry is no obstacle. Jack and I are en route to find it and whatever it's guarding.

perhaps another
Sigmon creature?
Local scorpions in the area have structurally
different claws than the Scorpion Man, but
the tail stinger/scorpion mans claw look
similar. Fusion gone wrong?

Mummies

Killed: 1

First Encountered: 2024

Known Location: Egypt/Mexico

Description: - Ceremonial bandages in place of skin; flowing sand underneath
- Swarming with scarab beetles
- Glowing green eyes

Abilities: - High-Level Hypnosis
- Form can be that of sand, providing strength and durability
- Access to the Astral Plane
- Vampiric speed — possibly faster
- Immortality
- Command over acolytes (Scorpion Man)
- Necromancy — Can summon an army of undead followers

Weaknesses: - Gwen Siodmak.

Gwen Siodmak

Killed:

First Encountered: 2024

Location: ?

Description: – 6' or 7' tall
- Large, stocky body type of a full-grown werewolf
- Grey fur covering grey skin
- Hybridized face; The long, protruding snout of a wolf with a set of red vampiric eyes
- Retractable fangs amidst a long row of perfectly-symmetrical teeth
- Long, translucent talons
- Ferocious appearance, but an otherwise sophisticated demeanor

Description (Human): – 5'3" approx.
- Long, dark hair
- Hazel eyes

Abilities: – High-Level Hypnosis
- Near-instantaneous healing factor
- Immeasurable strength, thus far unmatched by any of the entries in this journal
- Vampiric speed
- Hyperawareness: Vampiric/Lycanthropic senses, brought to their peak by Rebecca's serum
- Expert tracker/hunter, for reasons aforementioned

Weaknesses: N/A — Each species' weakness appears to be counteracted by the other two's healing factors: A stake through the heart/silver bullet would have no effect since Rebecca's serum would heal the wound, and Waylon's antiserum would have no effect due to her vampiric/lycanthropic regenerative abilities.

GWEN SIODMAK, BY ALL ACCOUNTS, IS THE SINGLE MOST DANGEROUS CREATURE ON GOD'S GREEN EARTH. If an opportunity for assassination presents itself, it will take priority over all else and must be enacted immediately.

SOLACE

AN EPILOGUE IN EIGHT PARTS

The Phantom awoke from a short-lived slumber.

The room was empty, lit only by a cheap overhead bulb. It was either somebody's unkempt spare room or a one-star motel, the Phantom wasn't sure. He looked down at the ground and saw the urn with the lid removed, but with all of the ash still confined inside.

Hoxton made himself visible from the shadows, with a small bag hanging by his side.

"Why?" the Phantom asked.

Ignoring him, Hoxton reached into the bag and pulled out one of the Gargoyle's jars. He wasn't sure which creature's blood was filled to the brim. It didn't matter terribly much. Also from the bag, Hoxton unfolded a small piece of crumpled notebook paper from one of the Gargoyle's many books. He squinted his eyes, interpreting the symbols.

Around the urn, Hoxton started drawing symbols in a very specific manner. He copied the style and formations of each written symbol on the note, maintaining their sizes and shapes as best as he could, encircling the Phantom as he went around the room.

The Phantom recognized these symbols and their precise order.

Hoxton finished drawing them and wiped his finger clean of the blood, then crumpled the page back into the bag. The Phantom could tell that they were drawn by somebody who'd never practiced magic before.

Hoxton glared at the Phantom.

"Marie Moffat Hatton," Hoxton said with conviction.

The Phantom looked down again at the symbols, then back up to his adversary.

"If you cast that spell," the Phantom said, "you will never see me again. Never be able to hunt me down for the rest of your days."

Hoxton remained silent, and the Phantom didn't press his luck any further.

"You get one minute," the Phantom clarified.

Hoxton nodded.

The Phantom's head tilted back, those spectral eyes of his turning completely white. From nowhere, as Hoxton expected, a faint breeze started to circle the room. Mist emanated from the Phantom's incorporeal form, and swirled around him progressively faster and faster. Hoxton flinched from the changing air pressure, then looked back and saw that the Phantom was no longer there.

It was Marie.

She was spectral and intangible, but prominent enough for her brother to recognize her. She stood in the room's center, not a day older than when Hoxton last saw her.

The Brute Man almost dropped to his knees, overwhelmed by the sight of her.

"*Hoxton...*" her voice rang, as if whispered and echoed by a dozen people surrounding him. It somehow came from all directions, yet was so quiet as to be barely audible if one weren't paying strict attention to it.

"I'm so sorry," Hoxton said.

"Don't," said Marie. "It's you who deserves the apology."

"How?" Hoxton pleaded. "I left you when you needed me most-"

"You left me because I drove you away," said Marie. "I should have told you differently. Told you *sooner,* at that. Oh, Hoxie, witches are not the Devil's work-"

"I know," said Hoxton. "I've made my peace with mages."

"If I hadn't gone to her..."

Hoxton just nodded. Without her saying it, he accepted her apology.

"I only hope you haven't spent your lifetime in rage and pity," said Marie with sincerity.

Hoxton bowed his head in embarrassment.

"It works its way in," said Hoxton.

Marie smiled. *That* was the boy she remembered.

Hoxton noticed Marie's body starting to fade away. He wanted to ask her another question, but she cut him off with one of her own:

"Has the pain gone away?" Marie asked.

Overcome with emotion, Hoxton replied as fast as he could: "Yes it has."

The very last thing Hoxton saw was Marie's face brightening up, smiling in relief at hearing his response.

"That's all that matters..." Marie said as she slowly faded away, out of existence once again. The same place Hoxton was destined one day to be.

Hoxton's head was in his hands. He was still processing everything that'd just transpired in this room, as he would continue to for a very long time to come.

When he removed his hands from his head, the Phantom reappeared in his view.

"Commence," said the Phantom.

"I didn't get to tell her-"

"*Commence-*"

"I want more time!" Hoxton yelled, his voice bouncing off of the surrounding walls.

The Phantom was unamused. He thought back to his six years spent with Nivalthnesser in his dying few seconds. Nobody'd given him any more time. He'd only been awake for several minutes before one of Hoxton's allies tore out his heart.

"You won't live to see eternity, Brute," said the Phantom. "It may take centuries. You might hit your first millennium before it happens. But eventually, the reaper's blade will pierce your mortal scales. You have that privilege. I do not."

Hoxton gathered himself. He resented the fact that somebody so despicable could be so accurate.

"Whatever it is, tell her *then*," said the Phantom. "She'll be happy to hear it."

Hoxton took a long, deep breath.

From the bag, Hoxton grabbed the page and flipped it over. The reverse side of it had the spell's Latin text, which Hoxton had practiced correctly pronouncing.

The thunderous winds in the room returned as Hoxton spoke the spell into existence. The bloodied symbols lit themselves ablaze on the hardwood floor, but the raging winds prevented the fire from spreading or burning the entire building to the ground.

A swirling cyclone of mist emanated from the Phantom's intangible body. Hoxton felt the winds quickly die down, sensing the room return to its status quo before the spell had started. Looking past the dissipating mist, Hoxton saw the symbols on the ground put out, and the Phantom still floating in the room's center.

The Phantom looked down at his spectral hand. He wiggled his fingers. Clenched them into a fist. Opened them up again. It was as if this form, though identical, had been completely *altered* from head to toe. It was hard to describe how.

But the Phantom knew how. That spell Hoxton had just read was designed to break the Phantom's enchantment. And that, it had just done.

"If we meet again," said Hoxton, "I will find a way to vanquish you."

The Phantom moved to the room's opposite wall, about to phase through it.

"We never will," whispered the Phantom before finally disappearing.

The crypt below the manor stank of the unwashed bloodshed of recent cataclysmic events. Practically every being trapped in those cells tore it and spilled it from one another once freed from captivity. The gateways to the cells all remained open, except one: The final cell, where the Scorpion Man and his sarcophagus were trapped. It was the one between Gwen and the crypt's only entrance.

Inside, the room had been cleared out completely. No furniture, no desk. Not so much as a carpet over the cold ashlar floors. It was some twisted cross between an asylum's padded room and a prison's detention cell, in both aesthetics and practicality. It housed a man who'd begun losing his hair since he started tearing it out of his own head. The man had no pen or paper to write anything, but still transcribed a message on the opposite wall of the cell's gateway. He'd used his own nails to etch it in, wounding his fingertips and occasionally drawing blood.

"Waylon?" asked a recognizable voice.

The man in the cell stopped his grotesque writings. He quivered into a fetal position and tried to stop himself from shivering, to no avail whatsoever. He'd already signed over his estate to Robert Maks, a man whom he'd met on one of his many expeditions. If anybody grew suspicious, of course.

"What are you writing, Waylon?" the voice asked again.

Waylon's body was blocking the message from the Underlord's view. Still shaking, he did not move from his spot.

Though he was too afraid to look in the Underlord's direction, he could sense the inescapable feeling of disappointment. It bore down on him like a thunderstorm in this moment.

"Let me see it," asked the Underlord.

Waylon hesitated.

The very act of resisting his Master was revolting to him. He had to move, right then and there, lest he throw up all over the only floor he had. Waylon moved aside and turned to see the Underlord, immediately being immersed in his otherworldly vision.

The Underlord smiled.

Waylon had made him happy. He smiled too, becoming giddy at the prospect of it.

I AM THE GREATEST GAME

Half-dripping in blood, spelled with perfect grammar. For all of the brain cells Waylon lost decomposing before being revived, he still had some very rudimentary understandings of basic penmanship. Things like his charm, charisma, wit, or much else of what comprised his personality were all forcibly removed. Subsided, in a way. They were worthless in the presence of Master's cardinal will.

"I am the greatest game," Waylon repeated out loud. "I am the greatest game."

It was spoken like a prayer, as if the phrase gave him power and energy. The more he said it, the better he began to feel from the inside out. A grand catharsis was taking hold on his psyche.

The Underlord held out his hand through the cell bars.

Waylon marveled at Master's reach. How he longed to touch it... To again feel the skin of the one who treated him so well. Feast on his open, bleeding wrist. But that was not what Master wanted. His black blood provided a source of vampiric strength to his underlings as they drank. Waylon hadn't earned any of that, and he was told never to expect it.

Tiny, closeby critters began scurrying in through the bars of the cell's gateway. They swarmed around the Underlord's menacing body as he commanded them and converged towards Waylon at the far end of the cell, their little appendages grazing the cold ground with unexpected speed. Waylon became delighted, seeing there must be at least two *dozen* of them for tonight. A full day's meal not to be wasted. Ravenously, Waylon began picking them up with both hands and eating them, biting their little heads and legs off first before finally devouring their bodies.

The Underlord lowered his hand and released the insects from his will. Waylon tried to eat them all before they began scurrying away on their own.

"*I am the greatest game,*" Waylon exclaimed through the many chewed-up bugs in his mouth. "*I am the greatest game... I am the greatest game.*"

Abraham's Progeny had undergone a great deal of maintenance since the Underlord overtook Waylon's estate. It sailed across the ocean with a crew of only three: Tryg, now permanently human, looked out over the railing, and the Gargoyle oversaw him at the ship's helm.

The third was asleep in the cabin.

Arriving at the island was an easy feat for the centuries-old creature who mentally cataloged almost everywhere he went. This island was not very far from Norway, sharing its frigid temperatures and constant rainfalls. Tryg stepped off of the ship and watched as the Gargoyle flew overhead, landing in a very specific spot.

"What are we here for?" Tryg asked, having received only vague, cryptic answers from the Gargoyle during their entire journey.

The Gargoyle enjoyed speaking in Old Norse for a change.

"The reason why I've kept you alive," said the Gargoyle.

The Gargoyle grabbed what looked to be a Herculean boulder and lifted it over his shoulders like Atlas. He tossed it aside, shaking the ground beneath Tryg's feet. Tryg stabilized himself and walked over to his ally, who was removing another stone almost as large.

And beneath it, the runestone rested.

"This is how I knew," said the Gargoyle. "This stone in this place. I was searching for..."

But Tryg had stopped listening. He was busy reading the runestone's inscription: A Viking Saga lost entirely to time, preserved accidentally beneath an old wickie's lighthouse for many years. The runes told Tryg of a tale of adventure and loss regarding a mighty Viking captain at the hands of an evil God-King, spinning stories of a man transforming into a Scorpion.

Tryg recognized the writing and style. It was his son, Hjalmar, who had inscribed the stone.

The Gargoyle watched Tryg fall to his knees, worshiping the runestone like an idol. He placed his hands on the lettering and felt the grooves his son had made when creating the warning. Tryg had taken his son's fighting hand but left him his writing one. Hjalmar could not live a life of a raider and hunter like his Viking ancestors once did. Evidently, he instead lived as a prophet and scribe.

"My son..." Tryg started to say.

But the Gargoyle already knew.

"Without him, I'd never have known," said the Gargoyle. "The group of us may never have stood against him. The world would be forever changed."

The Gargoyle placed his slender, clawed hand on Tryg's shoulder.

"You have only *him* to thank," said the Gargoyle.

Tryg would've responded, but his airway was filling and his eyes were swelling up. He'd been tricked into sacrificing himself at his own son's hand. That guilt followed him for the entire intervening millennium inside of that tomb. Despite this, and every other way Tryg had felt for failing his son, Hjalmar had persevered in spite of everything. The burden of what he'd done had been stuck to Tryg for so long, he'd forgotten how powerful relief truly felt. It was all-consuming, and melted away all of the negativity from his mind.

At last, Tryg turned back to the Gargoyle, who had spent this moment drawing symbols on the runestone's surrounding rocks. The ring of them encircled Tryg.

Tryg nodded, content for the very first time in over a thousand years.

The Gargoyle conjured the inverse of the same spell used on Tryg not terribly long ago. The inverse of the one Hoxton had received in 1693.

The symbols around Tryg caught fire from the Khronomancy, wavering slightly in the growing winds encircling Tryg.

Lightning struck.

When the wind calmed and the flames died out, Tryg laid by the runestone and allowed his wounds to overtake him.

The Gargoyle watched over Tryg's body, taking a moment of silence and solitude.

Before heading back to the ship, the Gargoyle paid a visit to the hand-made tombstone residing over his dear friend's grave. It seemed that the wickie, along with his faithful dog Neptune, had been resting peacefully for the past three hundred years, though centuries of weathering had brought noticeable wear on the stone's facade.

The Gargoyle smiled, trying to recall whose turn it was last to ask a question to the other.

Before he could, a noise in the cabin drew his attention. It sounded of something crashing.

The cabin had an open window barely large enough for the Gargoyle to pass through, and that's precisely what he aimed for when he leapt up into the air and flew straight over. When he landed inside, the Gargoyle saw the bed turned on its side, its inhabitant trying unsuccessfully to escape the bindings around his wrists keeping him against the bed's frame.

Upon seeing the Gargoyle, he calmed down.

"Just being cautious," said the Gargoyle affably. "No need to rebel: You're still on the payroll. Just under new ownership."

The man said nothing. Despite the searing pain from the bandaged-up stab wound on his chest, he remained completely silent as blood slowly dripped down onto the floorboards. Instead, the Gargoyle followed the man's eyes, and noticed them glaring at the nub where one of his horns used to be.

"Yeah, I'm not really over it," the Gargoyle muttered, rubbing the spot on his forehead. "Don't think I ever will be. But the Underlord's a powerful friend to have... I was possessed, if you could believe it."

"Where's my suit?"

"You've missed a lot, Jack," said the Gargoyle. "It's time to catch you up to speed."

When *Abraham's Progeny* had finally returned from its days-long voyage, Paula's child had gone out for a fly with the Gargoyle, as only the two of them knew the unbelievable bliss that flight could provide. Left to entertain herself, the inquisitive Ape-Woman roamed the mansion with all the world's wonder and reverence for every open doorway. It was the set of deadbolts on one of them that gave her pause. Expectedly, they did nothing but motivate her to break them off with little struggle.

In Waylon's old trophy room, where all of the poacher's favorites were either mounted, taxidermied, or diced up and layed out in display cases, Paula went wide-eyed and treaded with a hint of fear in her step, as though something were about to jump out at her and bite off her head. This, she would come to realize, would've been preferable to what she *actually* found in that room.

Paula saw the bodies and bones of many, but none haunted her like the skeletal structure of an old friend: The exoskeleton of a man-sized spider, with a human skull staring back at her.

In that same display resided the giant shell of the One Who Hides, and beside that, the gelatinous tentacle of the One Who Swims. These were only some of what Waylon had found and preserved from that island after exhuming the graves of Paula's family. The graves that she'd helped Dr. Sigmund plot out and bury.

Her animalistic side was about to unleash right in that room and bash every piece of glass into smithereens as she screamed and cried for an audience of nobody. A hundred years of pain could not be repaid in any fair way, no matter what damage she created. She knew that whatever was left of Waylon lived in the crypt, his soul gradually wearing away until a mindless corpse was all that remained of the Underlord's toy. Her vengeance could not be sought against him.

Before tears could fully swell her eyes and blind her vision, Paula saw a loose page resting on the display.

It was a copy of a page from a strange, hand-written journal.

Paula picked it up and studied it: There were two sets of handwriting, both alluding to a species of "Sigmans" living on an island in the Atlantic. The notes told the story of Waylon's grand capture of her and her child, and all of the detailed, scientific notes he'd taken of Paula during her time in the cell. It was a small, anecdotal sentence of Waylon's notes that triggered a trauma she'd forgotten she still had, buried away somewhere deep inside of her unstable mind:

Paula does not know that Hoxton killed her family. When and if she learns, it may be detrimental to any relationship they might have in this community I am trying to create.

The air was thick with the smell of decay as the last rays of sunlight disappeared behind the trees. This ordinary night was one of a full moon, and that moon shined brightly down onto the extraordinary manor formerly belonging to Waylon Ross. Currently, Robert Maks.

Not far outside of this manor, there was a young girl hidden away in the thickets of the land's natural fauna, stalking the place like a panther before it pounces on its prey. Hope had arrived at the property's edge, and was about to exit her camouflaged position when she stopped herself. Her left hand was always hesitating over her vest pocket, ready to provide the weapon beneath at a moment's notice. Was it this simple? Surely not, she reckoned. This was something she'd been preparing a long time for, but aside from a few sharpened wooden stakes and a couple of krav maga classes, Hope had no idea how to approach the situation.

She only knew where the Underlord actually was.

And there she stood, barely a hundred feet from the front door. A hundred feet from her goal. The only sounds were the whispers of the wind and the pounding of her heart as she made her way closer to the manor's massive, unwelcoming entrance. She probably couldn't sneak inside of a place like that. Her approach would have to be straightforward. Perhaps she could reason with whomever answered this door...

She didn't know what was right. She didn't know which choices would grant her entry, and which would get her killed. But she did know this: The only thing that she *couldn't* be was indecisive. Especially when death was only a heartbeat away.

So she stepped forward onto the open grass.

It was the calm chill of a bitter night that passed her by. To the untrained, it was nothing more than that. But Hope knew exactly what it was. And exactly what caused it. Her hand no longer needed to hesitate.

Hope spun around, in the same motion pulling the stake from her vest, and forced it into the chest of whatever was behind her, not expecting Ilona's firm hand to catch her wrist in the air.

The two froze. Deadlocked. Hope looked into the eyes of her target and saw the vampire's wicked gaze. She *hated* the feeling of it on her. Likewise, Ilona scanned the intruder up and down, then released Hope's arm from her grasp.

Hope scoffed.

"Don't try and stop me," said Hope in a demeaning way.

Ilona cocked her head curiously.

"Why do you wish to kill him?" Ilona asked.

Hope scoffed again. The answer seemed so blatantly obvious.

Again, Hope tried to strike the Underlord's youngest, but Ilona grabbed the stake from Hope's hand before it ever swung again, and tossed it to her side. Hope watched as the stake drove itself into the nearby grass, kicking up leaves and soil.

"Why?" Ilona asked again, this time more pertinently.

Hope's eyes went wide. She turned white, having no good response whether verbal or physical. With no other option, Hope conceded in playing Ilona's game.

"I... He ruined my life."

"Master?" Ilona asked.

Hope gritted at the term. With that word came so much history she'd been trying to ignore. A biting little synapse deep in her brain that wouldn't keep quiet when it was triggered. Frustrated, Hope stepped away, seeing only a nearby tree stump to sit on.

Ilona recognized Hope's pain, but didn't know how to console her.

"I was young," said Hope. "Vulnerable. I felt the crushing weight of disappointment when I lost that day. It was my last year to compete. We'd spent thousands... Five, six, seven years of my life went by for nothing. Not a thing in the world..."

Slowly, Ilona came in front of Hope's stump and looked down on her.

"You loved that night we spent together," said Ilona.

"Because he *made* me," said Hope. "Took advantage. Manipulated an innocent girl."

"He made us happy again," Ilona continued, almost robotically. "He made *you* happy for fifty years."

"Would you call that happiness?" Hope insisted. "I remember the taste of his blood on my tongue. There was *nothing* like it. Not one thing. It was bliss, distilled down to a fluid that replaced all food and drink in this world."

"Isn't that what happiness is?" Ilona countered. "You've got, what, eighty years here? Ninety at most? Then you decompose, and become no different than the ground we're walking on. To let him bite your neck... It's akin to freedom. No more feelings of worthlessness. There's only a bright, beautiful power to hold on to. A power you never have to let go of."

"He cuts his wrist and feeds you *lies*. You're so worthless to him that he'll replace you like chattel when you die. All the while, you're actually *dependent* on him and nothing else. It's how the obsession starts. It lingers at first. Somewhere deep in the back of your mind. A desire so subtle, it makes you fixate on his every little detail. The way he moves. The way he smiles. The way he touches you..."

A rage swelled up in Ilona's eyes. She didn't realize her hands began forming into fists. A decision subconsciously driven by her passion. Hope recognized how defensive Ilona had just become, and dropped the subject.

"I was straight, you know," said Hope. "I'd never found a girl attractive. It's another part of his... whatever you want to call it. He makes you *want* things you hate, *hate* things you used to love."

"He's more than that," said Ilona, more relaxed now. "Every woman he courts is *stuck* where they are, whatever that situation may be. I remember the feeling of powerlessness before he found me... Master offered me the same thing he offered you. The same thing he offered Lillian and Gwen. A better path. I live whatever life I choose."

"*His* life," said Hope. "Think back to when he made that offer. Did you choose that path? Or did looking at him just... *bring* that desire out of you?"

"I wanted it," Ilona replied.

"Did you want it *before* he asked?" Hope pressed. "Before you looked into his eyes?"

Ilona sat with this thought for a moment.

"I don't know," Ilona finally said. "I remember a fascination with him... Of all the men I'd encountered, he was the most appealing one to talk to. It felt like he always knew what to say. Always had the right answers."

"Of course he did," Hope scoffed. "'Answers' become 'commands.' Before long, he's making you target people he sees as a threat."

Upon speaking those words, Hope was struck with a hideous realization, and looked up at Ilona with a tinge of fear. Ilona solemnly looked back. She could only watch as Hope stood up off of that stump and pieced it all together: Ilona was here specifically to kill her.

That also meant, for whatever odd reason, that Ilona *hadn't* followed her master's orders yet, and opted instead for this line of questioning.

The conversation had died down. And the two women were left only with their thoughts.

"If we are destined to kill each other over this man," Hope asked, "must we do it now?"

Ilona took a moment. She turned from Hope and, herself, sat on the nearby stump, looking on at the manor. Without hearing any response, Hope took it to mean an approval.

And they waited.

Hope fidgeted with the stake in her hand. She'd spent a half hour sharpening it to a razor-thin point, only to carefully twirl it between her fingers as the two of them put off their inevitable conflict. Insects made their usual noise in the nearby woods and shrubberies, and the calm chill of night passed both of them by in this damp, quiet grassland.

"This is my favorite," said Ilona, staring stoically at the manor.

"The mansion?"

"No," said Ilona. "Master told me about this once, something Gwen had said to him. It's when the light is so dim, only the little details of something can be seen."

Hope looked again at the mansion, seeing what Ilona saw: The moon's light came down gently, coating the area like a warm blanket on a cold autumn night. The outlines, the highlights of the building could be seen, but not the finer details of the walls or surfaces. The leaves of the trees around it were visible, but not the branches underneath, and the trunks were half-shaded by their own massive sizes.

It was a black-and-white canvas painting of a worldview, looked down upon by a blazing moon and a trillion stars. *Almost* darkness. But not quite.

A knock on the mansion's door drew Lillian out from her daytime slumber. It was a steady three knocks, evenly-spaced as though a robot had made them. Lillian moved from her faraway room to the mansion's chateau in less than a passing second. To not arouse suspicion, she waited a few moments before answering the door.

It was a plain-looking man in everyday, unremarkable clothes. He almost blended in with the environment behind him.

"Hello," said Lillian.

"Is this the house of Waylon Ross?"

"It was."

"What happened to him?"

"He's sold his estate," said Lillian. "All of his assets were purchased by my husband, Robert Maks. Our family lives here now."

The man paused, but showed no signs of confusion.

"I see," said the man slowly.

Lillian stared straight into his eyes, probing for an answer. Probing for anything at all.

"How did you know him?" Lillian asked.

"I'm an old friend," said the man. "I was hoping to catch up."

Lillian looked him up and down. Even the most cold-hearted of people usually have something to offer a beautiful woman with the powerful eyes of a vampire, but she was getting absolutely *nothing* out of the man. The blank slate excited her. A real challenge presented itself. And it'd walked right up to her home's doorstep. *What mysteries this man must keep...*

For a split second, Lillian let out a smirk. She quickly recanted it.

"Would you like to come inside? My husband will be home shortly. He could tell you more about where your friend went."

The man weighed his options. He wasn't stupid - That devilish smile wasn't anything imagined. She knew a lot more than she was letting on. And he was no stranger to reading into people.

"I'd love to," said the man.

Lillian smiled again. This one did not disappear so quickly.

Lillian let the man inside of Robert Maks' mansion. The man kept a steady pace as he walked inside, not an ounce of fear on him. He took in the interior of the manor in a diligent sort of way, making sure everything was in its proper place. The man pondered what secrets this place was holding, no doubt related to where and why Waylon Ross had fled. Or so the mistress alleged.

"My name is Lillian," she said as she shut the door behind him.

The man turned and looked down at her extended hand. He grabbed it, and shook firmly.

"Kerry," said Officer Blake.

In the light rain of what felt like an endless night, the vampire fled across the quiet town's street, too fast for oncoming cars to notice. Entire city blocks passed him by in mere seconds. The vampire was desperate, and becoming exhausted.

Through an old church's unlocked window, the vampire leapt inside and shut it behind him.

In ancient times, priests often warded their homes and churches with Isolation Spells against vampires and similar unholy creatures, giving rise to the myth that they couldn't enter hallowed ground. In modern times, too few humans believed in magic at all. Fewer still could actually practice it.

As the vampire shut the church's window, he looked back and saw nothing. It allowed him to catch his breath. The vampire fled further, dashing across the hallway and making his way up the building's stairwell. He didn't need to use most of the steps at all, skipping five, six, seven at a time at his supernatural speeds.

At the roof, the vampire came to the edge and looked down.

Nothing.

The vampire closed his eyes and listened to the nearby blood flowing. Almost everyone in the adjacent buildings were either asleep or going about their life. Almost everyone in their vehicles seemed calm, yet impatient. This was the world of men through the lens of a vampire's senses, and it provided him with nothing about his pursuer.

A noise came about from somewhere closeby.

The vampire froze. There was nothing around him that could've caused that noise. This church's roof was as plain as he imagined, with sturdy shingles and buttresses adorning simple architecture. Crucifixes adorned every pinnacle. No men, monsters or mages were present whatsoever. Turning back around, the vampire looked back down at the city's street, watching it get covered in rain.

The noise repeated.

The vampire looked again behind him, picking out what he could in the dark. His nocturnal eyes weren't as useful in the rain. But still they worked, and found nothing. Nobody atop any of the roof's crowns or points. Nobody approaching.

Far, far away, perched on the building opposite the church, was a figure even larger than the Brute Man.

The vampire was transfixed on the figure. It was unclear whether or not it was a part of the building's design, or another creature looking back at him. The figure's frame was tall and wide, but too distant to pick out any defining details or traits... but it *had* to be real, and it *had* to be alive, because as soon as the vampire dwelled on the sight, the figure was no longer there at all.

The vampire panicked, turning to run in a new direction.

That new direction had the figure in it as well, perched on the farthest pinnacle of the church the vampire was taking refuge on.

The vampire spun around and dashed away, coming face-to-face with the figure once again. Whatever it was, it was so unbelievably *faster* than the vampire's top speed. It was as if it were teleporting, except for the fact that the vampire could feel the powerful gust of wind pass it by whenever the figure moved.

The vampire stopped right in front of the figure and took in its details for only a fraction of a second: A large gray mass of claws, fangs and fur. A set of pointed ears that heard every sound the night made. A pair of blazing red eyes that could see beyond infinity.

Before the vampire could turn away again, the figure snatched him by the throat, digging its thumb into the vampire's collarbone. The harder the vampire tried to wriggle free, the deeper those claws drove into his shoulder blades with just one set of its fingertips.

The vampire rose higher, the arm of the figure bringing him closer to its own animalistic face. Here, the vampire saw the beast in its entirety: The gray skin of the humanoid face with fur running down the sides of it, and the powerful, hypnotic stare of the most intense eyes the vampire had ever looked into. The gaze of the figure immobilized its prey. No longer did the vampire struggle in the figure's grasp.

The figure's mouth opened, revealing long, perfectly-symmetrical teeth. The jaws belonged to a werewolf, but the fangs, to a vampire in its prime. The vampire in her grasp could only watch as his fate was foretold, rather spectacularly atop that unsuspecting church.

The undead fed exclusively on the blood and flesh of the living. Gwen Siodmak fed exclusively on the blood and flesh of the undead.

The Mummy awoke.

His hands laid over his own chest, crossed in the usual way. Stagnant dust from the bandages around his eyelids separated and floated through the air by some unseen energy, and the preserved, ethereal air of his tomb kept God-King Nivalthnesser breathing once again. The Devil's League was a brief interim in the scope of his timeless plan, and in terms of the Mummy's perception of time, the entire ordeal was comparable to somebody blinking their eyes once amidst their day-to-day life.

It had been one thousand years since that fateful eclipse over Waylon Ross' manor, and the Mummy would finally have his vengeance.

This had been long-delayed: Once by Vikings in the Middle-East and again by a dozen abominations of magic and science. Both times were wholly irrelevant. Whatever society of petty men, false gods, or universal monsters were waiting for him, the God-King would meet their challenge. And he would not wait another millennium to do it.

The Mummy's eyes opened for the first time in ten centuries and saw nothing at all. A strange sense of weightlessness befell Nivalthnesser as the top of the sarcophagus cracked open, and it accompanied the pure, total darkness. It was like a dream, so immersive as to be indistinguishable from reality itself. But he had been dreaming for a thousand years. It was long past time to awaken.

The air in the ancient stone coffin freed itself as Nivalthnesser's tomb finally reopened.

Nivalthnesser rose from the tomb and discarded the old stone lid, but found himself unable to stand. Seeing nothing, he moved his mummified hands up to meet his face and rub away the ancient dust and bandages around his eyelids. Perhaps they were obstructed. Doing so, he felt his blood shift weirdly through his body, as though submerged in a large body of water.

Nothing impeded his vision. Darkness was what he truly saw, and as he kept squinting, all that became visible was a limitless array of tiny stars, speckling the boundless sky around him.

This was the vast, endless expanse of deep space, and the God-King's tomb was hurtling through it with the average velocity of an asteroid. With no wind resistance, and no frame of reference, it felt no different to him than being completely stationary. The Mummy's hand clung to the edge of his coffin for fear of careening off of the side in an unexpected way. As he pulled it closer, the rest of his body counteracted this motion and began a slow semi-orbital spin, almost jettisoning them apart.

Though terrifying, none of this Newtonian motion would matter to him much longer.

Nivalthnesser's immortality was fueled by ancient, immutable magic. These most recent moments were where the very, very last traces of Earth's Extromyte had left his tomb. Every ounce of air had been slowly drawn out of his resurrected body.

Untouched by the Extromyte's reach, the bandages encasing Nivalthnesser deteriorated to thin shreddings of old paper and dust. The skin, transforming from sand to organic matter, aged millennia in a matter of seconds to a rusted nothing. The muscle tissue disintegrated, and the bones beneath it turned black and lost all of their strength, many of them snapping and breaking internally. The Mummy quickly devolved into a suspended pile of grime and dirt, forming only cosmic stardust with whatever particles were left.

The last and only person he thought of in these final moments was his greatest friend, Alfred Louis, whom he could only hope had made it this far too.

God-King Nivalthnesser, High Priest of the Temple of the Summit Karnak, was no more. All that remained of the Mummy's presence were the sullied makings of a boundlessly-drifting sarcophagus and the deteriorated flakes of ash and dusted bone, aimlessly wandering through our cosmos, carrying with it no semblance of human life.

Milton Keynes UK
Ingram Content Group UK Ltd.
UKHW010631061123
432055UK00001B/196